BENEDICTION

BENEDICTION

OLIVIER
DUFAULT

TRANSLATED BY
PABLO STRAUSS

ARACHNIDE

First published as *Bénédiction* in 2017 by Marchand de Feuilles
First published in English in 2019 by House of Anansi Press Inc.
www.houseofanansi.com

23 22 21 20 19   1 2 3 4 5

Library and Archives Canada Cataloguing in Publication

Title: Benediction / Olivier Dufault ; translated by Pablo Strauss.
Other titles: Bénédiction. English
Names: Dufault, Olivier, author. | Strauss, Pablo, translator.
Description: Translation of: Bénédiction.
Identifiers: Canadiana (print) 20190067438 |
Canadiana (ebook) 20190067462 | ISBN 9781487005993 (softcover) |
ISBN 9781487006006 (EPUB) | ISBN 9781487006013 (Kindle)
Classification: LCC PS8607.U323 B4613 2019 | DDC C843/.6—dc23

Cover design: Alysia Shewchuk
Cover photograph: *Will James, prison mug shots, April 1915 /*
Special Collections, University of Nevada, Reno Libraries
Illustration on page 383: *Photograph of drawing by Will James /*
Special Collections, University of Nevada, Reno Libraries
Text design and typesetting: Sara Loos

We acknowledge for their financial support of our publishing program the
Canada Council for the Arts, the Ontario Arts Council, and the Government
of Canada. We acknowledge the financial support of the Government of
Canada through the National Translation Program for Book Publishing,
an initiative of the Roadmap for Canada's Official Languages 2013–2019:
Education, Immigration, Communities, for our translation activities.

Printed and bound in Canada

There was a few questions asked me and then I was asked for my name, which I gave wrong, and where I was born and so on. I gave that all wrong too.

—Will James, *Lone Cowboy: My Life Story*

Prairie Oysters

A clutch of men by the chuck wagon waved the rider over. Others, with hands cupped to amplify their voices, hollered at Will to come join them. But all their efforts were in vain. Will had caught whiff of that unmistakable stench of "calf fries" sullying the prairie air long before they started kicking up a fuss. He pulled up on the reins. Prairie oysters, the cowboy's caviar, revolted him. But since everyone else seemed to love them, Will had to follow suit. So, for appearance's sake, when it was the time for branding and castrating the bull calves, he always sucked one back, and made sure to do it with a smile.

As slowly as possible, Will approached his fellow cowboys, many with their eyes half closed, chewing on the sliced testicles floured and fried in an inch of lard over an open flame. The herd boy ran over to welcome him, helped Will unsaddle his bay and, with a slap on the hindquarters, sent the horse off into the corral where a hundred head of geldings impatiently awaited the moment they'd be needed again.

Will deftly rolled a smoke. The paunchy cook, Big Moose Tim, was known as "Chief" rather than "Chef" by a lot of the men, or sometimes just "Big Moose." He glowered at Will. He didn't like this young kid's accent any more than he liked his girly face, prominent cheekbones, fleshy lips, or that stunned look he sometimes gave when he managed to overcome his shyness.

"What, James, you too good to come over here and have a prairie oyster with us? Now there's one I never seen before!"

The cook's mean little eyes were hidden behind a pair of eyebrows as thick as his painter's brush moustache.

"Thought I saw a pack of wolves out there, Chief. Just wanted to make sure we don't run into trouble with sick cattle tonight."

"Like I got nothing better to do than sit around waiting for a bunch of ingrates to come eat! You know my day's just getting started. I still gotta finish cooking supper . . . not to mention tomorrow's breakfast!"

Big Moose Tim neglected to mention that he earned more than two dollars a day, same as the foreman and double the pay of the fifteen or so crew breaking their backs wrangling ornery cattle from sunup to sundown before riding back to camp, where, sure as rain would fall, they'd be greeted by an earful of insults and invective as they guzzled down the often inedible contents of their lunch pails and broke their teeth on biscuits even harder than the lot of the cowpuncher.

"You got any idea how long it takes just to skin them bull balls? I don't have to do it, you know. It's not one of my chores. And it certainly ain't that one there gonna help me do my job any faster."

Big Moose Tim threw a withering glare at his flunky. The young kitchen helper shrugged it off and melted into the background.

"Well, lookee here!"

And with that, Big Moose, the terror of the cook-pots, thrust an iron plate at Will with a smoking-hot double helping of sliced-up fried testicles. The cowboy suppressed a nauseous burp at the thought of them making it past the bandana covering his mouth.

"How about a cup of mud to wash it down, Chief?" he asked.

"Sure. And why not a little gravy while you're at it?"

The flunky, who'd had a soft spot for Will since the cowboy gave him a sketch of a galloping colt with its mane flowing in the wind, served him up a piping-hot cup of that foul brew the cowhands were in the habit of drinking without batting an eye. Will nodded his thanks.

"Someone tell you to move, kid?" yelled the cook at his ever handy minion, who scurried about even more, if such a thing were possible.

The season looked to be a long one. Will was thinking he might get out of having to eat when a horseman rode by the tent a touch too close for the Chief's liking, which always raised his hackles. On windy days especially, riding too close by the chuck wagon tent, or the Dutch oven suspended over the fire pit, could earn you months of short rations and a heaping portion of ire from the man charged with feeding you every

God-given day. If that happened, who knows what you'd end up eating—if you got to eat anything at all. And this was just one of the ways in which prairie cooks exercised their tyranny.

Will tried slipping away during the hubbub but Big Moose didn't miss a thing.

"James! Where'd you think you're going? Get your ass back here!"

Will resisted the urge to pretend to trip and flip over his dish. The dogs who'd savvied his intent were already licking their lips. The young man came back to the tent, knowing full well what awaited him.

Big Moose Tim crossed his arms. Tapped his foot.

It was important not to rile the cook but, on the contrary, to get on the man's good side. He had no choice. If he didn't, his summer would be hell. He summoned his sweetest smile, the one he used to open almost any door, winning over even the most leathery-tough of cowmen. This smile had been honed over the years, since Will's earliest childhood. It had been tested on every member of his family, all of his teachers, and pretty well everyone he'd crossed paths with since. Will had mastered his routine as though it were a birthright.

He started in on a slice, masticating with great difficulty. He closed his eyes as he swallowed, then immediately set in on a second one.

With his mouth full, Will began.

"Mmm. Say, Chief, these are the best prairie oysters I've had in a long time—maybe my whole life! And I've eaten my fair share since I was yay high. I grew up in Montana. We sure love us some good prairie oysters out there."

Will had hit pay dirt.

"I'm from there too!" said the cook in amazement, holding back a smile.

"Yup, that's what I was telling myself. That you make 'em just like we do up north. And that's where they're the best. But these are just scrumptious."

"Knock it off..."

"I swear it, *Chief*! This here's a little taste of Montana!"

Will took another forkful from the plate and looked it over a moment. But just for an instant. He needed to swallow it. He'd have to first chew, then swallow, then take a gulp and make sure it went down the right tube. Not that it looked bad. No, it looked good, even succulent. What kind of man would turn his nose up at such a feast of fried and battered grub? But what some found hard to stomach was its downy texture, the way it melted in your mouth. You had to be accustomed to the taste from a young age. In his late adolescence Will had struggled, despite his best intentions, to get used to eating those fuzzy little bull testicles. He could never quite shake the sensation of semen running down his throat. How could you eat testicles without batting an eye? How did other men do it? He was being tested, he was being mocked, he told himself again and again. Surely no man worth his salt actually ate this for the pleasure of it. No way this could be a delicacy.

Will put another morsel in his mouth, shut his eyes, and chewed it vigorously.

"Mmm! Chief, amazing, really!"

"Don't go pulling my leg now, James!"

"Now why would I be doing that," he answered, little chunks of meat between his teeth.

"Well, at first you didn't want any."

"That was before I knew what a great cook you were, Chief!"

Will had to concentrate not to say "*Chef*" as a French speaker would, and uttered the word "Chief" with an exaggerated American twang. As for Big Moose Tim, he was waiting patiently for a few more compliments.

"Let's just say there are cooks out there who serve 'em up cold. Even wrinkly, sometimes. You gotta be able to see that ain't right."

"Sure."

"But then yours — mmm! — they're nice 'n' crisp and hot enough to burn the roof of your mouth."

The cook's face relaxed. You never knew what kind of notions to expect from these young folk born at the turn of the new century. They looked like a bunch of layabouts, but maybe, after all, they'd been taught some basic values, like respect. And camp cooks undoubtedly had a hand in the game. Which is why you had to teach them the hard way. At the end of the day, they'd respect you for it.

Big Moose Tim almost said a few kind words to this young Will James, but caught himself in the nick of time.

"You fixing to finish that plate? You know my good-for-nothing flunky needs to get the dishes done before supper. If we leave it too long we just might end up waiting all night!"

"I'm savouring 'em, Chief. Gotta savour 'em," Will answered with his mouth full, doing everything in his power not to grimace and spit up everything onto the cook's boots.

"Well, go finish your plate somewhere else. Somewhere I can't see you now!"

Will did as he was asked. He walked away, and tossed his plate to the dogs. They fought over the last few morsels voraciously. It didn't matter at all that they were covered in a layer of dirt.

Will imagined he would be eating plenty more prairie oysters in the months ahead, before he finally turned his back on the ranch, never to return. But he'd managed to win the favour of an important figure in the camp. The sweet-faced young man with the outlandish accent would even join the very select company of the cook's favourites. From then on Will would be among the first to be served, always generous helpings, and sometimes even see a choice cut land on his dish.

With his back against one of the rare poplars that provided shade for the clumps of scrub brush whose roots drew nourishment from what could only at a stretch be called a watering hole, Will smoked a cigarette, then pulled his hat over his face. A little nap wouldn't hurt. The boys had started work at dawn, and they'd be asked to perform God knows what tasks before, in a few hours, the sun finally disappeared behind the smoking peaks of the Great Basin.

PART ONE

In the Name of the Father

1

Will turned up the collar of his slicker. Riding tall in the saddle with his hat pulled down to his ears, the cowboy stared at the hazy line in the distance where the mountains amounted to no more than a slender band on the horizon. He'd just finished the last roundup of the year. Most of the saddle horses had been put out to pasture for the winter, as well as the cattle from the last circle not held back and sent to the slaughterhouse — mature cows mostly, along with some heifers and calves. The ranch owner, James Riordan, had of course kept a few head to feed his family and the men who'd stay on the ranch in the off season. All that remained was to bring in the last of the cattle, and collect fall wages and the end-of-season jug of liquor.

The main buildings of the Riordan property were spread over a few dozen miles in northeastern Nye County, Nevada. The chuck wagon operated by O'Brien, Riordan's faithful cook for going on ten years now, had quit the ranch several hours before. They'd have to saddle up quick if they wanted to get a decent meal before morning. But everyone was taking their time, as if doing their utmost to drink in just a little bit more of the prairie landscape, the snow-capped peaks of the blue and brown Pancake Mountains in the distance, and the fresh sagebrush-scented air. This, before hunkering down for a few months of hibernation and letting the whiskey distill in their veins and, somewhat less placidly, addle their minds.

Will sat on his horse and smoked a cigarette. His expression was deadpan and meditative. He wondered whether or not Riordan would let him overwinter at the ranch, and whether he'd enjoy spending an entire winter in one place rather than, as he'd been doing since he left Quebec seven years earlier, drifting where the wind took him. He'd never been this attached to a ranch. It was as if, after all his peregrination, hardier roots were showing signs of taking.

But maybe he just wasn't in tight enough with the foreman to be able to stay. They'd clashed a few times during the season. Riordan, like most ranchers, liked keeping some of the men on for the hard work of December through February. Come spring, when it was time to ride out after the yearlings, older calves, and emaciated livestock, all hands were welcome. Every cowpuncher was standing by, itching to get to work and wasting no time doing so.

Jennie—Mrs. Riordan—could certainly put a good word in with her husband on Will's behalf. They got along well. She liked his sketches very much and had always been happy to supply him with pencils, and pads of elegant, thick, high-quality unlined paper. In exchange, he gave her some of his more elaborate drawings of bucking wild horses, with all four hooves in the air. Will was torn. But after eight months of knowing no floor but the prairie grass, and no roof but the capricious, wide-open sky—no company but his fellow cowpunchers in their dusty chaps, and no womenfolk twirling in skirts or summer dresses with their hair in long, soft braids that were enough to make a man fall out of his saddle—he was probably ready for a little distraction.

A fellow horseman rode into Will's field of vision and snapped him out of his reverie. Will acted like he hadn't seen a thing. Didn't stir, didn't so much as blink and let the crisp air of late fall tease out protective tears. Aware that he was being watched, and that his face conveyed as much nostalgia as confidence, Will adopted a calculated version of the natural pose he'd found himself in just earlier. He couldn't help himself, it was a reflex.

The rider approaching him was Lew Hackberry. Will had met Lew and his two brothers in 1911, three years earlier. They'd chased and tamed—"broken," in cowboy jargon—wild horses in Idaho, near the state's borders with Utah and Nevada, then sold their spoils, around three hundred head, and gone their separate ways. With his thick neck, greasy hair, tanned oily skin, sneering beady eyes, and incomplete set of plaque-ridden teeth, Lew looked like he'd seen better days. But he was good company for a late night of rousting about.

Will knew all too well what the old cowboy was about to say. He took a last puff on his smoke, crushed it out in his yellow fingers, and rubbed the neck of his horse Pepper, a cantankerous young pinto he'd taken a liking to that autumn. Pepper immediately understood that he needed to meet this man advancing toward them. Lew was also mounted on a saddle horse that had once been untamed, a proud but aging buckskin who'd not always been treated well.

"What say, Will? What you up to?"

Lew looked over the younger man, who appeared both relaxed and timid, smiling and vulnerable; a kid whose pleasing features were a million miles from his own world-weary mien.

"Was just asking myself the same question. Not exactly drowning in options."

"Me, I only see one."

"I'm pretty sure I know what you're thinking," ventured Will.

"This head of mine ain't overflowing with ideas... but this one's been hounding me for days now. I'm thirsty. And not just for drink. We could throw in for a spell?"

"Weren't you heading out tonight?"

"Why not? If we don't waste too much time, in five or six hours we could be in Ely with as many beauties as we want. Before daybreak, at any rate."

Lew lifted up his nose, as if to ask, "What next?" Will wasn't convinced. He didn't want to head north; he'd prefer to try his luck in a state with less inclement weather. New Mexico maybe. Santa Fe was a great place to spend a winter. As for Lew, well, all he could think of was hightailing it to the nearest town to drink until he was penniless and naked as the worm he was born to be. Will was well acquainted with Pioche, a fairly wild little town lower down. Hackberry was all for it.

Each man rolled a cigarette without saying another word. Once the rest had gathered—the foreman, and the several cowboys who hadn't ridden with the wagon train—they set off at pace in the direction of Riordan's ranch. They'd be there in a little under two hours.

2

The Riordans struck it rich at the end of the nine-teenth century. Now independently wealthy, it was their love of the prairie and the cowboys who rode and the livestock they tended that got the proprietor out of bed and to work every morning. He'd sold off the better part of the family land—his father must have been rolling in his grave—and had retained only a choice patch of the most fertile and unusually well-irrigated land: twenty thousand acres where the grass grew thick through rain and drought. The result was that his herd, just shy of ten thousand head, was worth its weight in gold.

A small crew of around fifteen men kept the ranch going: the cook, his helper, and a dozen-odd cowmen. Most of them overwintered on the property, and when there wasn't a blizzard, and with it the need to save the stock from certain death, the men weren't above stooping to farm work, normally viewed as an insult to the trade. Taking a blow to their pride in exchange for the day's hot meal and a spot around the stove was the lesser of two evils. And this rancher had a good reputation. Despite appearances—his crafty, prickly front (what man worthy of the name was any different?)—Riordan liked his employees and paid them accordingly. Getting taken on at his outfit wasn't easy. Quite by chance, Will had been the only man hired the previous year, when a member of the old guard hung up his boots for good. Hackberry was new this year. He and Will were the only two cowboys who'd decided to quit, aside from a couple of men whose families lived nearby who were spending a couple more days at the ranch before returning home.

Riordan took Will aside. He felt an affinity for this likeable kid. In truth, Riordan's entire family had fallen for Will's charm. Riordan offered to keep Will on for the following year, at least until Thanksgiving. In confidence he told Will that he didn't think hiring Lew had been a smart move, and he wouldn't be keeping him on, but that he liked Will, and would even let him break horses that winter if that would help convince him to stay. Clearly he'd not forgotten the conversation they'd had a few months back, when Will had boasted of his talents as a bronco buster and lamented not having the opportunity to put them to use.

"Young feller, don't ride with that guy," said Riordan. "He ain't nothing but trouble."

The "young feller" was all of twenty-two, and took umbrage at the expression. He said he'd think it over. He could at least urge Hackberry to stay the night, and then set off at first light. Lew didn't prove hard to convince—not once he saw the bottles of liquor lined up beside the sides of beef, and Riordan's blonde teenaged daughters hanging around the table set up for the going-away feast.

The men got good and drunk and caroused into the wee hours. They played cards, and someone pulled out an old fiddle from which he managed to extract only plaintive squeals as another fellow blew his harmonica. But the nights were already cold in that autumn of 1914, and word was a few snowflakes had fallen further north, so everyone headed to the main bunkhouse to keep drinking, have a little more fun — and, as any self-respecting cowboy is wont to do, spin a few yarns.

Will especially loved listening to the tales of the seasoned hands, of the real old guard: stories set in the last century, in an almost mythic rangeland that had existed long before it entered ranchers' minds to litter the landscape with fences that horrified Will because they marked not only property lines but the end of an era, the loss of a world where a man might still ride free. Will sketched these hirsute old-timers — tough, tired old men with bent backs and sandpaper hands. Or else he'd put down on paper the scenes they described: the hunt for a pack of mustangs, a stampede of cattle, a human cadaver discovered in a cave, Christmas in a cow camp, a rider sizing up an outlaw bronc, riders battling through a blizzard to save their livestock. A lot of folks asked Will for drawings, with no idea they'd be worth a tidy sum one day. They'd pat him on the back and, intrigued and charmed by his natural talent, share an admiring word.

But the thick bunkhouse smoke soon got to Will's head. He went outside for a breath of fresh air.

Will rolled a cigarette and headed for the corral where the men left their riding horses in summer. The Riordan family took good care of them. After a few months out working, their masters came back to find the animals in fine fettle: well-fed, happy horses with glossy coats, ready for adventure. Will hadn't seen Happy and Duffy since the spring. They were both greys — Will's favourite coat for a horse — and both did their best to ignore and pretend not to recognize him, but once they heard their names a few times they approached, breathing heavily and craning their necks over the fence for their owner to stroke from ears to withers. All things taken into account, the horses seemed to be thinking, no amount of skill or practice could make the cowboys' calloused hands any bit as pleasant as those of the rancher's teenaged daughters.

Will caught a glimpse of Mrs. Riordan wrapped up in a big coat of her husband's that wasn't quite long enough to conceal the hem falling over the tops of her boots. Her thick, loose, abundant hair, normally hidden under a bonnet, was flying in the wind. He had a moment of doubt. It took a lot of nerve for a lady to come out to the corral at this time of night, and even more to approach a hired hand. It was the kind of move that could bring trouble — or, worse yet, gossip.

"Something wrong?" asked Will, regretting his words the moment they left his mouth.

"I can't sleep."

"I guess we're kind of loud?"

She lingered a minute on Will's gentle face and full lips.

"No. I always have trouble sleeping. And don't worry, my husband's snoring is louder than you boys, even when you're drunk and rowdy. You wouldn't have a cigarette, by any chance?"

Will rolled two. They smoked in silence. Jennie rubbed Duffy's muzzle. Duffy knew this woman's tender hand and happily let her. Will would also have liked to know her better, would gladly have traded places with the horse—he hadn't known a woman's touch in ages, and never the touch of a woman like this. She couldn't have been much more than ten years older than Will, and though you could tell Mrs. Riordan had seen a great deal of life, it had done nothing to diminish her beauty. Her lips had just a hint of sternness, her cheeks a few bran-coloured freckles; her eyes were green, her nose gently upturned, and her almost-red hair smelled like fresh air and blonde straw.

Will should have spoken up, said something inoffensive and sweet, but the men weren't big on conversation, especially with women, and even a supposedly sensitive artist like Will was at a loss for words.

"And you wouldn't also have something to drink, would you?"

"Sorry."

She reckoned just smelling his coyote's breath would be enough to get her dead drunk. Seeing that Will, as usual, wasn't about to steer their conversation, she took the reins.

"Does my husband know you're leaving?"

"Yes, ma'am."

"Call me Jennie, will you? We know each other by now, don't we?"

They smiled and, for the first time, looked each other in the eye.

"You shouldn't. Leave, that is. You're not happy here? Don't we pay you enough?"

"May just be the best ranch I ever seen."

"And so? You aren't really about to go back to chasing stray broncs all winter, are you?"

"I'm no thief, ma'am. When they got a brand on 'em, I let 'em go. The young ones too. They don't pay enough, anyhow..."

He hesitated a moment. Looked at the distant mountains, dark shapes barely perceptible in the clear night.

"I'd like to settle down a bit. Maybe try my luck in San Francisco, or Los Angeles. I've never been."

"You're lucky...you men."

Will didn't feel like arguing the point. There was a strong undertone of resentment to what she'd said. Will took a last drag of his cigarette, almost burning his yellowed fingers.

"Will you write once in a while? Maybe send me a drawing or two?"

"You have my word."

They shook hands and said a somewhat stiff goodnight. Both looked slightly sad.

Will would only see Jennie one more time. In a few months, she'd come visit him in prison.

3

W ill and Hackberry had got up early with monumental hangovers. It was extremely cold, and Will's first thought was that they weren't going to be adequately dressed for riding on such a cruel fall day. And he was thinking the same again now as, on Happy's back, he made his way southeast. He'd need to make sure to buy himself a good coat before blowing his pay on whiskey and women.

The other men had overslept in a symphony of snoring that sounded like an earthquake. The bunkhouse reeked of alcohol, stale farts, and bad breath. People called it horse breath, but while horses' breath did stink, the odour was nothing next to that of a hungover cowboy. In most any way you could think, horses were better than cowboys, and no one who knew them would ever claim otherwise. As Will had waited for the coffee pot to boil, Lew brought over a couple of beers. They were cold; the temperature had almost hit freezing during the night. The beers were almost enough to get the men back on their feet and thinking straight. They'd made a quick breakfast of a hunk of bread and that good old Western staple, pork and beans. The Riordans had a small chicken coop, so they could have cracked a few eggs and tossed them into the skillet for a change, but neither man was much in the mood for cooking. Rough morning.

Lew tiptoed into the cook's cabin to make off with some victuals for the days ahead, as Will saddled up their two horses apiece. Then the two men and four horses left the ranch.

Now it was past noon and the pair's hangovers had more or less dissipated; the day was a hot one, and the sprawling Railroad Valley was behind them. They made their way around the south side of Currant Mountain and saw a watering hole. The snowy peaks of the Grant Range extended to the east, and Hackberry suggested they stop for a bite to eat and to water their horses. It wasn't that he needed a drink. The truth was that he hadn't stopped drinking since they'd left the ranch. He was well in his cups, still riding the wave of the night before, and thus incapable of shutting up for even a second. Will, on the other hand, cherished peace and quiet. He liked to pass his first hours of freedom in silent contemplation. And he'd hoped that, between bites, a little of that quiet might come to him. But Lew, with his mouth full and bits of pancake between his teeth, was rambling:

"So, what about you, kid? Where'd you say you came from? And where'd you get that accent?"

No matter that Lew was also shy of thirty, he still called Will "kid" or "young feller." It didn't help Will's cause that he wasn't actually very big—his feet, especially. He wore a six-and-a-half boot—had child's feet, really. But they were good feet for riding. They didn't get caught in the horse's ribs if he reared up or started crow-hopping. Out of necessity, Will trotted out the story he'd first developed years before, a tale he never stopped altering and embellishing, often confusing himself in the details. He'd already told it to the Hackberry brothers when they were out hunting mustangs in Idaho, but obviously his drunken partner didn't remember. A good thing too; Will was worried his current version might have changed quite a bit from the one he'd told back then.

"I was born on the wagon trail, in Montana. My parents were on their way to Canada."

"So your parents are Canadian?"

Will looked away from Hackberry, and stared at the ground.

"My dad was a Texan, born and raised in West Texas. My mother was from Southern California . . . I was about a year old when I lost my mother, and, by the time I was four, my dad went and joined her acrost that Range Beyond."

"So you grew up in an orphanage?"

Will grimaced, his smile pained, as if it hurt for him to go on.

"No. A friend of my dad's raised me. An old trapper and prospector up north, barely spoke a word of English. He died too. When I was fifteen. Showed me all I know. Owe him everything, and I've been riding solo ever since."

It always bore down on Will's conscience to have to deny his parents, who were, last he heard, alive and well. They were good French-Canadian country folk who, the way they told it, had banished themselves to the city at the turn of the century, when Will, born Ernest Dufault, was nine. If you were to believe the grandees of the Holy Roman Church, all manner of indignities would befall a family reckless enough to turn their back on their heritage and leave their paternal homeland. And maybe those men of the cloth weren't wrong.

"So you got no family? No people at all?"

"Nobody."

Lew remained silent a minute and pinched his lips. Will pictured his mother Joséphine, a pious, provident woman, wearing a dress and smiling, exhausted by her labours; and his father Jean, an unassuming, awkward man, but the sort who had worked with the public his whole life. Their voices came back to Will; he heard the peals of laughter of his brothers and sisters at supper, talking over each other in their shared eagerness to speak, no one really listening but everyone exuding good cheer.

"May be better that way," mumbled Lew, after knocking back a long draft of whiskey.

Now it was his turn to look down at his boots.

"Y'know, family ain't no good. Just another mess, trust me. Mothers, take 'em or leave 'em, but fathers...Jesus. When they ain't messing with your sisters and cousins and neighbours, or breedin' bastards with every whore in town, well, they're flayin' you with their belt buckles or rearranging your face with their fists. If I wasn't so tight with my words, I'd say you was lucky."

At that, Lew squinted and spat, fighting to swallow his anger. Now it was Will's turn to knock back a shot from the jug as he thought about his mother's kindness and his father's decency. Like all fathers, Jean played it strict, but he was a loving man, and sometimes even an understanding one. After all, hadn't he let his son set off at fifteen—*fifteen!*—to go work in Western Canada? Will apologized to his family under his breath.

He figured he was on safe ground now. Lew wouldn't ask him any more questions. But he'd piqued his partner's curiosity. Who doesn't enjoy a good yarn with their meal?

"So, tell me more," Hackberry pleaded.

"Don't know that I can, Lew."

"I ain't about to ask you twice!"

Will gave a reticent smile. There was no getting out of it. So he started to recite the story he knew by heart now.

"My dad always figured he'd be off to the Pearly Gates doing what he did best—mounting a rough bronc, swingin' a steer at the end of his lasso. But the actual story was much sadder than that."

Will had Lew's full attention now, and paused for effect.

"*He was peacefully prodding cattle thru the chutes to the squeezer when his time come. There was quite a herd of cattle in that same corral where he was working, and amongst that herd was a big 'staggy' steer that'd just broke a horn. The blood from that broken horn was running down that steer's face to his nose and he was on the fight, not with his own breed, but with anything strange, like a human... the big steer caught him broadside with his one good horn, hoisted him in the air, took him on a ways and then flung him against the chute. The horn had pierced him thru the stomach like as if it had been done with a knife, only worse.*

"*They said there was a smile on my dad's face when, after a while, he opened his eyes, and the first words he'd said was, 'Well, boys, I'm due to join her soon now'... Then, after a while, he'd added on, 'The only thing I regret is to leave little Billy behind... Tell old Bopy that all my gatherings are his and to see that my boy is well took care of. I leave him to him.'*"

"Bopy?"

"Beaupré. Jean Beaupré."

"Bopway," Lew tried again.

"The Canadian trapper who raised me."

Will, who'd been living a double life for some time, had plenty of good reasons to change his name.

After setting out on his own, he'd rambled around Western Canada for the rest of his teens and then spent a few years in Montana, where, true to their reputation, old-timers in the camps and ranches had teased him mercilessly. To hold his own and explain his accent—his incomprehensible manner of speaking which often made them roar with a laughter that crushed him every time—Will had come up with the story of Bopy, and the claim that he was an orphan. Will's admiration for the old cowpunchers knew no bounds; he'd hang on to every word of these grizzled veterans who, whether or not they knew it, were moulding his very being. He'd wanted to impress them. To be accepted. And the Bopy story had worked. Or at least, it hadn't hurt. Once they heard it, the men would leave Will more or less alone.

"When I was four, I reckon I must have talked in English with my father. But then I pretty much forgot everything I knew—the English, I mean. Old Bopy spoke French and some Indian languages too, but not much English. I learned to read and write from magazines and old horse-gear catalogues gathering dust in the cabins we were in."

"School ain't but a waste of time."

"You can say that again."

"Between four walls all day," Lew grumbled. "What's that gotta do with real life?"

Will felt his face relax.

"Real life," Will repeated with a smile. "For ten years, Bopy and me, we rode both sides of the Montana–Alberta border. In winter we got by trapping and selling furs. When we saw the geese and the other birds heading back north, well, we knew it was time to go south again. Bopy did a little prospecting. Never did have much luck though. He was a real woodsman.

A *coureur des bois*, they used to call 'em. An adventurer, like we had back when the New World was new. That breed's pretty well lost now. Bopy, he always found a way to keep me in pads and pencils. It was during those tough Canadian winters, when we'd be laid up for a spell, that I drew the most. Always from the same old magazines and newspapers. And those you could always find in his cabin, stacked up higher than me."

Will lifted up his arm and stretched his hand out flat to give Lew a better idea of just how high the stack of magazines was. Lew liked the picture he was painting. Wanted more.

"He must have drowned one day, I'm sure of it. Carried off by the current when he was chasing some nugget he figured might be worth a little."

Will stopped speaking to show reverence for the old trapper and mourn his loss with dignity. Old Bopy relentlessly searching for nuggets. Will wasn't lying, was thinking back to that time.

"And after? What happened after?"

Ever since he'd left Montreal, in 1907, Will had never stopped seeking out the company of men he'd been drawing years before seeing an actual cowboy in the flesh. Not something that was easily said.

"I worked..."

Lew spat out his whiskey.

"Ha! Look at you, kid. There isn't a ranch woulda put you to work at fifteen. Hell, you barely look a day older than fifteen today!"

Lew was exaggerating a little, but also closing in on

the truth. Will's early years working cow camps in Sage Creek, Alberta, and Kelvinhurst, Saskatchewan, had been difficult. The ranchers had laughed at him, hazed him, ridiculed him, and finally sent him packing. Some put him to work as a farm boy, though they never let him near a horse unless it was to shovel its shit. He was forced to travel from place to place, racking up experience and improving his English, always having to lie about the last job behind him.

Will turned serious, raised his voice a little.

"I was sure and certain I'd be a cowboy one day, like my old man and his old man before him, and I even knew I could be a good one. We were in Canada when Bopy disappeared, but I knew the territory and told myself I could stay where we'd been for a while. Thing was, no one would hire me as a cowboy. I worked as a flunky for some real bastard cooks and as a gopher in the bunkhouses of a few big outfits, and even as a farmhand. Barely got to touch a horse, let alone ride one. I'd had enough, knew I was worth more than that. I drifted east a bit, into Saskatchewan, where I met Jackson, one of the biggest ranchers in the region — Fred Jackson, I think, from the 76 Cattle Company. Told him I was a cowboy and he believed me. I was around for the final roundup of the season, and after rounding up the stock once, I had a pretty clear picture of how it worked. I wasn't nervous about it anymore, or at least not *as* nervous. Saw that I could hold my own. So I came back to the States."

Will wasn't telling the full story. In 1910 he'd been on his way back from his first trip to Montreal to see his parents since leaving them behind three years before. He'd already learned to play the part of the seasoned cowpuncher, and couldn't resist laying it on a little thick: he'd saddled up a piebald stallion and paraded around Viger station. Onlookers gathered, and the Dufaults didn't know quite what to do — any more than the police, who had a hard time dispersing the crowd.

When Will got back out West, the pressure was on. He did meet a certain Fred Jackson, who was foreman (not owner) of the 76. Jackson found Will's way of mounting a horse bumbling and comic, but the kid seemed so keen that he offered him a job as a herd boy. There wasn't a whole lot of difference between being a herd boy and a farm boy, but Will accepted anyway, despite himself. While the real cowmen rode off to round up the stock, he had to stay at the ranch and tend to the horses roped up in the corral, waiting to be put to work. He needed to stand by and be ready when the riders came in to swap their exhausted horses for fresh legs. Still, Will had picked up a lot. He'd learned the unspoken rules and hierarchies of the camp and the rhythms of the roundup.

And he'd sent his parents a postcard full of hope and pride — he always wrote to them in French and signed his name "Ernest."

Dear Parents,

I'm doing very well, everything is great. I'm working for the 76, a 3,000 head outfit. I haven't made it to Saco yet but I'm on my way, so please address all letters to Saco, Montana. How are you? I hope everyone is doing well, Mom and Dad, and above all don't worry.

Ernest

Lew squinted.

"That must've been not long before you met me and my brothers."

He was insinuating that Will had had no real experience when they'd gone out chasing mustangs together. And he was right. Will had introduced himself as an experienced horse-breaker. He was one of the best in the whole of the North, he assured them, and he never broke a horse's spirit or knocked the fight out of it. In truth, all he'd lassoed up to that point—and with great difficulty—were a few docile calves. And though he had been able to observe several men breaking horses at close hand, he'd not yet had the opportunity to try it himself.

Will's mind was racing to come up with an answer.

"No, not right before. I worked a spell in New Mexico, and in Texas a while. In between roundups I went out hunting stray mustangs in the region. There were fewer and fewer of them down there, and they were a lot more skittish. It was good training. You ever meet John Crouch?"

"No."

"No John Crouch, eh? You sure? He'd vouch for what I'm telling you."

Will had, in fact, travelled as far as Saco, Montana, but at that point was still lacking many of the basic skills that made a decent cowboy—and not just twisting a lasso, though he was particularly bad at that. He was being yelled at all the time, and was often fired in the middle of a roundup. More than once it felt like he'd hit bottom, convinced that his only option was to go back to Montreal. Will rode solo, wandering the plains, haunted by an unbearable melancholy that only got worse when he tried, without success, to capture stray horses. He'd headed back up north to ranches he'd worked before, making the most of the experience he'd gained since he'd left them.

Then there'd been the incident in Saskatchewan.

Will had charmed his way into the company of a few American competitors in a Regina rodeo. They'd done the rounds of all the hotels in town, and in between stops they'd put on little horse shows—if you could call them that—gathering a crowd, wreaking havoc. Will followed them everywhere and, too young to have built up any tolerance, drank till he fell off his barstool. The three rodeo men eventually went their separate ways, drunk as soldiers on leave—or cowboys after a roundup—though Will, his manhood on the line, had insisted on one last drink at the fleabag hotel on the outskirts of town where he'd met his new companions. Maybe half an hour went by before some loudmouth grabbed him by the elbow. Will, collapsed on his barstool, was leaning against the bar. He turned to the dirty bearded man glaring at him with a condescending stare.

"You cowboys," the man said. "Always taking up all the room."

His strident voice and crooked teeth made Will think of a witch. The man had spoken loud enough for every person in the bar to hear. This stranger was looking for trouble.

"Still," he went on, "I know damn well a simple shepherd like myself won't have no problem showing you the door."

The barman did his best to calm the man down. But his words seemed only to add fuel to the fire. Suddenly the man pulled out a knife and everyone in the bar stood up at once. The sound of tables and chairs being pushed over and falling down rose in a cacaphony. The barman jumped on the man, and Will followed suit. They gave him a good working-over. By the end of it, the shepherd was spitting blood and teeth, wheezing, and holding his stomach. Will's memory was hazy. They might have broken his ribs.

In the middle of the night, Will was woken up by a knock at the door of his fifth-floor room: the Royal Northwest Mounted Police, and they were not amused. They dragged Will into a tiny, freezing cell littered with straw. The bartender was lying in the one next door. They kept him locked up for a week, no one saying a word, and then released him without explanation. The rodeo was done by then, and Will had lost track of his new partners, and the barman had lost his job at the hotel where the fracas took place. A stalwart of the tavern was kind enough to let them know that the enraged shepherd had rounded up an armed posse that was looking for them all over town. Terrified, Will sold his horse and took a series of southbound trains.

"John Crouch? Really? You sure? I saw him not so long ago and I'm pretty sure we talked about you. Or maybe one of your brothers?"

Hackberry didn't get how Will could have made his way south so fast, if he'd been stopping at ranch after ranch as he claimed. There was something fishy about the whole story, but Lew wasn't the type to give him a grilling. Who knows, maybe he was the one who'd mixed up the timeline.

"If you don't mind, kid, I'm going to have myself a little siesta. How about it? Great story though. Helluva story."

Before following the lead of his partner, already stretched out under a scraggly pine with his dusty hat over his face, Will rolled a smoke and pulled out a drawing pad. The size of his pads was always changing. The one constant was the lousy quality of the paper. He filled up a dozen or so pads a year without thinking. Drawing was Will's escape. A third lung. A parallel life. It occurred to him to sketch Lew while he slumbered, but his model and the scene were of no interest to him. Someone else was on his mind, and had been since they'd left. A few crudely shaded and hashed lines soon formed the silhouette of a tall, willowy woman with a slender waist: Jennie Riordan. He drew her with her hair down, like she'd been wearing it when they'd spoken the night before. Will often drew her from memory, but the result was never as beautiful as Jennie was in reality. The nose was never fine enough, the eyes never as piercing, the lips always a little too full. He'd never have admitted that he was lovestruck, but that was the truth of it. Their conversation kept replaying in his mind. Will regretted every word he had uttered and all those he had not. She'd come out to say goodbye and he hadn't known how to respond with any class, how to be a gentleman.

Will crumpled up the drawing and then threw it on the fire. Immediately, he started another — a scene this time, rather than a portrait. A couple was dancing close and tight. Jennie and Will's alter ego, a good-looking young cowboy with handsome features he drew as faithfully as he was able, though he did exaggerate the thrusting line of the jaw a little. The man, slightly the taller of the two, was staring deep into the woman's eyes, his chest pushing against her breasts. She was wearing a simple yet fashionable dress with a belt above her navel; he'd taken his hat off. Soon enough, Bopy appeared in the background, wearing his plaid shirt, and Will drew him an enormous black beard and put a fur cap on his head. He was watching over the couple benevolently, like a guardian angel.

4

The travelling companions had been back on the road a few hours, and Lew had picked up his drinking where he'd left off before deciding to nap. As they made their way south through Spring Valley, on the northwest edge of Lincoln County, near the borders of White Pine and Nye counties, they caught sight of a herd out to pasture less than a mile away.

"Interesting," Hackberry mumbled.

They approached slowly, and the herd didn't scatter. The animals scarcely paid the two cowboys any mind. Will and Lew counted thirty-odd head, no horns.

"Thirty-one," said Will.

"GS?" asked Hackberry, checking the brand high on their hindquarters.

"The Lazy GS. The Swallow brothers' outfit over in White Pine. Got a whole post office just for them, up in the district they call Shoshone."

"You know 'em?"

"By reputation, mostly," said Will. "Smug bastards.

Don't treat their men good. Horses neither."

Will and Lew stayed on their horses a minute, smoking in silence and circling the herd. The wheels in Hackberry's head were turning, as if he were focusing every ounce of concentration on the task of sobering up so he could think clearly for a moment. He opened his mouth a few times but nothing came out. Will put him out of his misery.

"Something botherin' you, Lew?"

"You reckon they just wandered all the way out here?"

"Sure do look that way."

Nowhere did they see the slightest trace of horse tracks, either fresh or old. No one knew that these cattle were out here with the two men, some twenty miles south of the Lazy GS Ranch and the county line.

"Figger you could blot that brand?"

"I don't have my gear on me," answered Will. "Plus we'd have to wait for it to scar. Risky."

"Well, we can't just go and sell them in Ely. Word would get around too fast."

Ely was the biggest livestock hub in this part of Nevada. Ranches from all over the eastern, central, and northern parts of the state sent their cattle through Ely on the way to Denver.

"Not sure what to do. The Swallows may be bastards, but we could still bring them their cattle back. They'd pay us handsomely."

Lew sat up tall on his horse.

"Really, Bill? Really?"

"What?"

"Did they castrate you along with them steers over the summer?"

Will thought for a moment.

"I know a place not far from the Utah state line. Oasis. Kinda place where they don't ask questions."

"You took the words right out of my mouth. Oasis! Now there's the Will James I thought I knew."

Now it was Hackberry's turn to think a little. He was positively reinvigorated, and grinning like a kid.

"From Oasis, I'll catch the train to Denver. I know people there. It'll be easy and we'll be rich. I'm sure we can get thirty-five a head, at least, maybe forty, who knows — maybe even fifty! Those sure are some nice fat cattle!"

Fifty a head was over the top. Will wasn't about to get carried away, but the prospect of making somewhere in the region of five hundred dollars for a bit more than a week's work was nothing to sneeze at. It would be enough to set Will up for the winter, maybe even the entire next year, without having to worry too much about what to do next. He'd finally have time to draw, maybe even travel to the West Coast and study at art school. He could visit his idol, the great cowboy painter Charles Russell, in his studio.

"Okay then," said Will. "We should get there in ten days or so. But you're gonna have to follow my lead. I know the area better than you, and you're pretty damn drunk. You got many of those jugs left?"

Hackberry indicated that he did not, and adopted a malicious look that had been known to get him into trouble. Will steered them back to the matter at hand.

"Once we get to Oasis, I know I can trust you. But, until then, it's me who's in charge. And for God's sake, try to sober up a little."

Lew bared his rickety yellow teeth in all their splendour.

They decided to wait until sundown to make their move. That way, if other riders showed, they could always say they'd just arrived on the scene and were wondering what to do. Lew had no problem finishing his jug — he still had three left — as Will tried to convince him to get some rest. The next several days — or, rather, the next several nights — would be long.

5

A coyote lying in wait on one of the ridges above was watching the herd of cattle grazing, drinking, and resting near a hidden spring on the eastern flank of the Snake Range. The furtive animal poked its snout out from its hiding place from time to time. When it did, Happy warned his master, but the two of them knew the scavenger wouldn't come too close. The cattle were healthy, they didn't smell of illness or exhaustion, and above all, the crafty coyote had taken note of the two cowboys, those peculiar bipeds, always climbing onto horses and riding off and leaving a trail of their nauseating yet somehow sweet signature odour, which he hated with a passion. You couldn't be too careful. They had a way of shooting something at you with a horrible racket that could sting you and burn your flesh and cause no end of pain—even kill you.

The coyote had been following the herd for days.

Spurred on by the cowboys, the cattle had traversed a sprawling valley, headed northeast, passing the Cedar Range and the Fortification Mountains.

Then, strangely, they had climbed back in a south-easterly direction, toward Utah. The coyote had no idea why, on top of it all, the herd was travelling at night and then laying low during the day, higher up in the hills. At dawn, he'd left them for a few hours to go after some easier prey. He was dying of hunger; what choice did he have? He'd picked up their scent again in a little oasis of a verdant valley tucked away in the middle of the desert, just over the state line. But now something was wrong. No matter how many times he looked, checked, and checked again, one of the men was missing.

That morning, Lew had run out of liquor. Withdrawal was making him delusional. He'd been knocking back at least a bottle a day for three days now. The gaseous burps in his throat felt like burning embers and threatened to send up all the bile stewing in his stomach. He desperately needed coffee, and Will had to remind him that a fire was out of the question.

"Especially here, so close to town."

He regretted the words the second they were out of his mouth.

"A town, Bill? Where's that? Which one again?"

"Nothing. I didn't say nothing. Forget it."

"I asked you a question, boy. What town you talking about?"

"Try and get some sleep. I'll keep watch."

Lew grabbed a hold of Will's collar and yelled, "Which town?"

Will sighed.

"Baker, I think. Two or three miles north. But I could be mistaken."

They were, in fact, just a few miles south of Baker.

"You said you knew the area."

"Sure I know it. But we usually stick to the beaten path."

"I'm going," said Lew. "I'm going to town. I'll be back in a few hours with supplies."

"You're gonna stay right here and get some sleep, while I keep watch. You'll be leaving traces all over the place. Stop right now and listen good. It's dangerous!"

"I don't think you heard me," said Lew, clearing his throat and speaking a little more quietly. "I told you I'm going and I'll be back in a couple hours."

Will punched him hard in the face. Hackberry fell down flat on his back, didn't get up, and for the first time since they'd left Riordan's ranch, the lone cowboy had some peace and quiet and was able to savour the wide-open desert without distraction.

Maybe an hour later, Will woke with a start. He'd fallen asleep, and was angry with himself for it. Lew had disappeared. Will wanted to kill him—he truly could have killed that man. But he didn't move. He waited, fulminating and smoking cigarette after cigarette even though he needed to ration his tobacco. A few hours later the coyote spotted the second man galloping back, a grin stretching from ear to ear.

The two cowmen started arguing loudly, which agitated the horses. Lew drew his revolver and pointed it at his companion. Will caught him with a right hook and they rolled around in the dirt for a good while, kicking up a cloud of dust. The coyote almost convinced himself this was the moment, now or never, but instead decided to enjoy the show. When they finally did calm down, the two men made a fire—it smelled good—and got to drinking and smoking. Lew had brought a big store of top-quality Bull Durham tobacco to make up for his transgression, and when the sun went down over the horizon, they got back on the road as if nothing had happened. Strange animals.

6

The nights grew colder and colder. The wind chilled the two riders to the bone, whistling in their ears, red from the cold. Their bodies were cramping, their frozen fingers stiffening and turning blue. Each fresh gust of wind came as a reminder that they were terribly dressed for the weather. In Snake Valley, detouring around the hamlet of Burbank, they came upon an abandoned tent on the mountainside. Will wondered what fate had befallen its owner that he would flee and leave half his gear behind. Had he been chased off by a pack of rabid wolves, or maybe an implacable mountain lion? A bad end to a reckless expedition, the scene told the story of the mirage of riches that went hand in hand with a foolhardy stubbornness that keeps men digging despite diminishing supplies. They weren't waiting to see if the camper was coming back, instead cutting up the canvas to fashion their own makeshift slickers and mittens. Though "mitten" was a generous term for their jury-rigged hand-warmers, and their "slickers" were no more than squares of cloth with a hole pierced in the centre, poncho-style. Hackberry put his head through one, and out popped his inimitable drunken grin and filthy teeth. They both looked like raving madmen, but at least they were somewhat better protected from the cold. And they didn't care what they looked like once the first snowflakes started falling and a blizzard swept the prairie to the sound of its telltale song, its deathly whistle.

"The snow will cover our tracks," Will said, happily.

There was always something enchanting about the first snowfall of the year, something peaceful about the way the snowflakes gently drifted down and rested on the ground a moment before melting. But though the snow would cover their tracks, it made the driving of the cattle that much more difficult. After five or six nights of travelling, the animals were showing signs of exhaustion, and Lew seemed to be approaching the limits of his mental fortitude. The cattle repeatedly came to a halt, refusing to take another step. And Lew grew increasingly irritated and proceeded to yell and to whip them until he was out of breath. The animals were mocking him, he believed.

"I swear, Will. I can see it in their eyes."

"Calm down, Lew. And lay off the jug a little, okay?"

"Shut up!"

And with this rejoinder, Hackberry shot Will a withering look that said he wanted to kill him; his drink-addled expression hardly intimidated his partner as he would have liked, but Will grimaced all the same. Since their fight over Lew's trip to town, the two had been acting like nothing at all had happened, but something was different, you could feel it in the air. The partners watched each other with a wary eye. Conversation between them was rare and never amounted to much.

"My ass hurts. Let's stop."

"Keep going," Will implored. "The sun'll be up in less than an hour."

"You gonna make me say it again? That really what you want?"

"Okay, Lew. I got it."

"My ass hurts!"

By day they took turns resting, but never managed to get much sleep. To Will's dismay, Lew took to the bottle when it was Will's turn, and when his own came around, Lew blundered about uncontrollably, pitifully—dangerously, even—and Will managed only feverish, fitful sleep. Laid out on his meagre bedroll beneath a stiff, stinky ragg-wool blanket, he would constantly jerk awake and look around to see what Lew was up to. Sometimes he'd be snoring with his jug as a pillow; other times he'd be staring right at Will and clocking every reaction, every change in his expression. Will was wary of a rock to the head. The seasoned drunk could make off with their four horses, and just as easily kill Will in his sleep.

One morning, after they'd ridden all night—as light returned to the sky in the east and the exhausted cattle were shivering with fatigue—Lew noticed the little coyote boldly trying to sneak up on them. He started running after the coyote and shooting at him. Just like that, for the sheer pleasure of actually doing something, and being the person he'd always wanted to be. He chased the animal and threw up a great cloud of dust—the ground had completely absorbed the snow days before—before appearing a half hour later with the poor coyote on the hindquarters of his old bay. With a cry of triumph, he threw the animal down at Will's feet. The tiny body of the coyote hit the ground with a thud Will would never forget.

Lew spat a gob of saliva an impressive distance, then suggested they cook up the animal and keep his pelt. Will forbade it.

"You leave that be. Unless you want to join him."

Lew did not. Especially because, right after setting off the evening before, good fortune had crossed their path in the shape of a nice fat black-tailed rabbit, almost two feet long. Aside from jerky, dry biscuits, and coffee, they hadn't eaten much of anything since they'd set off, and Lew was licking his chops at the idea of gobbling up every last scrap of hare and not leaving any for that punk Will James.

"We've gotta move if we want to have breakfast and get any sleep before noon," said Will, climbing down from his horse.

Once the fire was crackling, Lew skinned the rabbit, starting at the front paws. It didn't come easily, and he swore vociferously as he yanked at the pelt to no effect. Will had pulled out his pad of paper and a pencil, and was sitting a ways back from the fire, smoking and taking it all in. And Lew wasn't done with his raging. Their Dutch oven was too small, so he'd have to do some butchering as well. He began slicing the air with his knife in big semicircles, as if he was wielding a meat cleaver.

"These rabbit bones sure do break easy."

"I can see that," Will replied.

The scene wasn't giving Will much of an appetite, any more than the aroma of the rabbit rising out of the pot did an hour later, by which time Lew had nodded off without eating so much as a bite. Lew wasn't just buzzed, he was roostered. The phenomenal amount of alcohol his partner was capable of ingesting had long ceased to impress Will, with Lew sometimes drifting off into sleep mid-sentence.

"I'm so hungry I could . . . I could . . ."

Will left the rabbit meat to simmer and went off to collect his thoughts next to the dead coyote. The body was completely cold. Will kneeled and, without thinking about what he was doing, took out his knife and started cutting off small tufts of fur, beginning with the animal's bushy tail and proceeding to its withers and neck. He clasped each tuft between the thumb and index finger of his free hand, making sure all the fur was pointing in the same direction. In certain places, it was hard not to cut off clumps of flesh along with the fur, and the corpse of the animal started bleeding in spots.

Pelt in one hand and knife in the other, Will figured he didn't have enough. He went back toward the fire. Lew was snoring loud enough to keep the wolves away. Will walked over to his partner's bay—the poor horse had drawn the short straw in the rider lottery. When Will gave the horse a pat it barely even shook. He felt the animal's black tail, running his finger through the horsehair. This would do, he thought. He cut a good six inches off the end of the tail, which he compacted against the coyote's hair he was already holding in his other hand.

He went to sit near the fire to warm up a little, and then started fashioning that irresistible object he'd been dreaming of for so long: a paintbrush, his first-ever homemade paintbrush. His hands guided him. The trick was not to think too hard—what was the point, since he had no idea how to make a paint-brush anyway? His thumb, index, and middle fingers gripped the bristles a little more tightly as he used the other hand to pull away a few of the longer horsehairs and fashion a tight knot around the rest. After tying the first knot with his teeth, the whole enterprise got easier. He repeated the operation a few times. The tuft of bristles was more compact now. He was able to run it over his face like a barber's shaving brush, without worrying that any of it would blow away in the wind. The caress was as sweet as it was soft, and he opened his eyes again.

Next, Will picked out one of the straighter, thicker branches from the pile of kindling. The problem of attaching the bristles to the stem was easily solved: he cut a three-inch strip of leather off his belt, then rummaged around in his bag and found a length of jute string that he cut in two. He wound some of the string around the clump of hair to hold the bristles together in a clump and then fastened it to the shaft using the strip of leather as a makeshift ferrule. Then

Will used the rest of the string to secure the brush.

A wide grin animated Will's face, golden in the firelight. He was more than a little proud of his handiwork, though his spirits fell once he realized he'd only solved one small part of the problem, and so he started mulling it over some more. He remembered that Lew had a dried chili pepper in his saddlebags that he'd hardly touched. That would be a start. He crushed the chili in his pan with the end of the brush, a move he would come to regret when he learned, the hard way, that he needed to be careful not to rub the brush and then touch his eyes. He passed the brush through the flames and then cautiously let it rest in the coals for a moment. It came out black. This gave Will a whole new idea: charcoal. He poked a still-hot ember away from the fire. He'd come back for it later.

Three pigments would do. There were plenty of evergreen bushes around. Perhaps he could pull off their leaves and extract their green essence. He stood up and walked down to explore the valley a bit. He would have loved to find some yellow-petalled desert marigolds, wild lilies, flowering greasewood, or white-budded purple malva. When there was enough rainfall, spring in the valleys was an explosion of colour that lasted right through June. Purples and yellows and bright reds and pinks burst into heady flower, with all the delirious ardour their ephemeral life permitted. Come November, the valley was back to its usual unyielding brown.

Will found a prickly pear bush that the cochineals had not yet stripped bare. But his smile soon turned bitter and his lips pursed in a tight pout. Caterpillars were waddling on the surface of the fat plant, revivified by the new day. He picked a few up and threw them into the mix with the pigment. Maybe they could serve as a binding agent. With gloved hands, he carefully ripped off one of the paddles of the plant—the thick, fleshy, branchlike section of the cactus called a "cow's tongue." The ligneous, pulpy interior, with its sticky sap, reduced to a puree and cut with a little water, might serve as a solvent.

As he went back toward the bivouac, Will came upon a juniper so massive that four men would have been unable to link their arms around it. He had no idea when the fruit of this tree ripened, but he did know that his chances of finding its fruit at this time of year were slim. Birds, cougars, wolves, and other big mammals had undoubtedly devoured everything. Will ran his hands through the fragrant branches and couldn't believe his luck. There were thousands of them! It was the time of year when the deep black juniper berries were ripe, and the fruit had not yet started turning white. Will remembered how, during his winter hikes, he used to admire the way that, rather than turning the usual red and black, the bushes would be covered in berries a shade of pale purple, almost white. He pressed one between his thumb and index finger, and squeezed out a trickle of dark juice. Just what he needed.

Lew, still sleeping, would surely be unconscious till evening. Will fed the fire. He felt hunger pangs, and chewed on a rabbit thigh right over the pot. Not bad under the circumstances. Just needed a pinch of salt.

He got to work. First, he crushed a few caterpillars up into the pigment still in the pan. The paste didn't look like it would be easy to spread, so he added a little water and then — why not? — a splash of his partner's whiskey. It was starting to look almost like paint. Like a really lumpy gouache. He found his iron dish to use as a pallet and a spoon that would do as a spatula to separate out the worst of the impurities, and started experimenting.

He didn't quite manage to squeeze enough juice from the cactus. Even adding water wasn't enough to get the paint to gel. Then, when he mixed ground saltbush leaves into the concoction, he found himself with a brownish soup instead of the green he was looking for. His pallet was now covered in a bronze-coloured paste.

The juniper berries yielded something a little more appealing. Mixed in with a few caterpillars, the paste took on a mauve hue. Somewhere between pigeon blue and plum, or perhaps bishop's purple, though Will did not yet have the vocabulary or experience to put a definitive name to this earthy purple that would pair uneasily with his mess of green.

"Des nuances de brun, ç'a l'air," he said in his native language.

It didn't matter that Will painted until not a single drop of homemade pigment remained in his iron dish; the cheap paper wasn't absorbing enough water, and the resulting brushstrokes wouldn't have passed muster even with a grade school teacher in a one-room school. Will hadn't touched a brush since he'd been a child in Saint-Nazaire, Quebec, when his overenthusiastic father would order far more art supplies at the general store than little Ernest had ever asked for. Still, after letting a little meditation, visualization, and alcohol ease him into a more creative frame of mind, Will started to see himself as a worthy successor to his hero, the painter Charles Russell. In his new state, Will tried to get his idealized, if sorrowful, visions down on paper, and to imbue them with form, texture, and life. With each new brushstroke, Will wondered whether he wouldn't be better off getting back to drawing, but there was no way he was going to waste this paint, no matter how bad it was.

Many pages were lost in the attempt to capture the vision troubling him. And under the colourful yet sombre sky (the hue of juniper berries) shot through by a few tentative rays of the setting sun (the cater-pillar pigment), the totemic coyote, a sentinel, was heralding the night as always, this frail creature that had never harmed anyone, and was simply following his instincts. The yip-yips and howling in the distance did nothing to yank Will from his creative trance. He wouldn't have been able to tell you whether the sounds were real or in his head.

Will returned to his drawing paper. He couldn't resist testing out his charcoal to blacken some of the features. The artist within him was guiding his hand, determining his choices. Though he was powerless to improve them, Will found the result of every attempt more disappointing than the last, and burned each one immediately after finishing it. The sheets crackled in the flames. Toward noon, obstinately sucking on the empty bottle, Will ate the second rabbit thigh before pissing on the fire, saving a little for the stew in the pot; he wasn't going to eat any more, but Lew was sure to wake up famished. He unrolled his mat next to Happy and fell asleep. All the while, the cattle watched him uneasily. Without any newborns to protect, they were gregarious but also docile. It didn't occur to even one of them to flee while their two guards slept.

7

For ten days they journeyed through the frozen Utah mountain deserts. They traversed Millard County from west to east, hewing to a route well away from roads and populated areas. The riders took a detour south of the Confusion Range and then toward Thomas Peak, then followed the pass between the mountains and Sevier Lake. North of the lake was an immense salt plain that felt, to Will, interminable.

The most trying part of their journey was travelling alongside the river to Oasis: two days of bleak and unrelenting flatness. True, the cattle were able to drink, but being so exposed was dangerous. There was nowhere to hide. And the wind! More than once, Will thought his ears might fall off from the whistling and the cold.

One especially hard night during the blizzard and winds that bit right through their clothes, Will saw, less than a mile off, the lights of a small, solitary house on the prairie. He had visions of being inside, toasty warm, as the little ones told naughty stories of

which his mother would have disapproved, or lying
in bed reading a magazine by the light of an oil lamp,
while a wood stove full of cedar burned. Its crackling
epitomized all the happiness its warmth provided. The
mother was washing dishes and the father rocking
gently next to the stove with a pipe hanging from his
mouth and a jug on his knee, gazing benevolently over
his progeny. But suddenly the cowboy was seized by
the cold and his fantasy dissolved. The house seemed
a thousand miles away. Will was trembling, and shivering in the glacial black-and-white night, driving the
exhausted cattle on. With only hunger in his belly,
Will forged on, incessantly glancing over his shoulder
to survey the horizon and on the lookout for cowboys
or sheriffs who might be chasing them.

More than once, the rustlers passed between
Joshua trees whose gnarled silhouettes in the black
of night took on the shapes of riders with rifles at the
ready. Will would give them a scrutinizing second look,
squinting and short of breath, ready to bolt. He wasn't
sure which he feared most, these apparitions or a real,
flesh-and-blood bounty hunter. A week of travelling,
deprived of food and light, had made him unrecogniz-
able — his face emaciated, his cheeks hollow. As for
Lew, he'd come to resemble a cadaver long before
they reached Oasis.

Late in the evening of the ninth night, after they'd
been wending their way in darkness for three or four
hours, the cowboys found themselves less than a mile
from Oasis. They were on the verge of reaching their
destination at last.

They forded the river. It was freezing cold, but at the point they'd chosen, the water didn't even reach the cattle's knees. They would survive. Happy coughed a few times — had what they called a horse cold, which would be forgotten twenty minutes later. They let the herd and horses drink, and opted for rest that was as sorely needed by the animals as by the riders. Hackberry came over, scowling as he spoke. Will's attention was listless, as if he was having an out-of-body experience.

"You stay here for an hour while I go into town. I'll reserve us a cattle car, and sign the herd under my name."

"Your real name?"

"Yeah, you're right. I'll use Bradberry — that okay by you?"

Will, unsmiling, agreed.

"When you arrive, we'll load 'em up and I'll leave. Then you can sell the horses and buy a ticket for Provo..."

"Why Provo?" Will asked.

They'd never said a word about the place.

"I know someone there — the sort of person we haven't seen in far too long, if you catch my drift. Lord, I hope she's still there. Provo ain't too far for you, either. I'll introduce you, if you want."

Will shuddered.

"No thanks," he said, and then, "What about after?"

"After? Well, kid — *after*, you can do whatever the hell you want. We'll go our separate ways and you can be King of England for all I care."

An hour later, Will drove the herd on for the last time. Even by himself he could have done it with his eyes closed; they were so exhausted they'd go anywhere you told them. Happy trotted joyfully through the town, as if he knew their journey was coming to an end.

As an outpost in the middle of the desert, the hamlet of Oasis was aptly named. It was forgotten in time, an islet of green irrigated by the river. Home to just fifty people, Oasis nevertheless boasted a hotel with a restaurant and bar and a general store, a train station, a barber shop, and a clutch of houses built along the muddy main street.

It was around eleven when Will parked his herd in the pen next to the railroad track, with the assistance of a well-fed man who asked no questions. Lew wasn't much help at all. Clearly, he'd found himself the time for a round or two at the hotel bar, and followed it up with two or three more. Mostly Lew seemed detached, restless, and nasty, but Will was too exhausted to give it much thought or put two and two together. Around midnight, the two cowboys went over the plans they'd made earlier that evening one more time. Will would sell the horses and—along with the wages Riordan had paid him—would have at least enough money to get by until Hackberry met up with him again in Provo.

"You got something to complain about?" Lew asked him.

Will shook his head, though he found it difficult to understand how a man could be so cavalier about leaving his horses behind. The prospect of parting with Happy was unthinkable to Will. But he didn't complain.

"I don't see why," said Lew. "We'll be rich!"

The pair had time to kill until the train left, and the wait seemed endless: Will hadn't eaten in at least twenty-four hours, and he felt as if he could sleep a full month without fully recovering from the fatigue and paranoia; his stomach was even emptier than his eyes. They finally caught word that the train would be at least an hour late, so Will took the horses to the stable, where the animals could warm up and chew on some excellent hay. Then he went to the saloon and ordered prime rib, fried potatoes, bread, and coffee.

Day was dawning when he watched the freight car disappear into the distance, and the sun was already high in the sky when he finally got to taste the meal he'd wanted hours earlier. He ate voraciously, though his stomach was troubling him. When, briefly, he looked up from his plate, Will caught a glimpse of his reflection in the mirror behind the bar: gaunt features, a pained expression twisted into a scowl, and greasy, dirty hair. He looked no better than a tramp. Enough to make his mother proud. It was time for a bath and a trip to the barber's for a haircut.

8

Richard Swallow Senior was an influential figure in Salt Lake City, feared and respected in equal measure. His family, persecuted in Missouri, had been a part of the first wave of Mormon pioneers to make their way across the country, and Swallow was one of the first sons of the Church of Jesus Christ of Latter-day Saints to be born in the promised land of the Utah Territory. His father was a talented carpenter, cabinetmaker, and mason; a successful builder who'd become a pillar of the community. His son hoped to live up to the family name, and real estate had provided him a profitable calling. Swallow owned many of the small buildings in downtown Salt Lake City, as well as large tracts of good land in Northern Utah, to the east of the Great Salt Lake—land that would be worth a fortune one day. Now, he was enjoying a well-deserved retirement, either whiling away the hours on the beautiful patio behind his palatial home, reading whatever he could get his hands on—a luxury he would never have permitted himself during his working years—or trotting around his acreage on one of his thoroughbreds, or his Morgans, or his Quarter Horses. Swallow's stables held no fewer than a dozen geldings and prize stallions possessed of an innate dignity many men would never summon.

Swallow's wife had passed in 1905. He'd loved her until the end, and had never seen a need to remarry. He felt he was too old for that—preferred the company of his horses and his hares. Occasionally, he would sleep with one of his Black servants. In private, it was said, he was at least a gentle, considerate man. Swallow had four sons, if we ignore the rumours of illegitimate offspring in the area. The two eldest had grown into men of little worth—spoiled, in every sense of the word, from infancy. The brothers, a capricious pair who held nothing sacred, owned a mid-sized ranch in the Mormon parts of Nevada.

Sitting, on this almost temperate November morning, in a green velvet suit out on his glassed-in patio, Swallow was flipping through the newspaper and sipping on the day's third cup of coffee (taking care not to stain his white moustache) when his manservant brought him a telegram on a silver platter.

= DEAR DICK SMALL HERD BRANDED GS PASSED THROUGH OASIS
TOWARD DENVER ALL WELL I HOPE BUT WANTED TO WARN YOU
IN CASE = YOUR FRIEND CALVIN

Calvin Tuttle, a long-time acquaintance of Swallow's, had lived in Oasis as long as anyone could remember. The evening before, he'd consumed a little more than a man with a fragile liver should at the Oasis hotel where everyone knew everyone else, and strangers only rarely stopped in for a drink. In the middle of the night an unfamiliar young man, dragging his feet, had entered the saloon and then walked out of it. An hour later, the stockyard and railway employee had come in and taken his place at the bar. He was a short, fat man whom Tuttle pretty well despised but whose loose tongue was something of a virtue. In no time at all, Tuttle learned that two men had loaded up a wagon with pretty but exhausted-looking cattle.

"What did their brand look like?"

"Oh, they weren't from around here, that's for sure."

"I figured. But what about the brand?"

The man scratched his head under his hat, and remembered the few dollars he'd been given to stay quiet.

"GS?"

Tuttle paid for the man's drink and left the hotel. Apprehending either of the men in the streets of Oasis wouldn't be a wise move. But he still took a walk around the settlement to see whether or not he might catch a glimpse. No such luck. He decided to go home to bed. By the time Tuttle drifted off to sleep, Hackberry was already long gone and Will was back at the hotel feasting on a healthy hunk of meat and thick slices of generously buttered bread.

Swallow Senior placed his glasses on the table and summoned his manservant.

"Earl."

"Sir."

Swallow handed back the telegram.

"Bad news?"

"Would you please write a cable to Junior and Ray relaying this information, and add that I'm sending someone they can trust right away—they'll catch my drift. Say I'll dispatch someone discreet to Denver before the police are called in, and tell them that if we want to see justice done, we'll have to find these rogues before the authorities do."

"So I'll write that they shouldn't contact the police."

"No, they have to. Let's play by the rules. Say something like, 'You good-for-nothing boys have been rustled again,' so they understand this is no laughing matter and that their father is always here watching over them, because they have no earthly notion of how the world works."

Earl didn't quite understand the end of Swallow Senior's tirade.

"Right away, sir," he said.

"And while you're at it, bring me the phone, along with another coffee and a little brandy."

"You know what your doctor—"

"Take your time."

Earl made himself scarce.

IN THE SANCTITY OF their respective quarters at the Lazy GS Ranch, Richard T. and Ray G. Swallow were sleeping in later than usual. The night before, they'd been pleasantly waylaid in the arms of a pair of saloon girls, in the sort of dimly lit establishment you were always sure to find in backwaters like Ely. They'd come home before dawn in their expensive automobile, and both had pretended to listen to their wives' complaints before they were finally able to hit the hay. It was the cook's flunky who woke the older brother with the father's message. The room reeked of bad breath, sweat, and alcohol. The son may have inherited his father's towering height and deep voice, albeit with a blockish head that somehow always seemed dirty, but Richard Junior had been graced with none of his father's elegance. He frowned as he woke up, and then coughed and spat. He had a splitting headache and couldn't make heads nor tails of what he was reading. The letters on the telegram were a blur.

SON YOU WORTHLESS BOYS HAVE BEEN RUSTLED AGAIN YOUR
FATHER IS ALWAYS THERE WHEREAS YOU USELESS BOYS HAVENT
THE FIRST IDEA OF ANYTHING CATTLE BRANDED GS LOADED IN
OASIS FOR DENVER A DISCREET TRUSTWORTHY MAN ON WAY
TO FIND THE CROOKS BEFORE THE POLICE EVEN THOUGH YOUR
FATHER SUGGESTS THAT YOU CONTACT THEM RESPECTABLE
FAMILY AND ALL =

    FATHER

A two-card telegram, Richard Swallow took note. Must have cost a fortune.

"*You*," Junior grunted.

His lackey stiffened and backed up a pace. More than anything, he feared the whims of this tyrannical, vicious person. His employer was a madman.

"Go get a couple of beers, then wake my brother, if he's not already up, and have the cook make us a feed. Coffee too. And hop to it!"

"C-co-coming up," the young man stuttered.

After gorging on a few hardboiled eggs, bread, and several rashers of bacon, and gulping down the coffee and beer, their hangovers were almost tolerable. The brothers even managed to loudly discuss what had happened.

The cows must have drifted south, into Lincoln County—nothing unusual there. They'd send a few of their best hands to track the livestock down and see how many cattle were missing. If the thieves had made it as far as Oasis, then yes, they'd most likely be selling them in Denver. The first order of business was to call the authorities and instruct them to keep an eye open and to inform them of any unusual cattle sales. The brothers also needed to contact C. S. Crain, the White Pine County Sheriff, so that he'd put himself in charge of the investigation. They didn't trust him—how could you trust any lawman in these parts, especially a liberal who'd shown he'd have no truck with lynching—but the Swallow brothers had no choice. This was a family matter.

Sheriff Crain had no hangover to nurse that morning. Formerly a notorious drunk, he'd found the remedy for his immoderate thirst. His badge depended on his temperance and, besides, he just didn't have the energy anymore. Which is to say that it had once been impossible for him to live a day without passing out cold, whether he was drinking to chase away his hangover, or the hangover from his hangover. Crain's come-to-Jesus moment came when he committed an act he'd regret as long as he lived. In the middle of an afternoon, ostensibly on duty, he'd stumbled out of a bar with a gut-busting quantity of whiskey in his blood and put two bullets in his pretty black horse's head. He'd felt the animal was pestering him. "I reckon you done nagged me for the last time!" he muttered as the poor beast drew its last breath.

When he sobered up, the guilt was so fierce he never drank another drop—except a cold beer now and then, two or three nights a week tops, to pass the time, and never more than twelve in one sitting. So Crain had a clear head when he heard the news that morning and it brought him no joy. He swore as he leaned back in his chair, feet up on the desk, sucking on his pipe with a faraway look. As he smoked, he smoothed his long whiskers, which did little to conceal the constellation of veins in his cheeks.

The prospect of running these fellows down for grand larceny was demoralizing. Hadn't he already been through that enough times? Given a rustling, a fight, and a shootout, he'd choose the rustlers every time, that was for sure, but darned if he could figure out why these men kept pushing their luck, doing the same thing again and again, generation after generation, when the cowpuncher's job, and prairie life generally, had evolved so much. The old West was long gone, though one thing never seemed to change, and that was ranch owners' atavistic desire to string rustlers up from trees—that is, when they didn't fire a bullet into their heads or a full chamber into their bodies.

Whenever a man went down in Sheriff Crain's territory, he viewed it as a personal failure and took a long time to get over it. Sure, men had been killing each other since the dawn of time; it was irrevocable and that was why they called it fate. Outside of White Pine County they could go ahead and kill each other all they wanted—like they were doing across the Atlantic, for example—but not in his county.

Crain got up from the desk, still smoothing out his long, unfashionable whiskers. He was thinking. Cables needed to be sent out to every ranch owner within fifty miles—only a few had telephones—in search of any drifting cowpunchers who had recently disappeared. There'd be a sizeable list to go through, what with the final roundups of the season just finished. Then Crain drafted another telegram to his colleague in Fillmore, Utah, asking him to send a few men to check out the town while he got there as quick as he could.

The light in the room changed, distracting Crain from his morning thinking. His right-hand man Bob was a behemoth who looked as if he'd been cut from a single block of granite; he was big as a hutch, with a round face that sometimes led people to underestimate his intelligence. He was standing in the doorway.

"Late again, Bob."

"Sorry, boss. Bit of a domestic situation."

"When you gonna stop letting your wife walk all over you? It's not enough for you to be my doormat all day, you feel the need to go home and do the same thing all over again?"

"I brought coffee."

"Well, that there's the day's first bit of good news."

"Trouble in White Pine?"

"You think the world's any less rotten here in Nevada?"

Bob remained where he was and said nothing.

"Bring the boys in for a meeting."

Bob stepped away from the open door, and the light in the room returned to normal. A few minutes later, Crain shared the news with his crew in the common room. Everyone had an opinion concerning how far the herd would have travelled and what the rustlers' whereabouts were—if hired hands who had finished up for the year had committed the crime, that is, because it could also have been the work of unsavoury characters passing through. The sheriff sent some men to Shoshone, a real hole, to take a statement from the Swallows and make a few inquiries of other ranchers in the area. And he had his secretary draft cables to send out to twenty-odd ranchers in neighbouring counties. As for Bob and himself—well, he laughed, there was plenty of adventure in store in Utah. Oasis was a hundred and fifty miles from Ely. It was not yet eight when they left the police station in the car; if they drove at top speed, they'd arrive before noon.

9

Once his stomach was full, a satisfied Will sat and waited for the barbershop to open at eight. A few drinks at the hotel, known simply as the Oasis, gave Will time to lower his blood pressure and let his adrenaline drop. Will was the only customer. The sight of the bartender, a permanent fixture by day and night, dozing behind the bar, did little to help Will stay alert. Not feeling safe loafing around in his empty room, where he was liable to fall asleep at any moment, Will spent the next hour with Happy, fighting off sleep in the straw of the stable. The warmth and odour of excrement and moist hay reminded him of his uncle Napoléon's farm in Saint-Nazaire, Quebec. He took out his pad of paper, but the first sketches were unconvincing. His heart wasn't in it; he couldn't find his rhythm. One drawing, depicting a herd driven by a pair of identical cowboys—two versions of Will—and the small head and slanted ears of the coyote tracking them poking out of the sagebrush, at least put a smile on Will's face. Eventually, he nodded off. When he finally set out, cloudy-eyed, into the cool morning air, the streets of the village were busy, and curious onlookers were gazing askance at Will.

The barber was a tiny, thin man with a ring of white hair around his bald head. He smiled, revealing a full set of teeth just as white. Will seemed to appeal to him as much as the barber did Will. He had the sense he would be well taken care of.

"I sure could use a bath."

"Right away. Good timing, I emptied the old water only yesterday. Coffee?"

"Wouldn't say no."

The barber beckoned him into the back room and showed him a metal tub that looked like it had been around the world twice. He was right, though: the water was clear and clean, not white from old soap and God knows what else.

"I'll bring you some hot water."

"Thank you kindly."

"Not at all, think nothing of it," said the barber congenially.

A few minutes later, soaking in the warm water and forgetting all about his coffee, Will stopped fighting and slept like a log, like a baby. The ash from the cigarette in his mouth dropped onto his wet chest. He dreamed of Hackberry and the little coyote, and afterwards of the little coyote on its own, wandering about the desolate prairie with an unfathomable woe in its gut. The little barber woke him up half an hour later.

"You sure seem to be enjoying it. But I don't reckon you're planning to spend all day in there, are you?"

"No, no."

"Give your hair a good wash, and I'll get going on that cut."

Will obeyed, and the barber returned to his chair and waited for him there. He didn't know what to make of the cowboy just yet. He was likely on the lam, something like that, though he didn't look like a dangerous criminal. Everyone made mistakes. What business was it of his? With or without the barber's involvement, the young man would get his just desserts sooner or later. Not in any cosmic or religious sense. In the barber's reckoning, there was no such thing as hell. Hell was this world, the material world here on earth. Everyone was entitled to their lot of pain and suffering. Some got a little more than their fair share, while for others, fate seemed an arbitrary thing.

The barber's chair was a lot more comfortable than many of the beds Will had slept in over the last few years. It had the same effect as the tub he'd just stepped out of. While the short man cut his hair, Will fought off sleep. The barber stopped asking him questions, the kid not looking like he'd had much rest lately. And rest was one thing the barber could provide. It was part of his service.

"You finished?" asked Will, when he came to again.

He almost cooed the word, the bristles of the barber's brush tickling the back of his neck.

"Yes. But a good shave would do you a world of good, don't you think?"

"I don't know. My skin don't much like the razor."

The barber sympathized.

"Don't worry about a thing. No one leaves my shop with marks on their throat. And afterwards you'll get a nice hot wet towel to relax you. That's if you're not already relaxed enough."

Will smiled.

"Let's do it."

The shaving brush glided over Will's skin, followed by a few long and precise strokes with the freshly sharpened razor. The barber was doing a few final touch-ups when three rough-looking men pushed the shop door open, revolvers clearly visible on their belts. Their faces were either dirty or turned leathery by the sun, and their three-day stubble didn't sit right with the barber. He had an inkling these men weren't here by chance, and that the reason for their visit might well be sitting in the chair in front of him. He laid the hot towel over Will's face before greeting the men, carefully placing himself between them and the cowboy scarcely daring to breathe.

After perfunctory greetings, one of the men asked the little man if he'd noticed anything out of the ordinary the night before, or perhaps on this lovely November morning.

"Well, that's a broad question, see. All kinds of things can happen that a man might call 'out of the ordinary.' Even in a little burg like this. Take three armed men marching into my shop. For example, see."

The one who had spoken dodged the barber's volley and gobbed a viscous nugget of phlegm into the spittoon.

"A herd of cattle was loaded up in Oasis last night. Cattle that ain't from around here."

"Really, now. And where were they from?"

"Nevada."

"Nevada's a big state," the barber replied with a broad grin.

"So you ain't seen nothing last night or this morning."

"And to whom, say, might these cattle belong?"

"That makes a difference?"

"Not at all, not at all. Just curious—and a barber. I have a duty to provide gossip. It's what my customers want, see."

"Swallow."

"Any ties to the Swallows of Salt Lake City?"

"His sons."

The barber detested Richard Swallow Senior, a smug Mormon waging war on anybody and everybody so that he could buy property on the cheap from the honest folk who'd for years nourished the land with the sweat of their brows.

"I'm afraid I just can't help you boys. But I'll sure let you know as soon as I hear anything."

"Right you will."

And then they left the way they'd come in, with a jingle of spurs.

"Geez, son. It looks like you've stepped into something."

Will gulped and thought fast. About the revolver tucked into his boot, among other things. But the next words the barber spoke reassured him.

"If I were you, I'd get the hell out of this town as fast as I rode in."

Will got up from the chair.

"How much do I owe you?"

"'Cause you intend to pay me?"

"Of course. What do you take me for?"

The little barber retreated a step.

"My apologies, young man."

"How much?"

"Fifteen cents."

Will handed over ten dollars. The old man furrowed his brow.

"Now that's just too generous," he said.

"It's been a long time since I've come across a good man. I'm not just paying for my bath and the cut, but for your kindness—and discretion."

"See, it's easy to draw hasty conclusions about who is and isn't a 'good man.' But men generally ain't especially well known for having good intentions. Or what you'd call a moral sense."

Will looked down.

"Don't make that face, now. I reckon you'll find a way to make amends. Won't you?"

"What, by turning myself in?"

"I didn't say that. You're a good man, and you're not stupid. Ain't that so?"

The barber smiled engagingly at Will.

"I'll give you something else to wear. You won't get far in your boots and cowboy hat—and don't you have anything to keep warm?"

Will shook his head.

"Wait here, I'll be back in a minute."

Three minutes later, the barber handed him a pair of square-toed work boots, a straw hat, and a thread-bare but double-lined overcoat that would help him stay incognito. Will put the new outfit on and the barber gave him a satchel for his old clothes.

They shook hands. The little man hoped that in a few days he wouldn't be told the kid had ended up six feet under, killed with a bullet to the head or his neck snapped in a noose.

"Take the back way out. I'll make sure no one's out there waiting for you."

No one was behind the shop. Will already had a foot out the door when he stopped short, remembering something.

"You'll find a grey in the stable," Will told the barber. "He's mouse grey and answers to the name Duffy. He's yours. Do what you will with him. Just promise me one thing: if you do sell him one day, please don't let him go to just anyone."

"Sure thing. Thanks! But...you sure, son?"

"I can't..."

Will suddenly had the strange impression that it was his old self he was renouncing; that by passing Duffy on, he was leaving the very last traces of Ernest Dufault behind. Duffy had been his first horse, paid for with his cowman's wages. He'd talked about the horse a lot in gushing letters to his parents, assuring them they'd not been forgotten, and that his new "friend's" name, short for Dufault, stood as a reminder of who he was and where he came from. An homage.

From now on there would be only William Roderick James. No matter what happened, Will would never again change names as he had done several times since leaving Quebec. C. W. Jackson had almost stuck, but didn't have quite the right ring to it; the young Ernest hadn't managed to slip into that skin. Going forward there would be Will James and no one else, even if this Will James started his life on the run. His story didn't quite square with the fantasy of a cowboy artist young Ernest had conjured up in such detail, an ideal that had swept him up for years. He'd envisioned a heroic, legendary rider who picked up his pencil to draw whenever he had a spare moment. And yet the life he was living was so much more entertaining, so much freer, and more fierce. More real. Stealing the cattle, Will managed to convince himself, had been the very best thing that could have happened to him. To Will James.

"Will you go find him?" Will asked.

The man agreed, trying the name in a whisper: "*Duffy.*" They said their final goodbyes, and the bald barber went back into his little shop where nothing ever happened.

10

Will wasted no time. If he'd listened to his inner voice he'd have razed the town to the ground, but that wouldn't have accomplished his aim. He walked the streets of Oasis with purpose, staring straight ahead, as if he had somewhere to go. The men who'd come into the barbershop would most likely be waiting for him at the town stables. And, sure enough, there was a man posted at the entrance, keeping watch, doing his best to look inconspicuous. Will hid behind a house and waited to see what hand Lady Luck would deal him. Providence showed up in the shape of a young boy pushing a wheel along with a stick. Will stopped the kid and pulled him behind the wall where he was hiding. He held out a silver dollar.

"See that, boy?"

The kid nodded and tried to grab for the coin, but it stayed between the fingers of the cowboy dressed as a shepherd.

"That's all yours, but I need you to do me a little favour."

A minute later, the boy — a talented actor who took his role to heart — was agitatedly pulling on the sleeve of the man in front of the stable, telling him his partners needed him right away, it was an emergency.

"They found a man! They got him!" he shouted, panting with excitement.

The man followed the kid, leaving the coast clear for Will. By the time the deputy realized he'd been tricked, the thief, with any luck, would be long gone. He saddled up Happy as fast as he could, picked up his stuff, and said goodbye to Duffy. Though he was well aware the man would betray him at the first opportunity, Will paid off the stable hand, then galloped right out of Oasis.

Once outside of town, Will headed east toward the Canyon Mountains, where he'd be able to hide out and graze his horse. He rode hard and fast for a good part of the morning, and when Happy could no longer keep up the pace, they slowed down but didn't stop, alternately trotting and pacing. After a long ascent, their journey finally brought them into the mountains. Will found a fine spot to lay up a while, a grass meadow between two ridges with the odd spindly pine tree and a creek running through it. The perfect place to pull out his bedroll and allow himself a luxury he hadn't known for days: sleep. He would happily have eaten something, but all he had left was a shrivelled-up flapjack. Best to save it for the uncertain days ahead. He let Happy graze freely on the frost-covered grass — a faithful companion like him wouldn't go far—and collapsed on his bedroll before he'd even finished laying it out.

Will slept into the early evening, though it seemed he'd been dozing less than five minutes when finally he woke. He felt a pressure on his shoulder, like a branch bending without breaking. He dreamed that the Swallows were punishing him for his crime, but his body kept snagging in branches as they tried to string him up on a tree. Everyone was swearing; everyone was trying in vain to unhook him. The branch was bothering him, interfering with his sleep. He cleared it away with a grunt, and noticed, through a half-open eye, something that looked like the mouth of a volcano. When Will tried to turn away and find a better sleeping position, a new branch stood in his way. When he tried to dodge that branch, it caught him again. And when he took it in his hand to push it out of the way once and for all, he finally woke up to find a six-shooter an inch from his face.

"Sleep well?" asked a gruff voice.

And then an equally gruff voice broke into laughter. All Will could see, deep in the night, were the silhouettes of two men of very different height. One was Sheriff Crain from Ely; the other his large and intimidating deputy. For now, the sheriff informed Will, there was no evidence against him, but they also had a duty to lock up any man hiding in the mountains just a few miles from Oasis the day after a suspicious load of cattle left town.

Will gingerly stretched an arm toward his satchel, where he knew one of his two revolvers lay—the other one was in his boot. The sheriff stopped him short with a boot on his hand.

"Don't bother, son. You won't find what you're looking for."

Crain lifted the panel of his jacket, exposing a prodigious beer gut. Will's gun was on his holster. The young cowboy groaned, wide awake and seeing the light. He'd never packed his revolver for anything but an abstract sense of protection. Pulling it on these lawmen was likely to backfire. Over the years, he'd met more than one man with an itchy trigger finger. Enough to know those types died young, or grew old and crooked in cold dark cells.

Will smiled. Once the officer took his foot off his arm, he was able to put his hands up.

"We'll hold on to your gun for you. Which don't have to mean you'll never see it again."

The sheriff tossed him a pair of handcuffs.

"Think we need these? I'd like to be able to trust you."

Will brought himself to his feet and handed them back.

"Whatever you think is right," Will said. "But you can trust me."

"You can put down your gun, Bob."

The second man demurred.

"*Bob*," said the sheriff.

Bob listened to his boss. Crain saddled up Happy, and Bob put Will's satchel on his second horse. Then they started riding down the mountains toward Oasis.

When they arrived back in Oasis late the next

morning, it seemed like the whole town was on hand to welcome them. The little bald barber was among them, though he was no longer sporting his gleaming smile. Crain played the part of the conquering general back from a long campaign, sitting with his chest puffed up and his back straight on his proud mount, and doffing his cap to each person whose gaze he met, the pretty local ladies especially. As there was no jail in the town, the sheriff's men assembled at the hotel. Crain ordered a meal for Will, who wolfed it down in a few mouthfuls. The men drank a few beers but didn't grant Will the privilege of quenching his thirst, real as it was. He sulked a while and then, sure he was being ignored, started to draw right on the table. The scene he sketched showed him riding off on a horse with its tongue stuck out and all four feet in the air. Bob scolded Will, but Crain took the fugitive's side.

"Lemme see."

Crain twisted around to get a better view of the drawing. He looked impressed.

"Not bad!"

They'd agreed not to head back to Ely before dinner. For the time being, what everyone needed was a little nap. Crain and his deputy hadn't slept in over twenty-four hours.

That afternoon in the hotel room, Will thought more than once of trying to escape. But every time he woke up—and he woke up a lot—there was either Crain or Bob, holding a rifle in his lap and staring at him. Will didn't let it get to him, as if all of this was happening to someone else and not him, or as if it was all part of a plan—his plan. He still hadn't been accused of anything, so what could possibly happen? Lady Luck would deal him a new hand, and he'd figure it out the way he always did. Only this time, she didn't hear his prayers.

11

There were telegrams waiting for Crain when his team left their rooms for the hotel bar, refreshed after a pleasant nap and the chance to wash up. The men he'd dispatched south of White Pine had stopped by James Riordan's ranch and not come back empty-handed. The whole county knew Riordan hired few seasonals, but Sheriff Crain had taught his men that proper investigations left no stone unturned. So they'd listened, and a good thing too:

CS CRAIN = OASIS HOTEL OASIS, UT =

TWO MEN LEFT RIORDAN RANCH DAY OF THEFT = LEW HACKBERRY

AND WILL JAMES BEST LEAD SO FAR BOSS =

TO BE CONTINUED

Crain furrowed his brow and looked over at Will James, who returned his gaze uneasily. There could no longer be any reasonable doubt, thought Crain—may as well take the offender's statement right away. He interrogated Will one-on-one in a small room off the hotel lobby that had stately wooden mouldings and was bathed in natural light. Will realized there was no point inventing some new story, especially as the kindly sheriff with a bulbous and veiny nose suggested to Will that the judge would look favourably on him if he co-operated. So the young man raised his head, met his interrogator's steel blue eyes, and got on with it. In less than ten minutes, the story of his and Hackberry's cattle rustling was down on paper. Then Crain asked where they'd agreed to meet, and Will again hesitated for a moment — or at least feigned to, for honour's or appearance's sake — but, after finding no reason not to, he named the town of Provo.

"But I got the impression Lew was making like a jackrabbit, and I think I would have spent a good long while chasing after him."

"That'll be all, young man. Sign here, please."

Will smiled disingenuously and signed the paper "William Roderick James," and Crain drafted a "Wanted" poster for the second suspect based on the traits Will had described: brown hair, tall, dark, bearded, unkempt; character, unsavoury. The poster would make the rounds of sheriffs' departments in the towns strung along the railroad line to Denver, all the way through Utah and Colorado. He dispatched Bob to the post office to send the cable, but Hackberry was likely long gone from Denver by now, and the sides of beef were surely swinging from hooks in the cool rooms or boiling in the melting pots of some slaughterhouse. Like Will, Crain had a feeling the thief wouldn't be tempted to retrace his steps, but would instead strike out in a new direction and stick to it. Then again, he might be totally unconcerned about anyone on his tail, busy blowing his cash and getting drunk out of his skull in some cheap Denver brothel.

Crain checked his watch. He was so thirsty his tongue was pasty. He went back to the bar to order his first cold beer of the day. On the road, Crain felt entitled to start drinking a little earlier than usual.

Three or four mugs later, someone came up to him.

"Phone call for you, boss."

"A phone call?"

"A phone call."

"You got telephones, all the way out here in Oasis?"

"Better believe it."

"But who could it be? Not my wife, surely."

"She know where you are?"

"No!"

"No chance, then. Caller's a man, anyways."

The caller turned out to be a constable from Denver who'd seen the bulletin. He said Swallow had contacted him two days earlier, the very morning the cattle were loaded up for Denver. He'd been on the case ever since and, in the course of his inquiries, had learned that a certain "Bradley" had sold, for the sum of fifteen hundred dollars, thirty head of prime cattle—all branded "GS." They were being held, for now, in a slaughterhouse corral, and Bradley was still on the lam. There'd been no sign of him save an unpaid bill in Albany under the name Bradberry, though the description fit.

"I'd be much obliged if you'd inform the Swallows, since the theft was committed on your turf," said the constable.

Crain agreed, and thanked his colleague politely though he despised officers of his kind, so quick to pass the buck because then they could keep on doing as little as possible. There may be exceptions, but the stereotype of the lazy policeman had still taken hold in the public imagination. The sheriff packed his pipe while he formulated a few choice phrases in his head. A few minutes later they were set down on the telegram card addressed to Swallow:

SIRS A MAN NAMED W. JAMES IN MY CUSTODY = ACCOMPLICE LEW HACKBERRY STILL FREE = BROWN HAIR BEARDED SCOUNDREL PRIORITY GREATER DENVER MAYBE ALSO PROVO IF HAS JUDGE-MENT WILL FIND ELSEWHERE AND MUCH LATER = SINCERELY DS C S CRAIN

Writing to the Swallow brothers appalled him, all the more so because he knew they'd left their ranch on the first day of the manhunt in order to find the rus-tlers before the authorities did. It was highly unlikely the ranchers would ever see his telegram, but Crain was nevertheless duty-bound to inform them, as they were the owners of the stolen private property. Without giving it much thought, he called the father as well. The manservant answered, and a minute later the patriarch was on the phone.

"Hello?"

"Mr. Swallow."

"This is he."

"Sheriff Crain here. I've got some news on the theft of your sons' cattle."

"I'm all ears."

"We have strong evidence suggesting we've identified the two culprits—Lew Hackberry and Will James. Those names mean anything to you?"

"Never heard of them."

Swallow was lying on at least one count. His man had found the stolen herd before the police, and knew the identity of the man who had driven it into Denver. Lee Bradley was the name he'd used to sell the cattle, though he'd given a different one at the hotel. Swallow's hired gun was still trying to get his hands on the man, but had assured his boss it was only a matter of time.

"I've got Will James under lock and key. Hackberry's still on the loose. Would you mind passing the news on to your sons?"

"You can count on me," said Swallow Senior, the calmness of his tone giving away none of his satisfaction. "But you might be better off dropping them a line at the ranch. Last I heard, they were waiting to hear from you."

Now there's a bald-faced lie, thought Crain. Like father, like sons. The sheriff kept his cool.

"Already done."

"Thank you, Sheriff. I don't know where we'd be without you."

"Don't mention it."

"Goodbye."

After he'd hung up, Swallow called for Earl. Then he brushed the dandruff from his anthracite suit with his slender hand.

"Sir?"

Swallow ordered his manservant to draft a cable to their man on the ground. They'd need to inform him of Will James's identity—though that part of the mission would have to be put on hold for now—as well as "Bradley's" real name. Likely enough the free man was holed up in a two-bit hotel in some backwater in Utah or Western Colorado.

"Tell him to use his police contacts, and such. Send a note to my sons too, at Tuttle's place in Oasis. Tell them, whatever they do, not to show their faces at the hotel in the village. The sheriff's there with his prisoner. They should head back to Ely today, and get back to normal life. Our man will know how to deal with those two when the time comes."

"With all due respect, sir, would you have me write that—word for word? You aren't afraid it might be a tad...incriminating?"

"Not word for word. Of course not. Write that our man will 'take care' of the rest of this business on his own. Make sure to mention that their efforts have, once again, proven completely useless."

Swallow looked up at the mountains and smoothed out his white whiskers as he gave it some thought.

SONS GO BACK TO SHOSHONE IMMEDIATELY YOU'RE TOO LATE
DS CRAIN HOLDING THIEF W JAMES OTHER MAN LEW HACK-
BERRY AT LARGE ABOVE ALL DON'T GO TO OASIS HOTEL SHERIFF

THERE RIGHT NOW OUR MAN WILL HANDLE OUTSTANDING BUSI-
NESS WITH ALL DUE RESPECT YOUR INVOLVEMENT FUTILE ONCE
AGAIN =

YOUR FATHER

The elder Swallow brother took no pleasure in this
cable for at least three reasons. One, they'd both been
looking forward to a good lynching, no trial necessary.
That was the first thing they'd have to kiss goodbye.
Two, they'd spent a good part of the previous day at
the Oasis Hotel—and not just the day, truth be told.
They'd closed the bar and left only in the wee hours of
the morning. It was now late afternoon. The brothers
were dying of thirst and dehydration, and Tuttle had
hidden every ounce of liquor in the house once he heard
who was coming to visit. Wouldn't even be having a
single beer with breakfast. Point three was the Oasis
Hotel itself: they were going to miss that place. And to
top it off, it had taken most of the day to get to Oasis
by train with their skittish horses riding the cattle car,
and the trip wasn't cheap. All that for naught.

"Hey, you," grunted Richard T. Swallow.

The cook's flunky stepped forward, entering into a
cloud of polluted air that made him snap his head back.
Layer upon layer of sugary, rancid sweat had soaked
through Swallow's clothing and dried on his dark skin.
The stench was impossibly foul, from beyond the pale,
and marinated in the alcohol of an extended bender. It
made the flunky feel like retching. Swallow was holding his revolver, spinning the open chamber around.

"Go to the hotel, and stay there. Then come back

and give me word the moment the sheriff and his men leave with their prisoner."

Richard's brother, Ray Swallow, who'd been too busy snoozing and nursing his hangover to read the telegram, stood.

"You're saying they caught the rustlers?"

"One of them, anyway. Will James. You know the name?"

Ray's attempts to think only harrowed his brain.

"Oof, dunno."

"They're heading back to Ely today."

"You thinking what I'm thinking?"

"You in any state to think?"

Ray was considerably taller and wider than his older brother, so that when they stood side by side he was the one you noticed. But Richard Junior, who was hardly slight, had always commanded respect on account of his age and vicious tongue. There'd only ever be one man running the show at the Lazy GS.

"My idea ain't complicated," said Ray in a gravelly voice. "Our men know how to handle a gun..."

"Nah, Ray. That's no long-term plan. Think how Pa would approach it."

"And you'd approach it just like Pa?"

Junior was losing his cool. And to avoid getting carried away, he cut to the chase.

"Say we post a man on the roof to take care of this Will James. Just what do you reckon would happen next?"

"Well, for one, he'd be dead. For two, we'd have our revenge."

"Huh, that's it, now? He'd be dead...Crain would investigate. Wouldn't be long before he figured out we were in Oasis, and then our lives wouldn't be worth much—seeing as how you were the one ordered the cowboy shot down in cold blood. Hell, I'd even say I was always against the plan, that you acted alone, and he'd have no choice but to believe me seeing as I'd have paid off everyone we know to back up my story."

Richard T. Swallow spun the chamber around one last time, and snapped the gun into place. Then suddenly a movement in the door frame made him draw it. He was pointing it straight at the cook's flunky, back already. The man almost pissed his pants.

"What's up?" asked Junior, without lowering his gun.

"The sheriff left an hour ago."

"Where'd you hear that from?"

"From the bar...the bar...keep."

"Who?"

"The barkeep."

"Good," Richard said at last.

He set the gun down on his lap, without taking it out of his hand.

"We'll go have a couple drinks, and then we'll do the same. You got something to say about that, Ray?"

Ray signalled his agreement with a disdainful pout. Was this the first time the brothers had sparred? Of course not, but containing their differences was neither man's strong suit. Ray tried to summon a mental picture of Will James, but couldn't have been wider of the mark. He imagined a grizzled man of imposing stature; a cruel, vengeful man whose size alone would be enough to intimidate all comers. He must be — after all, he'd dared to rustle cattle belonging to the Swallows. But Will was hardly that.

Any way you looked at it, flipping it this way and that *ad infinitum*, there was no denying Will's situation had gone from bad to worse. That, at least, was the conclusion Ernest Dufault had drawn, alone in the back seat of the rattletrap Ford as it bumped along the road to Ely. Bob, the sheriff's right-hand man, was sitting on the passenger side, lovingly cradling a Winchester and turning around to give Will a nasty look from time to time. Crain also glanced back from time to time, though the look he cast Will's way was much friendlier. Not that it mattered much to Will, who shot back the same hypocritical smile only he knew to be false. What else could he do? An unsavoury acquaintance had hoodwinked him, and he'd been left holding the bag like a rank amateur.

Unsurprisingly, the hundred and fifty miles to their destination was stark. Will saw nothing, was occupied with his thoughts, his back bent, his hands crossed; he was feeling morose and hardly up to playing a role for his audience of two. After hours of driving through the same valleys and the selfsame mountains he'd traversed in the opposite direction on horseback, Will was pulled from his stupor when he felt the car slow down on the outskirts of a small town. It came to a stop a few minutes later, in a yard he imagined belonged to the office of the White Pine sheriff. Will stretched his sore legs and took in a deep breath of fresh air.

He was craving a cigarette. Crain came over and put a pair of handcuffs on Will, if only for appearance's sake, and then he and Bob ostentatiously escorted him along the hallways of the modestly sized but recently constructed building. They came to a dark room with naked brick walls and a couple of cells. The door of the first creaked ominously. Will went in. On that cold mid-November day of 1914 in Ely, Nevada, the name that was entered into the prison register, as it would be in a host of other official documents produced in the months ahead, was "William Roderick James."

12

Richard Swallow Senior emerged with the dawn from the shack where he'd spent the night with his favourite, Mindy. The whole extended family of Swallow's maid, and occasional mistress, slept packed in a few rooms. Children young and old, Mindy's brothers and sisters and their husbands and wives and her parents all shared a bedroom with the eldest son and his wife. Only Mindy had her own room, what with Mr. Swallow's privileged visits. Swallow had given his lover one last look before leaving. Sweat was pearling on her large, gleaming black body. The damp sheet, barely covering her, left little to the imagination. He'd closed his eyes and inhaled deeply.

While her respected guest was lacing his shoes in the kitchen, the matriarch got up and yawned, and offered him a cup of coffee. Swallow declined, with the excuse that he was in a hurry.

"Go back to bed, ma'am, it's barely daybreak."

"No use rushing around at this hour, Mr. Swallow. Bad for the nerves."

But Mr. Swallow had business to attend to on this lovely morning in January 1915. Breakfast would have to wait. He thanked the large woman for her offer with a tip of his hat. Everything about him was in stark contrast to the place where he'd spent the night.

The next item on the itinerary was a series of visits in town. Swallow had favours to collect. First stop was the barber, who shaved him free of charge in exchange for a loan at exorbitant interest made over fifteen years ago—a loan that had at least let the borrower hang his shingle and get out of the mine before he died underground. Next stop was breakfast at a cafeteria of which he was part-owner, and where he also enjoyed services free of charge, and always had. He sipped a coffee before ordering, then asked for a second cup when his plate of bacon and eggs was served and quickly eaten. He followed his meal with a third cup of coffee, this one with a splash of brandy, as he gazed out the window at the spectacle of Main Street coming to life. He watched a parade of poor men who would die without a nickel to their name, passing on their way to work at the factory or elsewhere, bent over, hands in their pockets, no better than cattle to slaughter. You had to see how the men altered their posture and the way they deferred to Swallow to understand his conceit. Around this time of day, Swallow began smoothing out the curled ends of his immaculate white moustache.

His tour ended at the bank, where, for the sheer fun of it, he often terrorized the bank clerk he had in his sights. Swallow was always looking for an angle, a means of bringing everyone and their neighbour to heel. When, finally, the manager came out of his office, alarmed and contrite and wanting to make sure everything was all right, Swallow decided to take out a few dollars he didn't need just for the sake of it.

Swallow might have gone on to visit a few of his fellow men of property, or a private investigator from Salt Lake City who was chasing a few interesting leads and whom he'd quiz for information, or one of the several journalists and politicians with dirty laundry they'd prefer to keep hidden, or a few of the landowners he'd made it a habit of intimidating with visits as regular as clockwork. Enough to make his presence felt and, maybe, you never know, to bleed them a little more. But today he felt a certain torpor—something akin to serenity—and it pushed him back in the direction of his big white house rather than spending any longer in town.

Earl, professional but sincere, welcomed him with his usual affability.

"I'd like to . . . I'd like to . . . "

"Sir?"

If he'd listened to himself, Swallow would have ordered more eggs and bacon, pork and beans.

"I'll take the newspapers in the parlour, please."

"They just came in, sir."

"No rush. I'm going to stoke the fire."

Earl left the room. A few minutes later, Swallow heard the phone ring in the kitchen. Someone answered. Earl, probably. He strained to hear. Most of the calls to the house never reached him, but had to do with provisions or maintenance for the house. Day-to-day business. And yet they were always interesting. A minute passed before Swallow's manservant brought him — along with the *Herald*, the *Telegram*, the *Deseret News*, and the weeklies — his pedestal telephone, the cord extended so that it could be carried all the way into the parlour that abutted the glassed-in patio. It was the only ranch in the area that boasted such amenities, and Swallow was extremely proud.

"Sir, you have a phone call."

"From whom?"

"The caller did not wish to reveal their name. I insisted. To no avail."

Swallow's curiosity was piqued, and not without cause. It wasn't every day that one received a phone call, let alone one from a stranger. With a certain apprehension, he put the handset to his ear.

"Hello."

"Hello, sir. Recognize me?"

Swallow, a little angrily, did recognize the voice on the line. It was the killer he'd hired to go after Lew Hackberry. He remembered, with disgust, the tall man, thin and wan, with light blond hair and almost-transparent eyebrows, hollow cheeks, and a massive triangular nose — a deranged, sadistic individual. He'd have to hire someone less unsavoury next time.

Swallow placed his hand over the transmitter.

"Thank you, Earl, that'll be all for now. I'll ring if I need anything."

"Ring away, sir."

The two exchanged an uneasy smile.

"We need to have a parley," said Swallow into the receiver.

"I could come all the way to Salt Lake City to tell you what I have to say, but it's a long way. I'm calling from a hotel in Austin."

"Austin, Texas?"

"Austin, Texas."

Silence. Swallow was calculating the distance to be travelled and the fees his hired gun would demand.

"No need. I can guess why you called."

"That's right. Let's say I've finished the job you hired me for. There's one less thing to worry about. A stone shaken loose from your boot, so to speak."

Swallow didn't encourage him to elaborate.

"I know everything your man did, before our final meeting. You want details?"

"Certainly not. That's your business, and yours alone." Then he whispered, "Someone might be listening."

For two months, Lew Hackberry had been endeavouring, as so many criminals had done before him, to disappear to Mexico without a trace. He had opted not to head straight south through New Mexico, but had instead taken a series of trains between Denver and Wichita, through the Eastern Colorado plains and the inhuman flatness of Kansas. He'd then bought a cheap and decent mount, a bay with black legs and a certain elegance, and ridden briskly south over the equally flat centre of Oklahoma. Farmland was unfamiliar terrain to Hackberry. The absence of hills and mountain ranges distressed him to the point of his needing to expend a couple of weeks in an Oklahoma City whorehouse, where he spent a small fortune to get over the experience. Finally, before cutting back west for a final straight shot to Mexico, the cowboy meandered through Central Texas, country he loved dearly, where he'd worked so many years earlier and which was infinitely more welcoming and far less monotonous than the states he'd passed through. But he sensed trouble: while his horse was drinking in an elbow of the Colorado River, a few miles south of Bend, Lew realized a stranger was following him. Hunting him down, no doubt.

"You're the boss," the somewhat disappointed assassin told Swallow. "I took notes, so as to leave nothing to chance. Wanted to tell you exactly how everything went down."

The blond-haired assassin, through his network of "eyes" scattered throughout the West, had tracked down his prey in Oklahoma City. Hackberry, he said, was a man marked for death, a worthless filthy man, deeply tanned and with an unearthly sheen. He'd wanted to observe him before taking any action that might prove fatal. He needed to know what kind of man he was dealing with, and now that he'd snared his game, there was no rush. Only boredom and the prospect of a long trip home had made him break his cover. And when Hackberry finally caught a whiff of this killer on his tail, it was by design.

"Sir? Is something wrong?"

Swallow was jolted out of his reverie. He smoothed his whiskers, his expression grave.

"That's it, yes."

"Something's wrong?"

"No, no..."

Hackberry and his pony had not had the chance to rest and get their strength back. They'd needed to get underway quickly and to wander erratically to throw their tracker off the scent. Hackberry swore; his horse bucked. They rode continuously for twenty-four hours—the pony risked its life and gave everything it had, alternating between a nervous trot and an unchecked gallop. But in vain. The next day, Lew, sweating profusely, caught sight of the stranger less than a half mile away. His pursuer had been able to change horses several times since Oklahoma City, including in Bend, where he'd treated himself to a young and spirited new mount.

"I'm sorry to have to ask, but you're absolutely certain...that there were no witnesses," said Swallow.

The killer hesitated a moment, but caught himself in time.

"You've got no worries on that score, sir. I'm a professional."

"Professional."

Hackberry's pony was on its last legs when Lew spotted a small house about a mile off. He spurred the pony on to a fatal gallop. A small speck of hope remained—and it resided in the house. The people who lived there would have horses. He'd borrow one. Borrow two. By any means necessary.

At that same moment, just under a mile away, an old woman with a bent back and trembling hands broken by a life of hard labour was squinting out the window. She drew the curtains — less than a mile away, a man was galloping toward their Mason County home, a cozy little farmhouse in the middle of nowhere. Their closest neighbour, a successful sheep-farmer with a thousand-acre spread in the Texas flat-lands, was at least two miles east, toward Llano. In the other direction, but for the odd house scattered around Plehweville, not a soul resided between their property and Mason.

"Pappy! Pappy!" she shouted.

This fine January afternoon in 1915 saw Pappy dozing in his chair.

"Pappy!"

"What?"

"Come see this. We've got company."

The news interested the old man, though he didn't always believe everything his wife said. At least not any-more. He got up, dragged himself to the window, and peered into the distance as his wife had done earlier.

"I don't see a thing."

"C'mon, take a closer look."

He could just about make out a dot on the horizon. Might have been a shrub, maybe a lamb, or their kids back from town after selling their wool and stocking up on provisions.

"Could be plenty of different things," Pappy said.

"Different things that gallop? That kick up clouds of dust?"

Pappy went to pick up his trusty Winchester 1873 .38-40, and together they stepped out onto the front porch to wait and see. His wife was scared. The area had become a lot more dangerous in recent years, and fresh in her mind were memories of the land wars, of bloodthirsty natives, of the outlaws of the last century, and of the cruelty of cowboys who reserved their keenest hatred for the inhabitants of the Northeast and for the farmers — sodbusters, they liked to call them — and who hated shepherds worst of all.

The horse was dragging itself toward the house. Even once horse and rider were within range, the old man hesitated to pull the trigger.

"Shoot!" his wife urged him. "Shoot already!"

The woman imagined her old husband living out his golden years in jail while she looked after their two hard-working children — good people who would surely take care of her. She wasn't displeased at the prospect, not a lot anyway, but this was no time for daydreaming. The man had dismounted and, despite the saddle, the exhausted animal lay down immediately. Knowing just how difficult it would be to get up, its numb legs heavy and swollen, trembling, its panting body covered in whitish scum, the bay whose master hadn't bothered to give it a name turned its head to one side and exhaled a last, drawn-out breath. The horse would never rise again, and was now free of all further suffering.

Despite the awful scene, Hackberry greeted the couple with his most effusive smile.

"Howdy," he said.

The couple didn't answer. The old man started shaking. To get a hold of himself, he spat and hugged his rifle.

"Listen here," said the cowboy, heading toward them with one hand in the air. "Put the gun down. I mean you no harm."

"No way he's gonna lower his, hey Pappy?" said the wife.

"Hell no."

The old man spat again, and fired a warning shot less than a foot from Hackberry. The report rang out over the prairie. The dirty, sweating, bearded cowboy didn't exactly have a face that inspired trust. Best not to let the feller come any closer. Which is just what he did.

The cowboy took another step and his face started to turn red, to boil over as if ready to explode.

"I told you I don't mean you no harm," said Hackberry. "Don't make me change my mind."

"Go back where you came from, son," ordered the old man.

"Go back? And how exactly am I gonna do that?"

They gazed at the horse. As Lew turned to look at them again, he had the bad idea of reaching toward his holster. A second later, a bullet pierced his stomach. You could have heard Lew's cries a half mile away. Too bad there was no one within at least a mile to hear them. The cowboy fell to his knees, grimacing, barely understanding what had befallen him. He'd tried to draw to fire back, but didn't get a chance. A second bullet pierced his skull and sent his hat flying. It came to rest in the dirt a few feet away. As he slumped to the ground, Hackberry had a final thought for the thirty head of fine cattle who'd earned him a tidy sum, only to cost him his life. He died face down in the dirt before he even had a chance to see that it was an old Texan woman holding the rifle. The man was flushed with admiration, relieved that he hadn't had to take action himself. Once again.

"Exactly, sir. A professional."

The hit man had missed nothing. He'd been hiding behind a bush with a spyglass pressed firmly to his right eye that he closed only after observing what the old couple would do next. Amazingly, they did nothing. The spy could hear them having a discussion on their front porch and remonstrating loudly. Then they went back inside, without bothering to touch the body now fertilizing the ground with its blood.

The hired gun approached slowly and examined the corpse. Though the parched ground was absorbing a lot of it, the pool of blood was growing larger. He backed off and, squatting, rolled himself a cigarette. It wasn't long before they caught sight of him. Poor old folks, he thought, they figured their troubles were at an end. The old woman, still holding the gun, was pointing at the stranger from the doorstep, and before he'd had the chance to say a word he felt a bullet graze his right ear. Now that he could have done without.

The old woman didn't even have time to realize what hit her as the magazine emptied into her. The old man cried out in despair as he ran toward the man who'd just killed his wife. He'd saved a bullet.

This was his least favourite part of the job. But he couldn't have let them live. Didn't have a choice. It just meant two fewer shepherds in the world, no longer letting their herds graze relentlessly, eroding the once-arable land. If, in the hierarchy of the gun for hire, he hated most of all brazen cowboys who figured they were larger than life and free to do whatever they wanted—though he had to admit there would be a dearth of work without them—shepherds came a close second. Then, yes, it was true, he hated Northerners with a passion, the sodbusters. Dregs of the earth, they were—folk he hated more than cops and Negroes. He was hard put to think of any more parasitic than shepherds, perfectly capable of ruining a prehistoric landscape, in under a decade. You had to hand it to them. Even the oil prospectors who'd been putting down stakes in Texas for several years now, doing their level best to wreck everything, couldn't match their gift.

He walked over to the bodies.

"You gotta understand," he said, "it's nothing personal. Ain't no enjoyment in this for me. I'm just good at what I do. And the pay! You just shouldn't have gotten up this morning. Like every other morning, really. No matter. You'll get a good taste of some real rest and relaxation looks like soon enough."

The blond assassin took a puff on his cigarette, clocked his audience's reaction. The old man didn't look convinced.

"You got something to say, now's the time."

Go to hell! Or that's what it sounded like.

"Fair enough, then. Fair enough. I'll see you there!"

The killer buried his three victims together in a single hole, at a bit of a distance from the house. He hated burying the dead. It was a long, hard, dirty job, and by the end he was always sweating and filthy. But there was no time to spare and it wasn't a step you could skip. That's what his client paid him for: for his victims to disappear from the face of the earth. Yes, a few months from now the sheep would enjoy themselves some real nice, thick grass to graze on.

"You'll still come to Utah and tell me the full story?" Swallow asked. It was a ploy. He wanted to bring this intrusion in his day to an end, given that it could link him to the murders, and the bored switchboard operators were no doubt listening in.

"Sure. That's the other reason I'm calling, in fact."

"I'm all ears," said Swallow impatiently.

"I was wondering if you'd like me to . . . to go meet our other man."

"Nah," said Swallow, rocking in his chair.

"James will surely be transferred any day now. To the federal prison in Carson City. It's only a matter of time. I could be waiting for him outside. Somewhere not too close."

"Tempting offer, but it's water under the bridge. We can't have anything get back to . . . "

"Come on, that won't happen."

"What do you know? You here to teach me a lesson now?"

"No, sir. Of course not."

"Didn't think so. Time to let it go. Worst-case scenario, we can change plans later."

They exchanged some pleasantries and then hung up. They might well have passed for normal men having a normal conversation. The killer took several weeks to come back north, making his way from hotel to hotel, so that by the time he reached Utah he'd spent a good part of his thousand-dollar windfall from Hackberry. He put a few hundred in the bank, same as always, but never had the chance to spend it: a few months later he caught a bullet in the back, a revenge killing for some incident of distant and dubious origin.

Swallow returned to his newspapers. He caressed his white whiskers, telling himself the world was going from bad to worse, and that at least he was fortunate to live far away from so-called civilization, in a corner of the world that would never change, never fall prey to ideas—like communism, to give but one example— raging in parts of Europe. Groups of workers in the East and North (two parts of the country as lousy as each other) were also promoting various forms of socialism or unionism or liberalism or anarchism— multiple terms for the same abomination—but he knew these perturbations would be stifled at the source by politicians and police in no time, and the natural order of things re-established. Swallow Senior was pleased to be a citizen of a nation that would never be so improvident as to join the conflagration that was starting to get serious across the Atlantic. Such a mess over the assassination of an archduke who'd inherited the crown of a dying empire no one could care less about; a war that had come about because of the delusions of grandeur of a fistful of "worldly" aristocrats who'd never understood the first thing about men.

Now, Americans understood men. Real men, with a clear sense of their collective and individual destiny.

Real men were uncomplicated; they worked without complaining. They *worked*. Never said a word more than was necessary — and, sure, entertained themselves when they had too much time on their hands, but in a simple way. The effeminate decadence of the Old Continent was making inroads in the cities of the New World, but the men in this part of America would hold out. Here was the last bastion of manhood. Of men who loved ideas, who were curious, but the ideas had to be comprehensible, not artificial. Yes, it was necessary to know what your neighbours were up to, how your neighbours thought, but without succumbing to their decadence or imitating their weak manners and specious faults. A true philosophy was a pragmatic philosophy, though one that didn't announce itself as such. Populism was also a road to decline, to barbarism, so the intellectual elite, along with the pastors, had to show the way and not isolate themselves; they needed, at a minimum, to play the role of simple men, in order for their politics and privileges to be accepted. Later, behind closed doors, they could do what they wanted. Many would get rich at the expense of the common people, as long as they didn't lose sight of these principles and alienate people. And really, what was the point of aspiring to a glorious future when the present day was already so glorious.

Swallow looked up at the mountains, as was his habit. It was lunch time. Saliva flooded his mouth at the thought of his drink. And, afterwards, a nap.

He picked up the bell and rang it.

"Earl?"

PART TWO

A Turning Point

1

The road that travels west from Ely to Carson City
traverses the plains at the heart of the Great
Basin. For some three hundred miles, pretty well the
entire width of Nevada at that latitude, the route is
a succession of massive and desolate mineral valleys
fixed in antediluvian time and bounded to the north
and south by a series of peaks and the seemingly
endless walls of massive and craggy mountains. In
certain particularly arid valleys, nothing manages to
grow except the odd juniper tree or sagebrush that,
after a good rain, gives off a sharp, almost urine-like
scent which never failed to bring a smile to Will's face.

Still, in the 1910s, this was a land where mustangs were able to wander free and to proliferate; land
impossible for anything living to roam without knowing
where to find the tiniest oases and waterholes, hidden
in the foothills, frequented by the few wild animals
indigenous to the territory (reptiles, rodents, and the
occasional larger mammal in the higher altitudes). This
stretch of road was called the Lincoln Highway, though

later it would go by other names—"The Loneliest Road in America," Route 50, State Route 2. There were few drivers to care what it was called at that point. And what effect does a name have on an unpaved road running through desolate countryside?

Crain and his deputy set off in a car with the prisoner Will James one morning early in May 1915. They left the lockup at dawn; they wouldn't reach Carson City until evening. Will wasn't watching the landscape scrolling by his window. The expression he was wearing was inscrutable: he remained composed, but something in his soul was dying a slow death. Fundamentally, Will's five months in White Pine had been a vacation. He'd been a favourite of the guards, who were constantly doing him small favours and granting him considerable privileges. Will had paper, he had pencils, and he was always given plenty of tobacco. Crain was even in the habit of bringing him leftovers from his wife's cooking, when it wasn't one of the guards sharing their lunch or a thermos of coffee. In jail, Will was left at his leisure to draw bucolic scenes from the life of liberty he'd lost. But these were not the ones that inspired him. Will was drawing fewer and fewer horses and men, developing instead an obsession with the fractured lines of the horizon he'd come to know. The tiny window in the hallway leading to his cell looked onto a drab grey wall. To please his jailers, Will started adding the silhouette of a figure in a cowboy hat to his sketches, the rider mounting a four-legged silhouette with powerful hindquarters, but never without contemplating at length the fantastical and atavistic panorama unencumbered by people. As had always been his habit, he gave away nearly all his drawings. This elevated his status, bought him extra privileges, and strengthened his relationships with the guards. Without taking heed or even understanding what was happening, all of the guards were won over by the charms of Will James.

· But in the Nevada State Prison (which he was already calling the NSP), Will could surely expect no such special treatment from the guards. Winning them over would be a long game. First of all, he'd have to mix with the other men, with criminals likely notorious and vicious. And there was no guarantee Will would be able to keep drawing, or even lay his hands on pencils and paper. Already, riding along in the back of the noisy and uncomfortable car, he was suffocating at the thought. And they hadn't even travelled ten miles yet.

Crain was driving slowly. He preferred leaving the top down, no matter the weather. He'd insisted on transferring his coddled prisoner himself, loath to admit that he would miss him. They left Ely via windy side roads that took them through arid mountains where shrubs languished in the red clay soil, soon passing the outskirts of Ruth, a mining town, before — after a short climb — the country opened up. During the three-hundred-mile drive to Carson City they would pass through only three settlements: Eureka, with its main street of stout buildings they hardly realized they'd crossed; Austin; and then Fallon. Three hundred miles afforded a lot of time to think, and everyone was thinking hard — Crain most of all.

Over the preceding five months the sheriff had gar-
nered a real affection for the young cowboy. Whatever
despondency he felt was likely less than what the short
man in the back seat of the car was feeling, hard put
as he was to conceal his trepidation at the prospect
of his being committed to an enormous penitentiary
full of hardened criminals convicted of serious crimes.
Crain spent the entire drive swept up in a surge of
vague regret. Whatever could have caused a healthy,
genial young man like Will to get into a mess like this,
he wondered. One day he'd demand an explanation,
even if he already had a notion. He was aware Will
James never knew his parents, that he'd been raised
by a certain Beaupré, a trapper Will described as a
good man, though that didn't change what the man
was—a trapper, and, like all other trappers, surely
an outcast who rejected other people and society at
large; a man without roots or the ability to pass on to
his young charge the things that mattered most. And
hadn't this trapper met with a sudden end, leaving
the young man to fend for himself among roustabouts
as he drifted aimlessly west, and north, and south?
At least Will James had avoided the orphanages, and
a life of crimes far more serious than cattle rustling.
Will might have a lot of talent, but that talent would
come to nought if he didn't get his act together once
he was released from prison. If only he'd been brought
up in a good, stable family from either the city or
countryside, a loving family that would have catered
to a young man's needs; if only he'd grown up in the
happy bosom of a family where he'd have known love

and developed a sense of respect and discipline. Had
that happened, Will would never have found himself
where he was today: in transit to a penitentiary where
he'd be incarcerated for a year, at least; left to his
own devices, forsaken by his family, the community,
and society at large. This was what he was facing.
The poor young man could barely read and write,
and spoke with an accent that made him sound more
like an animal than a man. It was a crying shame,
an upbringing like that, a crying shame! He ought to
have gone to school. Every child needed to attend
school at least up to a certain age, or else what
hope was there for humanity? The sheriff figured
humankind had maybe two or three more generations before everything was an irreversible mess. If
the elites didn't relinquish the monopoly they'd held
on a decent education since the nineteenth century,
how could the average man hope to make his way
in the world? How was he to shape it in his image,
according to his will, and improve it?

Crain thought of Lockhart, the public defender
appointed to represent Will James versus the State
of Nevada, and grumbled. The way things were going
they would soon be left with nothing but incompetents
like Mr. Lockhart, Esq., to defend, advise, direct, and
sell whatever goods they were pushing, without anybody else having a clue about what was really going on.

Will asked Crain whether there was a problem, and
he grunted and spoke the name in a one-word reply.

"Lockhart."

2

Will grunted in turn, though mostly not to alienate Crain. Truth be told, he'd kind of liked his
repellent lawyer. By then, two long months had passed
since he and Hackberry had been formally accused of
grand larceny. Two long months of moping in his grim
cell, haunted by the thought of the punishment his
family would inflict if they ever caught wind of what
he'd done. The authorities had hoped to get their
hands on Hackberry and put the two cattle rustlers
on trial together, but Hackberry was nowhere to be
found. And then this odd lawyer had appeared.

Lockhart smelled of onions and sported the bushy
moustache and thick sideburns cowboys loved to
mock. His manners were awkward and brusque. One
moment he'd be smug and overbearing; the next he'd
be a panicky, contrite bundle of nerves. The first few
minutes of their meeting had done little to reassure
the young French-Canadian prisoner in the wilds of
Nevada. Regardless, Will set about explaining the difference between rustling, which involves doctoring

brands and waiting for the scars to heal before taking the cattle to market, and grand larceny, when a thief doesn't bother with such niceties and simply leaves the state to sell the cattle as he found them, in some faraway town, and Lockhart's interest was piqued. The lawyer was hanging on Will's every word, asking questions and insisting he elaborate. It was nothing he didn't already know, but the attorney glimpsed a certain talent, the gift Will had for capturing people's attention and holding it.

"We'll have to hope the judge feels the same."

They hoped in vain. On the advice of his attorney, Will pleaded not guilty at the preliminary hearing at the White Pine County Courthouse. Lockhart contrived to shift the bulk of the blame onto Hackberry, arguing that he and he alone had sold the cattle. The public, he contended, needed to understand that Will was a poor innocent who'd been pulled into the sordid affair and not pocketed a single penny from the theft.

"The three months he's spent behind bars have already taught him a powerful lesson, you can be sure!"

In what became a rather convoluted defence, the lawyer tried to convince the judge that the cattle were running wild, "at any rate." Will and the lawyer had prepared the argument together, but it didn't come out as the cowboy had hoped. He frowned as he heard his words issued from another man's mouth, like a game of telephone.

"And when you get right down to it, Your Honour: Do we really have any certainty, any proof *beyond a reasonable doubt*, that the cattle in question were, in fact, the property of the Swallow Ranch? How many miles must a cow stray before it is, in effect, lost — and another rancher is free to take ownership? The fact of the matter is that James and Hackberry did the Lazy GS Ranch a favour. Has not the ranch now pocketed a portion of the proceeds of the sale of the cattle intercepted in Denver? Did the accused not drive the cattle to the destination where, one day, they'd have been driven anyway? Or not! Without their intervention, the herd would likely have strayed even further and been lost forever. Some men walk away unpunished for 'stealing' hundreds of head of cattle — sometimes as many as five hundred — and now we're treating my client like a criminal for admitting that he drove a few dozen head hundreds of miles to the slaughterhouse? Is it even reasonable to speak of private property when we're discussing thirty-odd head born free in nature and left free to wander by their presumed owners after branding? We're arguing over a mark made upon the cattle with a searing-hot iron. When we get right down to it, were these cattle even born on the Swallows' land? What proof do we have the Swallows didn't steal the cattle in question?"

The judge straightened up. Lockhart, fire in his eyes, was on a roll. He forged ahead.

"And what if we *were* to stand in the way of these young men pushed to extreme actions by the precariousness of their circumstances, doing no more than what they needed to get by? Where's the dignity in a man's being forced to sell himself afresh every season, at a cut rate, to another man, imperilling life and limb without ever putting down a stake of his own, without ever laying by even a few dollars for the future? Where is the dignity in a man's living in such conditions? Is he not simply trying to escape the poverty of his lot? Fundamentally, he's doing no more than taking a step toward his liberty—even if the path to liberty demands he commit an act possibly transgressing limits laid down by the law. And we see nothing but limits, nothing but fences all around us! But some we believe to be real are merely propped up by the *symbolic* value we ascribe to them. Your Honour, you have only to consider how the law has evolved over the years. The law exists to protect the downtrodden of this world—it has been ever thus—and the accused standing before us today has never had the opportunities afforded our rich Utah ranch owners. He's an orphan, who has known only hardship and struggle his whole life; a boy who spoke the tongue of wolves before learning the language of men. Would you believe that the man before you has never been to school? We should be giving him a medal! Or, at the very least, a pardon. What did he steal, when we get right down to it? *Nothing*. Next to nothing. He simply borrowed a small allotment of hope from people with an ample supply. And when you live alone for too long—cut off from society and wandering this great and sparsely populated land—then it's only understandable that you may forget the laws and customs of man. It is the territory that makes us who we are, and there's nothing to be done about it! With my hand on my heart, let me say it again: I am utterly convinced that William Roderick James has learned his lesson."

The judge decided to interrupt Lockhart's outland- ish pleading.

"Mr. Lockhart, would you care to conclude?"

The lawyer mumbled a few words no one could dis- cern, then sat down. Back at Will's side, he smoothed his big moustache, and struggled to conceal his discomfort.

Judge Edwards's decision surprised no one. Bail was set at two thousand dollars to free the accused until the State of Nevada was ready to try William Roderick James on the charge of grand larceny, which would happen by the end of spring. The judge's gavel struck twice, in time to Will's furiously beating heart.

Two months later—the night before the trial was to take place—Will and Lockhart agreed on a new strategy: plead guilty. This would circumvent a trial, and perhaps yield a shorter prison sentence. Because here was the truth of it: Will was going to prison.

"Still no news of Hackberry?" Will asked, without much hope that there would be.

"Afraid not."

The two men could not help but look disappointed again.

The verdict was handed down on April 27, 1915: twelve to fifteen months in the Nevada State Prison in Carson City. A sentence to set an example for others: twelve to fifteen months! In light of Crain's good word and the five months he'd already spent locked up in Ely, Will had hoped the judge might be more lenient...twelve to fifteen months...He'd been expecting to serve perhaps a couple of months, maybe just a few weeks. Everyone had agreed he'd never get more than six, under the circumstances...twelve to fifteen months...He'd just have to find a way to serve his time while avoiding the blades of hardened criminals, and the sexual predators.

In the days and nights that followed, Will's thoughts turned to his parents. His mother would faint if she learned what had befallen her son. The news would break her heart, though it would also be difficult not to write for an entire year, or to send her his usual postcards without arousing suspicion: *Everything is fine, wish you were here!* He would figure out what to do when the time came. For now, the best he could do was wait.

The night before his transfer to the other side of Nevada, his lawyer had come to see him a final time. He gave Will a pouch of tobacco, some rolling papers, a virgin drawing pad, and a pencil.

"I've got one other thing for you," said the lawyer with a smile.

He passed a rolled-up newspaper between the bars.

"What's this?"

Will read from the *Ely Record* of April 30, 1915. War, misery, injustice, grandstanding—there seemed to be very little "new" in the news. Then a sidebar caught his attention.

SOMETHING OF AN ARTIST

Will James...has made many friends among county officials, and others. He is a natural artist and since confinement in jail has had time to devote to drawing. He is especially good with ranch scenes, and with proper training would soon be able to do first-class work. His confession was secured by District Attorney Jurich, who, however, made no promises as to clemency on the part of the court.

It didn't matter what Will actually believed, at that moment, about whether or not he'd be a professional artist one day. Regardless, this was his mention in a newspaper, and the laudatory tone warmed his heart. Will was a somebody! He bristled a little at the term "proper training," and would dwell on these words with a certain resentment for months, even years. He'd show that journalist! They'd see what he was made of! But the defiant attitude the article instilled in him proved short-lived. Will slumped in his seat, his shoulders drooped, and he turned away from his visitor.

Lockhart didn't stick around. For expediency's sake, he asked a few questions that went nowhere, and Will's answer was the same every time: he didn't know. Lockhart shook his client's hand in silence and left him to his foggy thoughts. *Twelve to fifteen months in prison.* Will stayed up all night smoking cigarette after cigarette, sprawled out on his back like a corpse, his eyes glued to the ceiling. Everything around him was crumbling. His soul, his reason, his life as he

knew it: all were slipping away. He couldn't understand what he'd been thinking. Not in committing what
Justice Edwards had adjudged a crime — the theft of
the cattle — but in imagining he might get away from
it with a mere slap on the wrist afterwards. He'd
been careless and foolish, a rank amateur. *Amateur,
amateur, amateur.* With two concurrent jail terms,
he'd end up serving close to two years before tasting
freedom again; he who thought he shared the beating
heart, unbridled joy, and indomitable nature of wild
horses! He who, as far back as he could remember,
had always felt stifled when confined between four
walls. And, riding for hours in a car that was finally
approaching a new town, nothing would dispel his
lassitude now.

3

The men began a new ascent. Soon the sheriff's car would be carving its path through the Toiyabe Range, one of the highest in Nevada. This time the travellers would reach an elevation of around eight thousand feet; enough to make their ears pop. They had the impression of being able to see as far as California, to the end of the world—and time. Then they began the arduous descent. The road wended its way down a steep slope alongside deadly ravines, extricating Will's mind from the mire of thoughts he'd been stuck in all day and the night before.

"Look, there's a town down there."

Will didn't.

Austin had probably been named after the capital of Texas. (There were competing origin stories, but none are any more credible.) It was just one of dozens of unremarkable settlements sprinkled throughout Nevada and the West. The territory was only tenuously settled, there being scant reason to stay once the long-abandoned mines and veins of silver started to yield little or nothing. In a town that had once been home to eight thousand people, by 1915 only a quarter of them remained. Within a century, Austin would be a ghost town lost in newly hostile country. The mining bonanza had lasted a few decades, until 1890. Just long enough for a handful of brick buildings to rise. Most of the rest were rundown, patiently waiting for time to run its course.

Despite Crain's wife having prepared the basket of roast pork sandwiches sitting at Will's feet, they found a roadhouse on Austin's main street. Crain wanted a beer, and figured the sandwiches would come in handy on the return trip.

The saloon was run by a woman. The men figured she was filling in for the real barkeep—her husband, surely. Time had left its mark on her as mercilessly as on the town, but she seemed a jovial sort and Will hadn't seen anyone of her sex for months. But for the occasional visit from Mrs. Crain, that is, a sorry woman who elicited only feelings of compassion from the prisoner. So the sight of this Austin barkeep with her generous curves and full, round face was yet another fresh torture for Will to endure—it's not that he was overcome with desire, but rather that any hint of sweetness now turned his stomach. He scowled and had a hard time finishing his meal. He'd ordered—to the chagrin of the sheriff, who'd paid for his inmate's and deputy's lunch as well as his own—a roast pork sandwich. They smoked a few cigarettes, and allowed Will a beer, the sheriff a second, before the men decided to stretch their legs and continue their journey.

"Lovely day, gentlemen!" said Crain.

Will swallowed with difficulty. The town, nestled between mountains on the west slope of the Toiyabe Range, was not exactly lively. Some houses were boarded up, others abandoned; there were still a few extant businesses and craftsmen's shops, and the odd person who appeared wealthy, but mostly the three newcomers were treated to the sight of old people on their balconies going about their habitual business of watching the world go by, staring at interlopers from behind long white beards and giving them the one look they were capable of expressing: a mean suspicion. Crain couldn't quite manage to avoid their stares.

It must have taken a great deal of courage to decide, a hundred years ago, to leave behind everything one knew and strike out for an unknown land and try to make a go of it. The region had made promises it hadn't delivered on. People had worked hard and said their prayers every night. Now their idleness was eating away at them, needing only a spark to ignite into a fire of rage and turn their hatred on the first person—man, woman, or child—so unfortunate as to find themselves nearby. And the children and their children's children, with as much reason to despair, would come of age in this toxic atmosphere, knowing neither labour nor its rewards, reproducing in turn their parents' and grandparents' trauma. Such was the lot of the gold-digger who traded his dignity for a patch of land to dig, or for inhuman toil in the mine. These people's lives couldn't have been further from the dream Will was chasing. They were its walking antithesis.

The travellers also crossed paths with two or three not-unattractive mothers with provisions under their arms, or pushing babies in prams; women readily returning the smiles of Crain and the deputy. Will kept his eyes to the ground, which took all the strength he could muster. Despite his respect for Crain, Will couldn't chase away the dream of escape that was forming in his mind. The scene started with him subtly picking up a stone, and continued with him knocking out his captors before they realized what hit them. Next he would take possession of the two men's weapons and tie them up — with what rope it was impossible to say — before speeding off in the Ford. There was just one catch: he'd never driven a car in his life. He could always steal a horse, though in this desolate and wholly unfamiliar country his chances of getting away were slim to none. But the details were unimportant; the main thing was that the men didn't believe Will capable of such an act, and that was where his chance of escape lay. Will snapped back to his senses as they came back toward the car. Stay on the straight and narrow for now, he told himself; later do as you choose. That's if there is a later, he ruminated, banishing the thought of some gang having their way with him in a dark corner of the federal prison, as Bob asked him, with something approaching a genuine smile, if he was ready to go. *It wouldn't happen. It wouldn't happen.* Will would hunker down, keep a low profile, and come up with a whole lot of stories that, once he was free again, would keep everyone on the edge of their seat. He'd reinvent himself. Again. After all, what self-respecting cowboy had never been caught rustling? It was pretty much a mandatory stop on the way.

The road became bleaker and bleaker once they left Austin. The mountains appeared smaller and smaller, the distant chains sprawling less, and further apart. The vegetation, already scraggly and sparse, disappeared altogether. Will fell asleep and started snoring. All three men were growing weary and having trouble keeping their tired eyes open. The beers they'd had with lunch, small as they were, didn't help. But the wind blew stronger, rousing Crain from his torpor, and for the next several miles it gusted up, buffeting the car. Crain struggled to stay on the road. The bad jokes he made fooled no one; the drive was making him nervous. A few hours after their departure from Austin, a solitary dune known as Sand Mountain appeared on their right. Will had never heard tell of the dune. Its sinuous crests and the wind howling off its dark slopes pulled him out of his haze. Crain was providing a rambling history lesson and describing a bygone era before even dinosaurs roamed the earth, a time when an ocean covered all of Nevada.

"Dinosaurs?" asked Will, the word only vaguely familiar to him.

"Massive reptiles that lived tens, maybe hundreds of thousands of years before mankind!" said Crain. "They were the masters of every corner of the globe, and now we've taken their place. Something wiped them out, though nobody knows what. Some say it was a plague, others that they just couldn't adapt. Whatever it was, the news was good for us!"

Will believed he might as well have been listening to a description of the cowboys of the previous century, of speculators and hired hands driving cattle for hundreds of miles without encountering a single fence; pioneers who'd been replaced (or conned) by giant, soulless companies not caring a whit for their animals or employees. The cowboys were a dying breed, fighting for their place in a landscape that was increasingly the stuff of fantasy.

Crain's lesson wasn't over.

"You know a mountain of sand like that signifies this must have been the highest point — and that's what caused the erosion. The plates shifted, and that changed everything."

"The plates?"

"That's right, plates. Plate tectonics! The earth is made of massive fragments, and when they rub together they can change dry countryside into sea, or the other way around. Like here! Just look at this landscape and imagine a sea teeming with prehistoric fish — twenty-footers with massive teeth and who knows how many eyes, fighting it out with other gangs of fish three times bigger than them!"

As they drew nearer to Fallon, Will decided to be polite and take a look, but the spectacle didn't interest him. The country was becoming more and more flat. A salty limestone flatness that Will wouldn't want to find himself in under the best of circumstances — even with a top-notch saddle horse and a packhorse behind him carrying gallons of water. The hills were now too small to be properly called mountains and seemed to be miles away; they were thin bands on a distant horizon. The car drove on, and for a few dozen miles they didn't see a trace of green—until, like a magic spell, the artificial oasis of Fallon appeared, making the men forget all about the miles of desert they had traversed.

Will had heard of Fallon. The town had started to prosper at the turn of the century, much to the detriment of its nearby rival, Stillwater, established on ground slightly further east when Fallon was nothing more than a dusty road cutting through desert interspersed with a few lakes and creeks that usually ran dry. Fallon had been a backwater, then; home to two or three families as headstrong as they were inbred. The land around Stillwater was much better suited to farming, but the settlers of Fallon had willed it otherwise, behaving like demigods to bring their vision of nature to fruition. Today, both Fallon and Stillwater were on a fast road to nowhere.

"But who'd ever settle for a lost hole like this?"

"Sheriff," said Bob, hurt. "Are you forgetting that my sister married a guy from these parts?"

Crain guffawed.

"Really though, what were they thinking? A bunch of politicians who never pitched a shovel anywhere near Churchill County think they can irrigate a half-million acres? Bring twenty thousand people into Fallon? What a bunch of sops! No surprise they made a hash of it, bought a bunch of tracts of worthless sand. I heard they were mighty proud of all the water they thought they'd bring in, but that it didn't take long for them to realize that all the optimism in the world wouldn't make their plan work. Some say the whole scheme was a scam—that, or politics as usual. I figure this part of the country will get by for as long as there's rock to mine, but there's no lode I ever heard of that doesn't run out sooner or later. The day will come when this whole area is nothing but ghost towns. Maybe you believe the politicians figure out some other plan and how to get there, and that's why they rise to the top and win elections. But hell no! They're taking it one day at a time, just like me and you. They can't see any further than the ends of their noses. They let themselves get corrupted, believing they can always start afresh and become 'financiers' or what have you. Doesn't matter what—anything the slightest bit off, they'll be drawn to it like flies to you-know-what."

There was something incongruous about such talk from a man who was himself an elected official—a politician, really. But Will had little to say on the subject, or about Fallon for that matter. The place just made him think of Bagot County, where he'd been born: the flatlands, greenery, a lively agricultural community reminiscent of Acton Vale, Quebec. There were plenty of young trees, a few rivers and creeks that were all bends and elbows. All signs pointed to freshly irrigated, arable, and fertile land—though not much more than that, if Crain was to be believed.

It was the sort of landscape that evoked timeless ways of living short on action and devoid of change, save the cycle of the seasons. A life of dedication to a job that would always be your master; a harsh existence without a spare moment to enjoy the idleness Will so cherished, or the daily exchanges with one's fellow men that he cherished even more. Everyone knew farmers were the loneliest men on this earth; that they spent their entire lives stuck on the acreages they were cursed never to leave.

A little beyond Fallon they came to a fork, and they left the Lincoln Highway that would have taken them to Reno, just north of Carson City, for another, less welcoming road. Just a hundred miles left to their destination: they were getting close. In this, one of his first car journeys, a disgruntled Will was rediscovering a landscape he'd crossed innumerable times on the backs of the best horses; a land of valleys and pictur-esque rolling hills, welcoming and green, and prairie as far as the eye could see. The sight of it turned Will's stomach, heart, and mind. He was already in a bad way, and the sight of the ranches they were passing pushed him over the edge. He stopped looking out the side of the car at the golden evening light, the very light he'd once captured so accurately in paint; he refused to watch the sun slipping behind the blue mountains of the Sierra Nevada. Something was eating away at him—a vague regret that in a single day he'd covered a route that would have taken him a good month on horseback. Will was at the end of his rope.

"Sheriff Crain."

"Yes, son."

"You mind if I smoke?"

"Of course not. Go right ahead."

Will savoured his smoke as if it were his last: with

reverence. As if he were on his way not to languish in a cell but straight to the gallows. The cigarette invigorated him, gave him a sense of composure; prepared him to face the danger ahead. And that way, danger did lie.

They made their way through part of the city. Though it had been chosen as the capital of Nevada, Carson City was still a small town; what you might call a sprawling but orderly town, even if for the three-thousand-odd folk who called it home, downtown and its main street at sundown were a hive of activity. The driver, his deputy, and the passenger in the back seat were able to feast their eyes on some local beauties. Will almost enjoyed it. He closed his eyes, telling himself he should do his best to hang on to images of what he was seeing; that it might help him survive the most challenging moments of his dereliction. Though Will may have never heard that word in his life, dereliction was the idea creeping up and occupying his thoughts. After only a few months in prison, and on the verge of a year of danger imminently under way, the feeling was palpable.

Dereliction.

4

The state prison was two miles outside Carson City, on the rim of Warm Springs Valley. It had been built in the 1860s on the site of a trading post where stagecoaches were once provisioned, home to a hotel that saw little business, though more than its fair share of robberies. The worn brown and green foothills of the Sierra Nevada provided the foreground to a majestic view of steep mountains and dizzying blue peaks capped in snow, and backlit by a burnt orange sky.

As they turned onto the dirt road leading to the prison, you could have heard a fly buzz, were it not for the roar of the exhausted motor. Will didn't take his eyes off his hands, laid flat on his thighs. He told himself that if he wasn't killed in the first week, or in the first month, he just might stand a chance.

They parked the car in front. The building was gleaming white. (Aside from the offices, the entire prison was white.) Two guards came out to greet them. They were on time.

Crain handed Will, his protegé, over to the guards without so much as a handshake. The sheriff contented himself with a timid nod of the head, as if to say, "I hope to see you again, for the right reasons this time."

He would never see Will James again.

Will was handcuffed and led to a sort of cloakroom, where the pungent smell of men brought wild animals to mind. On the other side of these walls, thousands of men were packed into the main wing, and already he could hear the low murmur of rumours circulating: fresh meat, that's what Will was. The two guards who'd escorted him took a step back when the lieutenant walked in. The man had a slender moustache and the brisk demeanour of someone without time to waste. He looked Will up and down.

"Right. You're going to listen up, and do exactly what I tell you to do. *Exactly*. That clear?"

The lieutenant let a moment elapse. His voice resonated powerfully, as if he were addressing an audience of thirty. Yet he stood only three paces from the new prisoner.

"Get undressed. Remove your clothing and place your personal effects in this box."

Will did as he was told. The room was fairly cold, and his penis shrunk like a snail crawling back into its shell.

"Once you're naked, put your hands behind your head."

Will saw no reason to disobey.

"Turn your face toward the guard. Lean your head forward, and rub your hair briskly! You heard: I said *briskly*! Good. Now stand up and open your mouth!"

A guard came over, with rubber gloves and a tongue depressor.

"Stick out your tongue and move it around."

He stuck his tongue out and moved it left to right, then up and down. Will wondered if the guard was checking for diseases, or for something he might have hidden in his mouth.

"Hands in the air! Show the officer your palms. Okay, now the backs of your hands. Good. Now, lift up your penis and testicles!"

There wasn't much to lift, but Will again did as he was asked.

"Now follow the line on the floor to the scales."

After Will had been weighed and measured, the guards gave him some clothes to wear: a pair of denim pants, a light denim shirt, white with navy blue stripes; a white shirt with short sleeves that would come to be known as a tee shirt; a grey linen vest; and a pair of leather shoes that had seen a lot of use. They were the typical work clothes of the prisons of the day, the black-and-white-striped uniform Will had been expecting having fallen out of use with the turn of the new century. Once he was dressed, Will looked around in vain for the hat they'd not provided. His jeans were no different than the ones he'd been wearing his whole life, but the lightness of his shirt and vest gave Will pause; nights in the prison would be cold, as temperatures in the desert could drop very low. He hoped his blanket would be warm enough.

Their immediate business done, the guards took him to the room next door to have his photo taken and complete his inmate's paperwork.

A cardboard label was pinned to his sleeve: N.S.P. *1778.*

"Do not smile, 1778."

Not a necessary instruction, as Will didn't see what there was to smile about. The two photos, front and profile, recorded a face more square than oval. The prisoner had a straight, pointy nose and smallish nostrils. His fairly wide, rounded, and prominent chin was thrust forward, and his almond eyes slightly droopy. His lips seemed unusually fleshy, and also dropped slightly at the corners of his mouth. Will's expression was dour for good reason.

The new prisoner's file registered the incarceration of one William Roderick James, aged twenty-two, his twenty-third birthday to be spent in prison one month later. By Will's own (and for once truthful) account, his date of birth was June 6, 1892; his height, five foot nine (eight and three-quarters, to be precise); weight, 135 pounds; shoe size, 6 ½. He was dark-skinned, with chestnut hair and green eyes that were almost brown. He was slim but nervous, robust more than he was skinny, but short for a cowboy. On many an occasion since he'd left his family to pursue his dream of riding the West, he'd been forced to prove that his short stature was no obstacle to imposing his will on wild horses and recalcitrant cattle. He would have to do so many times again. And, again, he would vindicate himself.

A guard issued Will a foul-smelling pillow and an equally nasty, hole-ridden woollen blanket. The young man understood the time had come for him to take his first steps into the prison and see his cell. They needed to pass through two sets of metal-barred gates to reach the square courtyard of the wing where he would spend the next year.

"Follow the yellow line!"

On either side of the narrow hallway, over four floors, tough-looking men were watching him. Some wore unabashedly perverted expressions on their faces. He was accompanied up two flights of stairs. The guard yelled at everyone to step aside and clear off. No one gave them any grief.

"Left!"

Will turned and walked into his cell. The stench of it! Old sweat, old piss, fresh shit. The room was between four and five feet wide and seven or eight feet high. On one side were two bunks; on the other, a wall of naked brick that had once been white. At one end was a rusty, brown washbasin, and in the corner, a toilet that looked no more inviting. Will hustled over to the little window to breathe in the fresh air. Through it, he could admire the peaks of the Sierra Nevada, which he would spend months obstinately drawing, like Ozias Leduc painting Mont-Saint-Hilaire.

The man on the bottom bunk sat up. The guard had other cats to skin, and left the two men to make their acquaintance. They exchanged barely a word. His cellmate was much older than he was, his greasy hair plastered to his head but for a single rebel strand, and he seemed to have been roused from profound hibernation. Will climbed up onto the top bunk, which had absorbed the smell of the room, and didn't move until the cell door clanked loudly shut. He didn't yet know that this knell would become a fixture of his days, repeated morning and evening with an undeterred constancy, as if the days could not begin without the repetition of this foreboding sound. The clanking of cell doors would be one of Will's abiding memories of his year in the sprawling Carson City prison, a detail he never failed to mention when, after a drink or two or eight, he would launch into the story of his days behind bars.

A few hours passed. Will concentrated on his anxious breathing. There was action in the cells — prisoners yelling at their cellmates to shut their traps, claiming they were trying to read, each sally invariably met with insults or just laughter. It didn't feel to Will as if he'd been landed among the unhappiest or most dangerous of men in the world. It was merely a facade; a way not to admit defeat. At ten o'clock, by Will's estimate, a gong sounded and a guard announced "Light's out!" at the top of his lungs. And every night some comedian on the floor would yell the same thing, *"Goodnight, ladies,"* which made everyone laugh — everyone except Will, that is. The same joke every night and the men laughing every time: he never quite understood why. Perhaps he'd have needed many years in lockdown for the reason to come to him.

It goes without saying that Will James, a.k.a. Ernest Dufault, the young French-Canadian from Saint-Nazaire-d'Acton who'd left Quebec a few years earlier and now found himself surrounded by thieves, rapists, and murderers in the Nevada State Prison, didn't get much sleep that first night.

5

D ay after day and especially night after night, in the silence of his stone cell, with both eyes wide open and staring at the ceiling, Will's thoughts turned to mountains and deserts, boundless prairies, cool clean springs, and the taste of the freshest air in the world; to the light when the sun set and that other light, suffused with hope, that early morning brought to the mountains and the deserts. He listened to the songs of cicadas and crickets, and, during the days, felt the caress of the sun on his copper skin and beheld the mountain ranges and the deserts, before, night after night, he trained his eyes on the ceiling in insomniac silence. Will remembered the joy of following the wind, independent and free, mounted on a saddle horse with a trusty packhorse behind him. For hours at a time on his uncomfortable bunk, Will replayed these memories and recalled the names and breeds and coats and markings of the horses he had known and the anecdotes he remembered them by: every horse he'd ever straddled; ones he'd worked with and ones that had become trusted friends. Maybe, thought Will, when you got down to it, these horses were the only creatures who'd ever really understood him. And for months on end, riven by guilt, he also thought of his mother and father, Joséphine and Jean Dufault, and his brothers and sisters: Philippe, Auguste, Anna, Eugénie, and Hélène. He spent hours, day and night— especially at night—absorbed in childhood episodes surfacing from the well of his long-buried memories.

It was all coming back to him.

The four sparsely populated streets in the small town of Saint-Nazaire-d'Acton, known as Saint-Nazaire for short. The large church square. The coarse sun-leathered faces of the farmers and villagers who'd patronized his father Jean's store, men and women who earned their bread by the sweat of their brow and had bent backs to show for it: some were solid, others faltering; all were simple and proud. He remembered the general store itself; its shelves and glass counters and displays and sacks of flour, sugar, and salt stacked in the centre—in season, you could also buy sugar and salt by the block. There was a small but decent wood stove, around which taciturn men gathered to rub their cold hands warm. Behind the counter was glassware of varying quality that his father sold to newlyweds come to settle the rural byways of this backwater at the ends of the earth. He remembered the sweets and candies set out to tempt people not inclined to succumbing to temptation; a wall of fabrics that was dusted every Friday along with the rest of the store. Boxes containing who knows what sometimes piled up—items not

paid for that would be delivered anyway because that
was the way it worked. And who could forget the big
brown leather-bound ledger under the enormous cash
register? A book that must have weighed a ton: one
that seemed possessed of magical powers and which
little Ernest stared at in fascination; one that held his
father spellbound for hours on end. The shelves behind
the counter also held footwear—work boots mostly,
though also the odd pair of beautiful little shoes for first
communions (black for boys and white for girls)—and
then the oil lamps and large stores of candles, and there
were boxes of soap in the display cases that were always
running out and needing to be reordered. For despite
what city people said, country folk did wash, and one
look at the size of their families would give you an idea
of how long one bar of soap would last. One popular
shelf held tobacco and smoking paraphernalia; another,
young Ernest's favourite, was stacked with stationary
and periodicals, and it was here that the young boy
whiled away the hours. His son's budding interest was
one reason Jean kept the stand so well stocked, and
in addition to the usual pads of writing paper, lined
or plain, he ordered heavier paper stock from Saint-
Hyacinthe dealers with Montreal connections, though
no one ever bought it. Ernest was not yet nine years
old, but Jean never hesitated—at least at the beginning—to order the paper he learned to draw on, along
with pencils and more sophisticated pens. He'd even
overcome his wife Joséphine's reluctance and his own
ignorance in the matter and brought in oil pastels, boxes
of watercolours, gouache, and charcoal sticks, though

when he saw the stains these left on the fingers of his son, whom he thought of as some budding Raphael, he held back a curse and realized he'd made a mistake.

"Everything okay, Papa?"

"Of course, Ernest. You can draw as much as you want. That's all that matters!" he'd concluded, ruffling his son's hair.

A tear ran down Will James's face. He shut his eyes tight but couldn't dispel the memories coming to him.

If the first floor — the main floor of the general store — contained plenty to occupy the thoughts of young Ernest, then the basement was a treasure trove that had terrified him every time he was sent down to find some item running low on the store shelves. This fear went back to his earliest childhood, though he could never put his finger on exactly what it was that scared him so. The troubling shadows, the humid dirt floor, the musty smell? All were enough to send a young child's imagination running wild.

To get there, you went through a trapdoor outside the store, and more than once Ernest's older brother Philippe had closed the trapdoor on him. Ernest remembered being imprisoned down there and, terrified he would suffocate in the dank hole, screaming at the top of his lungs until someone finally came searching for him. One day his mother Joséphine decided she'd had enough and reprimanded Philippe in front of the whole family — and with a stick, not her hands. His naked bum turned red before their eyes. Philippe begged, with tears streaming from his eyes down a face grown every bit as red. He never shut his little brother in the basement again, though he did pummel him in the stomach with his fists the next day, to get even. Ernest fell to the ground and rolled up in a ball; now it was his turn to cry hot wet tears.

Will turned over on his mattress, remembering in detail how he'd grown to love animals at the same time as his talent for drawing had emerged. He'd built a rich imaginary life populated by a cast of creatures both fantastic and realistic—farm and backyard animals capable of speaking; their creator wanted them to be able to talk to each other, so of course they did. Ernest ruled over them as king and master.

At the age of seven, Will had shown his mother one of his first drawings, in which he'd captured the shadows cast over a small group of grazing cattle perfectly. A simple broken line denoted the horizon, a radiating circle hung in the clear mid-afternoon sky, and a few aspen rising out of the arable land formed a rudimentary country landscape. Its starkness only made the cattle appear more real. Joséphine's mouth opened wide. She squinted and scrutinized the drawing, then declared she'd been blessed. Her son was a genius.

In his cell, Will shifted his position, lying on his back with his hands on his stomach, then with his hands crossed behind his head, then back on his stomach. From time to time, he could almost smell his mother's scent—a wisp of soap, a hint of sunflower. She was a generous woman and devoted mother who would occasionally partake of a drink when no one was looking, especially on their trips into the "big city," Montreal.

In the depths of night, memories of his uncle Napoléon Dufault also came back to him. Napoléon was a farmer with no children of his own and a great love for Ernest, his favourite nephew. Will recalled his uncle's loud and unaffected laugh, his beaming smile, and the way he had of showing people how to approach animals, treat them right, and understand them. And he thought back to the long walks he'd take with his brother Philippe, always with a spirit of adventure, to the farm on the 4th Rural Road of Saint-Nazaire. Sometimes, during the cutting of hay that happened around Saint-Jean-Baptiste Day on June 24, their father would let them stay at the farm for a week. Young Will had never gone so far as to say as much out loud, but deep down he wished he'd been born on a farm. Sure, it was back-breaking work. Farmers aged quicker than the rest, looked old at forty, and struggled to eke out a living. They were among the most boorish and uncultivated people who ever passed through the general store but, in the best sense of the word, they lived a simple life. Years later, as a new and zealous convert to cowboy culture, he learned to despise farmers and other sedentary country-dwellers. He adopted a different discourse, regarding them as slaves to the capricious whims of cruel, merciless, and ungrateful nature, no more able than beasts of burden to fathom life's meaning, or to know what it was to be free. They meekly accepted their yoke, lived out their lives like

half-men. But back then, when he was just a kid, he
loved his animals, and he loved his uncle who lived
surrounded by them: a man cut from the same cloth
as the hewers of logs who'd first cleared the land and
built the colony; someone who'd fertilized the land
with his sweat and asked no more in return than a
hunk of bread and portion of bacon each morning
and night. (His uncle must have made a meal of his
wife's ample bosom too, as a good Catholic, Will
imagined in the solitude of his cell.) His was a breed
of men not around anymore, and never to be seen
again. It was one Will had always longed to join,
though he was not quite sure he'd ever have wanted
to settle down.

Will would also be reminded—every time he saw a
fellow prisoner chugging a big glass of milk at the can-
teen—of his *annus horribilis*, 1900, in precise detail.
First came the accident that forced them to leave the
general store and their hometown. Will's father had
severely fractured his shoulder and the doctor was
unequivocal: there was to be no more heavy lifting for
Jean, especially none of the repetitive and heavy kind
that made up the typical day of a storekeeper. After
thinking it over long and hard, and after finding a
buyer for the store and a new job—Jean had invested
nearly all the family's savings in a new shoe factory
that failed to fulfill its promise—the Dufaults packed
their life up into a wagon and departed for life in the
big city, Montreal. Ernest was nine, Philippe eleven or
twelve, and Auguste, the youngest, was two. Ernest
arrived excitedly. He relished the prospect of being in

pursuit of adventure and striking out into the unknown without any idea of what their future held. But leaving behind the family's familiar country life proved difficult. The boy who had always run unfettered through the fields and enjoyed large open spaces where his imagination could run free, now found himself in the city and imprisoned in his thoughts. Reading and drawing were Will's only refuge.

Then, that same year, there'd been the poisoning episode, one that traumatized Ernest and would haunt his dreams until the end of his days.

One day, young Ernest had returned from one of his little adventures to find a tall glass of what he took to be milk on the table. Good timing: he had a powerful thirst and gulped down the liquid, which turned out to be diluted lye—sodium hydroxide—and it burned his throat and his stomach. Ernest's cries of pain and panic brought his mother—who was surely on all fours scrubbing the bathroom floor tiles—running. She called Philippe, who was playing in the alley, and sent him to get the doctor.

"Hurry up! C'mon!"

Ernest was writhing in pain. She made him drink large quantities of what he was terrified was the same liquid, but was milk, and it took all the mother's guile and tender words to overcome her son's fear. The doctor arrived, confirmed the seriousness of the situation, asked for a bucket, and stuck two fingers down the child's throat. Ernest threw up all over the bucket and the doctor's nice new pants. His mother's and the doctor's interventions saved the boy's life.

A near-death experience comes at a price. Due to the severity of his internal burns, Ernest was put on a strict diet for a year. He was allowed only liquids, no fruits or anything acidic, and had to spend several weeks confined to his bed. His drawing was better than ever, but the time dragged, and after twelve months Will still had stomach pains when digesting or excreting. Many years later, Will's brother Auguste would posit that there might have been a connection between the incident and Will's premature death; the alcohol that eventually killed him preyed on a liver already weakened by the lye. Certainly Ernest would never drink milk again, but then most cowboys didn't. They liked to say they'd been nursed on whiskey, that they were not calves, but men.

The Christmas after his poisoning, Will's grateful parents were especially generous. On top of the two oranges in his stocking, and candies as usual, he was given oil pastels, coloured pencils, and a revolver fashioned out of a quarter-inch plank. Philippe was jealous, but he'd always been jealous of his younger brother, because he didn't have the gifts and charms that came to Ernest naturally. Joséphine's first delivery had been difficult, and her labour long. Subsequently, the doctor had prescribed at least a week of bed rest. (Her husband almost starved, and, when she was finally back on her feet again, the house was a disaster.) But Ernest's birth was over in less than an hour. He slid into life like a fish into water.

Will's uncomfortable bunk made his back ache. He missed his brother. *"Philippe,"* he whispered to

himself, "*viens-moi en aide. Donne-moi la force.*" Come
help me, he thought, as he remembered the stare of
his brother's large green eyes, the way they searched
for something inside of Will with both apprehension
and animosity. His older brother had become sweeter,
and friendlier, after the accident. They'd all come to
understand that family was sacred.

The benediction Jean offered on New Year's Day
was especially heartfelt. It wasn't Philippe who'd asked
for their father's blessing, but Ernest. Nerves and an
otherworldly shyness constricted his throat as he
approached his father, tall and portly and with an
imposing build. The same discomfort gripped Jean
Dufault, a humble man of few words. The New Year's
benediction had always been a solemn moment. The
whole ritual was perennially awkward, tied as it was to
profound emotion. The father figure demanded respect
and represented authority. It was a heavy weight to
bear. And that year, as if it had not been enough for
the family to move to the dehumanizing metropolis,
a world of concrete and criminality and no place for
young children to grow up, his son had almost died,
and now the family business was faltering. Jean was
extremely worried and, though he did his utmost to
hide it behind the stony facade so typical of men of
his generation, he was a sensitive sort and beginning
to question everything. Jean Dufault worried he'd not
be able to take care of his family—the people nearest
and dearest to him, the ones he loved without ever
telling them as much. The New Year's blessing was
always a poignant moment for Jean, and this year he

needed to dig deep to summon the energy, first of all smiling at Ernest and ruffling his hair.

He looked around.

"Let's go into the hallway, there's more room."

The family gathered, and kneeled, side by side. Jean crossed himself and, in a quivering voice, recited the prayer that had remained unchanged over the years. Perhaps it was not God he feared, so much as life threatening to get the better of them.

"I bless you in the name of the Father, the Son, and the Holy Ghost."

After crossing themselves in turn, Joséphine and the children got up. Jean approached his wife, made a wish, and kissed her on the lips in front of everyone — a rare occurrence. Then he went around the table, doing the same with each of the children, kissing them on the cheeks from oldest to youngest. By the time he got to Ernest, he had a hard time choking back his tears. After Jean, visibly emotional, asked his son to never scare him like that again, Ernest broke down. The father's words hadn't come out as a reproach; his voice had been full of love. No one, and especially not Ernest, imagined that in only a few years he would again be the cause of so much grief by leaving the family nest before he was of age. If only they knew where he was.

Sometimes, in his freezing bed, Will wished he could relinquish his memories, cease to be his former self. Everything would be so much easier. But if Will slammed the door, they'd come right back in through the window, or the basement trapdoor of his childhood home.

Dawn was colouring the sky. Gradually, the light seeped into Will's cell. As Ernest Dufault, that boy from another time, dissolved back into him, Will finally went to sleep.

6

Five months served, and the metallic clank of the cell door still woke Will with a start every time. But not that morning. Will woke up long before the cell doors opened, before even the sun rose. And despite the enveloping blackness and relative warmth of his blanket — he'd been issued a new, thicker one — Will couldn't get back to sleep. Even in prison, Sunday was a day of rest, a "free" day you might say; but this particular Sunday would be unlike any other. No lounging around the yard, drawing, and smoking. Two weeks earlier, toward the end of September, a letter from the pale hand of Mrs. Riordan had reached Will. Jennie claimed she had business in the city in mid-October, and suggested a visit to her "good friend" Will. The letter had filled his cowboy heart with joy, the effect of which was that the days, hours, and minutes ticked by much more slowly. Nights already seemed interminable; now they were a personal hell. Might as well abandon all hope of sleeping, he thought.

Lying in his bed, Will imagined their meeting, sometimes fantasizing that he and Jennie might find themselves alone in some dark corner where she would know exactly what to do to make Will forget his loneliness. He fought off his erections by thinking of something interesting to say to her, a few questions that went beyond mere pleasantries, along with responses she might not anticipate to the questions she would surely ask—answers that didn't adhere too scrupulously to the truth.

But then, in the middle of a long night, Will had a prodigious erection he didn't feel like thwarting. His hand slipped into his pants. Oh my...Jennie, tall and blonde, her green eyes magnificent and her hair as it always was, gathered up in a bonnet that revealed her slender neck, her waist so trim. Jennie's scent and body permeated the space around him. Every man on the ranch had been in love with her, another way of saying they all wanted her. Yes, every one of them, like Will, had dreamed of being the one to—what, tame her? Men came to Nye County from all over Nevada for the sole purpose of working for Riordan and his wife. What did it matter that the men's labours were so far from the main ranch house? On rare days off there was always the chance to catch a glimpse of her. Unlike most of the roustabouts who'd drifted through over the years, Will had managed to make a good impression on the rancher's wife. She'd immediately taken to him, and the warmth she'd demonstrated was reciprocated; what an abundance of smiles and stolen glances his darling friend had given him. She

liked his drawings, and one day he'd even been so
bold as to express his wish for an hour or two alone
with her, somewhere, to draw her portrait. Then the
magic could have happened: she abandoning herself,
vanquished, won over by his caresses, his kisses on
her hands and arms and ears and face and lips, Jennie
lifting up her dress, exposing a bit of leg and his soiled
cowboy fingers sliding along her thigh as he went right
on kissing her neck. He'd tear her buttons and she'd
be wearing no corset; he'd plunge his face into her
bosom, and the two would breathe as one. Yes, it was
true, he'd vowed to paint her portrait. It was nothing
like what he'd fantasized: Jennie had simply looked
down, and replied that she didn't think her husband
would be keen on it.

When, from time to time, the men descended on
the ranch, leaving the solitude of their cabins and the
rush of the roundup for a few days of well-deserved
rest, Will would sometimes help her with the dishes.
At the end of some of the more trying and exhausting
days, she'd undo the top two buttons of her collar —
just enough to reveal an opening, a glimpse of the
canyon, sweat pearling on her fair skin, her breasts
rising with every inhalation. Each one was like a small
death, the most exquisite of tortures. How heady the
nights had been, the two of them lying side by side
with their eyes wide open. On one occasion Riordan
needed to travel to Arizona and, trusting him — or,
more precisely, in the good humour he inspired in his
wife — he'd asked Will to keep an eye on her. So it was
that one night she happened to join him after dinner

on the porch while he was having a smoke and doing some drawing. Will was paralyzed on the spot. Jennie's chignon was still in place, though a few stray strands fell onto her neck. Will took a long, deep breath.

Jennie was drinking, like a man, without wincing. The alcohol and her courage were catalysts, and it was only a matter of time before the confessions issued forth. Sometimes, she began, she got the blues. Like tonight. She felt a deep emptiness inside. Her husband was a boor. On the rare occasions when he did take an interest in his wife, he treated her exactly like he must have done the harlots he visited.

"You men are so . . . clueless!"

Jennie possessed a calm mettle. You could say anything to her.

"Why not show me?" Will answered.

He watched as she blushed and lowered her gaze a second time. Listened to her breathing. She stood up and told him she had to put her girls to bed, and that, after, she'd take a bath.

"If you'd be so kind as to pump me a little water and stoke the fire before going back to your cabin, it'd be much appreciated."

She'd said this more loudly than was necessary, as if to make sure the other hands heard her send Will away. But there was no one around. The bunkhouse was a good distance from the house and, at this hour of the night, the other men would be draining the last of the bottles and well gone, oblivious to the world around them; and that's if they weren't at the nearest bar or brothel, neither of them close.

As Will was carrying the last bucket of hot water to the house, Jennie reappeared in a flannel bathrobe, the open neck of it revealing much more than her unbuttoned blouse had done. Her naked feet—a man didn't see women's feet much in those days—had their own stirring effect.

"William," said Jennie, "don't get carried away. You know full well we won't do any of the things we very well could."

She came closer. The chirping of cicadas surrounded them.

"Do you get many chances to see women?"

"Not often, no. And the ones I do aren't what you might call...respectable."

"Roll me a cigarette and pour me one more drink, will you?"

As it happened, they didn't do any of the things they could well have done—and now he imagined in great detail all the things that never happened. Yet it seemed like she was the one who had started it. Will had been obstinately hoping she would take her bath in front of him, but the moment passed. The bath was forgotten. Instead, she took to the bottle. A few drinks later, she was still telling him how sad she was, how hard it was for her to get up some mornings. With no way of knowing it, Jennie was a woman of her time, and within her raged a war between desire and propriety. Life as Jennie had known it had gone on long enough—she would do whatever it took to make sure her daughters knew something different.

They drank until the sky was infused with blue. With the light of the sun's first rays, her face seemed undone. She got up, weaved a little, and then held Will very close and kissed him. Her breasts were soft and full; she burrowed her moist face in the crook of his neck and then, no longer able to contain themselves, the two kissed again, after which she ran back inside the house.

It wasn't enough, would never be enough. Too impulsive, not sexy enough. The night before Will set off with that bastard Hackberry—yes, that was the night—she'd come out to join him as he was petting Happy. Something might have come of it. Jennie couldn't sleep. He'd seen her coming, her hair dishevelled, bundled up in a roomy coat of her husband's that didn't fully conceal her scant nightie. It was an invitation, surely, an invitation following everything they had shared, an invitation he'd failed to heed. They'd smoked in silence. If not, Will would have told her he needed to feed the horses.

"This late?" she'd have asked, intrigued.

"This late," he'd have shot right back.

"Let me give you a hand."

Together they would have proceeded as far as the corral. She'd have glanced at him from the corner of her eye—an ambivalent look, or perhaps just an apprehensive one. Will was feeling sheepish too, but he knew that the moment they were in the barn, she'd be his. He knew she'd let him do whatever he wanted, because that was what *she* wanted—to give herself to him in the hay. They would go inside and that's how it would be. He wouldn't even pretend to be there for the horses. He would turn toward her, draw her in, wrap his arms around her.

Then their lips would find each other in the darkness. Then, though it's cold, her coat falls to the ground. He takes her in his arms again, more forcefully this time, envelops her, caresses her back and ass, sucks on her neck; their mouths fuse, their emboldened tongues meet.

"I've always wanted to see your breasts."

"Will, be reasonable," says Jennie, sighing.

"You're killing me."

She lets herself fall back into the hay and is breathing quickly as his rough hands slip under her nightgown. Will feels no trepidation and buries his face between her breasts. They have a marvellous salty smell. He could spend his whole life there, and the next one as well. She moans, but has enough of her wits about her to unbuckle his belt and unbutton his fly. His pants slide off now, revealing an impossible erection. He comes on her. She closes her eyes. They gasp together, like a scream.

. Will jerked a few times and could contain himself no longer. Suddenly on the bunk he felt ashamed. Had he dishonoured her? She was a decent married woman, one who exuded goodwill, and was coming that very day to pay a prison visit to the ungrateful cowhand turned thief. Perhaps he was paying her homage, a tribute that would remain with him until the end of his days. Will liked to think she'd understand, maybe even be flattered. The loneliness of his silent bed, the cell, the prison—this world—was overwhelming.

Will looked to the window, tried to estimate how long it would take for the sun to rise. Hard to say. He wanted to sleep, but in vain. Images of Jennie assailed his mind relentlessly. Will closed his eyes and gave up trying to stem the flow.

7

In the mess, a few hours later, Will's breakfast of porridge and boiled eggs washed down with dirty water was a trial—or at least, more so than usual. He had butterflies in his stomach; every mouthful made him sick. Will tried to control his chaos of feelings, to convince himself that hers was a routine visit, likely the only one he'd get for the duration of his imprisonment, and that she was just an acquaintance—a woman he'd coveted briefly, and another man's woman to boot. He tried to dispel the perverted images that came to mind as soon as they arrived, as he struggled to swallow his Catholic guilt, as he did the cat slop they served the inmates every morning.

By eleven, when he made his way to the visitors' room, Will's hands were sweaty and his legs like jelly. He splashed a little cold water on his neck and forehead, and tried to appear happy and relaxed. It wasn't easy.

She was there waiting for him, sitting bolt upright with her hands on her lap and her hair up in her trademark bonnet. She looked at him with a smile possibly even more forced than his own.

"Mrs. Riordan," said Will.

He sat down. His legs hadn't buckled.

"William, please. Call me Jennie. How many times do I have to ask you?"

"Jennie," he said, tipping his imaginary hat.

"How are you doing?" she asked.

Will stared for a moment at the wall behind her, then deep into her eyes.

"Guess I know how it feels now, to be thrown into a corral against your will."

Again, as a courtesy, she smiled. Will grimaced a little. His witticism had sounded neither as funny nor as lighthearted as, in his cell, he'd hoped it would.

"I brought you something," Jennie said. "But I don't know if I'm allowed to give it to you."

She pulled from her handbag some pencils and three high-quality sketchpads.

"Geez, you shouldn't have. Thank you."

"It's all right if I give them to you?"

"I think so. They already searched you, right? In any case, they let me draw in here. Because they figure I have a bit of talent, the guards give me paper and pencils — but not good ones like these! In exchange I give them drawings. Sometimes I can even sell one, or barter with the other prisoners. Really, many thanks."

What Will did not mention was the nature of the drawings his fellow inmates asked of him — erotic scenes of naked women in not-altogether-Catholic positions. Word of them had spread like wildfire, and there were weeks when Will simply couldn't meet the demand. And yet he was not the least bit interested in erotic drawings. The few undaunted peaks of the Sierra Nevada he was able to glimpse by pressing his face up against the window of his cell excited him a thousand times more.

"The light here transforms the atmosphere and colour of the mountains every time the sun moves," said Will. "It's real hard to capture it in drawings, but if ever I did want to paint professionally then I'd already have a few sketches and studies under my bandana. After all these months staring out my little window, I'm getting a real sense of the natural lines of the region—of the desert, which I can see a little, and the foothills and mountains."

Jennie urged him to keep at it, to focus on his art and pursue it when he got out of prison, rather than falling back into the life of the drifting cowpuncher. He looked down at the table. She was aware of his despair and wanted to follow up with something more positive, maybe even something mothering.

"You've been on my mind a lot, Will. A lot since I heard about your trial, but before it too. The truth is I've been concerned about you ever since you left. A premonition, maybe. A woman's intuition. You're not alone, you see."

Will blushed. "I always felt at home, on the ranch, and that's because of you. Not to say your husband isn't a good boss."

"I wouldn't believe it if you did!" she joked, with a laugh.

"How's he doing, by the way? Was the season good?"

Jennie's expression became sombre. It had been a tough winter. Many of the calves had died. Buried under snow, they'd been unable to scavenge anything to eat. Her husband and a few of his men had spent months riding the plains trying to help, but they were powerless before the sad spectacle of the herds decimated by the cold, the blizzards, hunger, and disease. When spring came, the ones that had survived were sickly. The cows and steers weren't much better off.

"And there were so many coyotes this summer, and they were much bolder than usual. Even gunshots don't scare them off anymore."

Will nodded, his lips pursed. Jennie observed the tightening in the large square jaw that had always been so attractive to her, but fought off the distraction.

"We made it through the year, but it was hard. We had to let some good men go, men who've been with us for years. You know how it is. The prices have been low — well, they're still low. We barely have enough to pay the hands and finish the season without going too far into the red."

Suddenly she was pulled away from her story, and turned completely pale.

"Sorry, Will. Here I am complaining, and here you are . . ."

"Think nothing of it, Jennie. Stop," he said gently.

He extended his hand toward hers, but not all the way.

"I came here to talk about you!"

"Ah, really?" he stammered, blushing again. "Hearing about the outside world does me good, though maybe I'll feel lousy tonight."

He swallowed uncomfortably.

"Are they treating you okay in here, Will?"

He stared at the back wall again, ponderously, and summoned up the little speech he'd rehearsed. Cleared his throat.

"The monotony of the clanging cell doors and three calls a day—it's enough to make a man die of boredom. But then you always have to be on your guard because there's no telling what the other prisoners will get up to. I just want to do my time and keep to myself, clear my name, walk out that door, and never look back. I don't want to make waves. Mixing with the others doesn't interest me. It was hard at first. People were always trying to pick a fight, insult me, threaten me, for no reason at all. I just let 'em do their thing. I did almost have to raise fists a couple times. I've made a few friends though, good people, and I'm left alone now. A few of the guards are mighty kind too. They give me some privileges. Like I get to help out in the main kitchen now. But I do hate it. I've fallen so low!"

Jennie nodded supportively, letting Will know she'd understood. In the cowboy hierarchy the cook's helper occupied the bottom rung: he was less than zero, constantly pushed around, a punching bag who gets no respect whatsoever and is stuck doing the very worst jobs. The kitchen helper was a lackey—a flunky—and so that was also the name he answered to. In prison, kitchen duty meant peeling potatoes, washing dishes, cleaning the kitchen, scrubbing the floor. Nothing to complain about, really, and a far cry from the thankless tasks of the flunkies in the cow camps and roundups Will had gotten his start in so many years before. Fair weather or foul, the cook's flunkies pitched the tent next to the wagon. The moment they reached camp they had to dig a hole and make a fire, or be prepared to catch an earful. After that they'd do their best, more often than not under pounding rain, to raise the three steel bars that held the S-hooks to hang the beaten cast-iron pans and Dutch oven. The cook, meanwhile, would mix, knead, and fold dough right in the pots the bread would be baked in. And as it baked, the cook's flunky would single-handedly run back and forth, arms full, while his boss stayed in the dry tent enjoying a smoke if he was not making the rest of the supper. And every man in the camp would be teasing him mercilessly, a gentle razzing during good times that turned decidedly less gentle when things went badly, or if the cook just happened to wake up on the wrong side of his bedroll, as he often did. No, Will's prison chores did not compare with the travails of a roundup flunky; he wasn't expected to keep up the breakneck pace of the chuck wagon, and everyone around him went about their business reasonably cheerfully, happy not to be breaking rocks in the middle of the desert or roasting under the noonday sun.

"It got so I was dreaming of the washing-up every night," said Will. "And potatoes! What a nightmare. But a friendly guard took pity and had me transferred.

I've been chopping wood and stacking it in the yard, for a few months now."

"They let you use an axe?"

"Yes, of course they do—but with a pack of armed guards watching, on top of the ones posted day and night in the watchtowers. And I kept up the charm offensive, giving the guards drawings and telling 'em my stories. So when a better job came up, they let me know. Now I serve in the officers' mess. Which pretty much means waiting, and I mean *waiting*, at the officers' table."

Jennie smiled politely at his play on the word.

"I ain't complaining, as I say. The trusted prisoners get to eat the prison workers' leftovers, and on real crockery. The food sure is tasty—nothing like the godawful slop they serve up on iron dishes in the mess. I swear it ain't fit for a dog. The problem is there's this other prisoner who's had his eye on me—a ruthless, stinking Mexican. I tried to ignore him, but once he crossed the line. I had time to break a bowl of boiling soup over his forehead before they broke us up."

"Did they put you in the hole?" Jennie asked, a note of worry in her voice.

"Not even. That's how much they like me here. Probably didn't hurt that the other guy was a Mexican," thought Will out loud.

"So what happened?"

"Well, I went back to chopping wood!"

Jennie chuckled. Will sat in silence for a minute, and finished rolling his smoke. He pointedly offered it to his visitor. She declined. He struck a match and took a few long puffs, the paper sizzling and the cheap tobacco popping as it burned. The lines Will had rehearsed the night before were now coming to him more easily.

"You know," he said, "it's not actually so bad in here. The nights are long and hard, it's true, and time drags, sure. But honestly, it's not that bad. I can abide. I know I'll land on my feet. I want to get back on the straight and narrow. I'm ashamed of what I done, and here I am paying my debt to society. For sure, I'll never commit another crime like that. I am not a criminal."

"I know you're not, Will."

"And there's other men got it worse. Families outside and, what with them locked up, their families might as well be serving time too. Women left without two pennies to rub together, children abandoned, mothers overcome with suffering and the shame foisted on the family. That must be hard, real hard! I'm almost lucky to be an orphan. I miss no one, don't make anybody suffer, and nobody worries about me."

"*I* worry about you, Will."

She placed a hand on his. Had he not been so composed, her gentleness would have made him weep. He'd been putting on a great show of pride, wanting to appear at ease but the truth was another story. All the crazies ready to jump at your throat for an innocent remark; men who could literally stab you in the back or ribs for nothing more than a sideways look, or on account of some inexplicable childish grudge, or just for something to do. Will also made no mention of the jailhouse homosexuality, a taboo subject that was

repugnant to him as well. He was not about to let her
know that, after fifteen years in the shadows, inmates
were not immune to the charms of the freshly arrived
ass of a new young prisoner. On the one hand, some
of the burly men with whom he shared the quarters
were pederasts and sodomites just waiting for the
opportunity to gang up on a younger man and have
their way with him — make him their doll, their toy;
on the other, there were men likely to pounce on a
man in some unsurveilled prison hallway and beat him
to death. Will had emerged unscathed so far, though
he'd also fallen back into the habit of praying.

He was equally mute when it came to the painful
and disturbing business of his parents. The thought of
them left him not a moment's peace. He didn't mention
the remorse gnawing away at his insides, or the shame
in his gut. He did what he could to quash the image of
his distraught mother, heartbroken on account of her
son; an image that haunted him constantly, kept him
from ever snatching more than an hour or two of sleep.

"And ever since this new feller turned up," said
Will, "things are much better. He's a cowpuncher like
me. He's a 'pardner'! Can you believe that I was the
only cowboy here in Carson? People made fun of me
when I told 'em all what I knew how to do. Nothing
but city boys in here — or that's how it used to be. It's
different now."

"Why's he in here? For the same thing as you?"

"Nah. Almost no one goes to state prison for rustling — they'll string you up first! No, he caught his wife
cheating on him. Beat her lover to death."

"To death?"

The colour drained from her skin. .

"In a manner of speaking. Let's say he hit his mark. And was given, what's the phrase . . . 'a sentence to set an example'? But he's a stand-up guy. We made it so we're in the same cell and at night we pass the time talking about the wide world outside, naming all the ranches we've worked and the broncs we've broke. Not that it don't make us miss the range."

This fellow prisoner was an off-the-cuff invention. Will couldn't have told you why he did it; he didn't really know himself. Maybe he didn't want to worry Jennie anymore. The conversation went on a few minutes longer like that: Jennie asking polite questions; Will providing polite answers. Will almost forgot where he was, and the life he was about to resume the moment Jennie got back to her own. Soon the conversation faltered, the silences lengthened. Jennie checked the time. Their visit had lasted half an hour. She'd have stayed longer, she assured him, but she still had a few things to do before catching her train back to the ranch. She rose from the table a little dolefully.

Will followed suit, and they exchanged a cordial handshake. Had they listened to their hearts, the two of them would have taken each other in their arms instead. But Will was aware that proper manners didn't really allow it—even between husband and wife.

Before she went back out into the free, civilized world—as civilized as you could call the American

West — he risked impropriety and asked her for a handkerchief as a memento. Any one would do, even the one she had hidden up her sleeve.

"I don't have anything up my sleeve. But I should have one in my bag," she said, blushing.

She looked for one nervously. God knows what purpose he would put the handkerchief to. As she rummaged through her handbag, her face took on an expression of surprise and embarrassment.

"Oh, wherever is my mind?"

"What is it?"

Jennie pulled out a packet of letters and postcards, tied up with string. It wasn't very thick: two or three letters, and about as many postcards.

"That was one of the reasons for my visit," she said. "They keep on arriving at the house, regular as rain. You sure ought to write them back!"

She spoke with innocence and candour. Will looked down.

"They're all from the same address: Montreal, Province of Quebec, Canada."

"Is that right?" Will was prolonging the moment, thinking fast.

"You have family in Canada?" she asked.

"Not exactly. Just the family of the man who raised me. A French Canadian. Haven't I told you about him before?"

"We know so little about you! But why that face? It's like you've seen a ghost!"

The ghost could have been the ghost of Will James, of Ernest Dufault, or of his parents Joséphine and

Jean, whose very existence he was in the habit of denying. The correspondence between Will and his family, first to Montreal and later to Ottawa, would last until the death of the cowboy impostor. At the time, Will wrote his letters in French and signed them "Ernest," but his parents, who would continue writing their son in their native French, had to mail theirs to "Will James." After his release from prison, his literary success, even after his father's death, Will would write only in English, stipulating to his brother Auguste exactly what their mother could and couldn't know, even the exact phrasing to use with her. In the twenties and thirties, at the height of Will's American success, he even went so far as to order his correspondents to burn every childhood photo, any scrap of evidence tying him to his true identity — even to destroy his letters, once read, if they were to receive any more. And all the while he said nothing of his success or of his marriage to a minor Miss Nevada, effectively lying to them as he did to his wife. When Will and Alice bought a ranch in Pryor, Montana, he rented a PO box for his exclusive use in Billings, so as not to arouse suspicion.

But back in 1915, Will James was still serving a sentence for grand larceny — and, as an impostor, was a relative novice. He had no idea what to say to Jennie Riordan, so said nothing at all.

"I couldn't help reading one of the postcards. I'm really sorry. They were right there and the writing piqued my curiosity. You speak French?"

"A little. Not much. It's a long story."

The muscles of his jaw stiffened and he took on an absent look. He, who had always been so open and genial with her, was now clammed up.

"Could we leave it for another time?"

"Of course, Will, of course. But you'll write me, won't you? Whenever. Whenever works for you. When you're thinking of me?" she suggested boldly.

Even years later, Will would think of Jennie, but he would never write to her. And, even though his desire was stronger than his shyness, he'd lost the courage to ask her for the handkerchief again.

"I'll write you, you can count on it," he said. "What would help me most, in the short term, though . . . I don't want to impose . . ."

"What? What is it?"

"You know . . ."

"Oh, yes! A handkerchief."

She smiled and plunged her hand back into her handbag.

"Give me a second."

8

For close to a week Will lacked the fortitude and couldn't summon the courage to read his parents' letters. Day after day, night after night—especially night after night, eyes open wide and fixed on the ceiling in the stony silence of his cell—his only thoughts were of the mountains and deserts, of the endless valleys with their cold springs, the taste of fresh air and of the particular light of evening and early morning. He could no longer remember the joy of riding on a good strong saddle horse, independent and free, wherever the wind decided to take him. He didn't go over the list of all the horses he'd ridden and worked with anymore. Gnawed by guilt, his thoughts turned to his mother and father, Joséphine and Jean Dufault, and of his brothers and sisters, Philippe, Auguste, Anna, Eugénie, and Hélène. For hours on end, in any moment of the day or night he tossed and turned in his horribly uncomfortable bunk.

He relived the many moves the family had made after leaving Saint-Nazaire: from Montreal to

Vaudreuil, Vaudreuil to Montreal, from Montreal to Saint-Hyacinthe — where his father operated a small inn for a couple of years, the Union Hotel, that welcomed drifters and travelling salesmen for a week or a month at a time — and then from Saint-Hyacinthe back to Montreal again. The last move was in early 1906, in the middle of the school year. They moved to Boyer, a village within the city that would later be known as the neighbourhood of Rosemont. North of the gentle slope known unimaginatively as *"La Petite Côte"* were fields as far as the eye could see, all the way to Sault-au-Récollet and the Rivière-des-Prairies.

He thought back on his family's quasi-nomadic existence, a life with no chance of putting down roots, of constantly having to make new friends only to say goodbye, and finding himself in new streets and neighbourhoods, with untamed territory to explore. Even after the Dufaults left the countryside Ernest escaped into the woods or took off through fields at every opportunity. He would explore everywhere he could, walking alongside rivers he would swim in, lounging on the banks, never coming home before evening, giddy with feelings of unchecked freedom, as everyone started to wonder what had become of him. But the family's moves also brought trouble, his father's financial woes chief among them. Will remembered the sad face his father Jean wore every time he had to tell them, yet again, that it was his fault, he'd made a terrible mistake and they'd have to move again. Jean would only bring a measure of stability to the situation when, in 1906, they returned to Montreal, where he'd work in the post office until he retired. By then he was a broken, nervous, defeated man, a shadow of the person he had once been and might become again. But Jean remained an adoring father who made his love felt with a scarcity of words, with a fond look or a pat on the shoulder. Will remembered his father's encouraging words when, in Saint-Hyacinthe, he had for the first time made drawings in soap on the mirror behind the bar. The hotel customers all took an interest in little Ernest, showering him in compliments. He was twelve or thirteen then, and already had grand designs. That was the hotel where Will started collecting the illustrated American magazines left behind by the flow of travellers passing through from New England. Hundreds of thousands of French Canadians of the diaspora, far from assimilated, came back to visit their families as often as possible. And when they did, they brought the best of the Western magazines with them. There was *Wild West*, which went for a nickel—full name, *Wild West Weekly: A Magazine Containing Stories, Sketches, Etc, of Western Life*— and, for twice that price, *Dime Western Magazine* and *The Jesse James Stories*. Young Ernest Dufault didn't understand a word of English, but effortlessly told himself stories of his own, based on the illustrations he'd stare at for hours on end. Along with the few Westerns he'd been allowed to see with his big brother at the movie theatre—a newfangled art form Joséphine feared like the devil feared holy water— these magazines were the impressionable adolescent Will's first contact with cowboy culture.

Will rolled onto his back, hands folded behind his head. There was always a hero towering over every-one — a strong, silent type with a steely gaze and a lightning trigger-finger — and a lady in distress, fallen into the hands of a desperado, a dangerous outlaw who held nothing sacred; and Indians who were stuck with unflattering roles. They were the bad guys, the enemies to be taken down, the savages who kidnapped good white women and — it was never shown but always clear enough — violated them and turned them into pagans. The stories were violent and action-packed, full of revolvers and shootouts and the quick-drawing legends of the Wild West. Young Ernest made the acquaintance of Buffalo Bill, Sitting Bull, Kit Carson, and others. He was equally enamoured of the notori-ous villains, especially the cantankerous Billy the Kid, who would be an inspiration when Will chose his own pseudonym a few years later. Ernest also spent hours scrutinizing the pictures and trying to understand how the artists had managed to depict horses in action. Such precise lines, with every equine muscle taut and defined. But he didn't often copy the drawings. Will had a true photographic memory, and usually drew without a model. That, according to Joséphine, her daughters, and Auguste — none of whom ever tired of singing the boy's praises — was young Ernest's true gift. His ability to accurately visualize a drawing on the still-blank page was breathtaking.

But despite his good memory, Will could scarcely recollect the long hours — long *years* — spent on school benches; just another kind of prison really. From ages

six to fourteen, what with the Dufaults being repeatedly uprooted, Ernest attended a number of different
schools: École Saint-Pierre in Montreal, the parish
school in Vaudreuil, École Casavant in Saint-Hyacinthe,
and, in 1906, when the family returned to Montreal
for the final time, École Saint-Jacques, where he
squeaked through eighth grade. All were Catholic
schools because Joséphine, sure that public school
teachers were little better than illiterates, wouldn't
have it any other way. Ernest hadn't always hated
school. Certain of the Brothers who taught him were
nice enough and, when he was very young, he only had
to watch his father toiling in the general store to see
where a lack of education got you. During Will's first
years of elementary school at the tiny Saint-Nazaire
schoolhouse, and his fourth, at École Saint-Pierre, his
quickness and curiosity and, on occasion, his persever-
ance, were noted. Outside of the family cocoon, he
discovered that he possessed a unique charm, a gift—a
magnetism, a charisma, that let him hold others in his
thrall without his even really trying. In fourth grade,
thanks to his mother devoting long hours to filling the
gaps in her children's education at home, Will began
to read extremely well and write with very few errors.
Math proved more challenging, but he did learn to add,
subtract, multiply, and divide. And though he found
Canadian history dull, the geography classes where
he learned the names of places by situating them on
maps always excited him. A visceral sense of possibility, of a brave new world opening up, gave Ernest
butterflies in his stomach and made his toes tingle. But,

unfortunately, the Brothers spent twice as long on religious instruction as they did on history and geography
combined. Catechism was studied in public schools as
well; there was no escaping it. The purpose of turn-of-
the-century Quebec's slipshod education system was
not to lead the French-Canadian flock to higher studies
but to entrench ignorance, and it worked. Close to 90
percent of francophone students, in city and country
alike, left school after sixth grade. Boys often quit
after just four years of instruction; girls left after six
years or less. Outside of the upper classes and some
progressive pockets of the middle class, education
was held in low regard. Children had to work like
everyone else, and often started aged eight or nine.
The children suffered. Or they were bored to the point
of desperation.

That, certainly, was what happened with Ernest.
Several of his classmates started leaving school to
work in factories or on the family farm, and Will soon
realized he'd learned all he needed to know, and had
little reason to stay in school. He was getting by in
French composition and even in math, and had learned
the gospels and Bible teachings by heart, and wasn't
that all that mattered? He blushed as he recalled the
trying, thorny conversations that always arose when
it was time for him to do his homework, a struggle
that went on for years. He was up to no good—that's
what they said. A pouting, grumpy Ernest, exhausted
by his long day behind a school desk, would get the
ball rolling. School wasn't even mandatory, he'd complain, so why do I have to go? Because it's important,

his father would answer. In a few years' time, he'd no longer look back on these years as boring and punishing, they'd tell him. No, Ernest argued, you're wrong. And insomniac Will James, tossing and turning and studying every fissure in his stone cell, still felt the young boy he had been was right.

Joséphine sent all her children to school until eighth grade. It wasn't up for discussion. Children were to listen to their parents, and that was that. If other people didn't see the value of a good education, that was their problem, but the Dufault children would go to school. For Ernest, each new school year began well. He got along with his fellow students, but in no time at all he preferred to take refuge in drawing rather than study French, math, history and geography, and prayer. Hundreds of pages, thousands of blackened margins in his school notebooks: monsters, caricatures of his teachers, a collection of fabulous characters born of his imagination, the view from the classroom windows, still lifes—and then the horses. Horses and horses and more horses. A hind leg drawn a thousand times until he got it right; until it was perfect; until the coat glistened. By fifth grade, and even more so in sixth, Will was paying scant attention to the teacher's lectures, interminable as a funeral service and reaching him only through the cottony gauze of his boredom. To get out of doing homework, Ernest would sometimes come home three or four hours after class ended, acting like it was no big deal, pretending not to understand why everyone, who'd been waiting until he arrived to eat dinner, was throwing him a dirty look. Then his misbehaviour burgeoned into a full-blown conflict. Joséphine admonished him solemnly on the importance of going to school if he didn't want to end his days in abject ignorance. And just as was happening with his teachers, Ernest stopped hearing his mother's harangues. His deafness was self-induced.

In seventh and eighth grades, in Vaudreuil, Montreal, Saint-Hyacinthe, and then Montreal again, as attendance at Ernest's classes began to thin, it became increasingly difficult for Joséphine and Jean to make their son listen to reason. More and more, Ernest played hooky. He'd wander, in fair weather and foul, out where he knew no one could find him; through the fields and forests and along the riverbanks again. They stopped badgering him for a while. After all, what could they really do to him—the teachers, the school administration, whoever. The days Ernest spent in the school of the great outdoors started to vastly outnumber those in class, and inevitably his parents needed to be contacted, if only as a matter of safety. Ernest was caught by surprise. He brooded for a while and then, one night, at dinnertime, said his piece.

"I want to leave. *Je veux m'en aller d'icitte.* Go live out West. Work as a cowboy. Or up north, in the bush camps. I'll be a lumberjack, a woodsman, something like that. Live with the wolves."

Live with the wolves, Will repeated, mumbling the incantation to himself *sotto voce,* deep in the abyss of this dark night of his coming of age. Joséphine's reaction reflected the intensity of her possessive feelings for her young son who was growing up too fast. She let out a piercing scream. She was devastated, as if she'd died on the spot and been trampled by a crowd — by the unwieldy mass of her son's chimera and foolish ideas. Ungrateful boy! Had he no consideration, no respect for his poor mother and father? Ernest looked bored. His mother thrust her fists heavenward. "Curse the night when I conceived this child of mine. You're nothing but a burden!" She crossed herself and swallowed the bile of her dread, at a loss to understand the designs of the Almighty. *Amen.* Jean, Philippe, and Auguste, on the other hand, didn't take Ernest seriously, didn't think he was capable of doing such a thing. Leave? Surely a love of horses and the great outdoors was no reason for Ernest to banish himself and embark on a precarious existence far from all those he loved.

"What about English?" asked his brother Philippe. "Are you going to magically learn English in no time at all?"

"Given that we're moving around all the time as it is, why not make a real move? Like to the States."

"To the States?" Philippe echoed. "Where in the States, then?"

"Umm...yeah. Well, Hollywood."

Everyone except Joséphine guffawed, and Jean just sat there in a daze. Ironically, a few years later Philippe would take his brother's cue and also migrate to the United States. He'd end up in Florida, where he'd try unsuccessfully to make it as a painter.

Afterwards, Ernest endeavoured to be more discreet. He went back to school, and tried to be more diligent in eighth grade and finish the year without incident. Oh, but the boredom of it! This was the thing he remembered most of all: the crushing boredom. It wasn't a specific set of memories that came to him, or anecdotes, but the generalized heavy feeling of terrible boredom slowly killing him; that the possibilities before him were being gradually, powerfully stifled. The cursed blackboard. The old ruler held high in the air and then snapping down with a dreadful slap. The sucking and chewing of interminable prayers. That face the Brothers made, clearly expressing that he was a worthless boy without a future. The ennui. Will was champing at the bit, but hid his dreams from his family. Which is not to say that he wasn't keeping the fire burning, but that he was only blowing gently on the coals.

Meanwhile, young Ernest's collection of cheap magazines was swelling. Two hundred issues! For years, he'd been buying one a week with the pocket money Jean gave him for odd jobs around the house, and the change dropped by customers that he'd snap up. But reading the treasured magazines was no longer sufficient to quell Ernest's wanderlust. He wasn't a child anymore; he was done with living vicariously through fiction. What he wanted, and badly, was a life of action, a real life, the thing itself—life at its most thrilling, nerve-wracking, and all-consuming. And in this other life, Will would be far too busy taming horses to have any time for reading stories in stupid cowboy magazines. After the family's return to Montreal, Ernest left the entire collection to his brother Auguste.

Drawing was another story. Ernest sketched compulsively, sometimes filling up a notebook in as little as a week. Drawing was second nature to him, and yet the possibility of becoming an artist never entered his mind. He was vaguely aware that there were, in Quebec, folk known as "artists," but not many. Even in a family as relatively open-minded as his, it would be an understatement to say that such a life was held in low regard. Better to become a doctor or a lawyer, you can always paint in your spare time, be an amateur. He'd have had an easier time pursuing his vocation in France, but he knew nothing of the country beyond the usual clichés and France wasn't calling to him. He knew that were he to remain in Quebec, in Montreal or in Saint-Hyacinthe, he'd end up at trade school, and perhaps learn to be a draftsman. But there were no desks in the "school" where young Ernest would find his calling. His parents must have seen it coming—made their peace with the obvious, one way or another. It was inevitable that Ernest would leave Quebec, the country where nothing needs to die and nothing to change.

Lying on his damp and uncomfortable bunk, his back full of knots, Will recalled the job he'd had as a porter and kitchen helper at Viger station, back in '06 or '07, and how it changed his life. Extraordinary men of the world, looming larger than life, standing tall like the forces of nature they were, passed through the monumental city hub. Smoking fat cigars, willowy ladies at their elbows, dressed in expensively cut black coats and wearing large hats, the men never failed to impress the young Ernest, who still felt he knew nothing of the wider world. He wondered where these men came from and where they were headed, and tried to imagine all the places they must have seen: New York, London, Bangkok, Peking. Imaginary scenes entered his mind and were gone the next moment. These men — among them Americans from the East Coast and the Midwest, "English" from Ontario and Western Canada, satisfied millionaires, businessmen, prospectors, and travelling salesmen, sure; but also musicians, actors, and artists — were living proof of other ways to live, of far-flung lands and something different to the life into which he'd been born, a life foreordained by birth and family, his country and his cross.

Ernest's parents let him earn a few extra dollars drawing on barroom mirrors. He would go from tavern to tavern with a photograph that a friendly American tourist had sent of the "fresco" he had drawn on the mirror of the Hotel Viger. He knew all the places, never far from a whorehouse, where woodsmen (trappers, laid-off lumberjacks, log drivers, voyageurs) hung out when they were in town. During his last year in Quebec, Ernest spent a lot of time in dark and smoky rooms, listening to the woodsmen's stories of lands unsullied by the hands of men, of strange beasts encountered, and life at its most elemental. He sketched out some of these scenes: the arms of a raftsman as he slipped into the water, surrounded by log booms; a black bear with its claws out, standing upright and bellowing; a log cabin at a lumber camp in the middle of the wilderness; a trapper in snowshoes, lost in a blizzard and struggling to advance, his body at a forty-five-degree angle; exhausted sled dogs, tongues wagging, eyes wild...He'd emerge from the watering holes giddy with feeling, too excited for even a wink of sleep once he was back in bed, his eyes open wide and staring at the ceiling. Just like that first night, that seemed to last an entire week, in the Nevada State Prison. Because of his youth, Will was frequently chased from the taverns. And the burly men, worn rough by years of living on the fringes, could be hard on the boy. They'd ride him and they'd razz him, but he could take it. Character-building, it was. He'd be back the very next week, asking for more.

Like someone wrestling with a puzzle, Will tossed and turned in his bed as he replayed key episodes from his final year in Quebec. Not an altogether easy time. Wholly absorbed by his fantasies of the Wild West, by his dream of becoming a cowboy, Will took a full day's pay—most of his wages went to his parents—to buy his first revolver, a .32-calibre six-shooter. A somewhat astonished salesman at a hunting and fishing outfitter (Lalancette & Sons) sold it to the boy, no questions asked. Ernest and his constant companion, his angel-haired younger brother Auguste, would not breathe a word to anyone and would head to the quarries in the east end of town. Just the tram ride to the edge of the island could take an hour and, once there, they still had to hop the fences and climb up piles of gravel giving way under the weight of their footsteps, and then leap over the ravines. Dust would fill their lungs and soil their clothing and hair. And when, finally, they found the right spot, Will would tell his younger brother to stand at a distance and keep watch as he taught himself to draw. Then Ernest would empty the magazine on bottles and cans they'd brought to the quarry. He'd become another person — Billy the Kid or Jesse James, usually — and spend hours shooting. He'd shoot until his arm was too tired or in pain and his child's thumb unable to cock the hammer, at which point he'd use his palm and keep right on going, unless someone surprised them and they needed to shimmy off on their stomachs.

After their mother Joséphine claimed she had "come across" the gun in Ernest's things, young Auguste, whom Ernest had not allowed to even touch the gun, succumbed to his mother's scolding and ratted on his older brother. Knowing her son had bought a gun, she cried and asked, repeatedly and with desperation in her voice, what she could possibly have done to make the good Lord give her a child like this.

Will closed his eyes tight and tried to chase away the image of his mother pulling his hair out. *I'm sorry, mother,* he said to himself. *Forgive me.*

Jean and Joséphine's desperation peaked a few months later, after Ernest stole the milkman's horse and disappeared with it. As the police searched for a runaway horse, or a thief, Ernest hid out in the woods and fields of Varennes, on the other side of the Saint Lawrence. For two whole days, little Ernest was on the lam. He walked and trotted and galloped and became familiar with his mount, trying to decide on a fitting name for the clumsy black-legged bay. He settled on Butterscotch, and observed the horse closely. He wanted to get a sense of who the animal was, and to learn to draw it. But poor planning thwarted his first attempt at escape. With neither adequate food nor gear, he was forced to return home with his tail and the horse between his legs. Jean didn't take the episode lightly and Ernest was given a good beating. Philippe made a token effort to calm his father down, as a big brother is supposed to do, though he also derived a certain satisfaction from the spectacle — maybe Ernest would end up being the black sheep of the family, after all. In exchange for Ernest's help, when he wasn't working at the hotel, the milkman agreed not to press charges.

Aside from these episodes of his early life, what most often came to Will in the confines of his stone cell was the recollection of his mother's kindness, her voice and her facial expressions, her scent, her hands, the way she moved. And on his first visit home, in 1910, from the very moment of his arrival in the cool house that cried out the name "Joséphine," it was his mother's scent that struck Will most forcefully. She smelled of sunflowers.

Where Ernest's father had been reticent with his affections, Joséphine fawned over the children, even Ernest, and showered them in love. And in truth, the rebellious Ernest may well have received a larger portion of her love. He'd been such a beautiful, talented, sensitive child.

Joséphine smiled in ways that left you happy all morning. She had a way of letting you know how much you were loved, and a lively sense of humour too; she knew how to find the right words for Jean to throw off his veil of gravity and become a living presence to the people around him, instead of fading into the background, as he so often chose to do. Like mothers through the ages, she worried constantly, about anything and everything. Over time, her children would learn to ignore her worries and obsessions, though paying them no mind failed to make her presence any less powerful. Joséphine was the strong arm that kept the Dufault family going, and Ernest was somehow an extension of this sensibility, one he felt in every fibre of his being.

A turning point came one Montreal evening in the summer of 1907, just after Ernest turned fifteen. He was on his way back from work with a train ticket in his pocket, preparing to tell his parents he'd be leaving in a few days. He'd always been secretive, so no one was surprised. The Dufaults took the kitchen chairs outside and spent a good part of the evening on the porch, as their parents enjoyed a few after-dinner drinks. Half an hour went by without a word, until Joséphine broke her silence as a river overflows its banks. She addressed her son in a clear voice, her every sentence an embarrassment to Jean, whose eyes didn't leave his shoes. But out the words came, one after another in slow succession, and Ernest listened to each one.

"You're still so young, son..."

The words were difficult to get out. Her boy had always been so shut off, but also under pressure, ready to blow his top. She could see the magazines weren't enough anymore, but also that, even if he still seemed too young to leave, he was not a child anymore. What could his parents possibly do? They no longer knew where to turn. Hadn't they always let him do what he wanted, she asked him. Had they not let him have all the freedom he needed? He'd stolen a horse and spent two whole days playing cowboy. He said he had the bug, but how long would it last? What would be the price to pay? And he was wrong to think that he had to leave—there was plenty of opportunity in Quebec.

"So much opportunity!"

He could become an artist—study drawing, painting, art. She would be a support to him; both of them would be.

Will answered that soon there'd be no more horses in Montreal. They were part of a disappearing world.

"And no more road apples!" joked Auguste.

The poor could still use them to heat their houses for free, said Ernest witheringly. All Ernest wanted to do was ride horses and see majestic mountains. Nothing else was on his horizon. And Quebec...there was no possibility, no future, no freedom for him here. He wasn't about to live out his days in a factory or on a farm, sacrificed on the altar of hard labour and the demands of his litter of kids. A life of poverty and pious destitution wasn't for him, he said.

But couldn't he wait a few more years before leaving. Out of love for his mother?

"I'll come back and visit," he said. "And I'll write all the time, Mama, Papa."

At the end of their long discussion around the oil lamp—a tense one, shot through with pregnant silences and the discreet tears of his mother as she repeatedly crossed herself—Ernest's resolute but heartbroken father gave his son a last pat on the back.

"Come home soon, son."

Ernest left the next morning with ten dollars in his pocket and a bag of biscuits. He wouldn't come back to Montreal for three years, and then only to leave again.

In the middle of the night, not long after falling asleep, Will James woke up with a start from a terrible nightmare. In his dream, someone had stolen the string-wrapped packet of letters and postcards from Jennie before he'd had the chance to read them. He picked them up and it felt as if his fingers were burning. Will tried in vain to fall asleep again. Sunk back into his memories. In the silent morning, streaks of blue illuminated the cell's small window.

9

Eventually Will read his parents' letters and post-cards, not once but many times, in chronological and then in random order. He read them until each word was committed to memory. They were written in French, some by Jean and some by Auguste, though Joséphine's presence was everywhere. His mother wasn't doing well. She was increasingly remote, isolating herself behind a wall of silence as she mechanically toiled away at the endless housework. She had also lost her eldest child, Anna, probably her favourite of the girls. Soon after Ernest's departure, Anna Dufault had joined the Congrégation des Soeurs de la Providence and now answered to the name of Révérende Soeur Cajetan. She could only receive family visitors once a month, and never for more than an hour.

The postcards, written first, were less depressing, and Will read them repeatedly. His family said hi, sent their love, hoped their missives found him well. Autumn was upon them, winter was coming to an end; it was raining too much, it wasn't raining enough. Snow was covering the city, or it was melting into slush that gathered in little lakes at every street corner. Will enjoyed the turns of phrase but, after a year without any news from their long-lost son, the tone shifted. Letters replaced the cursory postcards, and his family was concerned. In one of the last, sent just two months earlier, Auguste threatened to write to the Riordans if he didn't get a reply or any news. Will fought back tears. The shame of it. His poor mother. His *maman*. What if she found out?

For a week, Will ruminated over the words and sentences addressed to him, and fell into a deep depression. He barely touched the paper and pencils Jennie had given him, didn't bother walking in the prison yard when it was allowed, and mixed with the other prisoners even less than before. When he wasn't at work chopping wood, he lay on his bunk, staring vapidly into space.

His depression might have gone on forever had an officer not appeared at Will's cell door one morning, half an hour before roll call, with a summons.

"1778. Smith's office. Now."

Officer Smith was a high-ranking paper-pusher. On top of the tedious bureaucratic tasks he never missed an opportunity to complain about, he also served as prison counsellor, his favourite part of the job. He was a bald, hunched, cranky chain-smoker with short-sighted but alert eyes peering out from behind little round spectacles. During the first days of his detention at the Nevada State Prison, Will had dealt with the counsellor many times. Smith had explained the

workings of the institution, and done so kindly. He'd
been the first friendly person since Will arrived.

"All our inmates must keep busy," he'd started,
lighting up a smoke with his massive desk lighter. "It's
what they call 'rehabilitation through work.'"

The smell of the cigarette and the curls of smoke
rising in the air above him quickly entranced the
cowboy, who had been cut off from nicotine for over
twenty-four hours. He could barely make sense of the
words of the man sitting in front of him.

"Some of our men work as janitors, some are out in
the yard, chopping wood. Some even get to go outside
the prison walls, in a quarry, cutting building stone. It's
not too far away. Oh, and there's one more possibility.
With the lieutenant's approval, some men even get to
make up their own job. Tailor-made, if you will."

Will was paying attention now.

"Don't get carried away now. Unless you got some
hidden talent that fills a need here at the prison, these
jobs are strictly for veterans. Men who've *earned* the
privilege."

The "self-employed" workers made things like wool
coats, horsehair or leather bridles, crops, and nosebags, all of it to be sold in horse equipment stores
throughout Nevada and Eastern California. The oldest
of these men sometimes agreed to take on an appren-
tice, not least to make sure their art wasn't lost, but
the waiting list was long, and you had to pay your dues
as a journeyman for a long time.

"They're not driven by any special love of leather,
or horsehair, or wool," said Smith. "Thing is, part

of the proceeds goes straight into their pockets. Not much after the prison takes its cut, but it's enough for some sweets and tobacco, and to have the prison tailor make them some warmer clothes. The tailor — now there's another coveted position. And some of them send money to their families."

The officer stubbed out his smoke, then lit another using the same massive lighter. Will wondered if this was part of the game, of the little torture prisoners were subject to, a way for the guards to impose their authority on first-timers — on fresh meat. Smith's fingers were stained as yellow as his teeth were brown. Maybe he smoked like this from dawn to dusk — inhaling slowly and then releasing an enormous cloud of smoke. He asked Will what he knew how to do.

Will puffed out his cheeks. Aside from finding his way around in the wilderness, recognizing all manner of plants and trees, twisting a lasso, taming broncs, and rounding up cattle on a good strong saddle horse — well, there wasn't much.

"Plumbing?" Smith asked. "Carpentry?"

Will shrugged.

"You don't know how . . . "

Will didn't know how.

"So you're telling me those hands of yours don't know how to do a single solitary thing that could be of use to the prison."

"I can draw."

The words came out of nowhere. Smith sighed as he breathed out a fresh blue cloud of smoke. Will's head disappeared in its wisps and his eyes started itching and tearing up. The guard searched a drawer, looking for a sheet of paper. He pulled one out, along with a pencil.

"Since I don't like liars much, and jokers even less, and really don't like having my time wasted, you got thirty seconds to draw me something good."

"Thirty seconds."

"That too long?"

Without giving it much thought, Will started drawing the silhouette of a man assessing a bucking bronco with a menacing look in his eye. The lines were nervous, the result lacklustre. Smith yanked the page from his hands and took a long, hard look at it, nodding his head.

"Well, I'll be darned," Smith said. "Who knew we had an *artiste* in our ranks?"

Will blushed, smiling like a bashful schoolboy. Their encounter had taken a new turn and, although Smith hadn't given him pencil and paper at that first meeting, at the end of their second, a few weeks later, he'd dug up a crumpled old pad of paper from the bottom of one of his drawers and proudly handed it over to his inmate. The following week Will gave Smith a few of his drawings of typical Western scenes, mostly of lone mustangs with their heads down, wandering the deserted plains — nothing too subtle for the officer. From then on, Smith never missed an opportunity to summon Will to his office for a bit of fun.

And that must have been just what the old paper-pusher was looking for when he'd dispatched a guard to fetch the cowboy, his favourite inmate, if only to put an end to his boredom. There was something about the man's sketches and life that intrigued Smith; he admired his charge, a rare thing for a guard. And so Will was able to enjoy a moment of peace and quiet, have a chat, smoke some good tobacco, and even drink a decent cup of coffee. He could already taste the pleasantly bitter, hot brew on his tongue.

"I ain't got all day, 1778," said Harris, back in the cell.

Will finished buttoning up his pants.

"Ready," he told the guard with a smile.

Harris, a portly guard with a big ring of keys, led Will through a labyrinth of secondary buildings to the administration wing. Will, as he always did, asked after his family. He'd memorized the names of the wives and children of a dozen guards.

"James, I don't want to scare you or nothing, but I think Smith has a real bone to pick with you."

"With me?" he asked, astonished. "I ain't done nothing."

"You tell him that."

Will didn't slow down at all, but was feeling decidedly less upbeat. As he entered, Smith received him with daggers in his eyes, even more squinty than usual. Today he didn't look like a mole so much as a wolverine. Will held himself straight. Smith's office smelled like an old barroom.

"You know these walls don't just have eyes... they got ears too, eh?"

Will didn't flinch.

"Ain't we been good to you? Ain't we given you a lot of leeway, let you do whatever you wanted? There are limits, but we like to give inmates like you a bit of breathing room. We ain't monsters. We understand. We gave you your paper and your pencils. And all we asked in return was that you don't make waves, and keep your doodling to yourself. And now I'm hearing that recently some drawings—and nobody knew whose—have been passed around under the table. Some drawings that ain't exactly *respectable*, if you catch my drift. And the kicker? The drawings are a sensation. They're goin' all through the prison! We've got a whole new market created by the artist's carelessness. I hear they're fetching three or four times the original price now."

Smith butted out his cigar, sending ash flying up from the ashtray.

"What happened yesterday? Well, wouldn't you like to know! Here's what happened. The warden calls me into his office and questions me. He seems to have taken an interest. A *serious* interest."

Will was staring down at his feet.

"Shit, James. You're putting me in some hot water, some real hot water! The warden!"

What handsome shoes, thought Will.

"You want to do time in the hole, is that it? You want us to take away your privileges?"

Will lifted up his head, mouth round as a bowl, eyes like a dead fish.

"Don't give me that look," Smith grumbled. "Take a seat."

Will didn't move.

"Sit down and draw me a woman."

"Uh, sir . . . "

"That's 'Officer' to you."

"Officer."

"I'd advise you to come back another day if you're planning to test my patience, 1778. Do what you're told!"

Will sat down with a shaky hand and did as he was told. Once he'd established the outlines, he ventured to ask whether Officer Smith had any preferences. The officer shot him a look that said, "I'd beat you to a bloody pulp right now, if I didn't check myself."

"Make her nice and curvy. Light haired. And not too much in the way of clothing."

Will James could have made a fortune drawing pin-up girls. He gave them a slightly Western style, to get the blood pumping. Their proportions didn't always satisfy the artist himself, but it was nothing he couldn't improve in time. The pose this one had taken was much more demure than in his drawings for fellow prisoners.

"I ain't got all day."

Smith snatched the drawing out of Will's hands. His eyes stretched wide in appreciation.

"Not bad!"

He whistled.

"You got a dirty mind, James."

"This kind of drawing ain't for me."

"Then maybe you could explain to me why more than half the inmates in this here prison have drawings like it? *Your* drawings?"

"I didn't want to, Officer. It was a matter of survival."

Will adopted the contrite attitude of a man confessing at church.

"What would you have done in my place?" he asked.

"I don't get paid to put myself in your place."

Smith held out a box containing all of a smoker's needs: papers, tobacco, matches.

"Roll yourself a smoke and I'll think on it."

Smith leaned back in his chair. After rolling one, Will struck a match and took a big puff of smoke. It was good tobacco, the kind he hadn't been able to enjoy for months—for a year, in fact, save for the rare occasions when Smith gave him a little to smoke in this office. The taste of tobacco drove home the fact that one year ago he'd been a free man pushing a herd of tired cattle to Oasis on the back of an exhausted horse. A year! It may as well have been a decade. A lifetime. Someone else's life. Will closed his eyes as he inhaled.

"You know," said Smith, "I could help you get some more of this excellent tobacco. Every week."

The tobacco available on the prison's black market was the bottom of the barrel, cheap second- and third-hand leaf that only poor people outside would smoke, when rising prices forced them to.

"Every week a shipment comes in for the guards, so every week I *could* get you some. All you got to do is ask, James. Like I say, we ain't monsters. But you'd have to promise me one little thing. One little thing I'm confident we'll agree on."

Will smelled a rat.

"Anything. Whatever you want."

"Officer."

"Whatever you want, Officer."

"I need you to promise me, James—swear it on the Bible, and I ain't joking—swear to me you'll never give another drawing to an inmate. Not a one! No horses, no women, no nothing."

"Of course. You have my word, Officer."

"From now on, I'll handle all your drawings."

"Excuse me?"

"I said that from now on, the drawings go through me."

Will crossed his arms.

"Deal."

Smith sat up.

"Listen up. There's no 'deal' here. I don't think you've understood a darn thing. Don't go around thinking I led you into this. That the guards and the warden are encouraging you to draw."

"I could just stop," Will said. "We'd never have to breathe another word of it."

The officer gave his prisoner a long, cold stare.

"If I ain't mistaken, you must be selling at least three of your lady drawings a week. At least."

"I suppose so."

"Let's say three to five. From now on you'll hand over, to me, five drawings every week. You understand?"

Will understood all too well.

"Don't give me that long face, Will. You'll see, it ain't gonna hurt you none. Hell, you'll even make a tidy profit! You can't say we aren't generous, can't say we don't recognize your talent. Not good enough? C'mon, I'm listening. Name your price."

Will took his chin between his thumb and index finger and gave it a little stroke. What Smith was proposing was risky; he could very well be setting a trap for him. There was only one way to find out.

"Could I send a letter? To Canada."

Officer Smith, puffing away, leaned further back in his chair. For a moment he seemed to be looking right through Will, as if attempting to fathom a mystery, but he asked no questions. They'd had vague discussions about that French-Canadian trapper who was apparently the reason for Will's unlikely accent.

"Of course. Why not. Must be important. Something to do with all those letters in French that lady visitor handed over to you?"

Smith turned to Harris.

"We still ain't found a translator to read them over?"

The guard shook his head.

"All right. I guess there's nothing untoward about this. Is there, James?"

"Of course not, Officer."

As always, Will said as little as possible. If Smith wanted to learn more, all he had to do was ask. He didn't.

"Great then. You can translate them for me yourself, and we'll never mention it again. Which leaves us one final question."

"Question, Officer?"

"We've got to figure out what to do with you in the

short term. What to do with you right now. When I asked if you wanted to go to the hole, that wasn't rhetorical."

"I don't understand, Officer."

"Don't take it personal. We're gonna turn this prison upside down and track down every last dirty drawing you made. Everyone knows who drew 'em. So we've got to make an example. And the example is you."

"To the hole, Officer?"

"Of course not. But we are going to take away your stuff and keep you in solitary."

"Solitary."

"For ten days. In a little wing of the prison where you'll have a cell entirely to yourself. You won't go out, you won't see anyone. And you'll have all the time you need to draw your naked ladies."

Will couldn't imagine feeling deprived, so long as he had pencils and paper, which was pretty much all he had to his name anyway. His drawing materials, his letters, and a beat-up old copy of *Tom Sawyer*.

Smith ignored Will for a moment and rolled himself another cigarette. His fourth since their little meeting began, Will figured. He usually had a good supply rolled up in advance, but not today. Smith had smoked even more than he usually did. The night before, he'd worked his way through a bottle, not leaving his seat at all but thinking about Will and how to find a solution that would keep Will out of trouble and keep the warden happy. The large desk lighter spat up a flickering little flame. Will watched Smith suck on the tip of his cigarette in a slightly ridiculous manner that distracted him for a moment. How was it possible to smoke in such an unmanly way, with so little class, he wondered.

Smith wiped the smile off the corners of his mouth and blew out a massive puff of smoke, as was his habit.

"There some reason you're still here?"

"You tell me, Officer."

"Scram, then."

Will nodded and stood up.

"Harris, take him to empty his cell, and try to be discreet. For the rest, you have my instructions."

10

To his astonishment, Will was "confined" to the guards' wing. The prisoners who were favoured had individual cells there, so he was already well acquainted with that sandstone-walled section of the prison. For a whole week the cell door stayed closed, and no one in the prison had any idea what had been Will James's fate. For sure, everyone thought he was wasting away in the hole, and no doubt after a severe beating. If the way the prison had been turned upside down in search of dirty drawings was any indication of the severity of Will's punishment, he must not be a pretty sight.

But none of this was true. Will was eating much better, and his new quarters were warmer than the regular cell block, which made it easier to get through the hard desert nights. He was generously supplied with paper and high-quality pencils, and his new cell — you could almost call it *spacious* — was beautifully illuminated. The window was twice as large as the one he'd become accustomed to peering through if he wanted a glimpse of the Sierra Nevada and its changing light. And not only was he allowed to smoke in his cell, but he was actually provided high-quality tobacco — the same he would puff on from time to time in Smith's office, and regular stuff for the guards. He no longer had to rub shoulders with the other inmates or live with the constant fear that he might be the next victim of the prison's sexual predators. At first Will's isolation scarcely bothered him — far from it. If there were a way for him to maintain these conditions until his sentence was up, prison would be child's play. But he knew it was best not to entertain false hopes.

Again and again, Will struggled to find the words to write a letter to his parents, but he never managed to find quite the right words or tone. He was playing a double game: tricking the guards, and also deceiving his family. After several attempts in which he went to great lengths to conceal his situation, Will tossed off a letter in his mother tongue in just a few minutes. In it, he finally told his family the truth. He was far from losing his French, and in fact he never would, even if this was what he wanted others to believe. Unfortunately, the letter struck Will as perfect, and he didn't have the will to alter it. Nor could he know the letter would be burned, along with many of the others he had written in French, during his second trip back to Canada, in the 1920s.

Carson City, Nevada, December 16, 1915

To my dear parents, so faraway yet so near to my
heart;

I am writing you in hard times. I'm ashamed of
myself. The thought of writing you, and telling you
what I need to tell you has been gnawing at me for
months. I won't beat around the bush, so here goes, a
little over a year ago I was arrested for cattle rustling
in Nye County, Nevada. I let myself be led into this
sinful act by a man I wish I'd never met, but I have
only myself to blame. If I had spared a thought for
you at the time I made this foolish choice, I wouldn't
have strayed so far from the path of righteousness.
The prospect of easy cash is sometimes stronger
than the memory of our dear ones, the most honourable people we have known. I'm not going to justify
myself by saying that life out West is hard, since that
would be a lie, until this the West has been nothing
but good to me.

I've been locked up in federal prison in Nevada,
since last May, and soon I will be able to write to
the Parole Board and ask for an early release. Don't
worry about me, and don't take pity on me. Above
all don't be distraught, the idea of how this news will
distress you is worse for me than the time in prison
itself. I beg you, Joséphine and Jean, please don't
worry for me. Auguste, promise me to try to keep
mother and father calm. And if you ever get the crazy
idea of coming to visit me, put it out of your mind,

leave me alone to serve my time and my sentence, and when I'm free I'll come back to Canada, I promise. You can write me at the following address: Will James, N.S.P. Carson City, U.S.A., 89701.

With all my affection and humble respect.

Your son, W. J.

What humiliation! What a wicked son he had turned out to be—and that he should be writing all this so close to the holiday! The letter would likely reach his parents around New Year's and he imagined his mother nervously opening the envelope, and her reaction when she learned how low he'd stooped—so unspeakably low. Yet Will slept peacefully that night.

The guards were ordered not to speak to Will, and not to let him speak to them either. He'd have to wait until the end of his time in "solitary" to put his letter into the mail. When the other inmates left their cells, and just before they were put back in them for the night, they'd bring him something to eat, food they were trading for the pin-up drawings he'd produced between meals. And if he asked for tobacco they would give it to him, no questions asked, and discreetly.

Soon the guards would find Will waiting every morning with his hands on the bars of his cell. As the other inmates' doors were opened one by one, he waited for his own to be unlocked. The prison walls were starting to weigh heavily on him. He needed to be outside, to breathe a little fresh air and get some exercise in the yard, even if the privilege meant further dealings with criminals, dangerous or not. Harris was the guard on duty this morning. Will, not having a mirror, pushed as much of his head through two bars as he was able, and watched out of the corner of his eye to see which prisoners were being led out of their cells, and whether they looked lethargic or alert. Will's cell was at the end of the hallway. Harris looked at the list twice and went to see Will, whom he did not reprimand for smiling.

"Okay, I'd say it's your lucky day, 1778. Time to get out of here and go join the others."

"Well," said Will, "you don't have to tell me that twice."

"Hold on. You do a little drawing last night?"

"Yeah, yeah."

Will handed over a few drawings. One of them, a touch more risqué than his usual fare, showed a buxom woman kneeling, her back slightly arched, her bottom thrust out, her eyes shut in pleasure and her mouth open. The woman's tongue was sticking out a little, making the whole thing just dirty enough. She had slid one hand between her thighs, where it half disappeared in her crotch, as the other one squeezed a breast so plump it defied the laws of gravity—but then again, wasn't that one of the functions of art, to defy laws?

As was his wont, Harris couldn't help stealing a glance at each of the sketches. When his gaze landed on this one, though, he winked and lingered over it. A new smile lifted his lips.

"Oh, naughty boy," said Harris. "I know one person who's going to be very happy."

11

Sitting on his backside, comfortably ensconced in the aromatic hay in the little stable, casting an occasional glance at the horses he was supposed to be tending to, Will was drawing a stampede — the inimitable mad panic of a dispersed herd of mustangs. It was an ambitious picture he'd been working on in his spare time for a few days now. And he had spare time in spades. Will's daily work was to feed the horses, shovel their shit, and muck out the stalls. But he'd found a board to serve as a drawing table, the stables had excellent light — the sunny days were coming back again — and he had a steady supply of paper, crayons, tobacco, and rollies. In essence, at that very moment Will couldn't have asked for anything more. The hours were slipping by quickly, and he was a little surprised when he realized the light was waning and the cold was taking hold of the stable. He got up, stretched his legs, and went to pet the horses a little and take a look out the window: a tall wall of some kind of silica stone, topped off by a watchtower in which he could make out the silhouette of a guard against the setting sun. He could almost have fooled himself into believing the wall was something else—a horizon, a desert plain dotted with scrub brush and Joshua trees.

He was about to go back to the guards' wing when Officer Stone came into the stable.

"Inspection."

Stone was a tall, broad-shouldered man with a brush cut that made his head look square. Though he liked to act tough, he and Will got along and, during the months gone by, he'd bartered tobacco for many a cowboy drawing for his kids. Stone had pulled strings to get his favourite inmate into the prison stables doing chores that had been, until then, the purview of the guards—though, truth be told, they'd had enough of shovelling the shit of the nags they kept around in case of a prison break. The top brass had never wanted these chores to be assigned to an inmate, knowing they consumed very few hours of the day and thus left a prisoner a lot of "free" time. But Stone had found the means to convince them.

Will took Stone's inspection duty seriously, despite the guard's friendly smile. It had been less than a week since Will had been assigned stable duty, and the thought of going back to chopping and stacking wood with the others was altogether depressing. So he was careful to take nothing for granted. Stone and Will went through every stall. They were spot-less—except for one, in which a foal had just finished relieving herself.

"But, boss," Will protested, "there's nothing I can do about that!"

"*Officer.*"

"Of course, of course. There's nothing I can do about that, *Officer.*"

Stone nodded.

"There's just one other thing, 1778."

"Yes?"

"These nags look like they're getting fatter and fatter. Show me how much hay and grain you're giving them."

Will knew he should have been more sparing with the feed. His enthusiasm had gotten the better of his rational mind. Tending to horses in prison, who would have believed it? Will showed Stone what he was feeding the horses and the guard laughed.

"Shit, James. You're giving them at least double their normal ration. Keep it up, and you'll have to start taking them out for exercise soon," he said— with a wink.

"Really?"

"What, you think we'll be able to catch a runaway prisoner riding fat horses? They already ain't exactly ponies. Let me have a word with the higher-ups. I'll tell you what they say. Oh, and now that I think of it, find yourself one of those striped uniforms that prisoners used to wear back when I got my start."

"But, Officer," said Will, "I only have a couple months left here. What'd be the sense in bolting? You can't seriously think I'd pull a fast one, after everything you've done for me."

"Save it, James. And don't go thinking I'm doing you a favour. I'm doing this for myself and the other guards. You think I'm worried about your *well-being*? You're less than nothing, 1778. Just another brainless miscreant who wasn't smart enough to get away with it. No more, no less."

And Stone gave Will a pat on the back that made him blush for a good long while. Will coughed hard.

"Sorry, honey. Did I hurt you?" said Stone, mockingly. "Let's go eat."

Will went back to his cell in the guards' wing and waited for the evening meal to come around — the night-shift guards had dinner beforehand, around five, and an hour or so later a few privileged inmates would get to eat their leftovers. Will decided to keep working on his stampede drawing, now comprising no fewer than fifteen horses running wild. He was completely absorbed by the scene and the light was perfect. Will would have no trouble making himself at home in it.

Before becoming a part of a massive federal prison with multiple wings, this building had been the entire prison. Attached to the sandstone walls were rings and steel chains that were only rarely used now. And in the centre of each cell a large ring was screwed right into the stone floor. Prisoners tripped over them constantly, which occasioned some healthy swearing. The chains were vestiges of another era, and had given Will a number of unsettling dreams. He'd tried his hand at drawing the bandits, outlaws, and bad hombres of that golden age — the Old West of the nineteenth century. A white-bearded guard had even helped out, giving him the names of some of the outlaws who had been locked up between these walls.

"One time," he said, pointing toward the ring in the centre of the cell, "there was one guy, a real wild one, a real monster, almost managed to tear the ring clean out. Wasn't enough to chain him to the wall, we also had to bind his hands and feet. But that was a long time ago, long before you were born. Back in the 1870s."

A lot of men had passed through these cells; a lot of feet had worn the pre-Cambrian sandstone smooth. The same guard talked to him about the station for stagecoaches—a hub on the outskirts of Carson City— that had been attacked countless times, and about the executions they used to perform with guns and not nooses. Bits of flesh that would bake a while before rotting away, sticking to the walls.

"Well," Will ventured, "I sure would have liked to see that for myself. What it was like, back then."

"Don't fool yourself, young man. Things weren't easy back then. Life was hell."

It would have been hard to claim Will was searching for an easy life, in any sense. And the word "hell" had a nice ring to it, he thought, at least when it was quali- fied a little. He wouldn't have let on to anyone—he was far too proud, too *male*—but what he had been going through in prison was not far from his own idea of hell, if an ordinary one. The passive aggression, the constant fear too of your fellow man—not to men- tion the proximity to hundreds of men, which was hellish for someone who had always lived all alone in wide-open spaces or in cahoots with a few hand-picked partners. Given the choice, he'd have taken the hell of the old range wars and the conquest of the West every time—an era at once so close and distant, now past but living on in the memory of the ageing folks who'd been through it. An era marked by anarchy and violence, though also autonomy; a world in which fortunes were still to be made. Nowadays, everything was moving too fast. Money had won the day.

The bell rang, signalling mealtime. The inmates were obliged to serve the officers' meal, then clear the table, wash the dishes, and clean the wing. Only then were they allowed to sit down and eat. Most chose to take their meals in their cells, though some used a small common room. On his way to the mess, Will asked a veteran prisoner if he knew what they'd be eating. "Stew, dammit," he said. "What do you think? It's stew, like every other goddamn night." The bitter old man serving a life sentence, and for whom the mere thought of another helping of stew provoked the urge to kill again, frowned, and then hawked a massive loogie just a few feet from Will's boots.

12

A few months earlier, Will had learned he was eli-
gible for parole, and needed to write a convincing
letter to the parole board. All inmates in American
prisons serving sentences of less than three years and
demonstrating good behaviour had the right to have
their cases reviewed. If their application was turned
down, they could reapply after six months. Will wasted
no time in putting together what he believed to be
a sound application. Smith even agreed to help by
looking over his letter, the centrepiece of the request.

Nevada State Prison, Dec 15th, 1915
Parole and Release Board, Carson City, Nev.

Dear Sirs,

I am writing today to submit for your perusal my
request for parole. I was accused and pleaded guilty
of Grand Larceny on April 27, 1915, in Ely County
Courthouse, and then sentenced to serve twelve to

fifteen months in federal prison. I've been at N.S.P. for seven months now, not counting the five months spent awaiting trial. I'm a young man, twenty-three years old, and have never had dealings with the justice system until this.

I have a natural talent for drawing, and during my detention I had ample opportunity to practise and improve my skills. My aim, once released, is to develop as an artist through study on the East Coast or in California, and I feel that by seizing this opportunity to cultivate my talent I can make a promising future for myself. As a sample of what I am capable of, I have included a few drawings for your inspection.

My long months of detention have given me a great deal of time to think, and while this experience has been an unfortunate one, and I deeply regret the acts I committed that led me here, my fervent wish to become an artist has not flagged, nor have I lost faith in the goodness of life, or of men. If given the opportunity, I am certain that once free I will be able to live an honourable life, and make a positive contribution to society.

Rest assured, gentlemen, that if I am granted parole I will do everything in my power to be a productive member of society.

With my sincere regards,

Will R. James
Nevada State Prison

The rejection of his application was like a kick to the shins—he wasn't even granted a hearing, his defeat all the more devastating because he had been so pleased with his letter. Will had failed to perceive the hint of smugness he'd allowed to creep into his tone, or the unwarranted confidence that had undermined his letter's purpose. As well as his own, he'd gathered letters of commendation from Sheriff Crain, Justice Edwards, and the state prosecutor, Anthony Jurich. Crain had sung Will's praises, and all his referees had stressed how important it was that Will become an artist (a subtle way of saying that he should give up cowpunching), but the judge's letter, which could have carried a lot of weight, failed to state clearly that he was in favour of Will's conditional release. Jurich, the county lawyer who had prosecuted William Roderick James on behalf of the State of Nevada, noted that this Hackberry, still on the loose, was mostly to blame for the crime, and so it followed that Will James— especially in light of his good behaviour—had paid his debt to society, though his recommendation was tempered by his admitting it was not possible to be certain beyond a reasonable doubt that the inmate fully understood the seriousness of what he had done.

When the package came back, Will took another look at his drawings. He now saw them from a new and less forgiving, outsider's perspective. The proportions were not always right. Will often messed up his characters' arms or legs. The whole was not quite realistic, and lacking in depth. Will had made progress during his incarceration and, confined to the stables with the horses, would likely improve in the remaining months of his term. But his drawings were the work of an amateur—an above-average amateur, but an amateur nevertheless. The art schools he was keen to attend might not be impressed by his application. Maybe, he worried, he'd never get better; maybe he'd already pushed his talent as far as it would take him. Often, he was haunted by the drunken words of an eccentric and forlorn illustrator from Philadelphia he'd met in a honky-tonk one night.

"Any way you slice it, if you want to get good at something, be a real pro, you gotta put in the time. There's just no way around it. Do nothing but, for five years—and I'm talking full, tightly packed days. Not the short, lazy days of a dilettante. Six hours—six *consecutive* hours. Yeah, six, eight, ten hours at a time is best.

"And if I reckon the numbers—*hic!*—I mean if I start counting from my young days, then by now I've put in my time. Double my time! To be a bona fide professional—*hic!* Drinker, that is."

The illustrator, something of a dandy, knocked back a final drink and then curled up under the bar.

What with Will having had so much time to draw women in prison, he'd decided to submit one of his sketches to a Western romance magazine. Beneath it, Will had written the caption, "The only two people in the world," and the year he'd drawn it, 1915. He'd drawn two horses, a chestnut and a bay. A lady had dismounted from her horse to join her companion on his. She was nestled against his shoulder, and they

were getting ready to kiss. But he could see the problem: the woman was much too short. Her upper body
was perhaps three times shorter than that of Will's
square-jawed alter ego.

Two of the three parole judges had liked one of the
others, entitled "Turning Point." In three panels—
two up, one down—Will had depicted three pivotal
moments of his life: past (top right), present (the row
below), and future (top left). Everything is clearly
labelled, as if for an audience of children, and the three
panels are connected with a curved arrow pointing
from the past through the present to the future. In
the frame of "The Past," Will is shown from behind,
sitting on a bucking bronc and lassoing a steer. In
"The Present," he is depicted in prison, with a sombre
expression and drawn features. In "The Future," the
cowboy is in profile. He's wearing a dress shirt, hat,
and city shoes, and is no longer lost in thought but
absorbed by the easel in front of him. It is easy to
imagine the artist in a light-filled studio in New York
City or San Francisco. Beneath the drawing's title was
a summary of the letter he'd written, to make sure
the judges would get the point: "I've had all my time
to think," Will had written, "and now aim to move
forward in my art."

Pathetic, thought Will, with a lump in his throat.
How useless, how *pathetic*—when would it stop? He
realized that at this point in his life, another decisive
juncture, he had but one desire: not to become a professional artist, but to get back to cowpunching the
first chance he got. Everything in his attitude brimmed

with a contempt for people and the situation he was in: he was useless, he was a screw-up, he told himself, and all that he'd done until now was a lie. Not everyone could be won over with a few childish drawings. Apparently, the judges had believed Will James could benefit from a little more time in the shadows and some time to do a little more thinking. Since he was already on his knees, he got down and prayed to the Catholic God of his childhood. He addressed little Jesus in French—Jesus who had also known the aridity of abandonment.

Thousands of miles north, his mother was also on her knees, agitatedly gripping her rosary with a feverish hand.

13

That March of 1916, after he'd been working in the prison stables for another couple of months, Will was again allowed to try his luck with the parole board. He drafted a new and much shorter letter, and typed it this time. If his request was granted, he'd be spared a mere month of his sentence, but Will saw no reason not to give it a try, rather than languishing another month in prison. A month less was—well, a month less.

Nevada State Prison, March 15, 1916
Honourable Parole Board Carson City, Nevada

Dear Sirs,

I am writing respectfully to request that you grant me parole at the next meeting of your Honourable Parole Board in April.

On April 27, 1915, I was sentenced to twelve to fifteen months in prison by the White Pine County

Court, after pleading guilty to a charge of Grand Larceny, and when you meet on April 10, I will have already served a full year in Nevada federal prison.

I am asking that you show me clemency because I have worked to the best of my ability, and always been on the best behaviour in prison, and in any case am due to be released on May 19.

There is a job waiting for me in California, and I intend to pursue it immediately upon release, and to strive to live as an honest, respectful, law-abiding man.

I have enclosed a letter from William S. Hart, who has offered me work, and has assured me that this offer will still stand after your decision in April.

Respectfully,

Will R. James

The last two weeks of March felt like months—and those in the know say a month in prison is equivalent to at least three outside. The intense estrangement that came from being locked up took its toll, and more so than Will let on. It was the waiting, the subsisting in an infantilized state and being deprived of wondrous and essential things. In prison, Will was subject to forces beyond his control; he was at the mercy of time, and could do nothing but wait for it to do its work and heal all wounds. The few minutes of idly waiting for the lights to go out at nine always managed to drive Will slightly and perhaps irremediably insane. The path he was travelling grew clearer—it was easier and easier for him to envision and follow. Depression would mar the last decades of the life of Will James, of Ernest Dufault, and his affliction would always be tinged with what Will was feeling that night in his cell—a miserable, terrifying claustrophobia, a stifling sense of panic that clenched his lungs and paralyzed his brain, a total loss of self-esteem that was accompanied by an insurmountable insomnia.

The next day he was back in the stables and drawing the horses, but his heart wasn't in it. What was the use? He'd never be an artist. He could see that now. But then, of course, he'd never set out to be one. Drawing was second nature to Will, something innate, like a birthmark following him from Eastern Canada to the American Southwest that could not be expunged. And yet at no point had Will's love of art instilled in him the hope of one day earning a living from it. He might have dreamed on occasion of living the life of a rich and famous artist in San Francisco or New York City, surrounded by an adoring cortège of beautiful women, but that wasn't Will's style. Might as well laugh about it, he figured.

And yet, on other days, Will had to admit that being locked up for a year and a half had, if nothing else, given him the opportunity to draw more than ever before. And he might have drawn more, so much more, if only he'd had even more supplies; if only there had been light during those long and sleepless nights. He'd never be an artist invited to the Academy—but who wanted that? And he'd probably never be a professional artist, but he knew he could draw. No parole judge or art professor could ever take away that talent.

Right up until the end of his sentence, Smith continued to pressure Will into producing a weekly quota of titillating drawings. And Will almost wrecked everything when he lost his temper with an officer just a few days ahead of his release date. He made himself vulnerable to shakedowns, and was given a few warnings that were not far from threats. Will came around, lost interest in playing the game, started making more and more of a mess of his work, spending less and less time on his drawings and not bothering with details like fleshing out the shadows that defined the women's silhouettes. Were it not for Jennie's face making its way into half of them, the last sketches Will did in prison would scarcely be recognizable as the work of the same artist. Unsigned and undated, never to be seen or heard of again, these desultory drawings held no inkling of the life of Will James; their fate was to languor away in private collections and attics, if they hadn't been thrown in the garbage by jilted wives and sweethearts.

A few days before the parole board was scheduled to consider his second parole application, Will was given permission to write another letter to his parents — or rather, to a couple of his French-Canadian "close acquaintances." In English this time, Will wrote that he'd be out on parole by the month of May, and that, after taking a little time to get back on his feet, he'd head for San Francisco to study oil painting for a few months. He wasn't sure why he persisted with this lie from the letter to the parole board he'd written four months before. Maybe because it was easier this way, less awkward to have to pretend he had something waiting for him and somewhere to go. Certainly it was easier than admitting that the life of the cowboy, the very life that had landed Will in prison, was again calling his name. Deep down, nothing in him had changed. He'd go home with his head down. His family had pretty well believed him when, in his first letter, the prodigal son announced he would soon be home, but they'd not seen him for around five years. You can imagine his parents' confusion after reading the second letter. The Lord moved in mysterious ways.

14

Will knew the parole board was meeting in early April. And he'd been told they'd inform him of their decision quickly, a few days after the hearing—if a hearing there was—and that, if he was set free, his release would be immediate and unconditional. No longer could he contain his excitement. It was unbearable. Will spent hours on end in the stables, petting the horses and forcing himself to think about anything but his release. He knew by heart the name of every horse. They were all bays, with their distinctive black points, but some were lighter and others a mahogany brown.

These horses weren't like others Will had known. They were docile and friendly from the very first approach. They were never skittish or ornery, rebellious or just plain mean, like the wild broncs most cowboys ended up having to ride. Born in the stable to mothers who'd known nothing but the stall, these prison ponies had no notion of freedom. Under the circumstances, Will reflected, there was something moving about their condition. He imagined letting them trot right out the front door, how they'd be scared at first and then work up to a canter and then a gallop, discover a little more confidence before something in them burst like a dyke and they realized they were finally returning to their true nature.

They came to the stables to fetch Will in the afternoon. Smith had left his office to be there in person, an ominous sign. But no. The next day, Will was summoned to appear before the board of judges. He almost fainted. He hadn't slept at all the night before, though at least the insomnia had helped him to prepare for the interview as thoroughly as possible. He tried to predict the judges' questions, to imagine his answers.

The next morning, Will had a quick breakfast at the same time as the guards (special permission, exceptional circumstances), got dressed, and carefully combed his hair. He'd polished his shoes the night before, as best he could under the circumstances. He even went so far as to look at himself in the mirror of the shared bathroom. The face staring back at Will had changed. He had hollowed-out cheeks, black circles under his eyes, haggard features, and an empty gaze.

Just before nine, they asked Will to take a seat and wait in the hallway. He used the time to try to control his breathing, inhaling deeply and then exhaling until every bit of air was expelled from his lungs. His hands were sweaty and his legs were weak.

"*Crisse*," Will said to himself, "*ressaisis-toi*!" Get a hold of yourself!

"What?" asked the guard who was waiting with him.

"Nothing," he answered in English.

The door opened and his name was called. His legs fused and, curiously, this helped his resolve as he walked in to meet his fate. The room was much as he had imagined it: smallish, with a chair in the middle as well as a long table, behind which a line of judges sat ready to hear Will's case. He felt safe. The atmosphere seemed positive.

He was asked for the thousandth time to give his version of the crime. Who was he? How had he been drawn into this? It all seemed so distant to him now. The story had long ago imprinted itself on Will's memory, conveniently adjusted to the needs of the legend of Will James. This wasn't the first time he had told the story, nor would it be the last.

Will answered the judges in a clear voice, trying to smile at all the right times and stay humble. The judges also asked about the artistic ambitions Will appeared to have abandoned.

"In your first application, you claimed you wanted to study art," said one. "Now you say you have a job in Hollywood. Have you given up?"

"No, I'm not giving up, but a man has to live," said Will. "And I can make an honest living working in the movies. I'll get an apartment. I'm ready to start a new life. Find a woman if it's God's will—though it's not really up to me. Anyway, after all that—in a few months, maybe a year—we'll see what happens."

When the end of the hearing was announced, Will didn't know what to think. False hope could kill a man. And if even one of the judges was able to see that the letter of recommendation from William S. Hart was forged, then Will was done for. Not only would there be no clemency, but he would likely see his sentence extended by a few months and end up with an even more serious criminal record.

For the next five days, Will would go over every moment of the hearing. He revisited every word, dwelled on the judges' tone and intonation, relived every mistake he thought he had made. He asked permission to give up stable duty and stay in his cell as he waited for the board's decision. A little caustically, the guards told him not to push his luck or forget his station.

The morning post came in around eight, at the same time Will's work day in the stables began. Will dragged his feet, made himself late, and hid from the guards, doing his utmost to put off the moment of leaving the wing.

"James? You ain't about to pull the same move as those other days, are you?" said Harris. "Get over here!"

Still, every morning till the eleventh of April, Will got the better of Harris. He'd lost all interest in the horses in the stable and, having set his sights on riding another kind of horse, stopped taking them out for anything more than to stretch his legs. He'd still feed them and muck out the stalls every morning, but immediately after that he'd lie back down in the hay and not move for hours. Come the late afternoon, he'd stroke the horses and toss a few affectionate insults their way before he was called to supper. Every bite was an effort. He'd lost his appetite and his stomach was in a permanent knot, as if his insides were squeezed in a vice. After dinner, he'd go back to his cell, stretch out on his back, very straight, and lie without stirring until the next morning.

On the night of April 10, Will managed a few consecutive hours of sleep, which did him good. On the morning of the 11th, he had a premonition the moment he opened his eyes. There was something in the air, in the light. It was a beautiful morning, one of the year's first true spring days, and everything was suddenly moving fast. He was on his way to the stables, hands in his pockets, when someone yelled at him to turn around. Will rushed over to the guard who'd called him.

"Smith's office. Now."

When he arrived at the office, Smith was all smiles.

"No need to sit."

The cowboy's heart was beating hard. Smith got up, turned a sheet of paper that was lying on the desk 180 degrees, and slid it over to Will, holding out a pen.

"William Roderick James, sign here."

He could read the bold capital letters: PAROLE GRANTED. He signed with such vigour that the pen's tip almost tore through the paper. It was something to see: Will could barely contain the surge of emotion. He needed to live the moment like a man. Especially in front of Smith. And Smith understood. For even he was a little teary-eyed. The officer extended a hand toward the former prisoner and Will took it in his own and gave it a shake. The two men were now equals.

"I got you covered, James. Believe me."

"Excuse me?"

"If you ever really want to become an artist, don't worry about the drawings you did here coming back to haunt you. No one will ever know. You have my word."

"We can always hope."

"All you gotta do is never draw another woman as long as you live. That way no one will ever put two and two together."

The two men had a good laugh. Yet these were prescient words; Will would rarely draw women. Even his own splendid wife, Alice—a beauty queen— would barely make it into his work, save a few sketches from the early days of their relationship.

Smith pulled a folded piece of paper from his pocket.

Will could make out the words "Carol" and "Tarantula."

"Think of it as payment of sorts. Go find her. The first night's on me."

"Thanks."

"I also threw a little tobacco in with your personal effects. And a pad of paper and some pencils. Now go on and don't let me see you back here again. Get out of here, princess!"

They were going to miss Will. He'd trusted the guards and shown his vulnerability. He'd even made them laugh. And he'd always been ready to give them his drawings. They'd felt his generosity, knew it to be intact and precious, something the prison staff had lost years ago. Will James was one of a kind.

"All right, we'll escort you out of here," said Smith. "Harris!"

For the first time in months, Will passed through the main wing of the prison, where the murmur of voices had made such an impression on the day he'd arrived. Harris seemed even more emotional than his superior had been a few minutes earlier. The sight of the two high, barred doors through which Ernest Dufault had walked in as Will James a year before, entering the antechamber of his detention, this point of no return, struck him as an illumination, an epiphany.

He made his way along another sequence of hallways. Finally, they stopped in front of what looked like a warehouse. A tall man with a large flattened nose grunted as he slid a crumpled brown bag under the grille, along with a form to sign. Will was expecting to feel the weight of his rowel spurs when he took the bag, which would have made him the happiest of men, but no such luck. They'd been confiscated along with his two revolvers, back in Oasis. Next, they took him to the cloakroom, where a gaunt lieutenant with silver braid on his uniform stood waiting. Will hadn't seen him since he'd arrived, and as had been the case then, the man still didn't seem to have a moment to waste. The trick was to take the high road, be bigger than the surly brutes, if you were going to come out on top.

Will opened the bag and found his old satchel. In it were the pad of writing paper and two pencils as well as his squashed old hat, frayed jeans, dusty chaps, and well-worn cowboy boots that had lain dormant in a sooty pile for the better part of a year.

Even if he was allowed to shake the dirt off his clothes before dressing, there was no guarantee he'd be welcome anywhere. He looked like a hapless drifter—a beggar, even. An idle young man fallen on hard times. He'd wash his rags in a hotel come evening, he figured, so they could dry overnight. Will was then given ten dollars' spending money. God knows how far ten dollars would take him, he thought. Then he had to sign another form.

There was no one waiting for Will outside the prison walls. But he was greeted by the cool morning air and the sun breaking over the enormous, brown, sparsely treed mountains of the Carson Range to the east. Behind them lay the blue snow-capped peaks of the Sierra Nevada. Will squinted, and grinned like an idiot. Sixteen months had gone by between being caught a few miles out of Oasis and set free on that April morning in Carson City. Sixteen months for stealing thirty measly head of cattle.

"I've been ordered to put you in a car and take you to the station," said Harris.

"No need, I'll walk!"

"You got two choices. I can take you to town, or I can arrest you and send you back to jail. What'll it be?"

At least there was a choice there. The newly free man capitulated.

In the car, if Will had followed his instincts, he'd have let himself go and imitated the calls of dogs and put his head out the window. Driving through the desert of brush and tall grasses—sage and wild barley, speargrass and needle-and-thread grass—brought

Will back to himself. He could feel his rebirth in his back, as if he had great currents of fresh air instead of shoulders. When he compared this moment to another morning, nine years earlier, back in June 1907, when he'd left his motherland and his mother with ten dollars in his pocket, he could see that he was back at square one. He laughed to himself as he ran his fingers over the ten-dollar bill with Andrew Jackson's face on it, thinking how unlikely his story was — so much so that he could never tell it to anyone either. A decade of exile and living in English had moulded him into the man he was. The hard labour, the hazing of fellow cowboys, the toughness of the land, and the precariousness of life in the West had put him through an exemplary school of hard knocks. In truth, the years had added up to more than just a return to square one: the precocious young man who'd arrived at Viger station in Montreal one fine morning with only hope and harebrained schemes for baggage . . . that young man was no more.

PART THREE

Songs of the Sage

1

Will spent a wild night in a dingy room at the Tarantula, beside and on top of a small curly-haired and brown-skinned woman named Carol whose large store of natural charms included voluptuous curves and full, swollen breasts. Will was a step up from her regular clientele of idle, dirty old men unable to tolerate their wives another second, come to find a moment's forgetting between her legs. She whispered sweet nothings to her young client with shining, pale eyes, and bit his fleshy lips and earlobes, told him he was handsome, smothered him with audacious kisses and a thousand little attentions. Maybe her performance was not altogether genuine, but Will didn't mind. He liked the game. The two turtledoves talked into the wee hours, lying in the gleam of the gas lamp, with Carol's head resting on Will's chest. As soon as he recovered a bit of strength they'd go for another round. Drink followed fast upon drink, and before they knew it they had worked their way through nearly two bottles. Will was ecstatic, his thirst bottomless;

already, before he'd made his way to the back room with his lady, he'd bought a few rounds and downed jugs of beer. All night, and even in the midst of their lovemaking, visions would come to him of fried potatoes and bacon and slices of fluffy white bread piled high to the ceiling. He ordered steak, then chicken, and then spare ribs, the combination eventually chasing away the memory of the horrid prison food.

Will woke at around ten in the morning with a monumental hangover and half his savings gone. Carol made coffee in the hotel kitchen, brought it up to the room and slipped back under the covers, and then tried her best to help Will forget the vapours of his leaden fatigue with a few expert flicks of her wrist. Will was nauseous, and disinclined. It was no time for cuddling. If the last night had been about pricking his abscess, today would be spent staunching the bleeding. That, at any rate, was what he was thinking as he sipped his coffee in bed and started on the bottle again.

The clothes he had washed the night before with a little soap and then stretched out on the chair were more or less dry. The jeans and jacket were still a little damp, but a few minutes of walking under the implacable sun already high in the sky would be enough to make them perfectly comfortable.

Carol, barely covered, kneeled down on the bed and knotted Will's black bandana. He didn't object.

"I live down that way, with my sister and her husband. You could come by for a visit tonight, if you like. They're very open-minded," she said with a wink.

"But right now I can't really afford—"

"Don't worry about money. Dick gave me enough to cover two nights."

"Dick?"

"Mr. Smith?"

"Oh. I got you."

She adjusted the address on the sheet the old paper-pusher had given Will yesterday.

Carol, ~~*Tarantula*~~ *315 E. Proctor.*

"You can't miss it. We're right behind Chinatown."

"Chinatown?"

"There's a laundry and a Chinese restaurant on Carson, corner of Proctor. Folks call it Chinatown."

"Chinese restaurant, huh?"

Will never missed a chance to fill up on fried rice whenever he passed through a town with a Chinese greasy spoon. They'd cook a meal up in three minutes and he'd wolf it down in less time than that. Those coolies sure had the secret of cooking up something wild, all sweet and sour and salty at once. Nothing like anything he'd eaten before, often with more than one meat mixed in. Sometimes even meat and fish in the same dish. Had to be done!

"We could have dinner there, and then a drink at your house," said Will.

"You're the boss, good lookin'."

She flashed him a toothy smile.

"If I don't find work today, I'll be in front of the restaurant at five," said Will.

They kissed a last time, and Will tipped his hat and left the room. The hotel bar was dark. Three old stalwarts, each of them at a separate table, were nursing pints; a bit of the hair of the dog as they worked up a second wind. The barkeep, a large bald man with a scowling demeanour, was slumped in a chair and snoring, only his head visible, lying on the counter with a Jack London book for a pillow. The author's name rang a bell. Will hadn't read much; in truth, he'd never been much of a reader. He preferred talking to the written word, and the author he would one day become was still dormant inside of him.

The barman sat up when Will came over, but didn't bother standing. Will took a seat at the counter and ordered a cold beer and a coffee, then had the breakfast he'd envisioned: eggs, fried potatoes, and ham, with a half loaf of bread, each slice spread thick with the rich butter he savoured. Once he was done, brimming over with hope and enthusiasm, he made the rounds of the tables and asked each of the men if they'd heard tell of anyone hiring cowhands. In typical drunkard fashion, the men looked at him disdainfully and answered with grunts, grumbles, or monosyllables. But the innkeeper had a lead.

"You just missed him. A customer. Last night. He was here for the lady," he said, giving Will a knowing look. "But since she was otherwise occupied, he didn't stick around. Anyway, he mentioned that he was looking for a couple guys to work with him. Name of Bill Dressler, if memory serves."

"You know where he went?"

"Check the hotels, you'll find him soon enough. If I were you I'd start at the Bank Saloon. Fifth and Carson. He's been known to spend a few hours there."

"Really? You'd send your customers to the competition?"

The innkeeper didn't take the bait. He wasn't about to come up with a witticism for every customer who tried to be clever. Will paid his bill and found himself outside on Roop Street (and poor). He squinted at the sun. As he walked away from the hotel, he turned back to catch a glimpse of the facade. It was a squat one-storey building covered in clapboard that had turned grey with time. The curtains let almost no light in through the two front windows. A coloured sign advertised the "Only Cold Beer in Carson City."

"As if!" laughed Will.

A broad plank had been nailed over the door, on which foot-high block letters had been painted: TARAN-TULA. Will brought two fingers to his nose. He liked the smell, and would take a little bit of Carol with him as he set off in search of the Bank Saloon.

2

Roop Street marked the end of the eastern part of town. The sidewalk had only recently been constructed, along with the few wooden shacks facing the desert at the limits of the neighbourhood. Will walked south, skirting town rather than making any forays inside of it. He felt as if his legs were on springs, his every step a jump into weightlessness. He eyed the boundless brush-filled prairie warily, but before long just had to get out into it. He couldn't help himself. He raised his arms, breathed more deeply, closed his eyes as he made his way forward between the tufts of grass. Was there anything that urgently needed to be done? To live, maybe? Bill Dressler could wait.

The larks chirped their springtime melodies, lifting out of the tall grasses with a beating of wings and then falling right back down to the ground.

"*Turlututu!*" whistled Will, spurring them on.

A snake slithered into its hiding spot, leaving a long, zigzagging trail in the sand behind it. The rodents seemed less fierce around here. They'd stop moving a while, stand and take a closer look at the walker, their eyes like dark marbles, before scampering back into their burrows and nestling with their stomachs flat to the ground.

Will took a good mouthful of the fresh April air that smelled of sagebrush, and felt the kiss of the sun on his white skin, and the absence of bars, walls, watchful looks, and the number on his jacket. He was alone in the world. He stood astride a couple of slumps of foxtail barley and took a moment to clear his mind. It had been a year and a half since he'd been able to experience the world like this. His relaxation was total. He started walking again, and came back the same way an hour later.

In town, dazzled by the blazing sun, Will offered up full, enthusiastic, and toothy smiles through his tears at the few passersby he encountered. The scene was almost overwhelming: people who'd never once stolen, raped, or killed. Ordinary people! On Carson Road, residential houses and businesses stood side by side. Most were a single storey. It was the only street in the city where the buildings shared a common wall, as if the tenants were afraid of not using up all possible lot space. In the rest of the town, each building sat on its own lot. They grew larger and greener as Will headed west, and he understood that he had inadvertently stumbled into the wealthy part of the state capital. Everything was so new: the stone facades, imported shrubbery, even the odd automobile, not to mention the wooden sidewalks. It all seemed fake to Will, like so many dollhouses brought together to form a massive model. All he'd need to do was walk right into the first house he came upon and the whole charade would be exposed. It was as if no one lived there. It was all one big stage set. Will shuddered, turned around and headed east, and then, once he was back on the main street, south.

He tried every bar he passed (there weren't many), to ask if any person — there weren't many of those either — knew of a rancher looking for cowhands. But the cowboys had all left town for the surrounding valleys, fighting at that very moment a merciless cattle war.

Up on Robinson Street an outfitter selling clothes and horse gear captured Will's attention. He had noticed the shop the day before, and had wanted to visit before leaving town. The bell announced Will's presence, but he didn't see anyone behind the register. He strolled the aisles, salivating at the glut of gear that was enthralling for a horse lover like himself. There were bridles, nosebags, pelham bits, and hackamores — a rope bridle without a bit designed more for breaking horses than for riding — and all manner of spurs. There were straight spurs and swan neck spurs and ball spurs, and rowel spurs of every description — rounded and cloverleaf, with five, ten, or fifteen teeth — everything a man could ever ask for. And there were chaps: chinos, batwings, and the woolies Will would so often draw, with their visible lambskin lining, and felt hats of all styles: the Gus, the Cattleman, the Telescope, the Cutter — and, Will's favourite, the Boss of the Plains.

The boot section had Will in raptures. The tall cowboy boots were arranged by size and he picked up each one to hold it in his hand, then studied it more closely and breathed in the smell, examining the quality of the leather and stitching and durability of the heel. The most popular models had toes tapered to a blunted tip. There was even a new trend toward a more rounded tip. But even if the points of a new pair of boots started out sharp as needles, they'd round out once they were broken in. Will looked disgustedly at the boots on his feet. They were beaten and worn.

An entire wall was covered in whips and *latigos* (also known as lassos), and *reatas*—a Mexican lasso sometimes simply called a rawhide, even when they were made of hemp or agave. A lot of lassos were made of cotton as well, and leather ones were growing in popularity, even if the material wasn't as durable. (What leather lacked in toughness it made up for in its elegance.) The lassos measured between thirty and seventy-five feet, their length depending on who would be using them and what they'd be roping. The one Will was weighing in his hand was a magnificent sixty-foot specimen—and, going for thirty dollars, at the dearer end of the line. The fancy *latigo* would likely end up in the hands of a boss who didn't really know what he was doing, and wouldn't see much practical use.

Saddles were on show at the front of the store, in an area a little like a chapel. They were beautiful handmade objects, the work of master craftsmen. So-called Sunday saddles that—encrusted with conchas, silver shells that the rider would have to take care not to scratch, would also see little use — cost as much as three hundred dollars. One day, maybe, Will would find himself a piece of land, a few acres in Montana where life was still affordable, and build his own little ranch with everything a man needed in order to provide for himself. Maybe even find a wife too — why not? A man could dream. And when that day came, he'd purchase the most beautiful saddle three hundred dollars could buy. And on that day, a voice inside him whispered, Will James would no longer be an impostor. He was already there, said another voice, more grumpy than mendacious. Yes, he was already there.

A shadow approached.

"I sold one of them just last week," said the jowly proprietor with a laugh. "Local big shot. Can barely mount a horse. You know what they say: big saddle..."

His words weren't enough to pull Will from his reverie. The young man's eyes had grown big as saucers as he ran his hands over the fabric of a Native American saddle blanket with colourful patterns.

"What can I do for you?" the man asked.

"You're right," said Will.

"Beg your pardon?"

"Who'd really want a saddle like this?"

"On the other hand," said the salesman with a laugh, "my store would have been shuttered long ago if it weren't for the occasional rich prick come through to—"

Will cut him off. He wasn't here to lend the lonely man an ear.

"I need spurs. Something not too expensive, if you've got it."

"Come with me."

The man showed him the shop's collection of spurs, in a lovely mahogany display case.

"Cheapest we got are a dollar. Straight shaft, ball end."

"I'm looking for swan neck spurs."

"Well now, friend, you won't find a pair of those under three bucks. Try all over town if you want, you won't find a better deal than right here."

"Is that a money-back guarantee?"

"Excuse me?"

"Never mind. Anything used?"

"Nope, we just sell new here."

At that the man started laughing again. Each word emerging from Will's mouth seemed to engender more of the same. The man laughed before Will spoke, and again after. A real Buddha from Nevada, hawking a massive "clam" into the spittoon. Will bought a pair of white cotton underpants, as his own were full of holes and made him stink like a caveman even after being washed, and some good wool socks.

"Say, you didn't happen to hear of anyone looking for cowhands?" Will asked.

The salesman ran his finger along his lips, looked upward pensively.

"Not lately, no. There ain't many riders in town these days. It's been a good spring. Everyone went out to work three weeks ago."

"That's what I figgered. Thanks anyway."

The bell over the door rang again as he left, and Will found himself under the awning and feeling low. A woman sitting alone at the reins of her carriage passed by. Will doffed his hat with an impish smile and the woman wondered who this handsome stranger was, with his hair grown out all around his head and his sagging hat. Will watched her slip away into the distance for as long as he could. At the other end of the walkway an old man in a rocking chair shot Will a smile. Will smiled back at him with an expression of respect that was even more disingenuous than his smile at the woman had been, and noted that his easy charm was every bit as effective as before prison. Who could say, maybe he'd even upped his game. So many guards, and they'd all needed to be won over. Work like that kept a man's mind sharp.

3

A massive cauliflower cloud plunged the streets of Carson City into darkness during its passage through the sky above. Will spent a long time watching it, trying to understand its mysterious form and extract from it a shape that his hand might reproduce on command. The shading and chiaroscuro were problematic. Rays of sun soon pierced its tail end, illuminating the world below. It was as if every atom of the buildings, the sidewalks, the land and road were a part of an incandescent light bulb.

Will continued his walk south with no idea of where he was going. He squinted into the sun with his hat pulled down beneath his brow. On the corner of Proctor he found the laundry with its sign in Chinese characters, and the renowned restaurant, the House of Wei. His hunger was stirred and he started to salivate—but decided, not without disappointment, to wait until evening to eat. A hastily rolled cigarette cut his appetite.

Soon, the Capitol appeared. It had been built some fifty years before on what had previously functioned as the town square, a massive and unfenced empty lot easily located by the liberty pole at its centre, where auctions, public meetings, and other gatherings used to take place. Will was moved by the contrast of the Capitol's neoclassical grandeur and the whitewashed facades of the wooden buildings in the rest of the town. The trees were still young, their foliage sparse. Will wandered the square like a tourist, carefully scrutinizing its details. On the other side of the street he noticed a two-storey house with a sign; O'Flannigan's Ranch was a high-class inn that had been constructed long before the Capitol. He walked in and asked whether a rancher named Bill Dressler was a guest. The innkeeper stifled a laugh and pretended to check her ledger.

"I'm afraid not, sir!"

"No problem. Thanks anyway. And have yourself a great day."

The woman looked Will up and down as he walked out the door. He stopped in at two nearby hotels, still with no luck, before he saw "Bank Saloon" painted on the front of a stone building on 5th Avenue whose corner entrance vaguely reminded him of something. He realized soon enough what it was. The light yellow sandstone came from the prison quarry, as did the stone that had built the walls of the Capitol and the prison itself—both the new sections and the original outpost where Will had served the final months of his sentence. The thought sent another shudder through his body. He was tempted to keep on walking and not stop, but that didn't feel sensible.

A few men dressed for town were drinking at the tables. Another less smartly dressed character was slumped over the bar, his head nodding and a half-empty bottle in front of him. The room stank of beer, but the finely carved woodwork and selection of unfamiliar liquors suggested a degree of class. Will wondered what kind of drinker would frequent this saloon so close to the Capitol. He ordered a pint, then asked the barkeep if he had a customer answering to the name of Bill Dressler. The drinker at the counter also seemed interested.

"Why do you want to know?" he asked.

"Mr. Dressler?"

"Dependsh . . . whosh ashking. *Hic!* Whash your business?"

Will explained why he'd come to the Bank Saloon and declared that he was interested in working for Dressler.

"It's a sad story," Will added, "but I lost my spurs. I'd have to borrow a pair. Or rent them, until my first pay."

"Where we're going, you won't . . . need no . . . spursh."

"Come again?"

"Know how to milk a cow, shon?"

Will didn't blink. "Of course!"

"How many? Can—*hic!*—can you milk a day?"

"As many as you'd have me do, sir."

"That shirt shlooks awfully clean—*hic!*—for farm work."

"It'll be as dirty as you like, soon enough."

"Say, cowboy. Why ain't you out—*hic!*—out rounding up cattle on a beauti—*hic!*—ful spring day like
today?"

Will stared at the wall.

"I went to Los Angeles a few months ago. Tried my
luck in the movies. I know it's silly. No one wanted to
give me a chance. But I still managed to get work as
a stage tech...with William S. Hart."

"William S. Hart?"

The name never failed to make an impression.

"I decided to strike out a month ago, or there-
abouts. But I ended up staying in California for personal reasons, if you catch my drift. Stayed a little too
long. So I only got back to Nevada a few days ago, and
haven't found anyone willing to take me on."

The farmer thought it over a little, taking the measure of the young man in front of him. But evidently
his mind was in a haze, and he seemed to be having
trouble stringing a sentence together.

"Well, you sure don't—*hic!*—you don't look like
no milker, son. But I'll give you a shot anyway."

Dressler said he needed two men to milk his twenty-
five dairy cows three times a day. The first hand he'd
hired was out doing errands but he'd be back soon, and
then they'd set out for the Smith Valley farm Dressler
oversaw for the Plymouth Land and Livestock Co.

"Smith Valley?"

"You ain't from around here?"

"No, I'm from out East. I know the place though."

Will meant Eastern Nevada. Smith Valley was
around fifty miles south of Carson City, in Lyon County.

"We'll head to the farm today and you can get started tomorrow. But I'm gonna be on the road for at least a week, so I'll explain what to do today. That or my wife or son will take care of you. We'll figure it out once we get back and then you can decide whether you want to stay or not. I really only need one guy except that I've got to make a little—*hic!*—trip. Pay is six dollars a—*hic!*—week."

"Got it."

They shook on it, and an unsteady Dressler leaned against the bar again so as not to fall under his stool. Under any other circumstances, Will would have turned his nose up at a job so abhorrent to any self-respecting cowpuncher. And neither did the idea of wandering around town with a drunkard appeal. But Smith Valley was known as some of the finest pasture-land in the region, and sooner or later some cowboy would stop by the dairy farm—a commonplace thing—and ask after a place to sleep for the night. The cowboy might give Will the information he was seeking. And if the first cowboy didn't have any leads, another would be by soon enough.

A few hours later they were at the town stable, warm from the whiskey and bloated with beer. They hitched Dressler's two nags up to a beat-up old wagon and, as they trotted out of town, Will thought lecherously about Carol and regretted not having stopped at the Chinese restaurant when he'd had the chance.

4

Will spent two weeks on the very bottom rung of the cowhand's ladder. Work truly didn't get any lower than this. Hundreds of miles from movie sets or life drawing classes at the San Francisco Art Institute, Will was milking cows morning to night. His ass was sore, his back like jelly, his hands torn and cramped. After two days, his fingers were red and raw, and his thumbs and index fingers had swollen to twice their normal size. Even rolling a cigarette was torture, though fortunately the farmer's young son would roll up a few every evening for Will to smoke the next day. Will may have thought he'd hit rock bottom—that he'd landed in hell, not a dairy farm (at least, that was the thrust when he'd recount the story later in life)—but despite the discomfort and the pain, and once the swelling in his hands subsided, he accepted that, no matter how degrading, the work had done him a world of good. And, besides, there was no denying the beauty of the lush and windswept green foothills close to the state line.

Every night, his back to the stable, Will observed the changing light, the sun setting behind the pines, and the peaks backlit for a brief moment before the sun set completely, looking as though they were on fire, as a blue haze enveloped the base of the mountains, and then slowly rose, so the mountains appeared to float.

For the pleasure of this sight alone, Will would gladly have accepted the most mundane of jobs.

On his arrival, Dressler had led Will on a quick tour of the property, and explained to him what he was to do. The rest of the instruction he left to his wife, Rita, a minuscule woman who couldn't have been much over thirty but looked older. Rita only ever addressed her son—the poor boy was seven and still struggling to form a sentence—by shouting. Rita did try to be nice to Will when he helped her with the washing-up after meals, but she was completely lacking in natural spontaneity. She found it arduous and exhausting to squeeze a smile from the well of monotony that was her life. Perhaps, thought Will, she was simply trying to hide her broken teeth, ashamed of the image she must have known they projected. With so much to do in the gardens and the stables and the kitchen, she kept a messy house, and Will had feared that his own quarters would be no tidier, but the shed where he was put up with Larry, the hired hand, turned out to be very clean.

An awkward seventeen-year-old, Larry had no real sense of how to handle the cows, but Will did. Before the Dufaults moved to the city, Will's uncle Napoléon Dufault had shown him everything there was to know about milking them, and after a single day he'd rediscovered the dexterity needed for the job. Like riding a bike, Will figured. All that was missing was practice, stamina, and calluses. Larry was not much help. If they didn't find a way to pick up the pace, they'd be milking all night, all week. So Will showed him how not to try to draw all the milk in one shot, lest you end up with nothing at all, and instead how to give the cow's teats a wash with warm water, and then to relax her with a bit of massaging—what they called "bringing the milk down." Or, like the calves do with their noses, you could give her little nudges.

"Where'd you learn to do that, cowboy?"

"Watching other people in a previous life," answered Will ambiguously.

He showed his comrade how to hold the teat, and where to apply pressure: first at the base, between the thumb and index finger, and then along the entire length of the teat, pushing from top to bottom and then from the base to the tip, taking care not to squeeze out too much at once.

"Be gentle. Let your fingers do the work, not your wrists."

It took around thirty minutes to milk a Holstein—cows were much smaller in those days—but there were still several gallons to draw from each udder. Any way you calculated it, you had to get an early start, and even then the job would stretch well into evening. Only a couple of days after they'd arrived, Larry threw in the towel and left the farm before Dressler even got back. Rita wasn't sure she had enough to pay him. He took what he could get.

Will was left on his own to milk twenty-five cows, twice a day. It was too much, of course, so he milked each one once a day instead. With twenty-five head, even that was no small feat. When Dressler finally got back he gave Will a proper scolding, and his wife too. Will let him yell, and the next morning went back to work. Dressler watched Will go and stopped giving him a hard time, instead helping him out and seeming altogether more satisfied than he'd been the night before. Already, he was thinking he'd have to find a way to keep this kid.

He offered Will three extra dollars a week, plus a bonus bottle of drink every two or three days. Dressler put back a full bottle nightly, and that was on a slow night. The man was drinking away his farm — or at least the farm he'd been hired to manage, which was never a story that ended well. Often, as Will had a quiet smoke outside and admired the landscape, he could hear Rita yelling, or perhaps their son, or all three members of the family, the hollering sometimes accompanied by a pounding on the wall, slaps to a face, or the sound of a belt slapping the little one's bottom. The man was twice Will's size, and if Will had even thought of stepping in, Dressler would have beaten him to a pulp and sealed the deal with a bullet.

After fifteen days of working for the brute, Will was smoking against the stable wall one evening when he heard the clacking of horseshoes on rock and saw the silhouette of a rider approaching. The horse shaking itself off was a glassy-blue-eyed Appaloosa, and the cowman had a round face and bushy eyebrows. The two men said hello, and the stranger asked if Will had seen any strays in the area.

"Only cattle I seen are these goddamn Holsteins right here."

He gestured toward the cows grazing, in the light of dusk, in the enclosure beside the stables. The cowboy looked amused. Will held out a hand for him to shake.

"Will James."

"Pleased to meet you," said the other. "William Fletcher. But folks call me Curley."

Curley Fletcher owed his name to his head of blond curls. He was also blessed with a smile and a disarming ability to charm. He'd left a trail of broken hearts belonging both to a number of gentlewomen from good families and to the lowliest slatterns he'd met on his travels. The Californian took an instant liking to Will, who decided he liked him back. Will figured a stroke of luck had come his way.

"Say, Curley," he started, "your outfit wouldn't be looking for hands, by chance?"

Curley leaned back a little and took a good look at Will.

"Sure is. Can you handle a bronc?"

"Can I? It's my specialty! You want to twist 'em into shape without breaking their spirit, I'm your man."

For once, Will was telling the truth.

"What you doing working on a farm, if you're as good as you say?"

Will looked at his feet.

"They hired me to milk these here cows, but it

ain't really my thing... It's a bit of a long story," he hastened to add.

Curley thought that was funny. He picketed his pony and removed the saddle, and the two men made their way over to the small cabin where Will was staying. A full bottle awaited, and by the time Will had finished the story of his many mishaps it was much less full. Will, who felt an immediate kinship with Curley Fletcher, trusted him and didn't want to lie about anything, so he even told him the story of his prison time, and the reason he'd spent the last year inside.

"So after, when I met this farmer, I figured he'd hire me to work with the horses. Boy was I wrong!"

Both men guffawed.

"Instead he starts asking questions. 'Know how to milk a cow, son? How many can you milk in a day?'"

This set them laughing even harder. Curley, an entertainer, was slapping his thighs.

"I turned white on the spot, but what choice did I— *hic!*—have? So I say, 'Yeah, I know how to milk.' I tell him I can milk as many cows as he wants, only I'd never milked a cow in my life," fibbed Will. "All I wanted was a ticket out of Carson City, and to earn a buck or two."

Will took two big swigs straight from the bottle.

"Brrr! So let me tell you one thing, Curley." He wiped his mouth on his sleeve. "It ain't everyone knows how to milk a cow! I think he's been keeping me on just because he's in a jam."

Fletcher poured himself another drink and raised his glass, before speaking.

"Here's what I want written on my tombstone: 'He chose to die rather than to be a farmer.' Or a shepherd, come to think of it."

Curley downed his drink in one gulp. The burn eased its way down his gullet, like acid descending to his stomach.

"But what about you? You ain't in a jam no more, Bill. Except maybe with the broncs we'll give you to break. We got one there that's bested every cowboy tried to ride it, me included."

Will relished the prospect. The two men kept drinking until not a drop remained in the bottle. It was a matter of honour, draining it, and as luck would have it, they discovered they'd been born the same year, 1892. Their common age and similar build (both men were on the small side for cowboys) helped make them fast friends. There was a sort of tacit recognition that they belonged to something that felt real no matter how abstract it was, the same generation.

Curley woke Will up early the next morning, seemingly fresh as a daisy. He told Will he needed to collect his wages from the boss, and promised he'd be back in a few hours with a second horse. A smile came over Will's face, despite his splitting headache and sandpaper-dry throat. He pulled the blanket up and over himself, relishing the warmth that reached to his neck, and was still smiling when he fell back asleep.

5

Curley was good for his word. Just before noon he rode back up with a second saddle horse in tow, a strong young gelding with Will's favourite coat — dark fading to a kind of iron grey in patches. To speak of "grey," Will knew, was a fairly common mistake: all ponies will start to grey in time through depigmentation. Even bays turn to grey sooner or later.

Will mounted the horse, slid his feet into the stirrups, puffed out his chest, and spread his shoulders. He pretended to be holding a pistol in each hand, and took shots at the heavens. The pony was ready to buck but calmed down when its rider stroked its neck, settling instead for a little snorting and a bit of shaking.

"Curley, if I didn't know better I'd say you'd chosen this one special. It's like God himself was thinking of me because this horse was made to measure."

Both men smiled.

"I don't even think about whether or not we have a Master."

"Well, ain't you got a silver tongue."

"Not my words. I'm but a humble admirer."

"What you talking about?"

Curley rummaged through his bag and pulled out an old book he sent spinning through the air. Will caught it mid-flight, opened it, and read the title out loud, not without difficulty.

"*Rubáiyát of Omar Khayyám*. Translated by Edward FitzGerald."

Will looked up, confused and curious.

This world that for a moment we sojourn in:
We go!—no problem solved alas! discerning;
Myriad regrets within our bosoms burning!

Will couldn't suppress his hearty laughter.

"You messing with me, Curley?"

Wherever Fletcher went, he carried his treasured, worn copies of *The Sufistic Quatrains* and *The Rubáiyát* of Omar Khayyám, the eleventh-century Persian poet who left us these master works; a scientist and a freethinker confronting the fast-changing world he lived in and clearly acquainted with Epicurus. The *Quatrains* were Curley Fletcher's bible and his code, to the point that he wanted to be buried with Khayyám's work beside him. Will, curious, borrowed the book one night, but couldn't make head nor tail of it. All he could tell is that this Khayyám sure loved talking about pottery, tents, and alcohol.

Look not above, there is no answer there;
Pray not, for no one listens to your prayer;

Near is as near to God as any Far,
And Here is just the same deceit as There.
But here are wine and beautiful young girls.
Be wise and hide your sorrows in their curls.

The two cowboys soon left the farm and followed a long natural corridor east of the Pine Nut Mountains. It led them out of the valley in a southeasterly direction, after which they climbed in elevation for close to an hour. They reached the crest of a hill that had seemed smaller on the way up. The slope on the other side looked steeper. At the foot of it, the Walker River followed a meandering course. Will's eye was drawn to a white-bellied bird of prey with a massive wingspan—an osprey, no doubt. It was gliding high above, circling idly in the sky, letting itself be borne aloft by the wind currents before vigorously flapping its wings and moving on. The sound of the rushing river was enchanting. Will closed his eyes a moment, breathing in lungfuls of air and rejoicing in the sweet scent of the pine trees, and when he opened them again he admired the view to his right of snow-capped peaks against the blue sky.

"You getting some sun on those teeth of yours?"

They traced the river's path until they reached the hamlet that had been visible in the distance. Wellington was a minuscule settlement that time had left behind, home now to no more than fifty souls. A few shacks bordered the river, and the main street, Wellington Cutoff, was home to a post office, a small church, and a school. A saloon was attached to Wellington Mercantile, the general store that doubled as a train station. In an enclosure behind the store were some stray cattle and a few horses Curley had corralled during the winter.

They put their boots on solid ground and lounged around awhile, sipping sodas on the shady veranda of the country store. The drinks whetted their appetites, and they'd come to the right place. The store owner, Joe Winston, served delicious liver pâté sandwiches. Will enjoyed them so much he bought a few jars of the pâté so he could make more of his own later. It reminded him of the buttery, delicate taste of the pork liver his mother used to make. As for Curley, given that it was the middle of the afternoon and there was no roundup to busy them, he was getting good and thirsty for something a little tastier than room-temperature sodas. He bought a jug of whiskey to go with the sandwiches, and an apple pie. Will didn't say no when the bottle came his way, and the two cowboys ate and drank at their own pace, exchanging only the odd word from time to time. Then they had a smoke. Will savoured moments like these, of doing precious little and enjoying the landscape and life's fleeting pleasures — good tobacco, a warm shot of whiskey, the wind on his face, the baking heat of the sun, the wide-open horizon to the east, and the sweetness of it all. The silence he so savoured was just occasionally broken, in that way particular to two people learning each other's ways.

"I do love this place!" Will ventured.

Curley smiled. He told Will everything he knew about the village, founded in the 1860s, first as a trading post for the wagons and then as the railroad's final stop before Colorado. When the veins in the nearby mines tapped out, Wellington became an agricultural community and commercial centre of the valley.

"There's a trout lake a little lower down, by the border. Sometimes you can see women swimming naked. I heard they want to make an artificial lake by rerouting the river. Destroy all creation for farming. Produce, produce, produce! It's all they understand, I swear."

"They want to see the end of us, Curley. All the animals in their stables, and no rangeland left for the likes of us."

"Well they ain't gonna get us."

Will agreed, knocking back a slug of whiskey.

One comment led to another, and it wasn't long before the two men had a good buzz on. They passed the time talking about everything and nothing. Curley told Will about growing up in Owens Valley, north of Bishop, California, near the Nevada border. He said it was people of the Paiute tribe who'd taught him to cowboy, when he was just a young thing. He'd caught an earful for that from the other cowmen, who even called him the "Blond Indian" sometimes. He said he'd worked at a huge spread belonging to Tom Rickey, a big-time rancher. Curley's father, an English immigrant, had started off hating Rickey, but they'd ended up the best of friends.

"What happened next?" Will kept asking him.

Curley would just blush and make a face. He was a modest, high-minded man and never one to waste words, except in his happiest moments, and with his wife sometimes.

"After?"

"Yeah, after," Will insisted.

Will never missed an opportunity to steer the conversation away from himself, and was also genuinely fascinated by this man.

"Well, after, I got to riding the rodeos."

"Really? Rodeos?"

Will hadn't seen many rodeos, and he'd certainly never partaken in any. He believed real cowpunchers turned up their noses at that kind of foolishness, which struck him as little more than an excuse to get drunk and run wild in town. But, under Curley's influence, he would reconsider these prejudices.

"I don't go out every year. Only when I can afford it."

Curley had been dragged onto the circuit young, by his brother and faithful riding partner, Fred. Curley had talent, and a signature style, especially for roping steers, that never failed to turn heads. From his very first rides, Curley seemed to be bound for glory.

"I won right near every category in Cheyenne last year. Earned a tidy sum, enough to pay off some debts I'd been dragging around for a while. But then I lost it all at the card table. Wasn't my lucky night."

Will put on an expression of sympathy.

"Minnie was waiting for me at the hotel."

"Minnie?"

"My wife," said Fletcher.

"You got a wife?"

"Surprised? Good-looking guy like myself?"

They both laughed.

"She kicked me out of the room after she found out I'd lost everything. I tried every trick in the book, but she wasn't hearin' it. It was there, at the hotel bar, that I wrote one of my finest pieces."

"Wrote what?"

"A poem. A song."

Will chuckled. Fletcher was among the first of a new breed. Not all cowboys were ignorant hicks — many were musicians or songwriters, and a lot of others whiled away long hours in the camp cabins reading great literature (since it didn't take long to work your way through the magazines) — but Fletcher was one of the first to openly describe himself as a "poet of the West." And he was a genuine poet, someone whose verses went beyond the clichés of cowboy folk songs.

"I called it 'The Outlaw Bronco.'"

The title, he told a spellbound Will, he'd since changed to "The Strawberry Roan." Who would have thought that, to get back in his wife's good graces, Curley would have had to write a syrupy ballad. "The Strawberry Roan" became one of the most famous traditional numbers in the songbook. Curley Fletcher would publish his first collection, *Rhymes of the Roundup*, the following year, though his immortality was secured in the 1930s when "The Strawberry Roan" was featured in the popular film of the same name starring Ken Maynard.

"So how'd that night end?" Will asked.

"Well, I recited my poem and she let me in. I'll spare you the rest of the details."

"Yeah, yeah."

They had another good laugh.

"Guess you're better with words than the cards."

"You can say that again."

Just like Will with his drawing, Curley didn't take his writing too seriously. He'd scribble on envelopes and scraps of paper, and give his originals to friends, but he was blessed with a good memory and—even years later—could rewrite verses that had long since left his possession.

Writing remained something of a hobby for Curley, though; poker, despite the problems it brought him, was his real passion. Curley was an inveterate gambler, and the trials and tribulations of the game were much more serious than any caused by the bottle, his second love (or third, as we can't forget his wife, Minnie). Booze made Curley a sick man who completely lost his head the moment someone suggested a round of cards. Any game would do, and his wife was deeply troubled—not just about the cards, but also about the damage his work could do. Cowpunchers led perilous lives. Accidents happened in the blink of an eye. Whether out in the badlands or in the rodeo ring, you could always be thrown from the back of a wild bronc or catch the horns of a steer.

"I love her so much!" said Fletcher. "Every day she encourages me to pursue what she sees as my one true calling."

What Minnie so wanted her husband to do was

write ballads and odes true to the life of the prairie and the cow camps, the roundups and the wild horses. No need for Curley to use fancy words or write about things he'd not known first-hand—how the West was won, the territorial wars, the Texas longhorns. What he could do was portray real life as the cowhands lived it: a rough life that left many hunched over and deserved an unvarnished telling.

"But I'm a slow learner and I just ain't ready to settle down," said Fletcher. "Bill, I know every water-hole between Utah and the Sierra, and you know as well as I do that learning's as good as gold. Riding and working the horses, rounding up cattle for thirty bucks a month, travelling the length and breadth of this country—that's what makes me happy. It ain't poetry, or the movies—hell, not even cards! But I look back and I say to myself nothing will ever come close to these years in the saddle. These are our best years, man."

"Till you get hurt."

"Knock on wood."

Will gave the planks of the veranda a tap. But both men knew he was right. Every brave cowpuncher took a fall sooner or later. If they didn't end up with backs turned to mush from years of working horses, then a single bad fall or one injury too many would force them into retirement. And neither Curley nor Will would avoid this fate. A few years later, Curley would have an eye gouged out by a cantankerous steer. The injury shook his confidence, and he was never the same man again.

They sat in silence for a moment, each man lost in his thoughts, a flurry of ideas and emotions rushing around in his head. It was Will who broke the quiet.

"I ever tell you that I draw, now and again?"

"Is that right?"

Curley was visibly waiting for more.

"Show me!"

Will blushed.

"We're talking sketches, a bit of doodling."

"Like I said, show me!"

From his satchel Will pulled out a few drawings he'd not had the time to finish when he'd been milking on that miserable dairy farm.

"I haven't drawn much since I got out of prison," said Will. "My hands are too sore to hold a pen for long."

"Don't sell yourself short, Bill. These are great!"

Curley flipped through the drawings as if he was shuffling a deck of cards, stopping occasionally to take a closer look at certain details. He was partial to a likeness of Dressler's farm, with the pine trees and the mountains around it. As he'd seen the place, he was well equipped to understand what a good eye Will had, his gift for distilling the essence of a scene.

"Well, well. I didn't know I was talking to an artist! If I had, I would've cut the bullshit a little. Can I keep this one?" he asked.

"I don't know."

"Come again?"

"Well, what's in it for me? I still ain't heard a single rhyme."

Now it was Curley's turn to blush.

"Nah. Please, Bill, not now."

"Why not?"

"How about another time," said Curley, his expression imploring.

"I didn't hold out on you, did I? I let you see what I got. You think I wanted to?"

Curley shook his head a little as he drew a final puff from his smoke.

"Okay. Fine."

He cleared his throat. Even Joe Winston, the store owner, pricked up an ear behind his counter, not having missed a word of the two cowhands' conversation. Will had already taken the bait and had been drinking in the words of this innately dapper man who was able to spin a great yarn while somehow remaining discreet, and who, above all, spoke straight from the heart— but hearing the poet himself recite "The Strawberry Roan" was momentous. The story was simplicity itself. Man against horse. The noblest duel of them all. A story with a moral, but nothing in it contrived or too clearly spelled out. The magic lay in Curley's familiar, but also intelligent and deferential, way of describing the horse—"he could turn on a nickel and give you some change"—and his gift for capturing the life of the drifting, penniless cowpuncher. The way Curley told it meshed perfectly with Will's experience of cowboy life—prison interlude aside.

Will had a hard time holding back tears, his eyes red from the emotional power and honesty of the verse. Curley was waiting for a little approbation—any reaction at all, really — but Will let time pass. At last, Will told Curley he'd love to illustrate some of his work, if Curley ever published his poetry. Curley assured Will that he wouldn't forget to remind him of his offer. An empty promise, most likely — the kind of drunken promise one forgets as life goes by — but in the moment, neither man saw reason to doubt the other.

They rolled a couple more cigarettes. Curley noticed, for the first time, the resin stains on Will's yellowed fingers.

"Well," he said, "we better not waste any time if we want to get to camp before the middle of the night."

They bought provisions at Wellington Mercantile — Will had nearly thirty dollars in his pocket, no small sum — then untied their mounts and headed for the corral behind the building, where the horses turned up their noses at some cows that were trying curiously to approach. Curley twisted a rope above his head and then tossed the loop over the pretty black-and-white nag he'd been riding when the men first met the day before. His favourite. Meanwhile, Will unsaddled the buckskin he'd been riding all day. Then he brought the saddle blanket and saddle over to his partner and, saying nothing, grabbed the pony by the ears to distract it as Curley put on the blanket and saddled it up. They did the same with the horse Will was to ride, an old black a little shorter and scragglier than Curley's mount. Once they'd successfully mounted the horses, they let the animals fight a little, but all the two could muster were a few half-hearted bucks — more of a game, really, a convention understood by horse and rider alike, than an honest attempt to throw the riders. The horses were merely trying to retain a portion of their dignity. They'd become used to men and no longer felt that visceral, bred-in-the-bone hatred of their early years. Theirs was a way of not having to let on that they enjoyed being mounted. They knew what it meant, knew what to expect: a pleasant ride, or impassioned and dangerous work.

The two friends rounded up twenty head to bring back to the Rickey Ranch—a.k.a. the Double R, with an "ЯR" as a brand. Most of the cattle were orphans that had strayed from the ranch after being weaned. Leaving Wellington, Will and Curley drove the dogies along the trail that followed the river. They passed through a magnificent red-tinged canyon that brought them to the beginnings of a mountain range. Twelve more miles and they'd have made their way across the county line to Topaz, California, at the northern tip of Mono County.

"You'll see," Curley said. "It's God's country."

6

Just before sundown, around eight in the evening, after making their way around the foot of the brush-covered mountains and fording the Walker River several times, the two cowboys drove their herd to a higher elevation to get away from the swampy ground. On the other side of the pass they came upon a sprawling, lush valley where the cattle could finally graze. The animals couldn't have asked for richer pastureland than this clearing where the thick grass reached their knees. No surprise—hundreds of other cattle were widely dispersed and grazing the slopes.

Will had loved every second of their ride, driving the calves and bringing the most adventurous of them into line, just as he loved the ritual of dismounting and walking up to a ranch again after hours in the saddle that could feel like centuries.

Home to twenty-odd people, Topaz was less a proper hamlet than a clutch of buildings on the north side of the Rickey Land and Livestock Company holdings, used as the RR's winter camp. A few dwellings had sprouted up around it and, along with the usual cabins, corrals, barn, and stables for the horses and sickly cattle, there was a fair-sized blacksmith's shop with two stucco walls and two open sides. A tiny station where trains rarely stopped doubled as a store offering a limited selection of provisions. That the community's full name was Topaz Post Office showed just what a rare amenity a post office was in this remote area, though its presence also suggested just how much influence the ranch owner, Tom Rickey, wielded. In Mono County, he was known as "The Colonel."

Tom Rickey's ranch, such as it was—his headquarters, his spread—was in Bridgeport, forty miles to the south. It was one of the biggest outfits in the county, and very possibly the biggest, stretching over sixty miles from the Antelope Valley near Wellington, in Nevada, all the way to Bridgeport, California. The west portion of the Walker River criss-crossed the beautiful country that was Rickey's from end to end.

Will soon learned Rickey was unfortunately remembered for having lost his self-declared war against Henry Miller, a Californian beef magnate and rival cattle baron. Miller's holdings were massive—well over twelve million acres in California, Idaho, and Oregon—and made him the biggest meat producer in the West. The largest independent ranchers, like Tom Rickey, would have perhaps thirty to fifty thousand acres, herds running from ten to fifty thousand head, and the packs of horses and men needed to keep such an outfit running. These were large concerns. But compared to the company Miller controlled, they were nothing. The Californian had holdings belittling these, and a herd approaching seven figures. *A million head of cattle!* The Old West, with its longhorns and unfenced grasslands, had long given way to joint stock corporations and industrial conglomerates, and bosses whom cowboys would work for only when things were truly dire. The managers of these enormous outfits were often city men who could barely mount a horse, with heads full of book learning and fancy notions about planning and growth and the economy. The times were changing, and the turf war Rickey had waged with Miller over Walker River territory was one with no skirmishes, no shots fired, no bloodshed; instead the two sides fought it out and tried to wear each other down in courts of law. Then Miller took their dispute all the way to the Federal Court of the United States, the Goliath prevailed, and Rickey's dream of diverting the river into a natural reservoir to feed the irrigation ditches that would have made his lands even more fertile was thwarted. He'd ruffled a few feathers, and for a decade the family had to tighten their belts a little, but Rickey got back in the saddle and just did what he did best—raised stock, kept the old boys working.

Henry Miller was diagnosed with throat cancer right around the time he won the war. In October 1916, he died, leaving assets and real estate worth forty million dollars of the day to his progeny. When Rickey heard of Miller's death, he felt no compunction to quell his satisfaction.

"I hope he goes to hell!"

Curley and Will headed for the ranch buildings. They unsaddled their horses and released them into the corral among the other horses, then went off to take their gear into the stables. They hung their saddles on ropes nice and high, so the rats wouldn't chew the leather for their nests.

The bunkhouse into which Curley led Will immediately seemed familiar. In the middle of the room was a set of wooden chairs cobbled together by a not overly talented carpenter. On the table was a dog-eared deck of cards, an oil lamp, and a handmade ashtray filled to the brim. Next to a wall, an old wood stove fired up with poplar branches was keeping the quarters toasty. On the cooktop, a little off from the heat, a stew cooling in a Dutch oven didn't escape Will and Curley's notice. The interior of the cabin had been papered with dusty old rodeo posters; black-and-white reproductions of Western artists; photos of purebloods black as night, and others of cowmen who'd worked the spread over the years, and the kids and women patiently waiting somewhere for their fathers and husbands to get back home with something to eat. Double bunks had been crammed into every corner of the cabin, and a door beside the stove led to a second room—a small bedroom with two double beds for the rare men who travelled with their wives. The "beds" were naked mattresses onto which the men would place their bedrolls—as many layers as they could—to keep their sweethearts and the night as comfortable as possible.

Curley thought it over, then spread out his roll on one of the two beds. The other was occupied.

Gentleman that he was, Curley had considered leaving the bed for his new friend and taking one of the bunks, but Will assured him that he'd rather sleep next to the stove. He owed his partner an eternal debt of gratitude for springing him from the hell of milking cows; after that, sleeping arrangements were inconsequential.

A young man with his leg in a brace came in and threw a few logs on the fire. Curley shot him a smile.

"Bill, Dave Reed. Dave, Will James."

They shook hands. Then the young man leaned over to stoke the fire.

"How about that leg of yours," asked Curley. "Any better?"

"Hell, I ain't no expert. Damn horse only had one ball!"

Will suppressed a chuckle. So this was the man he'd be replacing. One look was enough to see that the kid was a tenderfoot. A horse might have one ball or two, didn't change a darn thing.

"So I'm gonna have to break an original?" Will asked.

Sometimes, as a yearling was being castrated, one of its testicles would rise back up into the body. When that happened, it was nearly impossible to get it to come down. Half stallion, half gelding, these "originals" or "ridglings" had a bent toward violence, like proud stallions, and a reputation for being indomitable — or better said, "unmountable." But Will was not especially worried. Tomorrow was another day.

They settled in, and before long Curley was trying to convince the boys to have a taste of the whiskey he'd picked up in Wellington. Wasn't that the best way to be sure of getting a good night's sleep, after all? It wasn't like they were working a roundup, he argued. Plus, the foreman was long gone and wouldn't be back for a few days. Who wanted to let this whiskey age without having a little taste first!

"And besides, how can we enjoy a game of cards if we're spending the whole time convincing ourselves we ain't thirsty?"

Will frowned.

"I don't know, Curley. I don't think that's such a good idea."

In theory, Will didn't see a problem. He'd be thirsty enough once he wet his whistle, and Curley sure could be persuasive when he wanted. But he'd also been in camp less than an hour, and he'd learned long ago to be wary of strangers. You never knew what someone would say about you the moment your back was turned, and in this line of work a man's reputation was all he had. He was glad to have hesitated when he saw Reed stand up apologetically.

"I'd play a hand or two, if I weren't sure I'd lose. Even against you, Curley. And you lose every time. Plus I'm already down to the scrapings of my last pay."

"You sure, Davie? I've been on a mean losing streak lately!"

"I don't know. There's a book I'd sure love to finish."

"Do what you feel. Bill, what about you?"

"I don't know, Curley. How about another time?"

"Well if that's the way it's gonna be . . . "

Reed went to grab the novel he'd been reading and camped in front of the stove after adding a little wood to get through the night. Will wandered around, then remembered the form he needed to complete for the parole board. The post office wasn't far away, why not get it over and done with?

Two weeks in Will's satchel had been long enough for the form to get good and crumpled. He smoothed it out with his forearm before filling it in. Then he sat down next to Dave, in front of the stove. The heat was wafting over his outstretched legs and rising up his body. The form done, he flipped through an old magazine, then read a few pages from the Omar Khayyám that Curley, zealot that he was, had lent him.

Heav'n but the Vision of fulfill'd Desire,
And Hell the Shadow from a Soul on fire,
Cast on the Darkness into which Ourselves,
So late emerg'd from, shall so soon expire.

Will would have done some sketching, but Dave's presence put him off. He might have asked Dave to tell him his story and then spin a few yarns of his own, but Will wasn't convinced this young Reed was worth the time.

Meanwhile, a grumpy-looking Curley was at the table, chain-smoking and playing hand after hand of solitaire. Occasionally he'd let out a heavy sigh, but neither Dave nor Will responded. He took out a notebook and pen and started writing to Bridgeport to let the Rickeys know Dave's replacement had been found.

"What they paying you, Dave?"

"Ten a head."

"And how many you got to take care of?"

"A dozen or so, counting that big buckskin with the white blaze."

The big buckskin with the white blaze was of course the original: the outlaw bronc that had injured Dave. It would now fall to Will to break it in the weeks ahead. He'd have to get all the horses gentled by the time the team got back from the first roundup.

Curley sealed the envelope by running it back and forth along his tongue several times, making sure everyone was watching. It wasn't easy, he didn't have a lot of saliva, and Will got the message: Curley was thirsty. But Will wasn't backing down and stayed where he was, and kept right on flipping through the *Dime Western* magazine he'd returned to after a futile attempt to wrap his head around Omar Khayyám. Curley was getting started on a new game of solitaire, which he'd never finish, and rolling a cigarette destined to go half smoked, sighing all the while. Dave, who was still green behind the ears, fell right into the trap.

"Darnit, Curley, go ahead and have a drink if it's bugging you so. I'm speaking for myself, but I'm sure Will is with me, when I say we won't tell a soul."

"We won't tell no one nothing, Curley," said Will, his tongue just a little in his cheek.

Curley went off to fetch the jug of whiskey from his room. They heard the sound of him taking one big swig followed by another. When he came back his face was flushed deep red, his expression peaceful.

"How about a little fiddle, boys?" he asked.

The other two agreed to it and Curley pulled a pint-sized instrument from a big oak chest filled with a little bit of everything the hands had left behind over the years. He tuned it, first by plucking and then with the bow. His left hand grasped the neck and the fiddle squeezed out a joyful, rhythmic melody that reminded Will of the Canadian rigadoons of his youth. He was impressed by his new friend's tuneful, sprightly playing, but above all he was moved by the music, so familiar to him because of his childhood spent a few thousand miles to the northeast.

Curley Fletcher handled the violin well, along with the guitar and the piano. His mother Benedetta was Italian, and had been well on the way to becoming a concert pianist before she'd emigrated to America. She was the issue of a bourgeois family whose fortune survived the upheaval of Italian unification, and so she'd received a rigorous artistic education and passed the same on to her children. At home, the children learned English, Italian, Spanish, and French (though Will would never find out), along with a smattering of Latin, and practised their elocution with readings from the classics of the European and Latin canon. And each child—it didn't matter whether their natural inclination was athletic, creative, or scientific—had to learn at least the rudiments of a musical instrument of their choice, and then practise it at least five hours a week until they turned sixteen. This wasn't negotiable, and over the years (and often at the cost of repeated blows to the fingers, and fits of crying to match) Curley had gone back and forth between piano, violin, and guitar. He was quickly bored of having to play a single instrument, so switching them up made coming back all the sweeter. On each, Curley came to master a decent repertoire of classical and folk numbers, but he insisted on calling himself a "middling" pianist, pointing out that he'd once known the second prelude of *The Well-Tempered Clavier* by heart, and now couldn't play it through without his fingers stumbling on the keys.

Will tried to remain stone-faced, but had trouble keeping it up. As the emotion welled up in him, his smile betrayed how much he loved the music. His head was moving to the rhythm of the song, and soon the sound of the knocking of wooden spoons, heels clacking on the floor, and an accordion accompanied Curley, his fiddle-playing having come to a halt. Will wiped away a tear with the tip of his finger, hoping no one would see. Suddenly he stood up and went outside for a breath of fresh air. He exhaled with relief when he was sure that no one had seen how emotional he'd been. Inside the bunkhouse, Curley had launched right into another piece, this one a plaintive ballad with lots of vibrato, and Dave's face was still buried in the novel he was reading. High in the sky, the stars shone, full of grace, and Will thought about how these same stars were shining on his own family those few thousand miles to the northeast. Back in the bunkhouse, he announced that he was going to bed.

"Big day tomorrow, but keep on playing, Curley. You're awful good!" Will said.

Curley played a few more songs, mostly variations on standards from the previous century. He had no time for the *ritournelles* suddenly fashionable, as they felt empty and overwrought to him. The music of his contemporaries generally did nothing for him, though his indifference didn't stop him from creating his own art and writing poem after poem about ordinary life. What's true for one person isn't necessarily true for another, thought Curley. And vice versa.

It took a while for Will to fall asleep. It wasn't that Curley's music was too loud, or that the guys were making too much noise, but the melody of that first rigadoon reverberating and crashing around the walls of his empty skull, echoing and amplifying, as if distilled into one single long lament. Without thinking why, Will put his hand in his pocket and pulled out Jennie Riordan's primrose handkerchief. He wrapped it around his face and, slamming his eyes shut determinedly, tried to inhale deep drafts of her perfume. But in vain: the handkerchief smelled like musk, with accents of human and horse sweat, maybe. It no longer held even the slightest trace of the miraculous scent of a woman, this handkerchief that had for days provided the aroma of her hair, with its hints of spring, and her milky, saline skin. He inhaled one last time, and was disappointed.

7

A month earlier, in late March or perhaps early April, 1916, the big buckskin with the white blaze had been peacefully grazing in low-lying pastureland with his pack of mares. It had been five or six years since the buckskin had seen a cowboy hat up close. When he wasn't busy defending his harem from roaming stallions who'd come sniffing around the mares the moment his back was turned, he spent most of his time, like a good patriarch, seeing to the education of the colts. He loved them, and more than anything in the world he loved playing with them, and the colts always came back charging, eager for more. The day would come when they would be the buckskin's rivals, eager to mount anything that moved—even their own mothers. And when that day came, they'd learn the hard way that there could only be one master. The buckskin was a fierce and violent machine, heavy and agile. A killer. None of which was enough to dissuade certain of the young mares from trying to slip away from the pack when they were in heat. Some succeeded, but the buckskin kept the rest in line, mercilessly. Sooner or later the ones that remained would all agree to stay within the barren pack.

The snow on the sunny peaks had melted a week earlier, yellow grass had appeared, and the horses no longer had to scratch away at the ground for something to eat. Green shoots were pushing up a good inch a day, clearing a path through the dry grass. Winter was behind them, the fine weather was back, and though it was still cool, the colts, the mares, and the buckskin were fattening up. They had a healthy layer of fat on their sides, were losing their shaggy winter coats and developing a healthy, silky sheen. At last, they'd be able to go down the mountain for some summer grazing in the foothills. Out there, thick grass covered nearly everything, and the creeks and streams were irrigating the plains and watering the roots of bushes and trees. The horses were building up the strength they'd lost during the long, tough winter months, and as they roamed they crossed paths with innumerable cattle grazing free on the green prairie.

Then the cowboys appeared in the distance. At a first glance they looked a little silly and certainly less dangerous than pumas, or a pack of hungry wolves, but the buckskin and his pack knew in their guts that these odd bipeds were the worst predators of all. The disturbance in their grazing was instinctual; they had the feeling that trouble was brewing and reluctantly left the flatlands at the foot of the mountain to head back up to the heights again. The horsemen weren't so easily deterred. A few days later one of them caught the horses' trace again, and now, less than a mile away, binoculars in hand, Curley Fletcher observed the pack for half an hour without dismounting. He came a little closer, to more easily observe the white-blazed buckskin. It was calmly grazing, at a distance from the rest of the herd dispersed along the ridge, aware of the presence of men among them. Fletcher whistled admiringly and took one last glimpse before leaving. He knew where to find them and would be back.

Curley was thinking hard about how and when to return. Chances were, the horse was a stallion. It was true that a ridgling, if it was big and strong and mean enough, could wrest control of a herd of mares and vigilantly keep them in its clutch, despite the impossibility of reproducing. That was Curley's hope, at any rate. If it was a gelding, he'd take a shot at gentling it; the better to work with the horse one day. And if it turned out to be a stallion, Curley consoled himself, he could always bring the horse back for the winter and introduce it to a few stable mares, which would produce far prettier offspring than bays breeding with other bays. Bays tended to be good, smart, hard-working horses that, even when they were domesticated, retained a touch of the wild in them, and Curley had always loved a good bay with a smooth glossy coat and jet black mane. For years he'd considered them the most beautiful horses in the world, but now what he liked were buckskins and light-coloured blondes.

Worrying about some cowboy had been the last thing on the buckskin's mind. He liked to pasture in the highlands, where the grass tasted slightly different than the fatter prairie grass. And in the highlands, you weren't liable to run into men the way you might on the plains. After a long winter, men were everywhere, always making a racket. Wild horses never understood how these devils were able to keep dozens and dozens of their fellow horses corralled together in a roundup. The men must have some sort of magical power, some spell they could cast over the horses—why else would their brethren not simply kill their so-called masters instead of marching along in step and serving them, obeying them, and running after the cattle? That a horse might actually come to like working for a man was something the buckskin with the white blaze would never admit. The way Curley Fletcher described the big, muscular horse to his partner, Dave Reed, left no doubt that the buckskin would soon find himself in a log corral. The time had come for him to be put to use. He'd enjoyed several years of liberty, but roaming free over the hills and prairies would soon be a thing of the past, something he'd only come to know again after years of hard labour and loyal service. That far-off day would be like being yanked from a dream, for the return to a previous reality is often brutal. It takes time to recalibrate. The vague memory of a paradise lost sometimes stays with us a long time.

The herd was grazing in peace when the long-legged cowboy on the back of a turncoat horse appeared on the ridge above it. He was backlit, so all they could discern was the ominous silhouette of his hat: a devil. Only a devil could appear out of nowhere like that.

Then everything happened very fast. The horses suddenly started and galloped toward the plains, to run unobstructed and the better to stay ahead of their predator. They covered a lot of territory, without realizing that the solitary rider was directing them toward a corral hidden behind branches. They were trapped before they knew it, surrounded. The camouflaged boards formed a chute leading the horses right into a big log corral, shaped a little like an ace of spades. At the point of the spade was a smaller round corral serving as a holding pen in which to tie up the wild horses.

By the time the buckskin and his pack realized what they had walked into, it was too late. Terror gripped their guts. The cowboys slammed a high gate shut behind them, hollering like maniacs. The buckskin could see other horses trapped in the smaller pen, all of them geldings around his age, though none as large. Curley was able to observe the buckskin up close now, and got a better sense of what a giant it was — a horse with lightning in its eyes, and its every limb quaking with fear. Might be a good one for the rodeo circuit, thought Curley. That was too bad. The cowboy opened the door to the smaller pen and made wild gestures in the air to push the horse through and separate it from the pack.

Through the bars of his new prison, the stunned buckskin saw that the others were being set free. One of the mares took the lead and galloped off into the mountains from which they'd descended. But it was every animal for itself now: the mares had stopped looking after their foals, and the little ones were struggling to keep up, and they understood in their bones that this flight was for their freedom, for their lives, and that what they'd been through was every bit as threatening as being chased by a pack of bloodthirsty wolves.

The big buckskin whinnied and stamped his feet, calling out to the mares, but not one turned around or slowed down. For all they cared, he could go to the devil—was already with him, for that matter. They'd been under his rule long enough and soon they'd be gone in a cloud of dust.

The sensation of another creature's hot breath on his hindquarters brought the buckskin back to the present moment. He leaped around, curving his neck and putting his ears back, and bared his teeth. This other, curious horse was a lot smaller. The buckskin could deal with him with a single bite. The other one got the message and backed up to show it hadn't meant to provoke him. But the buckskin pounced without warning and gave him a kick with his front leg, chomping on a bit of flesh as he did so. The poor gelding whinnied in pain and cowered behind his neighbours, who had to be wondering if they were next. The buckskin snorted furiously, and shot a murderous look at the other horses, who were too intimidated to meet his gaze. Then he charged the horse nearest to him, a pretty bay, and gave him a series of kicks to the flank. And he wasn't done. Next he trotted out to the centre of the corral— the rest of the geldings were clumped together against the log fencing—and bit anything in his path, kicking

ferociously. The animals started running. It wouldn't
take much for the situation to degenerate, and some
horses were trampling the others as they struggled to
escape. Eventually, the strain would be too much for
the corral's log posts, but before anything calamitous
happened, the blond curly-haired cowboy stepped in.
Given the agitation and frenzy of the horses, entering
the corral was dangerous, but there was nothing to be
done. The creaking of the heavy gate stopped them
short, and the buckskin halted his violent rampage.
He stood straight and proud, ears pricked, and ceased
his stomping despite still being upset.

"Where are your balls, big guy? You want to tell
me that?"

Curley took a second look. He saw nothing hanging down, which made him sad. A horse acting up
this way who was not a stallion was either an original
or an uncontrollable outlaw, and in both cases there
was nothing to be done. No one would ever be able
to master him; the only thing he'd be good for was
the rodeo. True, such a horse could still bring in a
pretty penny — and once he was caught in the cowboys'
nets, the foreman would never let him out of captiv-
ity until time came to sell him. But Curley was not
immediately put off. There were originals who, with
a lot of patience and care, could be trained to work,
and even if they didn't make the grade they could still
be mounted and ridden for a few miles, which always
made for an entertaining promenade. Sure they'd buck
a little, give a cowboy a run for his money. But that
was part of their charm.

"So you're an original, pal. Let's see what we can do with you."

Every word that came out of the cowboy's mouth sounded like the groaning of a three-headed Satan, but the buckskin wasn't about to let this demon pull his strings. Unlike the weaker horses, he was full of determination. The cowboy stepped forward. The buckskin snorted and stomped, kicked up a cloud of dust, and leaped over to the furthest reaches of the corral; taking refuge among the geldings he'd been bullying just moments earlier now seemed the best option.

Above all, he had to keep moving and prevent the man's approach. He decided he should wait a moment before charging and destroying his enemy. After all, the cowboy couldn't be that dangerous. Yes, he would charge and kill him, kick the man until his lifeless body lay in a heap of its own blood. Except that he didn't have time to execute his plan; the horses bolted as Curley twisted his lasso and took another step forward. A quiet whistling could be heard, and what looked like a snake gripped the buckskin's forelegs, brutally yanking them out from under him as he tried to break free. The horse spun around in the air and then landed on his flank. Immediately he tried to get up, but couldn't. Again, and again, and again, he tried to get up off the ground, each failure followed by another equally futile attempt. The cowboy spoke to the horse in a soothing, gentle voice, trying to reason with him, but the buckskin only answered with a look that was furious and threatening before it grew desperate.

"Be good now. You calm down. I wouldn't want to dirty that pretty coat of yours."

The horse was panting heavily. His brain ceased to function, his heart was pounding. Curley tied the horse's four legs together. The buckskin just couldn't understand how the predator had so easily bested him; the man had brought him to the ground and kept him there, had prevented him from moving anything but his head. The horse had proved capable of defending himself against a cougar or a bear and never once had he been in the helpless state he now found himself in. He could have fought for his life, with all the strength of his youth and his limbs, and all the strength of his proud breed, only now his predator was intent on taking his time. He didn't appear to want to kill his prey, to polish the buckskin off as soon as possible and leave him in a warm and bloody pulp. No, he was calculating. This animal had a plan, an endgame the horse didn't understand.

Dazed, he barely saw the cowboy leaning over him. The man's knee was on his neck, and his muscles twitched as if bitten by a poisonous snake. One hand touched his ear, another his forehead. He felt no pain, but he was so paralyzed by fear that he wouldn't have felt a thing even if the cowboy had been out to hurt him. Curley calmly slipped on the hackamore. The buckskin felt the bosal being eased over his nostrils, and the throat tie sliding under his cheeks, so that the muzzle strap could be cinched up mercilessly. All the while, Curley was talking quietly and doing his best to comfort the horse.

"That's a good boy. Yeah, like that. We're almost done. Don't worry, boy, everything's gonna be just fine."

The sounds emanating from this peculiar devil didn't seem nearly as dangerous or evil as they had only moments earlier. The buckskin was beginning to feel he could understand what the cowboy was trying to tell him. Maybe the little pats on his pretty white-blazed forehead were helping.

"You see I mean you no harm, boy. It'll take a while, but one day you'll understand we were meant to meet up."

Curley got up and untied the horse's feet. The horse felt the ropes loosening around his fetlocks. He understood he had a little room to move, though he was still confused. He was only able to rise to his feet because of the traction on the halter rope.

"C'mon, boy, get up!"

The horse came back to life. He abruptly arched his back and snorted. But the strength he exerted in a final escape attempt was not enough. His neck bent and he was forced to stop. That a one-hundred-and-fifty-pound man wielding nothing more than a rope was able to control a wild animal weighing more than fifteen hundred pounds was incomprehensible to anyone unfamiliar with the trade. But over the years, this cowpuncher had won over more than a few horses with this very same rope. The buckskin wasn't the first or the most intractable horse to feel its pull, and nor would he be the last.

The harder the original fought, the angrier he became. Watching as he was visibly unable to get the

better of this two-legged terror, the other geldings were
starting to make fun of him. He was putting all the
strength he had into trying to get away, but yanking
on the rope with all his might was tiring him out. The
cowboy could feel as much, and took a break to give
the buckskin a rest, which also might allow him to
reason with the horse. The buckskin tried to catch his
breath. His legs were spread, his coat glossy and drip-
ping with sweat. He scrutinized his enemy. Curley let
out a bit of the rope to give the horse a bit more play.
The original wondered if this was just another trick,
the psychological torture of false hope. Curley opened
the door and climbed onto a horse waiting for him outside the corral. The buckskin didn't have to think long
before leaping toward the open door, but was brought
to a sudden halt and pulled to the ground the moment
he passed through it. He'd not yet learned his lesson:
no matter what he attempted, the rope would beat
him every time. A painful reminder of this fact came
seconds later when, back on the plains, he felt the rope
slacken again and he tried to set off at a gallop. The
rope tightened and he was forced to stop and face the
cowboy. He watched in despair as the man dismounted
from his horse and tied the rope around a tree trunk.

"All right, big guy, now you're going to keep learning the lesson without me. Don't try playing tough guy
with this rope. Don't yank so hard. And stop fighting
it. Treat it right, and it'll do the same with you."

At that, Curley left the buckskin to learn for himself—there were other, less incorrigible horses waiting to be dealt with. The long cotton rope, thick and

supple, would—together with the trunk of the poplar tree—teach the original a basic truth that would serve as the foundation of his further apprenticeship in living with men: resistance was futile. Unfortunately, he would learn this lesson the hard way. In the days that followed, the stubborn and violent horse would hurt himself numerous times in attempts to break free. By the late afternoon, when Curley would bring the original back to the little corral he'd made for him alone, he'd watch to make sure the poor animal didn't bash his head in by banging against the logs. Many wild and untameable horses did, especially stallions, and killed themselves doing so, desperate to escape the harrowing condition of being a prisoner of men.

After days of fighting the rope, returning to the corral would be a small mercy. Freed from the infernal cord leading it by the end of the nose, the horse would once again eat grass where it was least trampled, where it tasted best, where it was nice and thick.

On several occasions, the buckskin managed to drag the log post he was tied to, convinced he could get away from his captors. But he never got far. All that would come of it was a sore neck that was still sore the next day.

It took a good few days before Fletcher saw any improvement. With considerable effort, the recalcitrant horse was still dragging the log post behind him, but he was no longer yanking on the rope to the point of breaking his neck. Now, when the buckskin reached the end of the rope, he turned around. He was learning.

After a week, most of the geldings were ready to make the trip to the Topaz winter camp, where their instruction would continue. With a rope tied around their front legs and just enough slack for them to walk and trot, but not enough to gallop away, they'd be led to their new home. And throughout this adventure the buckskin never stopped expecting the worst — that the day was approaching when he'd be killed and eaten, if he wasn't eaten alive. It was clear as day. Otherwise, why would they go to all this trouble? All that remained to be seen was how it would happen. These demons may wear strange costumes and have inscrutable customs, but that was no reason to let down his guard. Yet the buckskin often needed to fight hard not to develop a fondness for the cowboy, as on those nights when Curley — the horse had learned to recognize the man's name and smell — walked over with a cigarette in his mouth to give him a pat on the forehead, stroke his mane and snout, whisper kind words in his ear.

Surely this was all subterfuge covering up a sinister plan. He would not bend, would not flag, would not become one of these devils' henchmen, who let himself be mounted and who obeyed their every whistle, their every slackening or tightening of the reins. When Lady Luck smiled on him, he would act. He'd kill at the first opportunity.

After a while, Curley was called to a different task, leaving him without the time to finish what he'd started with his new horse. A telegram had arrived in Topaz informing him stray calves had been sighted a little higher up in the mountains to the northeast, near Wellington, Nevada. His job was to bring them home before farmers made off with them. Gelding the remaining ten head of horses was work that would fall to Dave Reed.

And we know the rest of the story: eager to prove himself, Reed tried to tackle the big buckskin first and was injured before Curley even had the chance to set out for Smith Valley.

As he travelled, Curley had but one desire on his mind: to get back to the winter camp and continue training the original he'd become so attached to. But his affection for his new friend, Will James, would lead him to hand over the horse he loved to someone else, a second time. There was so much to do; Curley wasn't merely twiddling his thumbs and leaving Will to break his fifteen-hundred-pound darling. The thing was, Curley trusted Will James, and his trust only burgeoned as he watched his new friend tame the other wild horses. Will was no greenhorn. He'd handle the buckskin exactly as Curley would. And besides, there was nothing to stop Curley from buying the horse he so loved from the ranch afterwards, and having him all to himself.

8

Will woke first. He'd slept badly, meaning not at all. First Curley put away his violin and nodded off, then Dave did the same, but the yip-yips of a pair of coyotes had kept Will up. Their sharp cries rang over the hill. After a while, the scavengers had joined in a plaintive serenade that was carrying far in this, the mating season. Their cries had only just abated when the interminable howling of a wolf drowned them out. Next to the wolf's doleful lament, the yapping and squealing of the coyotes seemed flippant and ridiculous. As if they understood they'd been outdone, the coyotes shut up.

Day was dawning when Will faced the facts: he wasn't about to start sleeping now, and might as well get up, have a smoke, and wait for the others. Like the coyotes, though lacking their animal charm, his two companions were making their own song and snoring in unison in the tiny room. Will stoked the fire and made coffee as quietly as possible, but to no avail. Before the coffee had finished brewing, Dave and Curley stumbled out of the room, yawning.

"Good morning," said Will, welcoming them with a smile.

"One way to see it, I guess," said Curley, his mouth dry and pasty.

Of the three, Dave was in the best shape by far. It didn't take a detective to figure out that Curley had spent the night furtively drinking whiskey. Will hoped he'd left a little for the next time his own thirst struck. Which would happen.

"What d'you boys say to an omelette?" Dave asked.

Both were hungry and agreed. Dave was a good cook. During the few days they'd work together at the RR—young Dave was eager to return home to his people, and didn't stick around long—Will would never once have a bad thing to say about the food, though when it came to the other qualities required of a cowman, Dave clearly didn't have what took. One look at his fancy saddle told the story.

Will and Curley helped Dave peel potatoes for him to fry in the skillet. Just this step took fifteen minutes.

"We ain't got all day, Dave!"

"You'll thank me later. And did you see the time? We *do* have all day."

He wasn't wrong. Curley was supposed to mend the fences, if he was back from his trip before the first roundup ended, but really he didn't have much left to do on the ranch. And as for Dave, other than sweeping the floor of the bunkhouse, cooking up the grub, and looking after the chickens, he wasn't expected to do much, though at least he tried to make himself useful by chopping and stacking wood.

Once the potatoes had turned a golden brown, Dave broke eggs over them and put the hash in the oven. He set a pot of beans to simmer on the stove. They'd be ready in time for the omelette.

The three men ate like kings, and Will repeatedly complimented the chef. There was no fresh bread, of course, and no one touched the biscuits. The potatoes had been enough to fill them up.

"One more cup of mud before we go?"

"I don't know, Dave," Curley answered. "I'd like to show Will the ropes — with your help, of course. What time is it, anyhow?"

"Going on eight?" Will guessed.

The bunkhouse clock had stopped working. Dave seemed a bit of a slacker, which didn't bother Will much — he was a kid, nothing to worry about yet. The poor guy tagged along with them to the post office, where Curley mailed a letter to Bridgeport and Will sent off his parole form. Then Dave followed Will and Curley to the corral, where the big buckskin with the white blaze stared at them lividly. Will's expression changed completely once he took a good look at the massive horse. He was high, long, and solid, his muscles large and rippling. His feet were swollen, tumours had deformed his hooves, and the "Я R" brand on his hindquarters hadn't scarred right. A yellow scab secreting pus in places covered the scar. The horse's dipped head, mean eyes, the pointed ears stretched back that touched at the tips, his strong neck, and

large, powerful jaw made him look murderous, like a
killing machine.

"Well, I owe you an apology, Dave!" said Will, who
was laughing and flabbergasted at the same time.

"What for?"

"For a while there I thought you just weren't cut out
for breaking broncs. But I gotta say—this one here is
quite a specimen. Really!"

He whistled in admiration, as Curley had done
when he first met the horse.

"You'll tell the others, Bill, that I did everything I
could to get him on side," said Dave. "There's just no
messing around with that one."

"Right you are, Dave. Right you are."

Will flashed a mocking smile, which cut to the quick
of Dave's pride. Then Will inspected the corral, where
a dozen young geldings stood chewing on what was
left of the hay Dave had brought the night before as
they waited to be broken. (What else was there to do,
without a pot of coffee to sip on this fine cool morning?) Curley made a few trips to get the horses fresh
hay. Will let them be a moment, a chance for them to
eat their fill, then caught their attention with a click of
the tongue and a gesture with his hand, and without
exception every horse grew fearful and backed up a
pace. They weren't about to help him impress his two
acolytes in the background rolling cigarettes.

"All right, boys. You ain't got nothing else to do?"

"Why," asked Curley. "We in your way?"

"Nah, it's just that I don't much feel like an
audience."

"Look, Bill. I hired you—or at least I got you hired, or pretty close thereto. Ain't that right?"

"True."

"So you don't think I got a duty to make sure you know what you're doing? That when you get down to it, you ain't just a phoney?"

Will crossed his arms, a stern look on his face.

"Don't take it that way. I'm just joking. You know what a joke is, don't you? Funny stories we tell for a laugh?"

"Hell, you boys do what you like."

Will opened the corral gate.

"Won't it be easier with a saddle?" Dave asked.

The question caught Will off guard.

"C'mon, let me help you with that."

They went off to the storage quarters, where Dave offered to lend Will his saddle—so much better than the ranch's, he said—as well as the rest of his gear, including a long halter rope he almost felt bad dragging in the dust, and a hackamore bridle. Every piece of gear was top-notch. The saddle was good as new and made by G. S. Garcia of Elko, Nevada, one of the most famous saddle- and concha-makers in the entire West. Will was in awe of its quality, and when he saw the name of the maker he said he needed to buy it from Reed. It didn't matter what it cost.

"I swear, Dave," said Will that night, "that's one hell of a saddle you got. You sure do have good taste."

Dave was cooking up dinner, a chowder with some rainbow trout and perch and carp he'd caught in the river. The aroma filled the room.

"Look, I got thirty dollars on me. It ain't a whole lot, I know, but I can pay you the rest when I get it. You can trust me, Dave, I'd never let you down."

"I don't know, Bill. I do love that saddle."

Will knew that a lot of people without a lick of talent grew attached to the trappings that let them pretend to be something they weren't.

"You see me out there today?" he asked. "You were standing there watching me, and you had a good laugh because I put the bridle on wrong—one little moment of not paying attention, that was all. But I didn't hear you laughing when I mounted that ornery bay. He was a real bucker and I stayed on him, didn't I? I could see you were impressed. At least a little. And I gotta say, Dave, this beautiful saddle of yours played a part in that."

"I ain't got much use out of it, truth be told," Dave volunteered.

"Now stop right there. You had some bad luck. Happens to everyone some time or other. That's how you learn. Tell him, Curley—about the rodeos. How many times did you go chasing clouds, get throwed and spun around and landed fork-end up?"

"A few, Bill. A few..."

"See, Dave? That courage, that call you heard one day, that's what makes a cowpuncher! You can't go hanging up your saddle on account of getting hurt just the once. Talk to guys who are thirty and thirty-five. Ask 'em how much pain they were in every time they found themselves on the back of a horse that kicked up and refused to be broken. But them guys are still out

working because they're men. You a man, Dave? Go
get a little rest with your family — lay up somewhere
and heal somewhere you won't need that pretty saddle
of yours, and give it some thought. Listen to yourself.
I'm sure if you do, you'll come to see you just had a
bit o' bad luck with that buckskin."

Curley thought Will was coming on a little strong.
The stream of flattering words might cheer the kid up a
little, but they also rang hollow. Curley was disappointed. His friend might be nothing but a con man when
you got down to it — the big-talking sort he viewed as
the bane of humanity. Seeing how low a man might
stoop to get what he wanted always depressed Curley.
Sometimes it took whole days for him to get over it.

"Let me think on that, Will. In the meantime, you're
welcome to use it all you want, it'd be my pleasure."

A few days later, Dave left the camp and agreed
to sell Will his entire outfit for a hundred dollars that
he'd never see. (He'd get forty, much later than he'd
hoped, but that was it.) Curley and Will wished him
luck and for him to get better soon. Theirs was nothing
but a "bye for now," they insisted. But they'd never see
Dave Reed again — neither on the trails, nor working
a ranch or riding in a roundup.

9

G entling horses in the RR winter camp, Will spent his days in a thick cloud of dust. He'd emerge with red eyes, fear in the pit of his stomach, and the feeling that he'd barely made it out of the corral alive, to say nothing of the teeth marks and bruises he'd accumulated from the near misses and blows he hadn't quite managed to dodge. After his days of working to break horses that never failed to resist more than he'd expected, chronic back pains would visit him come nightfall. In short, Will's time in the RR corral was a series of stupid and dangerous mistakes, failed efforts, and aborted attempts, with only an occasional small victory.

Every morning Will would bring hay for the buckskin in his solitary pen, where fresh grass had long stopped growing, and then go on to see the other ponies. He'd choose three or four broncs to work that day, and cut the rest of the herd loose. With ropes tied around their legs they never went far, but they did get to chew on thick grass with an appetite that helped them forget the dull-tasting hay that had become their staple since they'd been confined to the camp.

To do a good job, you needed a month to break a horse, working ten or so at a time, but Will had been given just two weeks for a dozen wild horses — hardly long enough to gently win their trust and break them in with a blanket before giving them a proper saddle. He needed to work fast, and that meant taking a few shortcuts, but without botching the job. His reputation was on the line.

Everyone in this part of the country had opinions of varying merit on how best to tame stubborn broncs. Ignorant folk thought cowboys used violence and cruelty to break their spirits and bring the horses around, box in their untamed souls. Not true. Sure, there were cowboys who shamelessly starved their horses a little and beat them; had their way with unfortunate animals often smarter and more sensitive than their masters. While their motivations ranged widely, most acted out of sheer malice. But these kinds of bronc-busters were few and far between, and they didn't last long in the trade because no one in the world was more eager than a true cowman to see a horse retain its spark, its elegance, its personality. A real cowpuncher was the first to know that a badly broken horse was no more than a shadow of its former self. To do it the right way took time. You'd sometimes have to discipline a horse, in the strongest sense of the word — but there was no good reason to resort to barbarity. Dangerous behaviour, left unpunished, was liable to congeal into habit, and that was when you had to fear a horse—one that might turn into an outlaw, a mean-spirited, dangerous animal waiting for the chance to turn against either its rider or the first kid unlucky enough to find themselves in its path.

Will did sometimes feel duty-bound to whip his charges a little, but he never gave them more than a tap on the fleshy part of their hindquarters. You'd never see him hit a horse about the head or neck or legs or knees, the way some people did. And he never put much force into his blows, because it was the mind, not the body, he was trying to whip into shape. You had to make the unbroken animals understand that certain behaviours wouldn't be tolerated, and they'd best not even try.

And horses had as many distinct personalities as humans. Some required a firmer touch, stricter discipline. Others were more sensitive and fragile, though also more inclined to turn deadly, and as such they required special treatment: a longer, more gentle and attentive period of breaking-in. All horses wanted to learn; what was crucial was to be attuned to their natural pace. And this time Will was struggling to get the balance right—except with the powerful buckskin, a natural-born killer who would demand an expert hand, an iron fist in a velvet glove. He chose names for the first broncs he made headway with: Big Tom, Old Smokey, Hammerhead. Most were based on the horse's coats, hence Brownie and Whiskey and Smokey. He was currently working with Midnight, a scrawny but powerful chocolate bay slowly coming around.

Will fastened the lead rope to one of the posts and saddled up the horse. The big gelding watched as Will put a hand on his belly, and then, when he felt the strap tightening, his back arched into a bump that pushed the saddle down over his hindquarters. No chance for Will to get Midnight ready for the saddle with a blanket, so he took him for a trot around the corral until he relaxed a little. He needed to calm the horse down before the upcoming duel, or he wouldn't learn a thing. Will pulled his hat down and his pants and chaps up, not wanting his belt to interfere with the horse's movements. Then he slid the gelding's eyelids down with his thumb to blind him before, as was his custom, he mounted from the left side. Suddenly Midnight felt an unfamiliar weight on his back — and could see again, though what he saw brought no joy. The rider was straddling him. Instinctively, the horse wasted no time, fighting with all the strength he could muster to throw off the man sitting comfortably on his back. He needed to make the man regret the day he was born.

The horse leaned his head forward and spread his legs, his neck arched as his back had been just before, and then took such a powerful leap that his rider felt as if the saddle were bending in two. As he jumped, the horse snapped his head from side to side, kicking violently in the air with his back legs. Idlers passing by, beware. Midnight was ready to fight for as long as it took to disburden himself of this weight on his back, but fatigue got the better of him. He was panting hard. The cowboy was still in the saddle, though he had lost his hat. He rubbed the horse's neck. After all, the boy had put up a good fight. His ears were still pinned back, but gradually Midnight eased into a more natural stance.

It never occurred to Will to punish a horse that gave him a hard time as he was breaking it. To rear up was a reflex, a valuable one and a habit that would serve a horse well in a roundup. The horses were as yet unaware, but in a few days they'd enjoy being mounted. They just needed a little time to get used to it, and if they did buck now and again, sometimes entirely without warning, they'd see reason soon enough and they would never again react as violently as the first time. And, deep down, cowboys were always a little disappointed when they came up against a horse with no fight, when the horse's every muscle did not rise up in revolt the first few times it was mounted. Some horses were made for movie sets, some for the city; some were born to the stable, and some were outright loco. And then there were the others: the genuine article.

During their breaking-in, the broncs had the whole night to mull over their situation. Next time that creature tries to mount me, you could almost hear them thinking, I'll find a way to free myself and trample the cowboy to death, first chance I get. And yet, even when they resisted twice as hard, the man still won, again and again. Will, who talked to the horses a lot, told them to wait a while before crying wolf, and assured them that in a few days they'd see that what he was asking them to do was not some diabolical torment.

"You're gonna like it, big guy. You'll see. You'll get to run like you've never run before. You'll be the one laying down the law of the flatlands, making life hard for those poor cows. You get to be the bad guy, not me. I'm telling you, you're gonna like it."

He mounted Midnight a couple more times. If the horse kept jumping so perilously, Will would have no choice but to discipline him. It was one thing for a horse to rear up and snap its head back; another for it to try to kill its rider each time. Even the most recalcitrant beasts figured that out sooner or later. And after the first two duels, Midnight fought his trainer merely as a matter of principle, and never for long. Just a perfectly amicable romp to start the day.

In order to teach Midnight how to react when he dismounted, Will kept his left foot in the stirrup while holding some of his weight off the horse's back. He'd stay in this position for a few seconds, the gelding wait-ing to strike or bite at the rider's first unconvincing movement. All Will wanted was for the horse to stay calm and not pull a fast one. With elegance and a light touch, in perfect control of the movements of his own body, Will swung his right leg and got back in the saddle. Midnight couldn't feel the cowboy's weight even when he climbed on his back again. So adept was Will that the saddle wouldn't even have moved an inch if not a single strap was holding it in place. Always keeping one foot in the stirrup, Will mounted and dismounted a few times. Midnight was coming to understand what was happening, and, as all of them did in time, calmed down.

Soon, the strap around the gelding's stomach would be undone and the weight of the saddle lifted, reliev-ing his tired shoulders. Before letting him go for his afternoon rest, Will gave the horse a good rubbing down with a jute sack. There was no better feeling in the world. Will was pleased when he saw the change that came over Midnight's face. His upper lip was quivering joyfully with each rub of burlap on his coat.

After these crucial early days, the real work could finally begin. Now was the time to ride the open prairie, to gallop at full tilt and teach the horse to follow directions and anticipate commands. He did this only with the most responsive horses, hoping that when the rest saw some of their number running stomach to the ground, they'd also come around. It was only possible to do this with three horses a day at most. Toward the end of the afternoon, he'd visit the other, envious horses, and continue mounting and getting the measure of them. (They were progressing quickly.) Then, at the end of the day, if he had the energy, he'd dedicate an hour or two to the big buckskin. He'd ease him in with a saddle blanket, rub him down a little to get in his good books, and then try to saddle him up, taking every precaution in the book because he still didn't dare dream of riding him.

The horse tensed up. All the precautions Will had taken would prove worthless. In a matter of seconds, Will would be dancing around to dodge the horse's biting and pernicious kicks. Once he had the saddle on the buckskin's back, he would cinch the straps under the horse's enormous midriff good and tight, then force him to take a few turns around the corral. The original might obey, but it was easy to see that nothing was sinking in, and that he didn't want to learn. The more

time Will spent with him, the more he doubted the possibility of ever mounting the buckskin, let alone staying
upright for more than a second or two. This horse was
one in a million. Only with an urgent desire to work
and make a name for himself would a rider attempt to
tame such an animal. Most cowboys valued their lives
above honour and glory. The animal seemed to have a
spleen full of hatred and a killer instinct stronger than
the wildest horses Will had ever ventured to try his
luck on. Maybe, thought Will, doing a little whispering
might relax him up a bit—it's a myth that cowboys
don't believe in the voice of reason.

"Don't you see where I got with the others,
Cind'rella?"

At first, Will had wanted to give him the French
name "Blondasse," but couldn't think of the right word
in English—neither "Blondie" nor "Yellowish" seemed
right. So he called him Cind'rella.

"Wouldn't you like to go take a turn, go out for a
run with the others? They sure do enjoy it. They may
be afraid at first, when I pull out my *latigo* and loop
it over their heads, but they get used to it, right? You
wait and see, it ain't that bad. Wouldn't you like to
sweat a little, go out and run around the bushes and
barrels and stumps? Learn to turn when I ask you?
Terrorize the cattle? It'd give you a new target for that
mean streak of yours. I ain't saying you shouldn't be a
bad guy. Just not with me. We could have some good
fun together, don't you think?"

Cind'rella snorted and shook. The horse had only
half understood what the cowboy was driving at, and

he wasn't about to give Will the satisfaction of seeming to agree. Over the last few days, the buckskin
had grown more accustomed to Will's presence, his
accent, his scent, and his pats on the side, and now
he had to be constantly on his guard to prevent his
being won over — or, at least, to keep the signs of the
struggle raging within to himself.

"Am I really gonna have to treat you like the real
Cinderella? Starve you, beat you, break you? I swear,
I don't want to. No, big feller, maybe I wouldn't go so
far as to say you're a pearl, like Curley does. Man, that
fool straight-up fell in love with you. Though you're a
handsome feller, true enough. And you got yourself
some charm, that's no lie. But all that's just surface
stuff. Even the devil must have charm to spare, I figure,
and there's plenty of pretty women who are stupid, or
cruel. Is that what you are? No better than a pretty,
cruel woman? No better than the devil? Go on, prove
me wrong."

Will reached out toward the horse's pretty blond
mane and pulled away quickly to avoid a nasty bite.

"I should spit in your face. I mean, I ain't paid much.
And here I am supposed to risk the best years of my
life for a knothead like you?"

Will gave him a good, hard slap on the ass. The
horse saw red. He immediately reared back and then
bucked a few times. Curley had witnessed the entire
scene from a distance and ran over, but Will was more
scared than he was hurt.

"Watch out, buddy. You sure you got the right
approach for this stubborn feller?"

"I've tried just about everything."

"Give him a couple more days, he'll come around."

"I wish I could believe it."

Curley patted him on the shoulder. Will climbed up to the highest bar of the corral and rolled himself a smoke. He hadn't eaten anything since morning. The tobacco, at least, killed his appetite. They observed the buckskin for a minute, with his bull neck, hooked nose, and evil eyes. Curley's were shining even brighter than the horse's glossy coat shimmering in the warm, hazy, late afternoon light, and Will knew what that meant: something that didn't often happen in a cowboy's life. He was falling for the buckskin and would do anything to buy him off the ranch, should the opportunity arise. But he certainly couldn't match what the rodeo organizers would be able to pay.

Curley snapped out of his reverie.

"I hope you're hungry. Because I cooked for four," he said.

"You can count on me, I'll scrape the bottom of the very last pot."

They made their way to the bunkhouse, laughing and joshing as they went. Will made fun of Curley's cooking, and Curley razzed Will for his horse-breaking. In their wake, they left a waft of sweat so thick the stench—particularly Will's—seemed to hang in the air. Will hadn't washed his shirt once since his first night as a free man back at the Tarantula. The smell of horses had glued to his skin. He wouldn't have gotten rid of it for anything in the world.

10

After putting in a long day of hard work — Will had taken every horse but Cind'rella out chasing stray dogies, and all of them were growing more responsive and obedient — Curley greeted him with a floral-patterned kitchen apron tied around his waist. He was covered in flour and red stains from head to toe.

"Tough day at the office, honey?" said Curley.

For a few days now they'd been playing at husband and wife, a running joke they wouldn't have dared trying in front of others. For now, the two men were alone in the world.

"Better than you, cooped up in here with your pots and pans, I figger."

"You'll never guess what I found at the back of the cupboard."

"What?"

"A can of tomatoes."

"And?"

"And I'm making us pasta. Pasta, son!"

Will frowned. It wasn't the reaction Curley had been hoping for.

"You ever even tasted Italian pasta—I mean real fresh pasta, made from scratch?"

Will had not. But, come to think of it, he'd no reason to doubt the pasta he'd eaten before was fresh. I mean, why would they serve it to him otherwise?

"Nah, didn't think so."

"What do you take me for?"

"Perdonami!"

Will walked over to the stove, not sure what to think. He had to admit it smelled pretty good.

"Taste this! Taste it."

Curley carefully brought a wooden spoon of boiling sauce to Will's lips. He had a taste, with his eyes closed, and pretended to be totally absorbed in the flavours.

"Damn salty!"

"It'll be perfect with the pasta."

"You call that pasta?" said an astonished Will, pointing at a large baking sheet laid out with something that sure as hell didn't look like any pasta Will had ever eaten: a bunch of cylinder-shaped chunks around a half-inch long and a quarter-inch thick. Unlike macaroni, this pasta wasn't hollow. No two of the shapes were quite the same.

"So you've never eaten gnocchi before?"

"Come again?"

"Gnocchi."

"Can't say I have."

"It's pasta made from potatoes. The gnocchi my mom made with butter and cream were delicious!

You can add whatever you like. But mostly cheese. Lots of cheese."

"You and your stinky cheeses!"

"Takes a real bumpkin to say that, but no matter. You can probably guess we're gonna have to live without Parmesan tonight."

"Fine by me!"

The water in the large pot on the stove was boiling. Curley salted it generously and then put the gnocchi in. The boil resumed a moment later and, one by one, the gnocchi rose to the surface. The cook educated his friend on the sacred art and religious science of cooking pasta correctly, explaining that it was crucial to keep an eye on it and strain it at exactly the right moment. A mere thirty seconds late, and you'd have soggy, overcooked pasta that could by no stretch of the imagination be called *al dente*.

"*Al dente?*"

Curley made a face.

"Not easy to translate that one. Crispy, maybe?"

"Crispy noodles?"

"That's what I said, and really, there's nothing better. You'll understand when you taste it."

Will's expectations were spiralling out of control.

"These gnocchi of yours better be good."

Sadly they weren't. Will was struggling to imagine this potato pasta with a stinky cheese to boot; he figured he was being forced to eat the most disgusting thing he'd been served in his life. But Curley was enjoying it so much he almost forgot to breathe between mouthfuls. He wolfed down a first plate, then a second, and was starting on a third before his pal was able to finish his first helping. Will liked the taste of the sauce, but the limp, doughy texture of the gnocchi turned his stomach. Surely that couldn't be *al dente*? And it was way too salty! While Curley stuffed his face as if he hadn't eaten in weeks, Will chewed laboriously, a fake smile painted on his face.

Curley had eaten so much his stomach felt ready to explode. Once he was done, he came back down to earth and interrogated Will, wanting to know if his cooking had had the same effect on the neophyte in Italian cuisine. Will smiled as best he could and said the first thing that came to mind.

"All that's missing is a good glass of wine."

"Don't remind me! You know my brother-in-law makes his own out in Sonoma. A good Primitivo — dark, kind of peppery. Can't believe how good it is!"

Curley seemed to drift a little, as if he were sipping his brother-in-law's wine at that very moment. His taste buds were filling his mouth with saliva and sending a signal to his sensory memory. He said,

> *And if the Cup you drink, the Lip you press,*
> *End in what All begins and ends in — Yes;*
> *Think then you are To-day what Yesterday,*
> *You were — To-morrow you shall not be less.*

Will gazed up to the heavens as Curley went on:

> *Whether at Naishápúr or Babylon,*
> *Whether the Cup with sweet or bitter run,*

The Wine of Life keeps oozing drop by drop,
The Leaves of Life keep falling one by one.

"Curley!"

"What?"

"You done?"

"Boy, how many times have you heard me recite Omar Khayyám since we've known each other?"

"Once."

"Fine. And don't you like wine?"

"Sure, it's okay, though I prefer the burn of a good whiskey."

Curley's eyes lit up.

"Maybe a little *digestivo* and a game of cards?" said Curley.

Will had hit pay dirt. Just the words he'd been waiting to hear.

"I don't know, Curley," he said. "You don't think that might be trouble?"

"What you talking 'bout—trouble? Do you see anyone else in this here bunk? I've got everything we need right here, enough for a couple of healthy young men such as ourselves to get right roostered."

"Who's talking about getting roostered?"

"In a manner of speaking, that's all. I mean, we could have a drink or maybe two and leave it at that. But then you do got to ask yourself what looks better. They could come back and find us here with a half a jug, and that looks bad, or they could find no jug at all on account of we'd polished it off and tossed it in the creek."

Will looked at him skeptically.

"And what if they did come back tonight?"

"What are you, green? Have you ever once seen a roundup crew come back to camp in the middle of the night?"

"Yessir. When something goes wrong I have."

Curley crossed his arms, regretting that he'd asked his friend to drink with him. Will realized he might have been a little brusque and he eased up.

"Okay, I'll have a little glass—just one. I deserve it, no? 'Cause ain't I been working hard, these past few days. After that, we'll see."

"Now you're talking!"

Curley clapped his buddy on the shoulder and got up out of his chair. He picked up his plate, then noticed that some pasta remained on Will's.

"Another helping?"

"No, I ate enough for two. That pasta sure is filling."

"If you ate for two, I ate for six. What are you saying? That I'm a big fat gluttonous Italian?"

"I didn't say nothing of the sort. But if the hat fits . . ."

"Enough, I got it."

Curley cleared the table and Will rolled a couple of nice-sized cigarettes. He lit one, and tossed the other to his pal. It spun in the air several times and Curley finished drying his hands just in time to catch it.

"You can wash up later," said Will.

"Fair enough. Give me a second."

Curley disappeared into the bedroom, came out a minute later with a half-full jug of liquor, and grabbed

a couple of glasses from the cupboard with his free
hand, smiling like a criminal about to commit an unpar-
donable but thrilling crime. Then he slammed the jug
down on the table in a way that made it clear there
was still plenty to drink — but only if they wanted to,
of course — and poured a good few fingers into each
of their glasses.

"We playing cards?"

"For money?"

"There any point, otherwise?"

"What you thinking of playing?"

"What you think, cowboy?"

"Not poker. I hate poker."

"What else is there?"

In the Dufault family there had only ever been two
card games: Hearts and cribbage.

"There ain't a cribbage board lying around here,
is there?" Will asked.

Curley guffawed.

"A what board?"

"A cribbage —"

"Now what exactly do I look like to you? An English
lord? Saddle up, Bill! We're gonna play some cards."

"I don't know, Curley. It's a nice night. Maybe we
could just take a couple chairs out and enjoy the fresh
air."

"No cards, then."

Curley waited a moment.

"All right then, have it your way," he said.

You could see that Curley was crestfallen. Will
wanted to make his friend happy.

"Maybe later? Right now I'm flat broke. I gave everything I had to poor Dave for that fine hackamore and saddle."

"I'll stake you if you pay me back when we get paid. Worst case — well, best case really — you win, and it's all cream for you. And I tell you, I ain't won for a good long while now. I can keep hoping for my lucky star to come, but I gotta face facts. I'm in a lean patch and it don't appear to be coming to an end any time soon. Started with the evil eye. My wife's. On account of she was tired of seeing me gambling all the time. And didn't that mess with the alignment of the universe — and my luck. It's not like I won that much before, but something changed, something that just don't seem to want to go back to the way things were."

"Maybe you shouldn't, Curley."

"I know! But what can you do. Just can't stay away from the poker table. Like a moth to a flame."

Will had pulled a chair outside with one hand, holding his glass in the other. And to continue telling his story, Curley had done the same. Almost reflexively, they were sitting outside on what could pass for a porch — or, as Khayyám would put it, a terrace. Either way, no more than a few dusty boards lying on top of the ground.

Will rolled another cigarette. He didn't have to look to see what his hands were doing — he could have rolled in total darkness without spilling even the tiniest leaf — and preferred to contemplate the immensity above, instead. The North Star was perched high in the sky, seemingly on its own, illuminating a large part of the bluish sky. Lower down, the majestic Ursa Major was watching over her offspring. It had taken some time for Will to get used to calling the constellation by its English name, the Big Dipper, rather than the "Great Bear," as the French more faithfully did.

"Care for another?"

"Don't mind if I do."

"As I was saying," said Curley, interrupting Will's reverie, "Minnie's perfect. I love her. I love her, I really do. Don't know how I could even live in a world where she didn't exist. I told you she gave me the evil eye, but plenty of women would have done worse."

"What are you saying?"

"Do you know a lot of married women who let their man go out working for months on end, far from home?"

"Really, did she have a choice?"

"We've always got a choice, Bill. She could ask me to change my life, change my job, go work in a factory, do absolutely anything—whatever I want, but within a mile of Bishop."

"You still live in Bishop?"

"Yeah, why?"

"I don't know, didn't you tell me your mom moved back to San Francisco after your dad died? I figured you and your wife lived there too."

"Ha, can you imagine me living in the city? One of my brothers bought the family ranch, and everyone lives there except my mama. How could she look after herself in the country? She comes to see us a lot, sometimes spends whole weeks at the farm, but for a

single woman—a widow—there's much more to see
and do in town. And all the Italian grocers are there,
selling everything she used to eat as a kid."

Curley paused a moment.

"What was I saying again?"

Will was hard-pressed to remember.

"You were talking about your wife?"

"Yeah."

Curley downed his glass. Will didn't need to have
his arm twisted to do the same. He was expecting a
few more verses of Omar Khayyám. But no.

"A nice little wife for you, Bill, ain't you ever
tempted?"

Will bit into his lip with his left canine, squinting
his eye closed on the same side.

"Sure! Why not? One of these days."

Will was blushing. He'd never given any serious
thought to marriage, dogged as he was by an irrational
fear of being a bad lover destined to be unmasked
by a wife—by all the women in the world, really. It
was a fear that never left him. Even on those rare
occasions when he had the chance to get to know a
member of the fairer sex intimately—ladies who were
not always drawn from the most respectable ranks
of society—the experience was far from memorable
for either party.

Curley raised his glass. Will did the same.

"To your future wife, my friend."

"To my wife."

"There must be one for you out there somewhere—
good-looking guy like you."

They raised their glasses again.

"Brr. One more?"

"And why the hell not?"

The two cowmen listened reverently to the music of the liquor flowing into their glasses.

11

The glasses were emptying as fast as the two cowboys could fill them, and the conversation on that starry blue night, like that on the shady veranda of Wellington Mercantile ten days earlier, careered freely from subject to subject. Curley was slurring and even weaving as he paced back and forth. He was talking about his mother, a highborn woman who'd taken charge of her children's instruction when she'd decided she couldn't trust the public school education on offer in Bishop, California. His mother was a difficult and demanding woman and gave her children a rigorous education, one that included music lessons in the evening. Each child had to practise at least five hours a week—hours religiously recorded in her little notebook.

Will had already heard the story but it seemed best not to point out to Curley that he was repeating himself.

To feign his great interest and curiosity, Will furrowed his brow and nodded his head at each new tidbit. Curley elaborated and digressed until he arrived at his maternal grandmother, someone who'd loomed large in the Fletcher household, and who had criticized her daughter relentlessly from sunup to sundown.

"And if she was hard on her daughter, she hated my father even worse. Swear to God, Will. Those two—*hic!*—they were at it like cats and dogs!"

"She still with us?"

"No, but she outlived my father. I swear being a horrible person only makes you live longer. Swear it on the Holy Bible!"

"When you put it that way, I'm not sure I want to live long."

"Same here! But I gotta say that there wasn't much she could do about it. Just the way she was. Believe me, Will, we change so little in life. No point fretting. We come into the world at a certain place and time, and who knows who raises us. Our days are counted, and there's only so much play in the lasso. Really, I don't think we're even able to change, to be anything other than who we are, deep down. Just like horses."

"Are you comparing your grandma to a horse, now?"

"Don't go putting words in my mouth!"

Curley paused for effect.

"That said, horses got better breath!"

That cracked them up, the two of them braying like donkeys and slapping their thighs, egging each other on with peals of laughter until Curley, red-eyed, was almost choking. Will clapped him on the back, as if that might help, even stroked it a little as he collected his wits, his composure, his legendary self-possession.

"You know," said Will, "there are times when I figger..."

He watched his friend catch his breath and wipe away a tear with his index finger.

"There are times I think the opposite, that maybe we can't change deep down, and yet still... in the things we do, in the present moment, every day we *can* choose to be someone else."

Curley sat up.

"I'm listening."

Will hesitated. He'd said everything he had to say.

"I dunno. What about you, when you're writing?"

"What about it?"

"Ain't you off in another place somewhere? Inventing some hidden world, something that didn't exist before you made it? You're telling other people: 'Lookee here, this is who I am. Add this to the rest of me, at least a little bit.' And then tomorrow, if you chose to, you could become a mineral prospector just like that, give up writing poetry altogether."

"I could, but it wouldn't really change me none."

"That's what I'm saying. But it'd change your—what do they call it—change your *persona*. And something would change. Think of all those people that inspire us, who've been everywhere, done it all. We see them differently."

"That makes a little sense. I guess."

Curley was fanning himself with his hat occasionally, struggling every time to put it back on. He felt a real affinity for this Will James; it was as if they were destined to be lifelong friends. Will's mendacity with

Dave Reed was water under the bridge. Only later, when he was putting together the pieces of his new opinion of the man, would he remember it. But on this drunken night he recognized Will as a brother. And you didn't find a new brother every day. If he'd listened to his heart he would have grabbed Will, squeezed him tight, and told him he loved him, because he did. Will understood and they avoided meeting each other's eye. Curley changed the subject, and stifled the idea that had been on his mind for days now.

"So how about that game of cards, then?"

"Please, Curley, enough of that!"

"Why not? A moment ago you said you might want to have a game a little later."

Will took a deep breath and then stubbed out his cigarette on his heel.

"Listen . . . I'd really like to talk to you about something a little, well, sorta touchy."

He knew what he wanted to do that night.

"And maybe after, we could have ourselves a little game?" he said.

Curley stood up. His eyes had a dead, glassy look, his eyelids were drooping, and he was trying to suss out his friend.

"I'm listening," he said.

Will looked down the neck of the bottle.

"Oh, I don't know."

Will stared at the point of his boot.

"I'm gonna need some help, I guess."

"Help?"

"Yeah, some help," said Will.

"Not with the horses, I hope. You don't want me to mount the buckskin?"

Curley sounded beseeching.

"No, no," said Will. "It's something personal."

Will grimaced. He was nodding, and swaying his upper body back and forth.

"It won't cost you nothing."

"Spill the beans, kid."

"I really want to talk about it with you, but you're gonna have to be...understanding. And discreet. Real discreet. You know that I trust you, right?"

"All right, you got me interested."

"Oh, I dunno, Curley. Let me think it over a minute."

"*Hic!* This your way of making sure I say yes right off the top?"

"No, it ain't that," said Will. "Look, forget it. You're right, let's just have a game of cards, and if I got something to tell you, you'll find out soon enough."

"It don't work that way, Will."

"Let's just leave it be. Like you said."

Will stopped talking, and Curley didn't push him. They rolled their smokes and filled their glasses in silence. The cicadas were stridulating, performing their evening concert to whoever thought to listen. It was late. Morning would come sooner than either man wanted—especially Will, who'd have to get back to tending the horses and be bearing the extra weight of a hangover. He shut his eyes and inhaled deeply, breathing in the night air as if it might do away with his drunkenness. He grew dizzy again. Curley was staring at him.

"So what about this favour, then?"

"Curley—*hic!* Just let it go," Will implored.

"What, you don't think I see what you're up to?"

"I ain't up to nothing! Who do you take me for?"

Will was being straight. He was relenting. He hated the idea of getting his friend caught up in his lies. He'd spoken too soon.

"You've come too far to turn back now," said Curley. "You don't think I want to know what you were gonna tell me?"

"You sure you want to?" asked Will.

"So long as we get there before the sun comes up!"

"Thing is, I'm gonna need you to give me your word. You're gonna listen to the whole story before judgin' me. And you're gonna have an open mind as I explain, and above all you're gonna swear never to tell another living soul what I'm going to tell you today."

"*Whoa.*"

"I got your word?"

But Curley shook his head.

"You can't ask that of anybody, Will. Not before they know what it is you're talking about."

"Great then. I'll manage."

"Hang on, hang on! All I'm saying is that you're demanding a lot even before you've asked whatever it is you want of me. Now I'll swear on my honour— *hic!*—you got my word: I'll take whatever you tell me to my grave...if you tell me. Even Minnie won't ever know a thing. But the rest—not judging you, keeping an open mind—I'll sure try, but I don't even know what it is you're gonna tell me. So maybe you tell me

you're a socialist, maybe even a punk. How am I supposed to take that, Will?"

"I ain't no socialist!"

Will had no idea what the word "socialist" meant.

"Well that don't mean you ain't the other—
hic!—thing."

Will looked up to the sky. Curley had hit the bottle
hard, it was starting to show, and he wasn't letting up.

"You got something to ask me, ask away. You know
damn well I'd never turn you down. Only thing I judge
you for is beating around the bush like this!"

Will put on his kid gloves.

"Well, sorry if I had to do it this way. I figgered I
didn't have a choice. You'd understand better if you
knew."

"Spit it out!"

"Look, I don't know how to tell you this, but I was
thinking since your mom lives in San Francisco and
you're still in touch with her, I was thinking...I mean I
figgered that...do you think...do you think maybe you
could post her a letter I'd written? Send her a letter
and ask her to mail it to someone on my behalf, like?"

Curley's head turned, as if to make sure he'd heard
right.

"I'm not sure I get it, Will."

"It's not all that complicated."

"So fill me in. What's stopping you from mailing
that letter yourself?"

His voice faltering, Will explained that the letter in
question, which hadn't yet been written, was intended
for the Dufault family in Montreal. That the Dufaults,

the extended family of the man who'd raised him, were pretty much the only family Will had, though he'd only seen them once or twice, growing up. They'd never stopped writing and, he had to confess, he'd lied to them in his last letters by not mentioning that he'd been locked up. They believed he was in San Francisco, going to art school.

Curley followed Will's convoluted story with his eyes closed. His nose was scrunched up and a constellation of wrinkles had appeared on his face. Will wished he could disappear.

"I didn't want to worry them. Didn't want to hurt them for no good reason. That's all."

"Look," said Curley, "I'd like to help. And I almost understand you. But do you really think if you send the letter from here, they're going to go looking at the postmark?"

"You never know. I'd like to make sure it don't happen, though."

Curley looked contemplative. Clearly there was a skeleton in the closet, and the body was not done decomposing. It didn't smell right. Stank, in fact. This kind of request was the last thing he'd been expecting but, at the same time, what wouldn't he do for a friend? Very little, fair to say.

"Okay then, Will. Give me the letter. I'll write one to my mama too and explain what's going on."

Will's shoulders relaxed, and his eyes closed again.

"We've gotta let her know as little as possible, Curley. I know it's a lot to ask, I know it seems odd. But I'm only trying to keep certain people happy. Older folks, who ain't in such a good way. I'd never want to hurt them..."

"And what if they want to answer? Where they gonna send their letter, then?"

Will opened his eyes wide.

"Would it bother you if I told them I lived at your mother's place? They could write me at her address, and I could go to San Francisco some day and pick up my mail, why not? Or if we're still riding together a while, she could send them to you, I guess."

"I don't know, Will."

Will gave him a pleading look.

"Well, I guess after—*hic!*—after everything..."

Curley, if reluctantly, had accepted.

"What you looking at?" he said.

Will was all smiles.

"After all," said Will, "it's not...it's not as if you'd never lied to your old mother before."

Will's kidding left Curley cold as stone.

"You're wrong there, Bill. I ain't never lied to her. Never once."

Will lowered his gaze and looked down at the floorboards of the porch. Mostly for effect, though guilt was gnawing at him.

"Have a drink," said Curley, laughing. "It'll pass."

Will heard his friend and immediately took a drink straight from the jug, the biggest swig of whiskey he'd ever taken, the biggest swig ever taken by any man—something in the neighbourhood of twelve ounces of contrition, burning his throat right down to the pit of his stomach with the hottest-burning fire of all, one that would keep right on burning long into the next day, when his head would be throbbing and his body unbearably dehydrated too. His guts were tied up in a knot.

Curley straightened up in his chair. He wasn't sure how to react. His friend almost spilled the jug when he put it back on the table, and Curley wondered whether he wasn't going to heave everything up on his boots, from the cups of liquor to every last bite of gnocchi and even the eggs they'd had for breakfast that morning.

"Come on then, Curley — *hic!* — it's your turn."

"What?"

Curley didn't see what his friend meant.

"Drink . . . drink . . . drink up . . . like . . . like I did."

"I don't feel like it."

"You said it — *hic!* You said we better not leave a single drop."

"I don't think those were the words I used."

"Well, your Khayyám said so — he did!"

Will shoved the bottle Curley's way, his riposte seeming to have had some effect. Curley lifted the jug up good and high, and then even higher for a second swig, though the two combined didn't come close to half the volume of liquid Will had just imbibed.

"Pour me out a couple glasses," stammered Will.

"Say what?"

"Pour 'em out — *hic!*" Will growled.

His friend listened.

"Again."

"Again?"

"Again!"

Curley poured one more finger into Will's glass.
The jug was a good deal lighter. Will knocked back
his drink in one gulp and then focused intently on
his friend, to the extent that he was capable. Curley
understood he'd be in for a scolding if he didn't keep
up, and emptied his glass. Will pounded the table so
hard the jug almost flew onto the ground.

"You there—*hic!*"

His squinty eyes were bloodshot and crazy-looking.

"You okay, Bill?"

"Shuddup. Never better. You, guy—*hic!*"

The scene was funny enough, but Curley wouldn't
have dared reveal even the hint of a smile. Especially
when he saw the revolver Will was cradling. *His*
revolver.

"Where'd you get that, Will?"

"In your—*hic!*—stuff!"

"There something I'm missing here, Will?"

"Not at all. If you knew..."

Curley knew nothing. If, since he'd left Montreal,
Will had met a single person he thought he could
trust, it was Curley Fletcher. No doubt about it. But a
chill had descended on the evening's conversation and
suddenly Will felt alone in the world. A lot more years
would go by before he'd meet someone else he thought
could be a friend, and now here he was, losing one.

"You," said Will, "you, I like you, I really do."

"Put the gun away, Bill. Would you?"

"Whassa magic word?"

"The magic word? Please, Bill?" said Curley, slowly
and carefully.

Will was overcome by an indescribable sadness. He was devastated, and passed the gun over, butt first.

"Thank you."

"Less finish the bottle."

"You sure, Will?"

"Don't make me have to take your Peacemaker by force! Pour 'em out!"

Curley poured the liquor into his partner's glass, and seconds later it was already empty, as if he'd not filled it at all. Now Will was trying to roll cigarettes. No easy feat in the state he was in. Curley wanted to help and Will let himself be pushed around, like a child.

"You think — *hic!* — you'll be able to work tomorrow?" Curley asked.

"Sure thing! Course I will."

"Stop it, Will."

"You're right — *hic!* I'll look like a right fool on the back of your buckskin. But trust me. A few hours' sleep — *hic!* — and I'll be good as new."

"You sure?"

"Trust me, I'm telling you. *Hic!*"

Will's face brightened up.

"Hey. Shall we go see 'em?"

"See who?"

"The horses, that's who. Shit. Who else?"

They lit their smokes and stood up nervously. Any more and Will would have fallen off his chair, never to rise again.

"Bring the jug," he ordered.

And the two hiccupping friends staggered off into the black night. Curley couldn't stop himself grabbing

Will by the shoulder and whispering a few lines of
Khayyám's.

> *I will drink so much wine . . . that this aroma of wine*
> *Shall rise from the earth when I am . . . beneath it;*
> *. . . when a drinker shall pass above my body,*
> *He shall become drunk . . . from the aroma of my*
> > *potations.*

"No one ever wrote another thing that beautiful . . .
hic!"

The writers of the world could eat their hearts out,
drop their pens. But not Curley Fletcher:

> *. . . the veil of our*
> *shame is torn in such a manner that it cannot*
> > *be repaired.*

The metaphor of the veil hit Will less powerfully
than the previous verse. The Persian poet's obsession
with tent cloth and dusty pottery left him indifferent.
Will wasn't encouraging his friend to keep on reciting.

Their eyes were soon accustomed to the darkness,
the shadowy forms of the mountains a reassuring presence in the distance. Millions of stars shone in the
cloudless sky, and the moon, their guide, led them
to the corrals.

"Brrr!" said Will, rubbing his arms.

12

The silhouettes of the horses were indiscernible until they were right up next to the corral. One of them trotted off to the far side, snorting and kicking up dust. They watched the cretinous humans with their usual expression of irked disgust.

Their animosity was palpable. Some had been lying down sleeping moments before, dreaming of verdant pastures only to be rudely awoken by two bumbling imbeciles barely capable of standing. The wildest of the horses, roaming paradoxically free within the confines of his sleep, was loath to return to miserable reality, had been picturing gliding over the region in flight, brushing up against the peaks of the highest mountains, buoyed up by the wings of gigantic, formidable, and powerful angels who, once set in motion, would cast a shadow over the entire valley, their every heartbeat setting off a tornado upon the earth below. The horse was ready to kill.

"*Hic!* They're funny, all the same," Will mumbled. "Pass me that jug."

Will was still drinking furiously, though the liquor burning on its way down, then going straight to his head and wreaking havoc with his mind, was beyond intense, and brought to mind the lye he'd ingested as a child years earlier. Maybe it was time to contain his ardour. He passed the jug back to Curley.

Leaning with their elbows on the fence — or, more accurately, with their whole bodies up against the fence — they called the geldings, but without much response. Frustrated at their being ignored, Will chucked the end of his cigarette at one of them. Instead of a reprimand, this elicited a hearty laugh from Curley.

"C'mon, boys—*hic!* Shit, c'mon over," he pleaded.

"Let it go," said Will. "You can see they—*hic!*— they don't want nothing to do with us."

"Let's go see the buckskin."

"Really?" said Will.

"Why not? *Hic!* Might as well while he's around."

"You miss him?"

Gamely, they took a few steps forward, one after another and each one feeling like an achievement. The big buckskin wasn't sleeping, and hadn't been since he'd heard the approach of the men and the verbal flatulence of which only their species was capable, notorious throughout the animal kingdom for its empty prattle and ignominious vapidity. Curley lit a match and held it at the end of his outstretched arm, and was (just about) able to see by its light a mass of hatred, the most beautiful mass of blond hatred he'd ever set eyes on. The cowboy bent his head forward, eyes gleaming and his lips pouting slightly. Will stood back, enjoying the show, and rolled himself another cigarette.

"Roll me one of those, will you? I can't see straight."

"And you think I can?"

Thirty seconds later the crackling of the lit match again ripped into the silence of the night. Now it was the buckskin's turn to have a good look at their faces. Sure enough, these were his two tormentors. The men had to wait a moment for their eyes to readjust to the darkness.

"Now, ain't this horse one of the finest specimens ever to walk the dry California earth?"

"I guessss—*hic!*"

"That was a *rhetorical* question. I don't give a damn what you think about him."

Curley clicked his tongue against the roof of his mouth, twice, each time extracting a little saliva, and Cind'rella made a come-hither face. The buckskin stopped short the second Curley stretched his arm into the corral. He imagined snapping off the intruder's arm. Maybe another day. His time had not yet come.

"Anyway, him—*hic!* He loves you, for sure."

"He just don't know it yet!"

That made Will laugh. Curley appeared to believe it wholeheartedly.

"Really, Bill. Really?"

"Sure thing—*hic!*"

Now anger got the better of Curley.

"All right, first things first. There's everything you

don't see in him. Then—*hic!*—there's the danger
if you don't manage to tame him at all. He's at the
crossroads, old partner."

"You're laying it on a little thick, ain't you?"

"No," Curley insisted, shaking his head emphati-
cally. "Want to hear a secret? You already gone told
me one. Now it's my turn."

Will was interested.

"I'm listening," he said.

"That there horse is mine."

Curley had raised a finger.

"Maybe not yet, but he will be. I've known it since
the moment I laid eyes on him. *Hic!* And I got myself
a plan."

"Seems clear as spring water, then," Will said.

"You don't understand. I'll steal him if I have to.
For now, though, I'm just letting him be."

"Why?"

"They'll take him away if I let them know how much
he means to me."

Curley said it with the deep sadness of a person
facing a travesty of justice.

"They'll take him away?" said Will.

"You know their sort. For sure, the foreman is
gonna ask me to sell him. Not right away. But he'll
suspect something. He'll put his best rider on him, and
you know what'll happen to him. And the next one—
hic!—and then the next—*hic!* And finally they'll realize there's nothing to be done with that buckskin."

Will saw where Curley was heading and let him
run with it.

"So the ranch will have a choice: sell him to me, their humble employee—and not for too much, since I'll be the one asking. Or else they could get three times as much from the rodeo men. That's how it works. It don't matter that I've been working for them for—*hic!*—for years. Money talks, amigo."

Will tried to reassure him.

"Seems to me, a horse like that—rodeo is where he belongs," said Will. "We could never get him to do much else."

Curley took a princely swig.

"Maybe—*hic!* You might be right. But I ain't sure. Not yet. I reckon a man like you just might be able to do something with a horse like that."

"What do you want from me, Curley? *Hic!* Tell me that much."

Curely's eyelids had drooped so much they were almost completely shut. He scratched his nose, then did his best to straighten up again.

"Nothing simpler—*hic!*"

"Well..." said Will. His breath would have woken the dead.

"You gotta gentle him."

Will nodded.

"You gotta ride him."

Will was on board so far.

"You gotta break him in before the guys get back, and you gotta be able to stay in the saddle when the bossman is watching. At least once. Enough so—so they can mount him too. It don't have to be easy," said Curley, weaving back and forth. "They gotta be able to mount him without getting trampled to death by this devil of a horse."

"We can only hope!"

"It'll be easy. Listen up."

The guys would all give it a go, and they'd all see that there was nothing to be done with this ridgling. Everyone would come to the conclusion that a horse like this was only worth the trouble if it was going to be the property of one man, and none of them would have the patience to be that man. Curley would work with the buckskin a while, make him his, and then man and horse would be associated with each other for ever more.

"You know how — *hic!* — how these things work!"

"I guess," muttered Will hesitantly.

"All I need to do is suggest I buy him. Then I could have him all to myself!" By the time he'd finished, his eyes were as round as silver dollars.

A whole bunch of objections looped around in Will's head, then made their way to his lips. He opened his mouth, with a hand in the air to signal Curley to hang on, then closed it again before even a word came out.

Curley said his piece:

"That's the horse I've been waiting for my whole life, Will. And I need your help."

Will now understood that Curley hadn't been letting him work the buckskin out of the goodness of his heart. Yet at the end of the day, the horse counted for less than a stranger in a bind whom Curley had saved from the purgatory of life on a dairy farm. Will sniffled. He was so moved he could barely speak.

"I'd sure like to help, Curley—*hic!*—but I've got my reputation to think of. Think what would happen if they ever figger out what's going on."

"You owe me one, Bill."

Curley had a point, and Will gave in. He turned toward that nightmare on four legs, and looked him in the eye: lightning on a cold night, but not a lightning of defiance. He even thought he could see a hint of curiosity in the buckskin's eyes. Will's bobbing head settled a moment, as if the better to think things over, suss out the situation from the depths of his inebriation.

"Watch me then," he cawed.

Will straddled the top bar of the corral. Even that took some doing. Cind'rella watched the scene, without batting an eye.

"Bill..."

"Trust me—*hic!* I've been working on him for days," he muttered as he held out an arm toward the jute sack.

"C'mon over here, big feller. Come see me."

And he clicked his tongue, just like Curley had done a few minutes earlier. To both men's great surprise, the horse ambled over—not with the joy of a lover approaching the object of his adoration after a long absence, mind you, but still with his head bowed and a certain determination in his step.

"Hold my smoke."

Curley took it.

"Okay, big feller," Will whispered. "C'mon over here."

It would have been hard to say what was on the mind of the hook-nosed buckskin with suppurating knee wounds. The main thing was that he came over to Will and let the cowboy stroke him with the jute sack, as had been Will's habit over the past few days. Emboldened, Will reached a hand onto his forehead, then behind his ear. The original didn't fight back. Curley was speechless. Even if he had the words, he wouldn't have uttered them. The horse gently backed away, without trying to bite even once. Will couldn't believe it, went so far as to call the buckskin back. Cind'rella ignored him.

"He's had enough."

"Hold on — *hic!*"

Will called him back one more time, whistling through hands cupped like a megaphone. He swung his arms to beckon the buckskin over but his histrionic gestures threw him off balance and he soon found himself on the ground, on the other side of the fence. The tumble hadn't been too violent. At least, that's what he tried to convince himself once he stood up and dusted himself off.

"*Hic!* Anything left in that jug?"

Curley frowned, did the math.

"About one drink apiece."

"Drink 'em back at the cabin?"

"Your call — *hic!*"

Will looked up at the sky. In one direction, black was turning a deep blue. A few pink streaks were already visible. It was maybe five in the morning, and in less than an hour or two, on this glorious May morning of 1916, dawn would break and the sun would illuminate the mountains that marked the limits of the RR Ranch and then the valley they found themselves in now. They already knew the scene by heart. The vistas had lodged themselves in their memories — images they'd be able to summon at will, years later.

"*Hic!*"

The coals of the campfire next to the cabin were still glowing red. They hit their bunks, as if drawn by a magnetic force, without bothering to drink their last shot. They collapsed and were as still as corpses, good disciples of Omar Khayyám. They may well have communed with God, or at least attained godliness, as God is present in all things — even whiskey.

13

In deference to their hangovers and burning throats, Will and Curley might have slept until eleven, but they considered themselves men of their word and hadn't been hired to sleep, so for better or worse they dragged themselves out of bed at nine, ready to work. And work they did. Curley shored up a stretch of the fence while Will tackled the last two horses still convinced that not a man on this earth would manage to ride them. The cowboys were busy congratulating themselves for setting about their various tasks when, just before noon, the boss of the RR rode up ahead of twenty men and two hundred head of horses. The team was driving several thousand head of cattle. Will and Curley heard them long before they saw them: a thunderous noise in a cloud of dust. To Will's ears it was the prettiest music there was, and to his eyes, the scene was truly magical.

He did a double take when he saw the portly cook lumber out of the kitchen wagon and realized it was none other than Big Moose Tim, terror of the cook-pots. The man himself. Will went over.

"*Chef,*" he said, pronouncing the word as the French would. "Amazing, is it really you?!"

Big Moose Tim couldn't find his hat. He placed his right hand above his eyes like a visor, and stared out at the cowboy with his myopic eyes. His bushy moustache and lips shook up and down.

"Will James. *William James!*"

"Who else?"

"Well now, I don't believe my eyes! Hell! What's it been? Five years?"

His voice carried so powerfully you would have sworn he was yelling.

"At least, Chief. *At least.*"

"You mind telling me what the hell you're doing in this godforsaken place?"

"I should be asking you that question. You get lost on your way somewhere?"

Big Moose Tim had always worked for outfits in Oregon, Montana, or Northern Nevada, which was where he'd met Will James years earlier.

"You know, I needed a little change."

The cook took a couple steps forward, unable to suppress a devilish smile, and landed a hearty punch on the shoulder of the young man never quite able to shed that accent of his. At least, after all these years, he didn't have that shy, stultified look anymore.

"You're on top of the world now, eh?" said Big Moose Tim as he lit an old cigarillo with a soaked end. "It's been a good couple years since anyone's heard a thing from you. What, did you up and disappear?"

Tim had caught wind that Will was in prison, and his mischievous smile and the twinkle in his eyes beneath brows as bushy as his moustache were enough to let Will know the cook was having some fun with him.

"Everyone thought you were dead—or worse! Gone to live in the city, maybe working some shoe factory. Coming home crying to your mama every night."

"If I didn't respect you like I do, Moose...I'd make you eat those words. Watch yourself, I'm not your flunky!"

Big Moose Tim smiled heartily, showing two rows of battered teeth. His fists were clenched. He was like a tinderbox waiting for a spark.

"Everything okay here, Tim?" asked the foreman, Jeff Nicks, mounted on his black horse. "Who might this be?"

The foreman had a slender moustache that must have required a lot of grooming.

"Not to worry, Jeff. Just a friendly argument I'm picking up right where this good-for-nothing Will James and I left it."

"Will James?"

"Will James," explained Curley, approaching his boss. "The bullbat I hired to break those broncs. I wrote to Bridgeport. Mr. Rickey knows."

"What about Reed—where's he at?" Nicks asked.

Will, still staring at the cook, butted in.

"Back home and hiding in his mama's skirts, I suspect. He hurt himself pretty good in the knee. Wasn't much help anyway."

Nicks hawked up an impressive stream of gob. He chewed on horseback and smoked on solid ground.

"I told him not to hire that punk. Just goes to show, never hire a man his father or uncle or mama or some acquaintance of his neighbour recommends. Them guys flop out like pancakes, every time."

"James replaced Reed and he's doin' pretty good with the broncs."

"Job was supposed to be done when we got back. Is it?"

Will stepped forward and held Nicks's big black by the bridle while the foreman dismounted.

"I'm near done. Most of 'em'll follow a hand signal or even the eyes, and they've got just one thing on their mind—chasing cattle."

"We'll see soon enough," said Nicks, who appeared more than a little happy to have his boots on the ground after such a long journey. He was sizing Will up, looking relaxed, and his face seemed to open up as he sensed that the young man in front of him was not afraid of hard work. He had an eye for that sort of thing. The only thing he wondered about was the kid's accent.

"You got something on the fire, Curley?" Nicks asked. "Tim's almost out of chuck. Nothing left but bread, and the men are hungry."

"I don't know that I have enough for twenty, boss. There's some leftover stew and a double batch of beans that ain't too old. Give me half an hour and I could rustle something up."

"That'll give us time to wash up and stretch our legs. Ask the flunky to give you a hand."

Curley had been planning on it. The cook's flunky rushed over. He was a lanky, pale guy with a downcast gaze and bent back.

Finally, the men got to enjoy a decent midday meal of pork and beans with bread. The lucky ones, the first to get in line, managed to snag a hunk of meat from the almost rotten stew Curley had served Will a few days earlier. Cubes of spoiling meat floated in the gruel that, for understandable reasons, the two men had decided not to touch. Will put a slice of bread in the oven, a fluffy treat he hadn't enjoyed in days. He felt like telling Tim the story of the pasta but kept it to himself, not wanting to offend the guy who'd been feeding him for the last two weeks.

Once the men had had enough to eat, they went for a nap in the bunks or just dozed off on the spot where they'd taken their last bite. After weeks of hard work, the impulse to rest was overpowering. Jeff Nicks had difficulty not following suit, and in no time he too was sound asleep, snoring in his chair, cigar ash falling onto the handsome shirt that had one day been clean. When Will coughed, the man leaped up, as if ready to charge after days in the trenches—a word that was in the air these days, starting to intrude upon the North American imagination.

"What was I saying?"

"Nothing at all, Mr. Nicks. Nothing at all."

He relit his cigar and almost nodded off again, but managed to control himself.

"Curley, did you brew that coffee before or after the Civil War?"

"Not far off, Chief. Want a cup?"

"Don't mind if I do."

Will and Curley also took a minute to enjoy a good cup of strong coffee. All morning, Will's hands had been shaking like leaves in the wind. Sometimes he had the impression, sweat on his face and his eyes spotted with yellow, that he was about to faint, like his centre of gravity wouldn't hold. Every second they could buy was putting off the inevitable moment when he'd have to prove himself. Curley, in the same sorry state, was even more aware of this than Will.

"You know, Jeff, we wouldn't go telling anyone if the sandman came to pay you a little visit. Lord knows you deserve it."

"Oh, I'd like that, Fletcher. Really, I would. I'll catch some shut-eye later though. I want to see these new horses right away."

Curley didn't flinch. He shouldn't have spoken, and regretted having proffered a choice. Nicks managed to stand up. He sniffed around, with his nose in the air, and then asked the question that had been on his mind since he first set foot in the bunkhouse.

"You boys didn't by any chance get into the liquor, did you?"

"What do you take us for, Jeff?"

"Cowboys, Fletcher. A couple of cowboys."

"Well you're mistaken, sir. With all due respect, we didn't touch a drop," Will assured him.

"And yet there's that smell, like a distillery barrel, filling up the room. I could swear it's coming off your bodies."

But Nicks seemed to lose interest in the question the moment Big Moose Tim walked back into the bunkhouse.

"If you like, boss, I'll make a run to Coleville, pick up some fixings for supper and for the week. If not, we'll have to water down the inedible soup that *Eyetalian* has the nerve to call beans."

"As you like, Tim."

Big Moose waited, tapping his feet with his legs crossed.

"What," said the boss, annoyed.

"Them victuals won't pay for themselves."

Reluctantly, Nicks handed over money for the cook to buy supplies.

"Don't forget canned peaches," said Nicks.

He turned away from the cook.

"What say, boys, should we go see if this new kid knows his way around the corral?"

Not many stirred, let alone answered. The men his question did wake up made like they hadn't heard. Not that they weren't interested. An unknown cowboy — a greenhorn, even better — going up against a bronc with all the talent he could summon, now that was a spectacle. Only, for later. Sometime later. Maybe tomorrow.

Big Moose Tim turned and gave Will a wink.

"I'd like to see how this young'un has come along. Coleville ain't so far. He was already a good rider before he even had hair on his face."

"I'm not your mother," was all the bossman had to say about it.

Will James, Curley Fletcher, Big Moose Tim, and Jeff Nicks went outside, squinted in the sunlight, and headed for the main corral.

"First off, show me what you can do with those strays you say you broke."

"Gentled, sir. Not broke."

Nicks pretended not to hear. He snorted, spat out a thin stream of phlegm, but his little show didn't intimidate Will at all. He entered the corral, a bridle in hand and a saddle under his arm, thinking fast. Instead of heading for the easiest mount, he chose a young horse who he knew had a bit of a wild streak, one of the wildest in the herd — Whiskey by name, a pretty white-legged bay who was still giving Will a run for his money. He bridled the horse, saddled it up, and mounted without a hitch. The horse didn't buck much, but the bay was an antsy one, and knew what it meant when this two-legged terror mounted him. Nicks himself opened the corral gate and, when the horse trotted by, gave him a slap on the ass. Whiskey bolted. But Will was expecting as much. Horse and rider headed off to where the cattle were peacefully grazing and enjoying the time they had to get stirred up before their masters came for them. Will twirled a lasso above the horse's head. Whiskey knew what that meant as well. His eyes opened wide, his blood started racing, his ears rolled back and his nostrils flared: he was thirsty to get the better of these cattle now. The calves bolted. One of them broke off from the herd and the horse caught sight of it as fast as his rider. In no time, they brought it back around, although the cow was giving everything it had. The loop fell, tightened, and Whiskey responded as he'd been trained to do: didn't come to a sudden halt, or pull too hard in the opposite direction. When Will jumped off to free the furious calf, Whiskey stayed by his side and waited calmly for his rider to get back on him. Once Will was back in the saddle, he rubbed the bay's neck to thank him, and the horse liked that. They were on the move again. Will wanted to show Nicks that, even though the geldings could be skittish and jumpy, they'd been trained for the corral, for patrolling and for sorting—though seeing that every new head brought in stuck with the herd, "sorting" would eventually mean cutting loose the calves that were too young, the fertile cows, and the mothers that had grown too old, and sending the others to be branded. The next step after that was the dinner plate.

The boss liked what he saw, but knew better than to let it show. Nicks had learned to wear the expression of a man who'd seen it all, but he was impressed. This kid knew how to break horses. Or *gentle* 'em, as he called it. From time to time Curley sang the praises of his protegé, though he was careful not to lay it on too thick. Nicks listened without objection, since Curley didn't get too carried away. The horse and its rider turned around and headed back toward the buildings. Some of the hands had gathered to watch. When he saw them, Will understood he was being observed, and liked it. If he was going to show his stuff, why not do so in front of a crowd? He minded his posture, sat up straight and proud in the saddle,

hat pulled down to his ears, and adjusted his black
bandana. With the look of the most confident man
in the world, he was hard put not to blink in order to
protect his eyes from the biting wind. He was powerless against the reflex.

After untacking Whiskey, Will asked the boss what
he thought.

"So?"

"Not bad," was all the foreman said.

Will lowered his head. Why did all these bosses
have to be such killjoys. Weren't they all on the same
team?

"If that's all for today, Mr. Nicks, I'd like to keep
on doing what you're paying me for."

"Hold on, there, James — it's James, right?"

"Sure is."

"I'd like to see what you do with one that hasn't
been gentled yet."

"What for?" Curley protested. "You can see as well
as I can this here's the man for the job."

Nicks was tempted to back down. He'd sussed the
new hand's character right away, and his first impression had been vindicated. The kid had a natural talent
impossible to explain, a gift denied men who'd try their
whole lives to attain it, and that others, surpassing all
expectations, had in spades. Jeff almost let Will go but
then remembered the big buckskin original Fletcher
had brought in. A real outlaw.

"What about that ornery buckskin? Where'd it
get off to?"

The question landed like a ton of bricks.

"James didn't get a lot of time to spend with him," said Curley, wincing.

Then Will piped up.

"I had a go with him. I did manage to get him a little more used to a rider's touch. He's coming around for sure. Leaves you thinking good things might happen but it stops there. I need a little more time, that's all."

Nicks said, "I've already told you where that horse belongs as far as I'm concerned, Fletcher. We could get a pretty penny too—with a nice finder's fee for you, don't worry."

"That ain't it, Jeff."

"You're right, it ain't. The question was, 'What ever became of that buckskin?' and what I meant was, 'C'mon James, let's have us a little show. You stay up even one minute on that natural-born killer and I'll double your wages. We're waiting.'"

"And we ain't got all day!" one raucous cowhand hollered.

Will turned toward the separate corral they'd built for the buckskin. His desire to get in there and put on a show was next to zero. Other men, still dozy, had joined them and were standing around, yawning and rubbing their faces. Will's reputation—and back—was on the line.

Cind'rella was watching the fair crowd of people walking over. He hadn't missed a second of Will and Whiskey's dramatic ride, but was proud to be off in his own corral and set apart from the pitiful and subservient other ponies. The mere sight of their docility put him in the mood for a good stomping. And now it was his turn. No doubt about it, his day of reckoning was around the corner—because that's surely where they wanted him to end up. It was him or them, him or them, and he was going to break *them* to pieces. This was a duel to the death, and the buckskin intended to leave his adversary slumped in a pool of blood mixed in with this foul, infertile earth that turned into dust and contaminated the air and polluted his existence a little more with each passing day.

"All these people around are making him nervous, Mr. Nicks. It ain't helping me none."

"You see anyone moving?"

Nicks looked first one way and then the other, then over his shoulder. Everyone was still. Will opened the gate to the corral. Cind'rella was unsure whether to rear up on him or bolt over to the other side of the corral. He chose option two, but only to give himself enough time to better plan his escape, his coup d'état, his revolution.

"Maybe a rope," suggested Curley.

"Pass me the blanket for starters," answered Will.

The buckskin calmed down a little at the sight of the blanket. His back had been itching all morning, and Will managed to rub him down a minute or two. The horse seemed on edge. Intimidated. Set to buck at the slightest false move. Nicks and the others were riveted. Big Moose Tim was standing at the back of the pack, arms crossed. Curley came into the corral with a saddle. Cind'rella snorted and shook.

"Whoa!" said Will, gently as he could.

A few heartless bastards let out a snicker. Will would have liked to see them in his boots.

"You really think you can mount him?" asked Curley quietly.

"I got any other choice?"

"I could talk to Nicks. I'm sure he'd cut you some slack."

"Let's at least saddle him up."

Against all expectations, the buckskin took the saddle. They even managed to get the straps cinched up before he bucked. At that moment, Will wished he were not about to do something foolish, but it was already too late. He'd started to believe he had a chance, that he just might hold on and catch a ride on this fierce animal, this dragon, this locomotive. He wouldn't stay up long, that's for sure, but he'd be able to mount him at least.

The original would rear up as he had never reared before, bounding forward and back and left and right in an infernal circuit that would make his foe dizzy. The saddle leather would stretch at the seams, fold and creak. Will's hat would fly up into the air. And the indefatigable beast, determined to throw this inter-loper off his virgin back, would be ready to buck as he'd never bucked before, buck to the death—until his muscles tore and ripped, until he didn't have another lick of energy or ounce of pride left. For a second the two would move as one. They'd fly and spin in the air as the outlaw horse executed a perilous leap, eyes rolled back in his head, four hooves in the air and belly to the sky. Will would be scared breathless. He'd surely leave his balls behind—but not his reputation, not his name. At the end of it all he'd still be in the saddle and it would be the other men who'd be breathless. And if he did fall, he would know how to put off the inevitable and earn the respect of these cowboys so ready to mock. From one end of the country to the other, they'd still be talking five years from now about a certain Will James, who'd stood his ground with the wildest outlaw that ever stomped its hooves in North America.

Unfortunately, things didn't pan out that way. Everything happened so fast. They slid on the bridle and Cind'rella didn't back off a bit. He even let Curley rub his neck. Will whispered his usual sweet nothings in the horse's ear.

"That's right, big boy. You're a pretty one. Yup, you're gonna be gentle, right? *Gentle.*"

"Ain't it true," said Curley. "He's a beaut."

Neither Will nor Curley had ever seen Cind'rella's hooked nose and devilish eyes so close. Will would remember the shape of the buckskin's Roman nose as long as he lived. He'd still be drawing it as an old man, making it even more pronounced in his pictures than it had been in real life. The horse's nostrils flared, and he loudly expelled two puffs of air. Will gripped the bridle strap. Short-circuit. The original snorted, then pivoted and gave a powerful, lightning-fast kick. Curley caught some nauseating drool in his eye; Will caught the back hoof in the jaw. He fell to the ground, stiff as a board. Every man heard the thud of his head hitting the bottom bar of the fence. They quickly dragged

him out of the corral, while the animal embarked on
a series of terrifying jumps, unaware that his mission
had already been accomplished.

14

When Will came to an hour later he had no idea where he was. The pain made him want to vomit. His abdominal muscles were contracting, his face was drawn and he was half blind. He threw up in the bucket some good Samaritan was holding out in front of him while gently rubbing his back.

"Well done, Ernest!" said Joséphine, urging him on. "You can do it, my boy!"

Will lifted up his head but couldn't see through his tears. Thousands of blood vessels had burst in his eyelids and around his eyes. People were speaking but he couldn't understand a word. Sounds came in little bursts, like ghostly, shapeless echoes; nothing reassuring. He grimaced some more and a new wave of nausea tied his stomach in a knot. His breathing accelerated oppressively, and he again stuck his head in the bucket. His teeth were loose in his mouth and some had fallen right out; he felt like his gums had been replaced with butter or candle wax.

As if through a layer of gauze, he heard a doctor

speaking quietly to Jean. He was saying that the burns were serious and the boy would have to spend several weeks in bed and be put on a strict diet. A whirlwind seemed to have swept him up and left him in total darkness. Jean, despairing, was struggling to hold back his sobs in the family's first living room in Montreal. He walked toward the boy, who was now standing, and begged him to never do anything like that to them again.

"I love you, son," he said.

His dad hugged him tight and tousled his hair.

"*Je t'aime aussi, Papa*," said Will.

A kiss landed on his forehead.

"Will!"

At last, he was brought back to reality. Curley had gently dispelled the world invading Will, snapping his fingers in front of his face. Will pinched himself to make sure. Tim, looking haggard and worried, was also by his side. They'd put him on a cot next to the wood stove. Curley held out a cotton square. Will brought it to his eyes, then blew his nose.

The pieces of his memory, at least those that wished to surface, started to snap together into a picture, one by one. There was him and Curley, drinking long into the night. The letter to San Francisco, Jeff Nicks, the beans he'd had for lunch, Whiskey the horse, the heartless cowboys, Cind'rella who let himself be saddled. Will could see his reflection in the dresser mirror. He craned his neck forward and squinted. A band of gauze was wrapped around his head, from his chin to the top of his skull. His jaw was badly swollen. Incredulously, he felt himself, though he was relieved

the episode with the caustic soda that had so traumatized his nine-year-old Montreal self had happened
long ago and was something he'd merely dreamed.
Will took a deep breath and wanted to smile at his
friends. The pain was unbearable.

"The buckskin really hit a bull's eye!"

"Is it bad?" blubbered the patient. "Don't hold back
on me now."

Now it was Tim's turn to grimace as he surveyed
the scene. The cook quickly dispelled any hope Will
may have been holding on to.

"Nearly all the teeth on the left side of your jaw
are gone. The three or four you got left are busted
down to the root."

Will gripped the bedpost tight.

"And on the other side," Tim went on, "a lot of
yer teeth were knocked clean out. You're gonna need
dentures, buddy."

Despite his young age, Will's teeth were already in
a sad state, visibly rotting after years of neglect. They
would have had to be pulled sooner or later. He lifted
his hand to explore the left side of his jaw. When he
realized just how bad it was, he looked distraught.

"The dentist'll take care of all that, Will," said
Curley, trying to seem positive.

His suffering made itself felt by the minute, by the
hour, by days spent moping around the bunkhouse,
the agonizing pain like the dragging of a cannonball, a
misery colonizing Will's every thought and determining
his every movement, down to the batting of an eye.
He tossed and turned, staring at the ceiling, its every

crack now familiar to him. He managed to sleep only a few minutes at a time, an hour at best, just like the worst of his insomniac nights in prison. The nights were still cold, and the lower the temperature fell, the more acute was his pain. Night after night, he tossed and turned on his infernal bunk, images of the little boy that he'd been, throwing up on the doctor's pants, returning to him incessantly.

"I'll be fine, no doubt," said Will, stoically.

His friends — if you could call Big Moose Tim a friend — raised their eyebrows.

"Roll me a smoke," Will asked feebly, but imploringly, so that no one would think of turning him down.

But the pain didn't pass. After more than a week confined to his bed, writhing in pain, with his back and stomach tied in knots, doing his manly best to try to eat and drink, when even sipping a cup of lukewarm broth made him want to die, he knew he needed to face the truth of it: he wasn't getting any better. The pain in his teeth worked its way down his neck, and from his neck stretched into the marrow of his spine all the way to the tip of his coccyx. Putting on his boots or taking them off — even the idea of it — was too painful even to think about. He didn't see how he could work again, or go on living for that matter, without an operation.

The cook tried to convince Will to go down to Reno, less than a hundred miles north of Topaz. He said he knew a good dentist there, and a family that would put Will up. Tim said the Conradts would welcome Will with open arms, and couldn't resist throwing in a word or two about the charms of the Conradt daughters, young and spritely blondes often to be found hanging around the house.

"You may not be much to look at right now, but all they're waiting for is the chance to spoil a young man like you rotten. And they're a real plucky bunch."

As for Curley, he thought Los Angeles was the place to go for a man looking to find a real good dentist.

"And don't even think about a horse. The train'll be hard enough. At least it won't take as long."

When he collected his wages, he'd have just enough to travel to Los Angeles and get by for three or four weeks without work. Yet there was something irresistible in the sonority of those two words: *Los Angeles*.

For years now, Will had been talking to guys about the studios and working for them as stuntmen, doubles, or extras. It didn't pay much, and some jobs could be dangerous, but the work left a feller plenty of free time and they fed you. Not bad, in the scheme of things. And it would give Will good stories to tell, he thought as he lay back with his hands on his stomach, behind his head, and then back on his stomach again. One more layer to add to the legend of Will James, if there was any legend there. (The term "character" came to him more easily.)

Aside from a few photos in the newspapers, mostly of San Francisco, Will had no idea what the West Coast would even look like—and, even less so, Hollywood. He'd be disappointed. Hollywood still wasn't much of a neighbourhood, let alone a city. You could almost say there was no Hollywood at all—just a bit of hilly country dotted with studios, each a good distance from the next. A lot of the studios weren't in Hollywood proper, but in Edendale, and that was where Will would stop, on the advice of a friendly cab driver who, after a few profitable detours, would also take Will to a dentist he knew. The following day, Will would find a ranch that rented horses to the studios. He'd hang around and make friends there, starting with the stable boys, and the bosses would hire him after the surgery scars on his mouth had time to heal and they saw what he was capable of. Riding a gentle pony, he'd show off his new — albeit fake — pearly white smile. If he'd wanted to, and hadn't grown bored so quickly, Will James might have had a career in the movies and spent the rest of his life in Hollywood. Instead, he made his career elsewhere. When he finally came back to Hollywood, it was to die of cirrhosis of the liver.

One of the guys entered the bunkhouse, burping away. Will turned onto his right side and convinced himself the pain was tolerable that way. But almost immediately, he rolled onto his back again. If California didn't deliver on its promises, he thought during his long convalescence, then he could always try his luck in Mexico. That was another mythic fantasy of his, one he'd been nurturing for years — he liked to say he'd worked there, just like he said he'd worked in Texas; neither was true. Northern Mexico was even prettier than the American Southwest, and you could live on next to nothing down there, they said. But you had to watch out; those Mexican girls could be dangerous for a gringo. And while Pancho Villa and his army were no longer the menace their acts of violence and hope had made them at first, rebels still came down from the highlands of the Sierra from time to time, mountains they'd made their refuge, keeping lawmen on both sides of the border busy. He'd have to watch himself, and yet the call of the unknown and of adventure would always be stronger than fear, thought Will. He put his hands behind his head. It was decided. He'd ask for his wages, pack up his possessions—not much to crow about—sell the saddle he'd bought from Dave Reed for a little more than he'd paid for it, and take the first train to Los Angeles. Of course, he didn't tell a soul that he hoped to get work in the movies. No, he was off to have his teeth fixed, and if he happened to make it in the moving pictures—well, so be it. That's if he could convince someone to give him a chance.

Curley came to see him every night, until he left. Even managed to sneak him a little booze. After all, didn't an injury call for anesthetic?

"How's it going?" he asked.

"About as well as you'd expect, with ten missing teeth."

And right then and there, Will spat into his palm a tooth that had come loose.

"You know what you'll do?"

"I got a few ideas."

A moment passed.

"How about that little buckskin? What'll come of him?"

"I dunno, Bill. But it ain't looking good."

The horse had slipped between their fingers. Curley's odds of buying him were now slim to none.

"I'm sorry."

"It's not your fault. Cut it out!"

Will still felt guilty.

"Never was able to put that plan of ours into action," said Will.

He grabbed his jaw.

"I don't know," said Curley. "Don't think about it. And don't talk too much. I'll see what I can do. One way or another, I ain't planning to stay here long. I miss my wife. Just got a letter from Bishop."

"Nothing serious, I hope."

Curley shook his head.

"I'm going to give my brothers a hand, take care of Minnie. I've gotta take care of her, right? As for the fall, we'll see. We could try to make a little money on the rodeo, Minnie and me. In Arizona maybe, something like that."

He looked at the floor for a moment.

"I'd like to make Nicks an offer right now but seems like a lost cause, no?"

Curley, slumped over, was giving up. He'd have to let go of the horse he'd been waiting for his whole life — his true love, his true friend.

Hope I see you soon, Will didn't have the heart to say.

Instead he contented himself with puffing on the smoke Curley had rolled him. After that summer of 1916, the two men would never meet again. Which is not to say that they weren't communicating telepathically for the rest of their lives—a strange way of saying each thought of the other man often, and that sometimes they did so at exactly the same moment, or close to it. Curley read pretty much every book Will James wrote, and gave them to his nieces and nephews for Christmas, though he was never fully sold on them. The first books weren't bad, but Will's prose disappointed him soon enough.

As for Curley's own story—well, after having an eye gouged at age twenty-five, and his every limb broken by steers and outlaw broncs as wicked as that buckskin by the time he was thirty, Curley Fletcher tried his hand at prospecting. He'd end up eking out a living of sorts from some second-rate mines, still joining the rodeo circuit a few months a year and hoping to sell his books of poetry—he called them "songbooks," as they were easier to sell that way. Curley and his brother fought long and hard to convince his publisher to print the books in a size custom-designed to fit in the back pocket of a pair of jeans. Curley's lungs were black as soot and his head addled by whiskey, but the new life was a step up from shepherding.

"I talked it over with Nicks," he told Will a few days later.

"That asshole," said Will.

"Not so loud."

"*Asshole*," Will repeated a little louder, though it hurt him to get the word out.

"He told me someone was coming in a car from Bridgeport to drive you to the closest station."

"That so?"

"That's what I said. But I'm warning you, it ain't next door. I think they're gonna take you to the station at Walker. Must be a good hundred miles, by the roadways."

"Beats ten days on horseback."

"Exactly."

"You think I'll make it?" Will asked.

Curley took a minute, lifted up his chin a little, and chose his words with care.

I've ridden afar on the trails of life;
And whether I've been right er wrong
In saddlin' the pleasure, ropin' the strife —
I've "follered" the trail right along.

Will pretended to ponder Curley's sentence.

"Khayyám?" he asked, playing along.

Curley's face lit up.

"A humble disciple — Curley Fletcher."

"The master's a good sight better!" Will teased.

"Don't I know it!"

They both had a good laugh, until Will's pain made him stop. Years later he'd remember the Persian poet without ever quite recalling his name — was it Kazam? Makkham? Karrack? — though he'd never actually bother finding out. He had other fish to fry, churning out stories at breakneck speed. Not that his work stopped him from claiming, in his frequently drunken state, to have read the work of an Arab poet of the middle ages or the seventeenth century or something, who had no end of things to say about alcohol and women, roses and pottery and terraces—not one word of a lie, it was the best thing he'd read in his life. *Hic!*

The two young men shook hands. Both smiled reservedly, showing no teeth: Will because he had none left; Curly, ever the gentleman, because it would be insensitive to flash his own set, all white and clean and neatly arranged in straight rows. He got up and left Will to his convalescence. Will shivered and pulled the wool blanket up around him a little. Oh, that cold! The nights of May 1916 were so cold that, later, as if before a mirror that distorted his (real and his dream) life, his memory would deceive him and he'd swear he'd been hurt not long after finishing the final roundup of the season in the fall.

Will pulled his hat down over his head to better fall asleep, but couldn't. The pain was too much and guys were playing cards and remonstrating loudly. Just maybe, they were watching him.

Letter to the Dufault Family

San Francisco, California, May 9, 1916

Dear Parents,

I'm doing fine, and everything here is great. I'm writing a longer letter today because I have a lot of news, and it's been a long time. But I think about you every day.

It's a little hard for me to write in French now, but I'm gonna try, because I'm free and have nothing to hide, and also because I want everyone to be able to read my letter.

For a few weeks now I've been living in San Francisco. It's a beautiful city and I'm starting to get set up real good here. I don't know if you've heard of San Francisco but it's one of the biggest cities in the States. It's real lively, there's all kinds of action and all kinds of folks here as well. You have to take a boat to get here, it's like an island. Or more like a bay, I guess.

I'm renting a room from the mother of a friend of mine. His name is Curley Fletcher, he's a good feller, born the same year as I was, and his mother's name is Benedetta. I met him on the train, and he told me about his Mama, who had a room to rent. She come from Italy, and also lived in Montreal with Italian relatives. Anyway, we hit it off right away, and she took me in, it's great to eat some home cooking, like what we eat at home except with more salt and tomatoes. I don't really know if I like this "pasta" or not yet, but we sure eat it often.

I may have caused you to worry or made you sad recently, please no [sic] that I am sorry, so very sorry.

I hope that one day you'll find it in you to forgive me. I know it may take a while, and I understand. If it helps any I can tell you that I'm back on my feet again, and I didn't come to San Francisco without good reason: I've applied to the best Art School in America and guess what, they took me! They call it Fine Arts, but I mostly do drawing, and I'm also learning to paint, with models who sure don't wear a lot of clothing.

My main teacher, Mr. Dave Reeds, is very encouraging. He tells me that I have real talent, and that I can finally do whatever I want, and earn my keep by drawing, you know how I love drawing cowboys and horses, mostly horses in action, that's what I love to do in life, as you know, and what I've always loved to do. I hope to make a real name for myself soon.

To cut a long story short, it's a fresh start for me, and I want to do things the right way this time, and try to stop straying down the crooked path, and who knows, maybe settle down and get married one day.

When I say that I've made a fresh start I sure do hope you'll believe me. I swear I've given up on cowboying, there ain't no good prospects in it, them cowboys are a dying breed and in ten or fifteen years there won't be any left at all. The big syndicates are buying up all the land they can get their hands on, it do make me wonder what sort of world we'll be living in tomorrow, you can't exactly say it's getting better for us little people and the average folk. But I know you don't like politics, so I'll stop this right there.

I want to change my ways, and never again make another mistake that will make you ashamed of me.

I promised in my last letter that I'd come back to Montreal, and it wasn't a lie, at the time I truly believed it was true, but I've put in too much work around here to pack it in right when things start to pay out.

Soon I'll be able to take a trip and come see you, I'll stay awhile in Montreal if my business is good, after all I can draw anywhere I want, right?

I wonder if everyone is talking about the war in Europe, the way they are here in the States.

People are always getting excited about the war, but it hasn't come here yet. Here people feel sympathy for the French, but they're bitter or just indifferent when it comes to the English. We don't care, they say, though to me it shore [*sic*] do seem that they care a whole lot. As for me, I don't read the papers much, and I stay away from that sort of thing, since I shore [*sic*] don't want to enlist and fight for the Americans. If I do have to serve, I'll do it for Canada, if it's mandatory. If duty calls I'll come back home to fight for my country, since that's what the good unmarried men are doing.

It's been three weeks since I wrote, and I'm struggling to stay awake and my hand hurts, but I'm happy I wrote this letter. I wonder what it'll cost to send all these sheets from San Francisco.

I think of you all the time, I miss you all the time, and I hope to see you soon, in fact I'm sure of it, you're always in my thoughts, day and night, and in my prayers in both French and English. I hope I'm in yours as well, I'm sure I am, you are such good parents. Say hello to Anna for me when you go see her in the convent. Tell her to pray for me.

With a warm embrace,

Your son,

Ernest

Translator's Afterword

"I was born close to the sod, and if I could of seen far enough I could of glimpsed ponies thru the flap of the tent on my first day while listening to the bellering of cattle and the ringing of my dad's spurs."

—Will James, *Lone Cowboy*

"Close to the sod": how ably this phrase from Will James's autobiographical *Lone Cowboy* captures the feel of his oeuvre and the rapidly disappearing cowboy life it celebrates. James's idiosyncratically spelled yet deceptively polished early writings are rich in simple images—ringing spurs, the "bellering" of cattle, the flap of a tent—that appeal to readers' eyes and ears and noses, just as his pencil sketches breathe life into a scene with a strict minimum of lines. Will James's mastery of cowboy lingo and the art of the Western tale gives his work an authenticity that has convinced and enthralled generations of readers, no matter how much untruth these stories may contain.

Benediction fictionalizes the true story of William Roderick James, né Joseph Ernest Nephtali Dufault, who is a distant relation of the novel's author, Olivier Dufault. Ernest was born not, as he claimed, "close to the sod" (i.e., on the wagon trail in cowboy country) but into a good French-Canadian Catholic family in the small farming community of Saint-Nazaire-d'Acton, Quebec, in 1892.

His father was a shopkeeper, his mother a home-maker. They were, by all accounts, loving parents who did everything they could for their son; that Will James was an orphan—the origin story of the persona Ernest Dufault created in order to fit in at the ranches and cow camps he worked throughout his youth—was a fabrication that would leave him with a guilty con-science for as long as he lived.

From boyhood, Ernest Dufault was quick-witted, creative, charming, and unruly. Before long he was playing hooky from school, even disappearing for days at a time on a stolen horse. The Western magazines of the era nourished his adolescent dreams of setting off to seek his fortune on the open range, and that's exactly what he did.

The rest is history—and fiction—and in this case the two are not easily separated. Anyone wishing to know more about the "real" Will James would do well to read *Will James: The Gilt Edged Cowboy*, an excellent autobiography and the inspiration for *Benediction*. (A full list of Olivier Dufault's sources, provided in the French-language edition of this novel, is reproduced below).

I WOULD LIKE TO take this opportunity to acknowledge a few of my debts in making this translation.

First off, in certain sections I have inserted whole sentences and paragraphs from Will James's *Smoky the Cowhorse* and *Lone Cowboy*; these are marked in italics.

Also quoted at length, and set off typographically, are character Curley Fletcher's quotations from the *Quatrains* and the *Rubáiyát of Omar Khayyám*, in the translations of Edward Henry Whinfield and Edward Fitzgerald.

Carmen William "Curley" Fletcher, who becomes fast friends with Will James in *Benediction*, is also a real historical figure: a celebrated cowboy poet and songwriter best known for penning the traditional song "The Strawberry Roan." Harry Jackson's rendition can be heard on *Cowboy Songs on Folkways*, a wonderful collection that not only provides a living record of authentic cowboy language, but also conjures up the atmosphere of this long-past era.

MOST TRANSLATIONS ENDEAVOUR TO carry a "foreign" language and culture across a gulf to a new readership, and this is effectively what Olivier Dufault accomplished in his fictionalization of the story of Will James. Dufault has recreated the rich world of the cattle camps for Quebec readers; as his translator, my job has been, in a sense, to "round it up" and bring the story home.

The outlook and parlance of the Wild West is perhaps more familiar to English readers than those from

Quebec. A further layer of complexity: the novel's subject was a French-speaking Quebecer *who wrote in English*. Beloved by readers of all ages, and edited by the legendary Maxwell Perkins, his bestselling illustrated books made Will James a wealthy man and household name. Few translators have the good fortune to mine the writings of their novel's subject, waiting for the right turn of phrase to flash in their pan.

I CANNOT OVERSTATE MY debt to *Western Words*, a dictionary published by the University of Oklahoma in 1945 (and available online through archive.org), whose author, Ramon F. Adams, describes his years spent fraternizing with cowmen and gathering notes on their lingo as "the hobby of a lifetime"; I affectionately recommend this charming and approachable work.

Equally invaluable were Will James's own writings. As these have become hard to find in print, I would like to thank the maintainers of Project Gutenberg Australia for making *Lone Cowboy* and *Smoky the Cowhorse* freely and legally available online in a searchable format.

Anthony Amaral's *Will James: The Gilt Edged Cowboy* is a masterful illustrated biography of Will James, and the fruit of years of research. It is an excellent companion to *Benediction* for readers keen to learn more, or make their own attempts to unravel fact from fiction.

I'd also like to thank this English edition's editor, Noah Richler, for his patient acceptance of this project's particularities and his sharp pencil, as well as managing editor Maria Golikova, copy editor Gemma Wain, and the rest of the team at Arachnide. Since I was born very far from the sod, and have never sat on a horse, I suggested to Noah that he find a "Western reader" to scrutinize the translation, and author Guy Vanderhaeghe obliged; I am deeply indebted to him for many crucial suggestions and improvements. The author Olivier Dufault has provided guidance on many points as well, and I thank him.

The list of sources below is from the original French version of *Benediction*: these are the works that informed Olivier Dufault's reimagining of the life of his relative. Will James may once have been a household name, but I imagine most readers today will approach *Benediction*, as I did, with no idea of who he was. For some, the end of the novel will mark the beginning of a longer voyage of discovery. The story they'll uncover, one wild turn at a time, is boundlessly fascinating—a tale so tall it could only be true. Which, in a certain sense, it just may be.

Pablo Strauss

TELL THE WORLD THIS BOOK WAS

| GOOD | BAD | SO-SO |

Author's Sources, as listed in the French-Language Edition

Biographies of Will James

Amaral, Anthony. *Will James: The Gilt Edged Cowboy.* Los Angeles: Westernlore Press, 1967.

Bell, William Gardner. *Will James: The Life and Works of a Lone Cowboy.* Flagstaff, AZ: Northland Press, 1987.

Bramlett, Jim. *Ride for the High Points: The Real Story of Will James.* Missoula, MT: Mountain Press, 1987.

Selected Works of Will James

Cowboys North and South. New York: Charles Scribner's Sons, 1924.

Smoky the Cowhorse. New York: Charles Scribner's Sons, 1926.

Lone Cowboy: My Life Story. New York: Charles Scribner's Sons, 1930.

Sun Up: Tales of the Cow Camps. New York: Charles Scribner's Sons, 1931.

The American Cowboy. New York: Charles Scribner's Sons, 1942.

Films about Will James

Clancy, Gwendolyn. *The Man They Call Will James.* 1990.

Godbout, Jacques. *Alias Will James.* 1988. (Available for viewing on the National Film Board of Canada website.)

Other Works That Inspired *Benediction*

Archives of Québec. "*Coutumes et cultures – Janvier – Jour de l'An – Clin d'œil sur nos traditions.*"

Fletcher, Curley W. *Songs of the Sage.* Los Angeles: Frontier Publishing, 1931.

Leclerc, Richard. *Histoire de l'éducation au Québec: Des origines à nos jours.* Quebec City: Richard Leclerc, 1989.

Treadwell, Edward F. *The Cattle King: A Dramatized Biography.* New York: The Macmillan Company, 1931.

Twain, Mark. *Roughing It.* Hartford, CT: American Publishing Company, 1872.

Author's Acknowledgements

I would like to thank Donnelyn Curtis and the entire Special Collections team at the University of Nevada, Reno, for their warm welcome and valuable assistance.

All my gratitude to my father and my grandmother, for providing information on Saint-Nazaire-d'Acton, and life in the "old days."

OLIVIER DUFAULT grew up in Acton Vale, Quebec, where he was raised on the stories of his distant cousin's exploits in the American West. *Benediction* is his first novel. He lives in Montreal.

PABLO STRAUSS grew up in Victoria, British Columbia, and has lived in Quebec City for a decade. His translation of Daniel Grenier's *The Longest Year* was a finalist for the Governor General's Literary Award for Translation.